R

Welcome back to Crystal Creek, Texas!

Ten years ago a devastating tornado swept
through town. And now Crystal Creek has a
Castle Enterprises whirlwind to contend with!
The question on everyone's mind is:
Can Crystal Creek weather more change?

Rumor has it that Castle's **Nick Belyle** is in
town to make some substantial offers for ranch
land. And **Claire Page** can be found out at the
McKinney ranch trying to forget about the
gossip she left back in Boston. Then there's
Teague and Kendra—he's leaving, she's
staying. But they belong together!

*Why don't you pull up a chair and grab a coffee—
we'll be waiting for you down at the Longhorn!*

D1306921

Vicki Lewis Thompson began her writing career at the age of eleven with a short story in the *Auburn Illinois Weekly* and quickly became a byline junkie. Then she discovered she could write books—and she's written over fifty of them! Vicki lives in Tucson, Arizona, and has two grown children and a husband who encourages her to write from the heart.

Cathy Gillen Thacker is a full-time wife/mother/author who began typing stories for her own amusement during "nap time" when her children were toddlers. Twenty years and more that fifty published novels later, Cathy is almost as well-known for her witty romantic comedies and warm family stories as she is for her ability to get grass stains and red clay out of almost anything. Her books have made numerous appearances on bestseller lists and are now published in seventeen languages and thirty-five countries around the world.

Bethany Campbell was born and raised in Nebraska—though we are sure she could tell you more about the town of Crystal Creek, Texas, having been involved in the series since it began in 1993. She has one son, who is an English professor in Tennessee. Bethany herself taught for eleven years before taking up writing full-time, and clearly made a sound career move. She has won the Romance Writers of America's RITA® Award three times, the *Romantic Times* Reviewers' Choice Award three times and the Daphne du Maurier Award of Excellence for mainstream romantic suspense. She and her husband now live in Arkansas, and their hobby is collecting cartoon art.

Return to Crystal Creek

Vicki Lewis Thompson
Cathy Gillen Thacker
Bethany Campbell

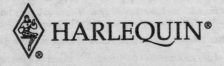

HARLEQUIN®

TORONTO • NEW YORK • LONDON
AMSTERDAM • PARIS • SYDNEY • HAMBURG
STOCKHOLM • ATHENS • TOKYO • MILAN • MADRID
PRAGUE • WARSAW • BUDAPEST • AUCKLAND

Special thanks and acknowledgment are given to Vicki Lewis Thompson, Cathy Gillen Thacker and Bethany Campbell for their contribution to RETURN TO CRYSTAL CREEK.

Special thanks and acknowledgment are given to Sutton Press Inc. for their contribution to the concept of Crystal Creek.

RETURN TO CRYSTAL CREEK

CONTENTS

Dear Reader,

Welcome to the twenty-eighth Crystal Creek book!

Harlequin authors and editors brought this warm, wonderful, lusty town to life almost a decade ago. It was a joy then to work on the original series, and it's a joy to return to it now.

The characters who began it all are still here—ranchers like the dashing McKinney family, and others of that proud and openhearted breed, the men and women of the modern West. You'll also meet new characters who bring fresh adventure and romance to the heart of the Hill County.

In "I'll Take Texas," the heroine is a woman all the people in town think they know. But none of them really does. Shelby Sprague finds herself pitted against a man even more mysterious than she is. But what's ultimately at stake is the town's very soul—and the stubborn hearts of Shelby and Nick Belyle.

There are two other brand-new novellas here. They're by writers that it's been pure pleasure to work with. Vicki Lewis Thompson and Cathy Gillen Thacker each brings her own special touch to a special place in Texas.

So please join us as you're invited to amble down to the Longhorn Coffee Shop, have Kasey bring you a cup of coffee, and lean back while we tell you stories....

Warm regards,

Bethany Campbell

I'll Take Texas
Bethany Campbell

CHAPTER ONE

CRYSTAL CREEK, TEXAS, WAS in the grip of insanity.

The fact was proclaimed everywhere. Each store window declared it. Children carried yellow balloons announcing it. In bright letters, a banner hanging above Main Street repeated it: May Madness!

The annual sidewalk sale was in progress. Outside every shop, displays offered their temptations. "Buy me!" the goods seemed to call. "Buy me *now!*"

At the display before Wall's Drugstore, stood a fat man with a mercenary grin. He wore a yellow T-shirt that said, Want To Buy? I Want To Sell!

This sentiment pleased the stranger.

He wanted to buy, and what he wanted to buy, some might say, was the town's soul.

He knew who all of these merchants were and what they owned. He knew about everyone of importance in Crystal Creek, although he had never before seen the place. It was a pretty little town. He liked it, and he would enjoy practicing his arts here.

The stranger paused before a small, neat building with flower boxes at the windows and a red-striped awning over the door.

The Longhorn Coffee Shop did not look like a significant place, but it was. This was where Crystal Creek's movers and shakers met and talked, made deals both big and small. It was the town's lively, throbbing pulse.

The stranger went inside. He was a tall, lean man, and his name was Nick Belyle. His Stetson was neither black nor white, but thundercloud gray. He wore a white shirt of western cut, jeans and gray snakeskin boots. His silver belt buckle glittered and was shaped like a dollar sign.

Crossing the threshold of the Longhorn was like stepping backward into the 1950s. The seats of the stools, chairs and booths were upholstered in red leatherette. Red-and-white-checked cloths covered each table, and each booth had its own old-fashioned individual jukebox.

The air was fragrant with the scents of coffee and fresh cinnamon rolls. It was an hour before lunchtime, but the place was already half-full and abuzz with conversation.

In a corner booth sat a trio of men, talking over their coffee. Nick Belyle was pleased, for these men interested him deeply.

Close to their booth was a small vacant table. Belyle moved to it and took the chair facing the corner booth. From beneath the brim of his hat, he watched the men, and his keen ears took in their every word.

"I don't like it," the heavyset one said. "Too damn many changes. Nothing's the same no more."

The hefty man was Bubba Gibson. In his mid-sixties, he had a jowly face and the band of his hat was studded with turquoises. On one hand was a wedding band and on the other a turquoise ring with a stone the size of a halved Ping-Pong ball.

Bubba owned the Flying Horse Ranch, eight thousand acres of rolling land—a very nice piece of real estate, wasted on raising ostriches, of all things. It was fairly profitable, but Bubba was getting too old and fat to chase ostriches.

Yes, someday Bubba could be ripe for plucking—or not. Nick sensed unpredictability in the man, a strange mix of the conservative and the reckless.

"Things have changed a lot since I got here," admitted a second, younger man. He shook his head as if in bewilderment.

Brock Munroe was a big man, well dressed yet somehow disheveled. He had a gentle air and pie crumbs on his shirt.

Munroe had come from Montana less than ten years ago and bought a ranch, fifty-five hundred acres that were more scenic than useful. He was hurting from the cattle-killing winter of two years ago and the drop in beef prices. Yes, Munroe, too, was a good possibility.

"There's new doctors comin'," grumbled Bubba, twisting his turquoise ring. "New *preacher*. My damn lawyer's gonna retire. I gotta find a new one. Don't want a new one. Want the one I got."

"Times change," said the third man. "You've got to change with them. Stop complaining. You sound like an old geezer."

"I am an old geezer, dammit," Bubba retorted. "At my age, I got the inalienable right to complain."

The third man, J. T. McKinney, only smiled. He was different from the others. If the town had anything akin to royalty, it was the McKinney clan.

J.T. owned the Double C Ranch, thirty-five thousand acres of prime Hill Country. His elder son had established a successful vineyard in its south quadrant; his younger son was filthy rich in his own right, and his daughter raised thoroughbred horses.

All three offspring were ferociously loyal to the land

and to their father. Their mother was dead, but now there was a second wife, Cynthia. She had borne J.T. his youngest child, another daughter. At this point Jennifer was the only McKinney who didn't wield formidable power.

Although J.T. was in his sixties, he was still trim, handsome, and looked as if he had plenty of fight in him. His hair was silver at the temples, but the dark eyes were alert and full of intelligence.

He was, in fact, discreetly watching Nick Belyle and taking his measure. Then a waitress made her way to Nick's table, coming between him and McKinney and blocking their view of each other.

At first Nick, irritated, saw nothing of the woman except her white apron trimmed in red rickrack.

"Sorry to keep you waiting," she said in a breathless voice. "We're shorthanded today. What can I get you?"

"Coffee, black," he said, and raised his eyes.

He was about to add, "And a piece of pie," but a freakish thing happened. The words stuck in his throat, unsayable.

The woman was beautiful. She was a goddess with a coffeepot in her hand.

What's more, she seemed strangely familiar, as if he'd known her in a previous life. Tall and slender, her long-lashed eyes were dark, and her skin seemed to have a sheen of gold. Her hair, gleaming and black, fell to her shoulders, and she carried herself like a queen.

"Pie," he managed to say.

"What kind?" she asked.

His eyes traveled in wonder up and down her body. She had full breasts, a small waist, and long, long, legs.

"Wh-what would you recommend?" stammered Nick. He couldn't remember the last time he'd stammered.

With one perfectly shaped golden hand, she filled his coffee mug. ''Everybody likes the coconut cream,'' she said. ''There's one piece left.''

''I'll take it,'' he said.

She smiled, and her goddess power doubled. She wore a denim skirt, a pale blue blouse, the red-trimmed pinafore, and no wedding or engagement ring. Over her left breast was a gold-colored pin that said Shelby.

Then somebody called her name, and she was gone, weaving through the growing crowd. He stared after her.

Shelby. Of course: Shelby Sprague. Back in Beaumont, Texas, she had been a preacher's daughter, five years younger than he was. The last time he'd seen her, she'd been only twelve years old. She'd been a child then. Now she was a woman—and *what* a woman.

She wasn't on his list of key townspeople. This meant she had no money, no status, no importance and no power—except her extraordinary beauty.

He raised his coffee mug and took a meditative sip. The second he'd looked at her, his plans had changed. This trip would not be strictly business. From the time he was a boy, he had wanted Shelby Sprague. As a boy, he'd been nobody. But now he was a man, and one used to getting what he wanted.

SHELBY STOPPED TO REFILL coffee cups for two other customers, Tammi Cooper and Angie Dunbar. She kept her hand steady, although her heart banged wildly. The stranger had unsettled her, and she was not used to such a reaction.

Although he was thirtiesh and completely masculine, his face had an almost boyish innocence. Much of the innocence was in his eyes; they were what Shelby thought of as angel eyes, a pure, heavenly blue.

She had seen such eyes once before—but where? They haunted her. His face was eerily familiar, too. He was square-jawed, but he had deep dimples when he smiled, and his smile seemed guileless and half-shy. His mouth had an intriguing sensuality, and his chin was cleft.

Shelby nodded and replied mechanically to Tammi Cooper's small talk, but the stranger dominated her mind. He was watching her, smiling slightly, as if he approved of what he saw.

Then, from the corner of her eye, she saw J. T. McKinney rise from his booth and approach. She was surprised when he put his hand on her shoulder. "Shelby, could I talk to you a minute?"

"Sure," she said.

He nodded toward the cashier's counter. "Meet me over there."

What's this about? she wondered. *He never does this.* J.T. always paid his bill at the booth, leaving his money and tip beside the napkin holder. She set the coffeepot on the counter and followed him to the cash register.

"All right," he said, pointing at the tins of aspirin in the display case. "Give me one of those and take your time. I want to ask a favor."

Puzzled, Shelby nodded and casually reached among the candies, gum and packs of tissue.

"That man over there," J.T. said in a quiet voice. "That man over there." He nodded discreetly toward the stranger. "He's looking at you with a lot of interest."

"Is he? I didn't notice," Shelby lied, hoping heaven would not strike her dead. It seemed an outright sin to lie to someone as principled as J.T.

J.T. said, "I saw him earlier in a white Corvette convertible. He was parked on a back road, right between Bubba's ranch and mine. He was taking pictures of our land. I was out on horseback, coming through a big stand of cedars. I don't think he even saw me.''

J.T. hardly glanced at her as he spoke; he seemed interested only in his purchase. ''I've heard rumors that somebody might be down this way. Rumors of things that could happen.''

''What sort of rumors?'' Shelby breathed.

''It's best I not say at this point. But I want to know who he is and what he's up to. I can't stick around and do it myself. I don't reckon he'd tell me anyway. Think you could chat him up? See what you could find out?''

Her hand closed almost spasmodically around the aspirin tin. ''Me?''

''You're a bright woman. Lynn's told me and I believe her.''

She smiled uneasily. Lynn was J.T.'s adult daughter. She and Shelby often went trail riding together—or they had before Shelby was forced to move to town and work at the Longhorn. She was a waitress by necessity, not choice.

''Will you?'' asked J.T., taking the aspirin and handing her a ten-dollar bill. ''Or would you find it distasteful?''

''I can try,'' she said with a lightness she didn't feel. She detested prying, but J.T. wouldn't ask her to do such a thing without good reason.

''Fine,'' he said. ''If you learn anything, phone me at the ranch tonight. I'm going into Austin, but I'll be home by eight.''

Shelby nodded wordlessly and started making his change. He gestured for her to keep it. She wasn't sure she liked taking it; it made her feel like a paid informant.

He smiled at her and walked out the door as if they
had discussed nothing more controversial than the
weather. Shelby closed the cash register drawer and
made her way back to the counter. She seized the plate
with the last slice of coconut cream pie and carried it to
the stranger's table.

He looked up at her gave her that bashful smile. "I've
never seen anything so beautiful," he said as she set
down the plate.

But he was not looking at the pie. He was looking at
her.

"Um," she said, toying with the strap of her pinafore
apron, "you're—you're not from around here, are
you?"

Oh, that was original, she scolded herself. *That was
really a brilliant and subtle stroke of detective work.
Great work, Sherlock.*

"No," he said. "You don't remember me, do you?"

"Oh," she said, all chipper brightness. "You do
look—kind of familiar."

"Nick Belyle from Beaumont," he said. "Once you
saved me from getting beat up."

"Oh," she repeated, this time with the shock of rec-
ognition.

Nick Belyle—Beaumont's bad boy. Or that's how
he'd seemed to her then with his swaggering walk and
his worn black leather jacket.

Her surprise must have shown on her face. Softly he
said, "So you do remember. Three guys had jumped
me."

"You'd stolen a girlfriend from one of them," she
said. *Oh, good grief, she thought. I had such a crush on
you after that day.*

He grinned wryly and shook his head. "I didn't steal

her. She decided she liked me, that's all. I never even asked her out."

Her chest felt tight, making it hard to breathe. Nick had been a striking boy, despite his ragged jeans and shabby cowboy boots. He'd worn his black hair unfashionably long, and he'd been much thinner. But the dark-lashed eyes had been that same unique blue.

He said, "I asked *you* out, though. Your father wouldn't let you go."

She swallowed in nervousness. "He said you were too old for me." She'd both resented her father's edict and been relieved by it. Nick had been too blatantly sexy for a girl as inexperienced as she'd been. He'd made her imagine things she'd thought must be wrong—like kissing and being kissed by him again and again.

He looked her up and down. "You didn't look twelve. I thought you were older."

"You've still got a scar," she said, staring at a slim white line near his temple. She had a ridiculous impulse to touch it.

"A permanent reminder," he said. "Two guys holding me, and one punching the hell out of me. Then you came around the corner and stopped in your tracks—for about five seconds."

"I was horrified," she said. "I didn't know what to do." She'd never seen anyone being beaten before. The violence and unfairness sickened her.

"You didn't hesitate long," he said with that dimpled smile. "You waded in kicking and yelling and swinging your lunch box."

Shelby felt the blood rising to flood her cheeks. She'd swung at the boy pummeling Nick, meaning to hit him in the back. He'd turned unexpectedly, and she'd smashed her lunch box right into his face, breaking his nose and chipping his tooth.

In pain he'd dropped to his knees. One of the other boys lunged for Shelby, but she dodged and banged him on the ear with the lunch box. By that time, Nick was back in the fight. He'd knocked the remaining boy halfway across the street.

A man with a golf club had run out of his house yelling, "You kids stop that, or I'm calling the cops!" The three attackers had fled, leaving Nick and Shelby alone.

Blood was pouring out of the gash in his head, his cheekbones were bruised, and he had a cut on his lower lip. The man had stalked back into his house muttering about young thugs.

Without a second thought, Shelby had pulled off her cotton half slip and pressed it to Nick's forehead to staunch the wound.

He'd looked down at her and said, "I don't know who you are, but I think I love you."

Her heart had turned somersaults, and feelings she hadn't understood swept through her in a tide.

Now he gazed at her the same way he had back then. "You ruined your lunch box for me. And your slip."

"I hated that lunch box," she managed to say. "It had Winnie the Pooh on it. You should have known I was only a kid when you saw that."

"I was looking only at you," he said. "I didn't think it was possible for a girl to be so pretty. Now you're prettier still."

Rattled, Shelby remembered J.T. "It looks like you've done all right for yourself. Where'd you go when you left Beaumont? Your family moved, right?"

"Up northeast," he said. "My mother went to live with her sister. I didn't think you'd noticed we'd left."

Shelby's heart took a staccato, trip-hammer beat. She couldn't admit it, but she'd been heartbroken when he'd moved away. Six months after the fight his family had left Beaumont. His mother was a widow with three sons, and they were poor.

They lived a few miles away, in a shabby part of town. He went to public school. She went to the private religious school that her father, a minister, had helped to found.

She said, "Did you stay in—the northeast?"

He shook his head. "I've been a lot of places since Beaumont. What about you? This is a nice town. You lived here long?"

"Oh, no," she said, twiddling with her apron strap. "Only two years."

"You've got a French book," he said with a nod toward her apron pocket. "You're a student?"

Her blush grew hotter. She'd forgotten the paperback grammar book stuck in the pocket. "Oh—" she said "—I hope to get back to school this fall. To get my master's."

He looked truly impressed. "Wow. A master's degree. At the university in Austin?"

"Um—yes."

He leaned his elbow on the table and his cleft chin on his fist, staring at her as if fascinated. "That's where you got your bachelor's degree?"

"Um. Yes." Her father had wanted her to go to a church college, but she'd held out for the University of Texas, promising him how well she'd behave.

"What'd you major in?" he asked. He had an intriguing voice; it seemed at once lazy and charged with sex. "French?"

"No," she said. "Biology. It's just—it's good to have a second language, you know."

He frowned thoughtfully. It was a most becoming frown, handsome, in fact. "So you graduated from college, but you've been here waiting tables for two years?"

She shook her head nervously. "I had a job as a naturalist. At a dude ranch."

"Oh, ri-i-ight," he said. "There *is* a dude ranch around here. I saw a sign when I was driving in. It's called—uh—"

"The Hole in the Wall," she supplied.

"That's right. Hole in the Wall." His smile was sympathetic. "Why'd you leave? Didn't you like it?"

"I *loved* it. But, well, Hole in the Wall had to downsize. My job was one of the first to go. So—for the time being, here I am." She gestured to indicate the restaurant. "It's not bad. Plus I get meals and a discount on a room at the motel."

She gave a philosophical shrug, but in truth she wanted to turn around and bang her head on the counter. *I'm babbling like an idiot. I've told him my entire life story and I haven't found out one thing about him. Mata Hari I am not.*

"Right, this is a motel, too," he said with an air of just remembering it. "Good. I need a place to stay. Are there any vacancies here?"

Oh, rats, thought Shelby. "Well, yes. B-but you could probably afford a nicer place. There's a wonderful old hotel, just restored—"

"No," he said. "This would suit me fine."

"You're—going to stay awhile?" she asked.

"I'm not sure. It depends."

"Depends on what?"

"A lot of things," he said with a disarming smile.

"And—uh—what are you doing for a living now?"

"I'll give you one of my cards," he said.

Her heart gave a cartwheel of relief. *At last, I'm getting somewhere.* "I'd love one," she said.

His fingers barely brushed hers, but the electricity of his touch danced along her nerves.

The card he handed her was expensive, the paper velvety to the touch, the engraving dark gold. It said:

Nicholas R. Belyle
Representative
Castle Enterprises
New York, Dallas, Atlanta, Memphis and Little Rock

Shelby studied it with new frustration. "You're a—a representative. What, exactly, do you represent?"

"Castle Enterprises," he said.

She tried to seem sweetly curious rather than snoopy. "What's Castle Enterprises?"

"A corporation."

She set her teeth delicately together. "So what's its business, exactly?"

He shrugged. "Its dealings are diversified."

"I mean," she said, "does it make things or sell things or build things or provide a service or—"

"All of..." He smiled. "It would take hours to explain."

I just bet it would, she thought grimly. Behind the heavenly eyes was a hellishly slippery mind, and the tempting mouth held a forked tongue. J.T., a perceptive man, was right to be suspicious of him.

Shelby put her hand on her hip. "What brought you to Crystal Creek?"

He tasted his pie. "This is delicious. It tastes like real whipped cream."

"It *is* real whipped cream. I asked exactly why you got sent here."

"Oh," he said with an innocent expression. "Here? In Crystal Creek?"

"Yes."

He seemed about to answer, when an impatient voice interrupted. "Shelby, I've asked you *twice*. You have two full tables waiting for menus, and the corner booth needs cleaning. *Puh-lease.*"

Shelby's face burned at the reprimand. Only she and Kasey, the regular waitress, were left to handle the May Madness crowd. Nora, the owner of the Longhorn, was home today with a sprained ankle.

Now Kasey pierced her with a disapproving look.

"It was my fault," Nick said to Kasey. "I was monopolizing her. My apologies to both you lovely ladies."

"Humph," said Kasey, but even she seemed to soften under his charm.

Shelby scurried away to get menus for the new customers. But she could feel Nick's blue stare on her, watching her, taking her measure, frankly appreciating her.

Shelby disliked the sexual power that gaze radiated, and she resented how he had dodged her questions. She was a private person herself—highly private, and she prized honesty as much as she hated deception.

From bitter experience she recoiled from men who were sexy and devious. Nick Belyle, unfortunately, was both.

When he finished eating he left a five-dollar bill on

the table and came to the booth where she was taking an order. He paused and whispered in her ear, "I'll be back, Shelby."

Her ear tingled as if he had breathed a devilish imp into it.

SHELBY WAS SHUTTING DOWN the Longhorn for the night when Nick appeared again. Kasey was already gone. Nick walked in the door just as Shelby was starting to untie her apron strings.

For an instant she forgot he was an assignment and was struck by the electricity of his physical presence. She had known he would come back, but now that he had, he seemed to exude an exquisite danger.

He was taller than she'd realized, and standing in the doorway, he looked less boyish than he'd first seemed. Far, far less boyish. His cryptic smile half hypnotized her.

Under the shadow of his hat brim, his vivid blue eyes were trained on her. "I heard you get off about this time."

"You heard right," she said, heart thudding.

"I thought I could walk you home," he said.

She raised her chin. "I *am* home. I live here." Her room was one of twelve units that formed the Longhorn's motel.

"So do I," he said. "You're in unit six. I'm in seven. We're neighbors. May I walk you to your place? *Puisje te marcher à ta maison?*"

His French took her by surprise, and so did his accent, which, drat, was perfect. She had the sensation of being expertly cornered.

He'd rented the room next door to hers? All the other units were empty, except for number one, where Albert, the elderly manager lived. Had Nick persuaded the old man to put him as near as possible to Shelby? *Albert,* she thought, *if you sold me out, may the devil take you.*

"Have you had supper yet?" Nick asked, his steady gaze still on her.

She picked up a paper bag and held it out as if it were a charm to ward him off. "I have a sandwich. I'm taking it with me."

"And I," Nick said, "have a sandwich I'm taking with *me.* Couldn't my sandwich and I join yours and you? We could go somewhere—have a picnic maybe. It's a beautiful evening."

"No thanks," she said as lightly as she could. "I've got my little routines. I stick to them."

"So I've heard," he said.

Her chin inched higher. "Heard from whom?"

"The manager, Albert. He says you're predictable as clockwork. He says it's strange that such a beautiful woman is such a loner."

She consigned Albert to an even hotter level of hell, one where the demons had sharper pitchforks. But she said nothing.

Nick moved toward her. "Everybody needs a change once in a while. Why don't we go somewhere? You asked me a lot of questions. I never had a chance to answer."

That gave her pause. She *wanted* the answers to those questions—and so did J. T. McKinney. Yet she didn't wish to seem too eager.

"I'm not dressed to go anywhere—" she began.

"You look fine," he said. His eyes told her she looked more than fine, that she looked beautiful, but she didn't like the feeling it gave her.

"I'll tell you what," she said. "I was about to put up

the Closed sign. We can eat right here. No frills, no fuss. If you really want to talk, it's as good a place as any.''

"Probably a better place than most.'' He paused then added, "I bought a couple of bottles of the local wine. You know, from the McKinney winery. Would it be against the law for me to bring one in and open it?''

She knew a drink in private at the Longhorn was all right. Nora had surprised her husband here once with a birthday party, and the champagne had bubbled, the icy beer had flowed.

Shelby herself rarely drank, but perhaps wine would make Nick Belyle's glib tongue less guarded. "That would be fine,'' she said. "If you mean it—that you really want to talk, that is.''

"I want to know more about you,'' he said. "Everything you've done since your father told me to get any ideas about you out of my mind. I never completely succeeded, you know.''

"That's all very nice,'' she answered. "But you said you were going to tell me about *yourself.*''

"All you want to know,'' he said with a smile. "Let me go get the wine.''

Half-reluctantly she nodded and watched him go. She spied on him from the window as he went to the motel parking lot and opened the trunk of the white Corvette convertible.

She remembered what J.T. had said about the Corvette being parked by his and Bubba's property, of Nick, thinking he was alone, snapping photos of the two men's land.

The shrill ring of the phone startled her. She whirled from the window and ran to answer it. She snatched up the receiver. "Longhorn Coffee Shop,'' she said. "Shelby speaking.''

"Shelby, I'm so *glad* to find you. I tried your room, but you didn't answer." The voice was J.T.'s oldest daughter, Lynn, and she sounded tense, almost desperate.

"Lynn?" Shelby said. "What's wrong?"

"Listen, Shel," Lynn said. "I heard there's a man who wants to see you tonight. He's from out of town. His name is Nick Belyle."

Shelby blinked in surprise. "How'd you know he wanted to see me?"

"This is a small town, Shelby. Word gets around fast."

"But—"

"He was asking about you. I'll explain it all later," said Lynn. "I don't know how soon he'll be there."

"He already is," Shelby said. "He went to his car to get something. What's the matter? Should I not see him?"

"No, no, no," Lynn assured her. "Just be careful, will you? He may want information from you—"

"From me? But what do I know?"

"What we need is information about *him*. Who he works for, what these people want here."

Shelby frowned in puzzlement. "What do you mean, 'we'? You and your father?"

"Good grief, no! Daddy's the last person we want you talking to. No—find out everything you can—and then talk to Valerie and me—please."

"Valerie?" Shelby said, her voice rising in bewildered surprise. Besides Lynn, Valerie Harris was her best friend in Crystal Creek. Until two months ago, she had also been Shelby's employer.

Valerie hadn't wanted to let Shelby go; she'd cried when she'd done it and said she didn't know what she and her husband were going to do about Hole in the Wall. She was afraid they were going to lose it.

"Lynn," Shelby said, "does all this have something to do with Hole in the Wall?"

"It could be about a lot more than that," Lynn said. "It could be about the whole future of Crystal Creek."

CHAPTER TWO

SHELBY FROWNED, PERPLEXED. "The future of Crystal Creek? What do you mean?"

"I mean Daddy got a tip that somebody might come snooping around here—somebody wanting land. A lot of it."

"Shopping for land? Ranch land? There's none for sale."

"But some people aren't doing as well as others. They *might* sell—if the money was right. Think about what happened to you."

Foreboding twisted within her. "You're talking about Hole in the Wall."

Lynn said, "Mostly. But Brock Munroe's had two bad years in a row. And Bubba Gibson's getting awfully old to run a ranch."

Shelby considered this. She knew that Valerie and Scott Harris's position was perilous. Besides their growing debts and shrinking profits, they'd been hit with a disastrous lawsuit.

She glanced nervously out the window. Nick was still in the parking lot, and now he was talking earnestly on his cell phone, the sack of wine set on the car's hood.

Lynn's voice was full of urgency. "Valerie said they got a call from a man named Armstead. He's affiliated with something called 'Castle Enterprises' and said a 'representative' would come to make them an offer on Hole in the Wall.''

"When did this happen?" Shelby asked, still watching Nick. He'd begun to pace as he talked. His conversation seemed intense.

"Late this afternoon."

"And this representative is Nick Belyle?"

"That's what he told them."

So that's it, Shelby thought. *Castle Enterprises wants Hole in the Wall.* She fished Nick's card out of her blouse pocket, studied it, and frowned.

"What do they want with it? To renovate it? Improve it?"

Lynn said, "We don't know. This Armstead said neither he nor Belyle are allowed to talk about the plans for it. Valerie has a bad feeling."

"What sort of bad feeling?" Shelby stole another uneasy glance at Nick. He was still pacing, now engrossed in listening.

"Well," Lynn said, "she heard a rumor a while back about some kind of big theme park being built near Austin."

Shelby grimaced. She thought of the countryside that she loved—cleared of its trees and bluebonnets and desert marigolds. She pictured the rolling hills leveled and dead beneath a shroud of cement.

Where the wild turkeys and deer and javelin now flourished, there instead would be roller coasters and other inane contraptions to make people spin, whirl, fly, flip, and most of all, scream.

"A theme park?" she echoed in disgust.

"It's possible," Lynn said. "But they could want it for *anything.* Shelby, can you please try to find out what these people are up to? And keep this confidential. Armstead told them his call was top secret.''

"How can it be top secret when she told you, and you're telling me?"

Lynn's voice grew more taut. "Valerie's scared that Scott's ready to sell to anybody. But she doesn't want to see everything they've built up torn down. She says she *has* to know what these people want.''

Shelby was more bewildered than before. "Your father already asked me to do the same thing this morning. I—I feel like a spy.''

"Oh, Lord,'' Lynn said with even more fervor. "You can't tell Daddy before Valerie and Scott know. It's their decision.''

"Would he try to influence them?'' Shelby asked.

"Daddy would try to influence *everybody*,'' Lynn said darkly. "He's got *very* strong opinions about how land should be used.''

Panic raced through Shelby. "But just this morning he asked me—''

"Don't tell him,'' Lynn insisted. "Scott and Valerie have enough pressure on them now without Daddy.''

"But—'' Shelby began.

"Am I your friend?'' Lynn asked. "Is Valerie?''

"Yes. Of course. But—''

"Then for now just leave my father out of it. *Please.*''

Shelby saw Nick putting away his cell phone. He picked up the sack from the winery gift store and started back toward the Longhorn.

"I can't talk any longer, he's coming,'' Shelby said hastily, slipping his card back into her pocket.

"Call me later,'' Lynn said. "After you've talked to him. I'll be home waiting.''

Shelby cringed. She had no desire to become the heart

of Gossip Central, and she disliked being caught between J.T.'s demands and Lynn's.

The brass bell tinkled as the front door opened. She hung up the phone and turned to Nick. Drat! He made her feel as giddy and excited as when she'd been twelve. "Hi—I had a little phone call."

He gave her the slanted smile that showed his dimples. "I had one myself. That's what took me so long. Sorry."

He hung his hat on a peg near the door. He carried the paper bag to a booth and set it down, withdrawing two bottles of Crystal Creek's local wine, one Cabernet, one Riesling. "Do you have any wineglasses?"

"No," she said, wiping her hands on her apron. Her palms were moist from tension. "Just regular glasses. Do you need a corkscrew?"

"I always carry one," he said. "Part of my trusty Swiss Army knife."

She brought plates, silverware and glasses to the booth as he drew out the knife and flipped open the corkscrew. He said, "I got a white wine and a red. Which do you prefer?"

"I have a tuna salad sandwich," she said. "So white, please."

"Fine. It's still chilled," he said, opening the bottle. "I got sandwiches from the pub. I hope that isn't sacrilege, bringing in food from another restaurant. There won't be a mob coming for me, will there?"

She managed a shaky smile. "They haven't made it a hanging offense—yet. Sit down. I'll put on some coffee for afterward."

"No thanks," he said. He startled her by moving toward her, turning her to face away from him.

"What?" she gasped, her arm tingling from his fleeting touch.

"You didn't finish taking off your apron," he said. She could feel his fingers picking at the strings. "No wonder. You've tied yourself up in a mean knot. There, you're free."

She slipped off the apron, then slowly faced him. She wished that such slight physical contact hadn't been so disconcerting.

"Sit," he invited with a wave of his hand.

She slid into the booth, her heart knocking against her breastbone. He strode to the light switch and dimmed the lights to their lowest.

Shelby's eyes widened. "Why'd you do that?"

He reached into the sack and pulled out a blue candle and a small glass candleholder shaped like a star. He said, "I thought if I got lucky, I might have dinner by candlelight with you. So I came prepared."

He thrust the candle into the holder, took out a pack of matches, and lit it. The golden light danced across the checkered tablecloth, twinkled on the booth's chrome jukebox. Suddenly Shelby realized the Longhorn looked almost romantic.

Nick sat down and poured the wine. He handed her a glass. "To the prettiest woman in Crystal Creek," he said, raising his glass to her.

"Wherever she might be," Shelby said, clicking her glass against his. She meant to make light of his compliment, but her throat was tight. He was moving in too fast. She remembered another man who'd done the same.

"The prettiest woman in town's right across from me," he said. "And she looks even more beautiful by candlelight. I knew you would."

Damn, he's an operator, all right, she thought. *But he looks pretty fine by candlelight himself.* His eyes seemed a darker blue, and the flickering light cast his cheekbones into higher relief, and made the cleft in his chin seem deeper.

She took a deep breath to steady herself. "You don't have to flatter me. In fact, I wish you wouldn't."

"It's not flattery," he said. "It's the truth."

Shelby set her jaw and hardened her resolve. "I agreed to this because you said you'd tell me about yourself."

"I'll keep my word," he said, unwrapping a sandwich. "But I want to know about you, too. You don't have on a wedding or engagement ring. Is there somebody special in your life right now?"

This was a question she was often asked, and she hated answering it. "No. Nobody."

He arched an eyebrow. "That's what Albert said. That as far as he knew, you never went out with anybody. He said, 'What a waste of a fine-looking woman.' I have to agree."

Incensed, she grasped the edge of the table so hard that her knuckles whitened. "He said *that*? How *dare* he talk about my private life that way."

"I asked him," Nick said. "I just wanted to know if you were free."

"I'm free, and I like it that way," Shelby protested. "I just want to do my job, save my money and go back to school."

Nick looked at her so steadily it unnerved her. She took a tiny sip of wine, trying to seem nonchalant.

"Somebody in your past must have hurt you pretty badly," he said, his voice quiet.

She was jolted by how he had guessed so easily; she had kept her secrets well guarded. Nobody knew her story and she didn't *want* it known.

"Are you divorced?" he asked.

"No," she said shortly. "I'm not." She took a bite of her sandwich. It seemed as tasteless as cardboard.

"Me, either," he said. "Never married. Never even got close. Did you? Get close to it, I mean?"

Oh, I thought I did. I thought I was about to say "I do" and exchange rings and live happily ever after. She recalled that delusion with shame, and Nick brought back the memory of her folly all too clearly.

She said, "Let's change the subject. You're wearing a college ring. Where's it from? What'd you study?"

"Harvard. Law." He took a sip of wine.

"You're a lawyer?" she said dubiously.

"I got the degree." He said it with a smile and a nod. His smile was self-deprecating, his nod was casual, and his answer was evasive, as usual. Her fraying nerves snapped.

"Is that why you can't ever give a straight answer?" she asked, pushing aside her wineglass. "Because you're a lawyer?"

"Ouch," he said, but his dimples deepened. "Is that how you see lawyers? You don't seem like a girl who thinks in stereotypes."

She reached into the pocket of her blouse and pulled out his card. She cocked one eyebrow as she read it again.

Nicholas R. Belyle
Representative
Castle Enterprises
New York, Dallas, Atlanta, Memphis and Little
Rock

She shot him a challenging look. "This doesn't *say* you're a practicing lawyer. Are you?"

He looked at her, his eyes narrowing as in admiration, his smile growing speculative. "I work on the corporate level."

"At law?" she pressed.

"Among other things," he said. "The law background helps."

"Helps with *what?*" she demanded.

"Many things," he said with maddening vagueness. He took another bite of his sandwich.

She slapped one hand on the counter and glared at him. "Stop playing cat and mouse!" She shook the card at him. "This thing looks good at first glance. Very expensive, tasteful. But it's—it's bogus."

He seemed unfazed. "Oh?"

She leaned across the table and thrust the card at him accusingly so he was forced to look at it. "It doesn't mention that you're a lawyer. It calls you a 'representative,' whatever that means. And it gives no address, no phone number, no fax number, no e-mail address. It doesn't even say *which* of these cities you're from—if any of them."

"You have a point," he agreed. "It's kind of ambiguous."

"*Kind* of ambiguous?" she retorted. "It's more than ambiguous. It's misleading. You could be anyone from anywhere and up to anything. For all this tells me, you could be the devil himself."

THE DEVIL HIMSELF. Nick liked that. He'd been called worse things—but usually at the end of his affairs, not the beginning.

He'd been vaguer than usual here because it was a small town; he expected that news traveled fast. But compared to his usual wheeling and dealing, he had thought that Crystal Creek would be child's play.

Shelby Sprague was proving him wrong.

She was too smart. He should toss out a few half truths to throw her off track, then get the hell away from her—and keep away.

But something about her was set in his heart like a hook, just as it had all those years ago. He didn't want to distance himself from her, not after just finding her again.

"So what do you want to know?" he asked. "I'm not doing anything illegal. But I warn you, there are certain things I can't discuss. For professional reasons."

Her midnight dark eyes with their impossibly long lashes looked him up and down. "Where've you been living?"

"Little Rock, Arkansas."

"Prove it," she said. Her gaze wavered no more than his did.

"Sheese," he said, half in laughter, half in frustration. He reached into the back pocket of his jeans and drew out his wallet. He flipped it open and showed her his driver's license.

Shelby studied it critically, then pushed the wallet back across the table. "And what were you doing in Arkansas?"

He folded the wallet, stuck it back in his pocket. "I'm sorry. I'm not allowed to discuss that at this time."

She tossed her raven black hair. "Were you working for Castle Enterprises?"

"It was related to that," he said. "Look, you've barely touched your food, you've hardly tasted your wine. Could you drop the interrogation for a minute? I, for one, happen to be starving."

He bit into his sandwich, which would keep him from answering questions for at least another twenty to thirty seconds. It also gave him a chance to watch the candlelight dance over her delicate features.

Her skin looked like the finest velvet in the golden light. He wondered if her whole body was that smooth and softly inviting. He'd bet his soul that it was.

But she'd taken on a regal aloofness, and he sensed that it didn't matter how desirable he found her; she didn't trust him. And if she didn't trust him, she would have nothing to do with him. She was off-limits to the likes of him, just as she'd been before.

She broke off a small corner of her sandwich and nibbled at it. Once again she reminded him of a princess, nibbling at ordinary food only to stay alive. If she seemed any more unattainable, she would drive him mad.

"What do I need to do?" he asked, pretending to jest. "Give you character references? Fingerprints? Take a lie detector test?"

She sighed and turned the glass of wine back and forth on the table. What she said next surprised him. Wearily she asked, "What exactly do you want with me, Nick?"

He glanced heavenward, as if he needed guidance. "What do I want? You're lovely. I thought so years ago. I think so now. I'd like to know you better."

Her smile was cynical. "You seem like a high roller. You went to Harvard. You drive a Corvette. I'm slinging hash in a small-town café. We have nothing in common."

"What about old times?" he asked. "I had a hell of a crush on you, you know."

When he'd found out she'd gone to the public library every Saturday, he'd made sure he'd be there, too. But he'd always been too tongue-tied to say much more than "Hi." And she'd seemed to shy to say anything at all.

"We were kids," she said.

"But we're not now," he said. "I mean it. I want to know you—finally."

Her smile grew sad, her eyes troubled. "How? In the biblical sense? Is that what the wine and the candles and the sweet talk is about? I'm not interested."

Nick frowned. Women never talked to him this way. He seldom had to pursue them; they pursued *him*. "You said you wanted to know more about me. Remember? You agreed to having dinner with me."

"I agreed because you said you'd tell me about yourself. 'All you want to know'—those were your exact words."

"About me," he countered. "But not my work. Not right now. In time, you'll know why."

She tilted her head as if she didn't believe a word. "And when I find out why you're here, will I be glad?"

"I sincerely hope so," he said.

She gave a little nod and took a sip of the wine. She said, "Did you want to see me again because I worked for Scott and Valerie Harris?"

Nick swore inwardly. That wasn't his main motive, but he had used it to rationalize pursuing her. Shelby was either sharper than he'd thought, or word of Armstead's call had already gotten around—or both.

"Why would you ask that?" he asked, feigning innocence.

For a second she seemed uncertain how to answer. "You were seen on a back road taking pictures of ranch property. The only reason I can think that a man might do that is because he's interested in buying it."

So he'd been seen. But where? And by whom? He

suddenly missed the city—it was a much easier place to go unnoticed.

He shrugged. "If a man did want to buy land, would his best bet be Hole in the Wall? Because if they're laying off well-qualified people like you, they've got money troubles—right?"

"I don't speculate about other people's money," she said.

You don't have to, he thought. *I know what they owe down to the last dime.* He tried a different approach.

He said, "That must have hurt, losing your job."

The corner of her mouth turned up, a new but wry smile. "Of course, it hurt. But that's life. It doesn't always go the way you want."

"So you have no resentment toward the Harrises?" he probed.

"They're my friends," she said.

"It sounds like they could use help," he said.

"I don't gossip about friends," she said.

Damn! He thought. She was beautiful, she was smart—and still as fearlessly moral as when she'd waded into that unfair fight to help him all those years ago.

"I might be able to help them," he offered, hoping he could appeal to her concern for the Harrises.

This time she did smile, but it was cool, mocking. "But you won't tell me how, will you? So how can I judge?"

Checkmate, he thought. His orders were not to discuss his business in Crystal Creek with anybody except potential sellers. He was not to reveal who wanted the land or why.

Brian Fabian himself had decreed this, and Nick owed him too much to betray his trust—even for a woman as extraordinary as Shelby.

So he tried again. "It's nice to know if people are worth helping—"

"Mr. Belyle," she said, "we're deadlocked here. You're not going to tell me what I want to know, and I'm not going to tell you what you want to know. So this conversation's pointless. Let's end it."

She slid out of the booth and went to the light switch and turned the lights up to their usual nighttime brightness. She said, "Why don't you recork your wine and leave. I'll clean up and close this place. I'm already half an hour late getting out of here."

"I'll wait and walk you to your room," he said.

"Don't bother," she said, turning to adjust the blinds. "I think you should go. It'd be best for everyone."

And it would, she thought. She had nothing to tell either Lynn or J.T., and in turn, she'd revealed nothing to Nick. Whatever was going on, she would stay uninvolved; it was the safest route. He made her feel far too aware of her own sexuality.

"If that's how you feel, I'll go," he said. "But I want you to know I'm just a guy doing his job. Part of the job at this point is being discreet."

"It would be nice for you to go be discreet somewhere else," she said.

One of the slats in the blinds was crooked. She started to adjust it. But just as her hand settled on the offending slat, she saw a car slow to a crawl in front of the Longhorn. It was a classic blue Mustang.

Shelby gasped. How many cars like that existed? It couldn't be—but it was. The window on the driver's side was down, and she saw him.

Alec. The familiar curling blond hair worn longish, the lean, aristocrat face with its surprisingly dark brows.

He was staring at the Longhorn with a speculative air.

Then he turned the Mustang into the lot next to Nick's Corvette and parked.

The driver got out, a tall man who moved with surprising grace. It *was* Alec—the man she had loved. He had broken her heart, stolen her self-respect, and made the prospect of sex as distasteful as muck.

"Oh, good grief," she said in panic.

Nick must have heard the emotion in her voice. "What's wrong?"

She didn't answer. She watched as Alec walked to her motel room, knocked on the door and waited. How, in the name of all that was holy, did he have the *nerve*—?

"Shelby?" Nick said. "Is something the matter?"

She watched, transfixed with horror, as Alec knocked again. He tilted his head as if to peer inside the window of her lightless room.

He tapped his foot as he waited. He wore black cowboy boots, black tailored slacks, and a white shirt. As always, his dress and grooming were impeccable. He turned and stared at the windows of the Longhorn, hesitated, then began to walk toward its front door.

"Oh, *no*," Shelby said. She could dart out the back door, but to where? Her car wasn't here; it was in the garage having its brakes repaired. What could she do on foot? Hide, cowering behind the Dumpster in the alley?

A desperate thought sprang into her mind. "Put some money in the jukebox," she said. "Play something romantic." It was half plea, half command. She dimmed the lights again.

Nick stood and dropped quarters in the jukebox. He pushed a combination of buttons. "*Now* what?"

She saw Alec only a few yards from the front door. She moved to Nick. "Dance with me," she said. "Please. Like you mean it."

"That doesn't make a lot of sense," he said, but he took her in his arms, pulling her close.

She heard Alec's knock at the door. She ignored it.

Her heart capered insanely. She pressed even closer to Nick. He began to move with her to the music.

She was waiting for Alec's knock. It came.

Nick stared down at her with a disbelieving twist to his mouth. "Somebody's going to get the wrong idea."

"I want him to," she said.

"Oh," Nick said and looked as if he understood. "Then let's do it right."

He bent and kissed her full on the mouth.

CHAPTER THREE

FROM THE JUKEBOX, Chris Isaac's voice sang "Heart-Shaped World."

Nick hardly heard it. Kissing Shelby set tiny firecrackers off in his bloodstream. He'd wanted to kiss her since he'd seen her years ago, and he aimed to make up for lost time.

He drew back with a wicked grin. "Did you leave your lipstick on me?"

She nodded, her eyes full of shock.

The doorknob rattled, then turned. The door swung open.

Nick and Shelby had stopped dancing. But he held her tight, so she had to twist to face the man who stood on the threshold.

He was in his late thirties, tall, elegantly lean, and handsome in a way that was almost pretty. He stared at the two of them with a combination of amazement and displeasure.

Nick felt the anxiety thrumming through Shelby's body and saw the vein in her throat pounding. Her hand gripped his more tightly, as if she needed him to stand united with her. He eyed the blond stranger more critically.

"Shelby—" the man said, then hesitated. He quickly recovered himself. "I didn't realize you were—entertaining."

There was accusation and more than a touch of condescension in his words. Nick didn't like either the man or his tone.

"If she were any more entertaining," Nick said smoothly, "I'd be smack-dead from pleasure."

"I know the feeling," the blond man said. "I remember it vividly. Well, Shelby, aren't you going to introduce me to your—friend?"

Shelby's body grew even more rigid in Nick's arms. "Nick, this is Alec Oliver. We used to know each other. Alec, this is Nick Belyle."

The two men nodded but looked at each other like two stags getting ready to charge, antlers down.

"Technically, Shelby," Alec said, "we *still* know each other. I came a long way to see you. I'd like a few words alone with you." He gave Nick a dismissive glance. "If you'd excuse us, Mr. Belittle?"

"Belyle," Nick said from between his teeth. Shelby didn't move away from him. He felt her soft breasts against his chest, and her hand still gripped his.

"I'm with Nick now," Shelby said. "You shouldn't just show up without warning, and expect me to drop everything for you."

"I *have* to see you," Alec said. "Just the two of us. Please, Shelby. Even if it's only for a few moments."

She raised her chin defiantly. "No. You can't just waltz back into my life as if nothing happened. You shouldn't have come."

"I sent you letters. I told you I wanted to see you."

"I never read them. I tore them up."

Alec gave her a stormy look. "I won't go until we've talked. I can explain things. Everything's changed—"

"Including me," said Shelby. "Goodbye, Alec.

Leave. This place is closed to the public right now. There's a sign in the window.''

Alec tossed his head, so that the streaked waves of his hair fell over his forehead. He swept them back with his hand. ''We'll discuss this another time, then. I told you—I won't go back until we have.''

Nick could still feel the fine tremor running through Shelby's body, still see the vein pulsing in her neck. He decided to act.

He released Shelby and stepped between her and Alec. ''Mister,'' he said, with his most deadly smile, ''the lady asked you to leave. I think you ought to be a gentleman and do it. Pronto.''

He locked eyes with Alec, and he could practically hear the wheels turning in the other man's head. Alec was taller by an inch, but lighter weight. Nick was broader in the shoulders and chest, but more important, he exuded *attitude,* and he knew it.

Without speaking, he could convey his message: *Make a wrong move, buddy, and I'll break you like a matchstick.*

Alec was the first to break eye contact. He tossed Shelby a sullen glance. ''I'll be around,'' he told her. ''I meant what I said. I'll be at the hotel when you change your mind.''

He turned and left, slamming the door. ''Oh, God,'' Shelby said, her voice almost breaking. She hurried to the door and locked and bolted it.

She pushed her hand through her dark hair and looked at Nick unhappily. ''I'm so sorry. I didn't expect him at all.''

Nick stood watching her, unconsciously clenching and unclenching his right fist. For once in his life, words weren't coming easily to him. He wanted to touch her, to hold her again, but he knew better than to try.

At last he said, "I got kind of aggressive with him at the end. If that was wrong, I'm sorry."

"It got rid of him," she said. "He was afraid of you. I could tell."

She turned to the door and stole a peek through its window.

Nick said, "Is he leaving?"

"Yes."

"He could come back."

Shelby let the blind drop back into place. "Maybe. But next time I won't be caught off guard."

She went to the counter and sat on one of its stools. "I regret dragging you into it, that's all. I shouldn't have done that. I just didn't want him to think he had a ghost of a chance, that's all."

Nick put his hands on his hips. "Look, tell me this much. Have you been hiding from this guy? Is he some kind of stalker who won't take no for an answer? Is he a threat to you?"

She shook her head. "No…I can't imagine him hurting anyone physically."

But he hurt you in other ways, didn't he? He's the one, isn't he?

He said, "I think he meant it—he'll keep trying to see you."

She nodded unhappily. "He'll get tired of it after a while."

"How long a while?"

She shrugged, shook her head again. "Not long."

Nick wasn't so sure. A woman like Shelby was worth a lot of pursuing. He realized his concern for her was real—real and deep. He moved to the counter and sat beside her. "Are you okay?"

She smiled, took a napkin from a chrome holder and offered it to him. "I'm fine. But you've got lipstick on your mouth."

He resisted the urge to say, *It was a pleasure getting it.*

Instead he took the napkin and said, "That was out of line for me. To put a lip-lock on you. I apologize."

She put her elbow on the counter and leaned her cheek on her fist. "It *was* out of line." But she didn't sound angry.

"I was improvising," he said. "Got carried away by my sense of the theatrical."

"I'm afraid I was theatrical myself," she admitted.

He smiled and wiped his mouth. "Long live the theater."

SHE LET HIM WALK HER TO her door. She worried about Alec coming back, and in truth she was almost glad to have Nick next door.

He seemed to read her thoughts. "If he bothers you again, you know where I am. If you need me, I'll be there."

"Thanks," she said. "Let's hope it doesn't happen."

They reached the door, and she began to say goodnight, but he startled her by saying, "Is green still your favorite color?"

At first, she could only stare at him in surprise. "Yes," she was able to say. "But how…?"

He gave her his strangely shy smile. "It was your favorite color when you were twelve. Your favorite movie was *E.T.* Your favorite movie star was Tom Hanks. Your favorite book was *Little Women,* and your favorite food was pizza. You played flute in the marching band. You made the honor roll and were in the school choir."

"How do you know all that?" she asked, truly puzzled.

"After your father said I couldn't take you out, I still couldn't forget you. I got hold of one of the school yearbooks and memorized everything about you. I asked around about you, too."

A blush heated her cheeks. She had done the same thing with him. She'd been surprised that in spite of his hoodlum looks and his rebellious reputation, he was a straight A student. People said he didn't seem to try or care. It came easy to him. When he got in trouble with a teacher, he could charm his way out.

Yet he'd taken part in no school activities. He'd run with no special friends. His nickname had been "Loner," and he'd been a mystery even back then.

Nick put one hand against the brick wall and leaned nearer.

"You had a cat named Ruffles and a dog named Buster. Your best friend was Heather Laine. You didn't have an official boyfriend. In fact, you didn't pay much attention to boys."

I paid attention to you, she thought in confusion. *I kept going to the library on Saturdays because I'd seen you there once. I knew sometimes you went to the park and shot baskets, all alone. You could do it for hours. You always carried a book with you. It was* A Shropshire Lad. *I bought a copy and read it so often I knew it by heart.*

He said, "Once I asked you for a date, and you said I'd have to ask your father. I couldn't believe it. It seemed medieval. But I did it."

She turned her face away. She prayed he didn't know the turmoil he'd stirred in her then and somehow was still stirring.

Nick said, "He said he wouldn't let you date until you were fourteen. He told me not to call or hang around. I figured I was just going to have to wait for you. Then my mom upped and moved us."

I cried when I found out you'd gone away, she thought. *But it meant nothing—I was a child.*

He said, "You have two older brothers and a younger sister. Your father was minister of the First Methodist Church. Your mother taught health and hygiene at the Methodist college. Right?"

"Yes."

"His name was John and hers was Judy. She ran a counseling service for unwed pregnant teens, too, right?"

Her face burned hotter still. "Yes."

"Are they still in Beaumont, doing the same thing?"

"No," she said and swallowed. "My father passed away my junior year in college. My mother died less than a year later."

"I'm sorry," he said.

"Your sister? Your brothers?" she asked.

"Fine. Just fine."

He drew back and hooked his thumbs on his belt. It was a strangely comforting gesture because it said he meant to keep his hands to himself. But he spoke the words she didn't want him to say. "I want to see you again."

"I'm not sure—" she began.

He shifted his weight as if some of his cockiness had deserted him. He said, "I'm going to be around awhile.

I don't know how long exactly. Then I'll be transferred to Dallas. I could come see you.''

She couldn't take the chance. Alec's appearance was like an omen, a sinister warning not to get involved again.

''No,'' she said. ''It's not possible. But I owe you a favor—''

''Then see me again,'' he said in a low voice. ''Please.''

''I owe you a favor,'' she repeated. ''So I'll tell you this. People are watching you. They're curious about you—and suspicious. If you keep on being closed-mouthed about what you're doing, it won't go over well.''

''That's too bad. Like I told you, I'm just a man doing my job. I have to be loyal to my employer.''

She smiled up at him sadly. ''And I have to be loyal to my friends.''

''Maybe someday I'll qualify as a friend,'' he said.

Her heartbeat sped and a fluttery feeling tickled her stomach. She remembered the strength of his arms when he'd held her and the touch of his mouth, warm and questing.

But she thought again of Alec. Her heartbeat slowed, the flutter vanished, and a deathlike coldness seeped through her. She tried to seem politely aloof.

''I never make predictions.''

ONCE INSIDE HER ROOM, Shelby dropped her mask of calm.

Nick had unsettled her, but Alec had shaken her even more. It was like having a terrible nightmare return and seize her.

Alec. She still could not believe it. She'd kept telling herself, *This can't be happening. It can't.* But now the reality was sinking in, and it sickened her.

In spite of the room's warmth, Shelby shivered. She sat on the edge of her bed, hugging herself, trying to squeeze the trembling and nausea out of her body. *Alec's here. In this town. He says he won't go away, we have to talk.*

She wanted to lie down on the bed and cry in frustration. Two years ago she'd told him never to come near her again. She'd been disgusted when he'd written to her at Hole in the Wall, and she'd told him the truth in the Longhorn—she'd shredded his letters without reading them.

But the letters had come months ago. She'd thought by not answering, that she'd warded off any further word from him—yet here he was. Could Alec be egotistical enough to think she'd take him back? It was impossible. He'd killed her love for him, perhaps killed her ability ever to love like a normal person.

She lay down on her bed, clutching a pillow tightly against her body, as if it could somehow protect her against her chaotic emotions. Not only was Alec back, he had turned up on the same day as Nick Belyle. She truly didn't know whether to laugh or cry about *that.* It was as if each man came as a symbolic warning about the dangers of the other.

Nick was a flirt and an enigma; still he'd been a godsend when Alec had the nerve to barge back into her life. When she'd needed him, Nick had *seemed* strong, protective—and absolutely dependable.

But *seem* and *is* were two different things; Alec had taught her that all too well. She sighed and loosened her hold on the pillow. She didn't need to see Nick again, either. The first thing she should do was to stop playing spy and counterspy for J.T. and Lynn. It was futile and somehow demeaning.

She sat up and looked at her watch. It was six-thirty, too early to call J.T, but she could call Lynn. Lynn took a long time to answer the phone, and when she did she was breathless.

"Oh, *hi*. I was out in the yard. We've got a new dog, a golden Lab pup."

Shelby said, "I talked to Nick Belyle tonight."

"Great!" Lynn said. "Way to go. What'd did you find out?"

Shelby put her hand to her forehead, which ached. "Nothing. He won't talk. It's useless to try to make him. I don't want to go through it again."

Lynn paused. "You say *you* don't want to go through it again. What about him? Does he still want to see you?"

"That's beside the point," Shelby began. "You've asked the wrong person to do this job. It's just not my—"

Lynn cut her off. "Has this got something to do with that other man? The one who showed up looking for you? What's his name? Oliver?"

Shelby winced in surprise. Lately Lynn seemed to know more about her private life than she herself did. "Who told you about him?" she demanded. "And who told him where to find me?"

"He turned up at Hole in the Wall," Lynn said. "He talked to Scott. Scott told him you'd moved to the Long-horn and you'd probably be there."

"Well, Scott *shouldn't* have. He doesn't have any right to—"

"Scott didn't think. And if it's any comfort, when Valerie found out he told some man where to find you, she *told* him off—in no uncertain terms."

"How do you know all this?" Shelby challenged.

"I know because I was with her. We'd been out riding and talking. About what's going to happen to Hole in the Wall. And about you. Hoping you'd get some information."

Shelby sighed in frustration. "Well, I can't. And that's that."

Lynn's tone softened. "Is it because of the Oliver man? Scott said he only told him where to find you because the guy insisted you were old friends—that he seemed to feel deeply about you."

Alec Oliver doesn't feel deeply about anything or anybody except himself, Shelby thought. But she said nothing. Before tonight, she'd never spoken to anyone in Crystal Creek about him. She still felt the same primal instinct—that if she didn't talk about him, she could somehow erase him.

Lynn misunderstood her reluctance to speak. Her voice grew even more sympathetic. "Shel, you've never discussed your love life. I've tried to respect that. If you don't want to pursue this thing with Nick Belyle because this other man's shown up, I won't pressure you, and neither will Valerie."

The idea of getting together again with Alec was more than Shelby could bear. "I have my reasons, but they're private," she said with finality.

"Then I'm sorry to have pushed you," Lynn said, and seemed sincere. She thanked Shelby, said she hoped there were no hard feelings, then said goodbye and hung up. Shelby sat on the edge of the bed, fidgeting.

She had disappointed both Lynn and Valerie. J.T., too, would be unhappy with her.

But she had done the right thing, she knew she had.

NICK LAY ATOP HIS BED, sipping red wine, and waiting.

He imagined Shelby lying on a bed much like this one, separated from him by only a wall. How did this elusive woman spend her lonely nights?

She couldn't be getting ready for bed already, could she? He wondered if she slept naked and decided she probably didn't. But Shelby naked was pleasant to visualize—her curves, her smooth, tawny skin...

No, he quickly decided, picturing her was pleasant but also torturous.

She still seemed as unattainable as when he'd been young. He'd been the punk whose family needed food stamps to survive. She'd been the daughter of one of the most respected ministers in town.

He'd had the gift of being charming or tough, whichever got him what he wanted. She'd been one of those girls who looked grown-up when she was twelve, and unlike him, she hadn't seemed to have a dissembling bone in her body.

There had been warmth under her shyness, and a simple purity in her morality that fascinated him. A girl who would pitch into a fight with three brawny guys, just to defend an underdog? A girl who wouldn't defy her father and sneak out to be with him because, she said, "I'd have to lie. It'd be wrong."

He'd been ready to play Romeo, but she wouldn't be his Juliet.

He wondered what Alec Oliver had done to Shelby to turn her into such an ice princess. No, Nick thought, not an ice princess. The pain on her face when she saw Oliver was all too human. And her lips didn't taste like ice. They tasted like—

The bedside phone rang, ripping his thoughts away from Shelby. He snatched the receiver. "Belyle here."

"Mr. Belyle." Brian Fabian's male secretary had a haughty accent. "Hold for a moment, please. Mr. Fabian's on another line to Australia."

Nick quirked an eyebrow. It was typical of Fabian to juggle multiple calls the same way he juggled million dollar deals.

"I can hold," said Nick.

Brian Fabian was as rich as Croesus, but he was a mysterious figure even to Nick. Though he'd worked for Fabian for years, he'd met him face-to-face only a handful of times.

Fabian was not only Nick's employer; he was his benefactor. Nick's mother had been a cleaning lady in Fabian's mansion, in charge of his private offices.

Minnie Belyle had been an energetic workhorse of a woman—honest, dedicated, funny and ferociously loyal. A widow with three sons, she was certain they were the three most brilliant boys in the world. She'd put aside every spare dime for their education.

Brian Fabian liked Minnie Belyle and said she reminded him of his own mother. When she proudly told him about her eldest boy, Nickie, getting nearly perfect scores on his SATs, it was Fabian who helped Nick get into Harvard.

He gave Nick summer jobs in the Fabian Unlimited law offices; he cultivated him, he saw that he was well coached, he brought him along. He did the same for Nick's two younger brothers, Jack and Mel.

Now Jack worked for one subsidiary company, Mel for another, and Minnie had retired early to a luxury condo in Atlanta near Jack. She thought of Fabian as a benevolent god; in her eyes he could do no wrong.

Nick had no such illusions. Fabian could be generous

to those in his immediate circle, but no one was truly close to him. He was ruthless to outsiders. His goal was to make money, and he didn't give a damn if his projects were questionable. And what he wanted to do in Crystal Creek was going to be as controversial as hell.

"Hello, Nickie." At last it was Fabian's voice, with its combination of raspiness and silkiness. "How's your mama?"

"She's fine," Nick said. "She sends her love."

"She's one in a million. You boys be good to her." The niceties taken care of, Fabian cut to the chase. "Does anybody in town suspect why you're there?"

Nick squirmed. "Yeah. A waitress. She guessed it was about land."

Fabian swore. "A damned *waitress?* How'd she figure that? The Harrises weren't supposed to talk. Did they?"

Nick bristled at Fabian's supercillious tone. "They might have."

"Or maybe," Fabian mused, "one of our own people let word out."

"Perhaps," Nick said. Fabian moved as secretly as possible, but his operations were vast—leaks could spring from a thousand places.

Fabian continued, "If that happened and I catch the SOB, I'll destroy him. He'll never work in investment again. The only job he'll be able to get is shoveling pig shit."

Nick knew this was true. Fabian expected absolute fidelity from his followers. Those who didn't give it paid dearly.

"Still," Fabian went on, "you think we can get Hole in the Wall, eh?"

"Yes," Nick said. "But we need to move fast and bid high."

"The high bid is what we have to settle. Who's down there who could start a bidding war?"

"If anybody could, it'd be the McKinney family," Nick said. "But they'd need most of it from the second son, Cal. He's the one with the midas touch."

"Cal McKinney?" Fabian growled. "I've heard of him. How much cash could he raise?"

"On short notice, maybe, oh, fifteen million."

Fabian laughed. "Chicken feed. That's the best they can do?"

"That's it," Nick said.

"My figures say the top dollar value of Hole in the Wall is twenty million," Fabian said. "Offer them thirty. Cash."

Nick swore. "That's *twelve thousand bucks* an acre. I know a place west of Rock Springs where you could get almost as much land for *seven hundred* per acre."

Fabian's voice went cold. "I don't want Rock Springs. Wrong location. I want land near Crystal Creek. And I want more than just Hole in the Wall. I'll by God get it, too. What about that Bubba Gibson character?"

"I don't think the time is right. Not yet."

"Then the other joker who's in trouble?"

Nick thought of the big man he'd seen in the Long-horn that morning, the handsome, rumpled guy with crumbs on his shirt, Brock Munroe.

"He's hurting. He's got more land than Hole in the Wall has, but it's worth less. It's scenic, though."

Fabian said, "Get in touch with him the same day you do the Harrises. Offer him nine thousand an acre."

Nick gritted his teeth. Munroe's land wasn't worth a third of that price. But Fabian said, "Don't go higher. If I get both ranches, I'll have eight thousand acres. That's a damned fair start."

Nick grimaced. He'd done this kind of work before; he was good at it. But this was different, and Fabian was raising the stakes to a wild and reckless level. Nick said, "I don't know how cooperative Munroe will be. Or anybody else."

"Then you don't know how powerful greed is," Fabian said in his silky rasp. "I do. That's why I'm rich. I'll make you rich, too."

"Yeah," Nick said, but suddenly he had a bad taste in his mouth.

"The more I look into Crystal Creek, the better I like it," Fabian said. "This could be the goose that lays the golden eggs. And lays them. And lays them."

The goose finally got killed for its golden eggs, Nick mused. It wasn't the kind of thought that he usually let trouble him.

Now it did. And he knew the reason for his sudden moral twinges. She was right next door.

CHAPTER FOUR

THE HANDS OF SHELBY'S watch finally crept to eight o'clock. She took a deep breath and dialed J. T. McKinney's number. He answered on the second ring, as poised in wait for her.

She forced her voice to be steady. "This is Shelby from the Longhorn. I talked with Nick Belyle this evening."

"Atta girl," said J.T., sounding pleased. "What'd you learn?"

She closed her eyes and recited the words she'd rehearsed. "Nothing. He says he has orders not to discuss his business. And he's sticking to them."

There was a moment's silence, and she knew J.T.'s mood had darkened. When he spoke, his words were clipped. "This was only your first try, Shelby. What you need to do is—"

She cut him off. "I'm sorry, Mr. McKinney. He's not talking, and it wouldn't do any good to try again. I won't do it, and that's that."

Good grief, she told herself. *I've just laid down the law to the great J. T. McKinney himself.*

"I see," he said. "Well, keep in mind whatever Belyle's up to could affect the whole community—adversely."

"Mr. McKinney, I don't want to spy or fuel the rumor mills. It goes against my nature, that's all."

"I can sympathize with that," J.T. said. "And normally I wouldn't ask you to do anything on the strength of a rumor. But the person who warned us that something must be up wasn't just anybody. It was Cal."

Cal? Shelby blinked in surprise. Cal McKinney was the younger of Lynn's two big brothers. But Cal hadn't been in Crystal Creek for months—he hadn't even been in the *country*. He was in Tasmania. How could Cal be the one to sense trouble coming?

J.T. said, "We just got word that he's making a special trip home. He'll be here tomorrow. He may be able to tell us more. If he can, do you want to know? Or do you just want to wash your hands of this?"

He caught her off guard, making it seem that if she refused to hear what Cal had to say, she was some sort of traitor to Crystal Creek.

"If Cal has facts," she said, "I'd like to know. Rumors I can always hear at the Longhorn."

"You'll know if he has facts," J.T. said. He thanked her for her trouble, said that he asked only that she keep an open mind, and bid her goodbye.

Drat, Shelby thought, fighting the urge to slam the receiver back into place. J.T. was trying to maneuver her back into the middle—the very place she'd made clear she was escaping.

ALEC OLIVER SAT IN THE pub of the Crystal Creek Hotel, feeling resentful, angry—and disoriented. When he walked through the door of the pub, it was as if he'd crossed a threshold into the Scottish Highlands.

The walls were ornamented with swags of clan tartans

and crossed broadswords. From the sound system, voices sang something lilting, yet haunting, in Celtic.

Over the glinting bottles that lined the back of the bar was a Scottish crest, a boar's head encircled by the words, *"Ne Obliviscaris."*

Alec knew that the motto meant "Forget Not." It seemed suitable, because he was in the mood neither to forget—nor forgive.

He was trying to dull both his memories and his ire with, appropriately enough, scotch. It was good scotch, but it wasn't doing its job. The memories got sharper and his rancor grew with each sip.

He hadn't eaten anything, the liquor was going to his head, but he signaled the waitress that he wanted another drink.

When she came, he could not resist asking her, "You know a woman named Shelby Sprague?"

The waitress, plump and thirtyish, wore a uniform embroidered with the name Margie. She lifted her eyebrow warily. "Shelby? Works at the Longhorn? Yeah, I know her. Just who are you to be asking?"

Alec drew himself up straighter. "I am Dr. Alec Oliver."

"You're a doctor?" she said. "Listen, I got this ache in my knee that—"

"I'm not that kind of doctor," he said impatiently. "I'm a herpetologist."

Her eyes narrowed. "That's just snakes and stuff."

"I've had a newt named for me," Alec said with an important air.

"Whoopty-doo," she said. But she put her hand on her hip and stayed planted in the same place, as if ready for a chat.

He said, "Shelby—what men has she been seeing since she got here?"

"The Invisible Man," said the waitress. "By which, I mean—nobody. That, of course, makes all the guys step on their tongues. I should have such a problem. She's a sweet gal. But she doesn't fool around."

He took a drink, hoping it would focus his mind. "She's fooling around with a man tonight. They looked pretty damn cozy."

"Shelby? Cozy? I don't know anything about that."

Alec's frustration built. "But this man she's with— who is he?"

"Is this the guy with the white Corvette?"

"Yes, yes," Alec said impatiently. "That's him."

She nodded. "I saw him earlier at the Longhorn, ogling her. And his car's in the lot tonight."

"So who is he?" Alec demanded.

The woman shrugged. "He's a stranger, far as I know. Just got here today, same as you. I hear his name is Nick something."

"You mean she just met him?" Alec demanded in disbelief.

"That I couldn't say," she mused. "He might have come out of her past."

"No. He didn't," Alec contradicted. Of this he was certain. He knew all about Shelby's past; she had held nothing back from him.

"Suit yourself," said the waitress. "And enjoy the scotch. It's your last one. The bartender's cutting you off."

Alec was offended, but his mind was too fuzzy to think of a withering reply.

THE NEXT MORNING Shelby, dressed in a denim skirt and white blouse, crossed the lot to the Longhorn at exactly 7:29. She, Kasey and Lorette the cook had to bustle to ready for the breakfast rush.

Nora, the owner, was still nursing her sprained ankle so Kasey was in charge. It was Saturday, the second day of the May Madness sale, and the Longhorn would be jammed until closing time.

Lorette had been at work since five, baking pies, cakes, bread, rolls and cookies. Now she was simultaneously frying doughnuts and mixing two kinds of muffin batter.

Lorette could do the work of three ordinary women, and everybody said she was the best cook in town since Dotty Jones, who, forty years ago, had made the Longhorn the institution it was.

Normally Shelby worked hard and was efficient, but this morning she was distracted. She was sorry about disappointing Lynn and Valerie and offending J.T. She dreaded seeing Alec and hoped Nick would stay away because he filled her with the deepest confusion of all.

Kasey unlocked the door at precisely eight o'clock and a dozen people flowed inside. The air was delicious with the scent of warm doughnuts, just-baked muffins cooling on the racks, and freshly brewed coffee. Soon the aromas would be enriched with those of bacon and sausage, eggs, hash browns, biscuits and gravy.

There was a slight lull in the bustle, and then in walked the thirteenth person, Nick Belyle.

He was dressed more formally today. He still wore the gray snakeskin boots, but he'd traded the low-slung jeans for gray slacks. The matching jacket of western cut made his wide shoulders seem even wider. His shirt was white, his bolo tie black and ornamented with a single onyx set in silver.

He was hatless, his hair as black as a panther's—he looked every inch the respectable and prosperous young businessman. He radiated such an unusual combination of confidence and bashful cheer that he seemed the sort of man you'd *want* to do business with.

Nick paused in the doorway, looked around the room, and when his gaze caught Shelby's, he gave her his thousand-watt smile. Her heart fluttered in her chest.

The crowd in the Longhorn got quieter. People stared at him, some in curiosity, some in distrust. He ignored them and looked only at Shelby.

"Whoa!" Kasey breathed in Shelby's ear. "Lorette's doughnuts just stopped being the most luscious thing in the place. I wouldn't mind licking the sugar off *him.*"

Nick nodded to both women and moved to the table where he'd sat the day before. It was Shelby's table, but she wasn't going near it. The vibrations he sent surging through her were too strong.

"*You* take his order," she said in a tight voice. "I can't. I won't."

"I heard he rented the room next to yours," Kasey said. "And he walked you to your door after work. I think he likes you. I think he really, really likes you."

"Look," Shelby said, "I want *nothing* to do with him. *Please.* If you'll wait on him while he's here, I—I'll do anything you want. I'll wait on Horace Westerhaus every time he comes in."

"Hmm," Kasey said, "that's tempting." Horace Westerhaus was the elderly curmudgeon who owned the newspaper and radio station. He was as pleasant as an asp.

"And," promised Shelby, "I'll always wait on Ralph Wall, too."

"*Very* tempting," Kasey murmured. Ralph Wall was the fiftiesh druggist, a self-righteous, meddling man who was given to furtively patting his waitress's buttocks. "You've got a deal."

Kasey grabbed a menu and a glass of water and headed for Nick, who seemed to be reading *USA Today.* Shelby felt certain that although his eyes seemed to be on the print, he missed no detail of what was going on in the café.

Shelby hurried to another table to bring menus to a pair of sheriff's deputies. But when she came back, Kasey grabbed her by the apron strings. "Deal's off," she said. "You've got to serve him."

"But you promised!" Shelby said in an accusing whisper. "What made you change your mind?"

"Benjamin Franklin," Kasey said, pulling a crisp hundred-dollar bill from her pocket. "I was bribed."

Shelby was shocked. "You sold me out? For *money?*"

"I need new tires," Kasey said, repocketing the bill. "And you need to face the truth. I'm doing this for your own good."

"The truth?" gasped Shelby. "What truth?"

Kasey nodded toward Nick's table. "That Mr. Blue Eyes rings your chimes. Ding-dong—hormones calling. Go answer, kiddo."

"Oh, Lord," moaned Shelby, but Kasey was already heading for the booth where Bubba Gibson sat with his nephew Dan.

Shelby headed to Nick's table. "Coffee?" she asked in her most businesslike tone.

"You know," he said in his low voice, "you wake a man up pretty good just by yourself. Looking at you is a mighty fine way to start a morning."

"Would that mean coffee yes or coffee no?" Shelby asked, not looking up from her order pad.

"That would be coffee yes, please," he said, amused. "Did you sleep all right last night? I lay awake, hoping you were—okay."

"I slept like a log," she said brusquely. "Do you want breakfast? The special is scrambled eggs, bacon, grits and gravy."

"Just a doughnut. That guy—Alec—he didn't bother you any more? Phone you or harass you in any way?"

"He called once. So I unplugged the phone. Plain, glazed, sugared, cinnamon, or chocolate?"

"I heard your phone ring once," he said. "It worried me. But after that, things were quiet, so I figured you were all right. Glazed—two. I'm going to see the Harrises this morning. Would you have lunch with me afterward?"

"Coffee, two glazed doughnuts. No. I can't. It's not possible."

"Let me have a glass of orange juice with that," he said, then added, "Supper then? We could have it here again, if you'd like."

"One orange juice," she said. "Not supper, either. This is my long day. Extremely busy."

"Ah," he said. "Could you make that a large orange juice? I guess I'll just get to *see* you at lunch and supper. I don't give up easily."

"One large orange juice," she said, scribbling the word and underlining it. Then she clenched her jaw and looked him in the eyes. She shouldn't have. *Good Lord, those sexy blue eyes.*

But she kept her own gaze steady. ''Why are you chasing me so hard?''

He smiled. ''Why are you running away so hard?''

''Because I think you're up to no good. You mean trouble for this town.''

''Do you think I mean trouble for you?''

''You mean *nothing* to me,'' she returned. ''If a man can't be open and honest about his business, it must be bad business.''

''And he must be a bad man?'' he asked, cocking his head.

''That would seem the logical conclusion,'' she said. ''Excuse me. I've got other patrons.''

''This isn't a matter of logic,'' he said. ''It's a matter of hearts being set free.''

She had already turned away from him, weaving through the tables to get his order. But his strange statement haunted her. What did he mean: *hearts set free?*

NICK HAD NO IDEA WHY HE'D said what he had. The words had simply leaped from his mouth as if they had sprung from some source beyond his control.

When he left the Longhorn, he could feel the inquisitive looks of the townspeople following. He ignored them. This morning had to be about Brian Fabian's business. He drove to Hole in the Wall Dude Ranch to meet Scott and Valerie Harris.

With them, they had a lawyer. Nick had hoped they wouldn't. Scott Harris himself had a law degree, but apparently wanted support and, possibly, a witness. Nick had asked for confidentiality, but legally, he couldn't enforce it.

The lawyer was Martin Avery, a silver-haired man in his early sixties who had been the former mayor of Crystal Creek. Nick liked this even less. A man with Avery's experience could understand all too well what Fabian's offer might mean.

But Nick forged on, and after the introductions, niceties and small talk, he made the offer.

"Castle Enterprises is prepared to make you a one-time offer of twelve thousand dollars an acre, in cash. That would be a total offering price of thirty million dollars."

The two men's jaws literally dropped. Valerie Harris's pretty mouth became a pink O. The three people stared at him, stunned.

Nick was used to this reaction and knew it could be to his advantage. He said, "You'll have until the middle of June to vacate the premises."

Valerie was a tall woman with a trim, athletic build, but she suddenly looked as vulnerable as a child. "There'd be so many things to take care of. And the animals—we have—animals."

"Castle Enterprises can add a clause making provision for the animals," Nick said smoothly.

She ran her hand through her auburn hair. She shook her head as if dazed. Scott Harris was speechless. Martin Avery moved his mouth as if trying to speak, but no words came out.

Nick said, "As I told you, this is a one-time offer. If we ever make another offer, it will be significantly lower. I emphasize that. *Should* we make another offer, it will be significantly *lower*. Do you understand?"

Scott nodded. His expression was that of a thinking man who had just collided with the unthinkable. "I understand," he said, but the words sounded hollow.

"I—I *don't* understand, Mr. Belyle," Martin Avery said, with a puzzled squint. "What's Castle Enterprises's interest in Hole in the Wall? For that matter, what's Castle Enterprises?"

Nick said, "It's against my orders to discuss that. Mr. and Mrs. Harris, the offer is thirty million dollars. You have until noon tomorrow to decide."

"Noon? Tomorrow?" Scott asked, clearly shocked. "This is a big decision."

Nick kept his voice cool. "It's big money, Mr. Harris. And needless to say, we'd appreciate your confidentiality on this matter."

He drew a sheaf of papers from his snakeskin briefcase, handed them to Scott. "This is a copy of our offer. I also have a check for one hundred thousand dollars earnest money to be held in escrow."

He snapped the case shut and stood. "You have my card. On the back I've written the numbers where I can be reached. We'll talk tomorrow. A pleasure to meet you, Mr. and Mrs. Harris. You, too, Mr. Avery. Good day. I'll see myself out."

He walked from the study of the Harris house and down the hall toward the front door. His heels clicked against the Spanish tiles. The house seemed as silent as a place where a death had just occurred.

Martin Avery sat in the study, staring at the unbelievable document Belyle had left. He, too, had the sense that something might have just died. And that something was the town, the countryside, and the home he had loved for more than sixty years.

Scott Harris's voice was hoarse. "We have to take it, Val. We have to. We'll never get another offer like this. We can pay everything off. We can make a fresh start."

But Valerie burst into tears. "No! I won't. Not until I know what he wants with it. Will he tear down everything it took so long to build?"

"Sugar," Scott said, "we've got no choice. We have to sign. Don't you think so, Martin?"

Martin, still dazed, shook his head. "I suppose so." Then, as if to convince himself, he repeated it, "I suppose so."

But Valerie rose angrily from her chair. "Well, it's no good unless I sign, too. And I *won't*—not unless I know what happens to this land. I damned well mean it—I *won't*."

Weeping, she stalked from the room.

NICK EASED THE Corvette back onto the highway. At eleven o'clock, he had an appointment with Brock and Amanda Munroe. He would make them an offer, too. Not as high per acre as that he'd made the Harisses, but temptingly, even giddily high.

He had time to kill until eleven. He'd drive and look over the land that Fabian coveted so much. He had to admit that it was beautiful country in its stark, spacious way and could understand why Shelby loved it.

This realization startled him. He had played his part at the Harrises' on autopilot, not thinking of the consequences. Now he imagined what this unspoiled land would look like when Fabian was done with it.

She's going to hate it, part of his mind said. *And she'll hate me.*

She's got to know it's inevitable, said another, colder part.

Yes, he told himself with finality, he would make her understand and accept. For now, he would take in the countryside. He would study it and try to figure out exactly how to tell her the truth—when Fabian was ready to let it be told.

Suddenly he wished he didn't have to go to see the Munroes. He wanted only to go back to the Longhorn and see *her.*

Again he wondered why he'd said such a strange thing to Shelby, about hearts being set free. Because he didn't feel as if his was being set free at all. It was taken captive.

CHAPTER FIVE

FOR SHELBY, THE MORNING passed slowly. She feared that Alec *might* appear and that, without question, Nick *would.*

When Nick was there, he left her breathless and distracted. It was as if he were a hypnotic flame that consumed all the oxygen at the same time he ravished her attention.

When she'd gone to clean his table, he had left a tip that was generous but not so lavish that she'd feel uncomfortable. But clipped to the crisp bills had been another of his cards.

On it, he had written "If that guy bothers you again, call me at either of these numbers. I'll be there for you. Yours, Nick."

Her heart had knocked at her ribs. She should have torn the card up and thrown it away. But she hadn't. She'd put it into the pocket of her apron, where it radiated tingles she felt through her whole body.

So I'm attracted to him, she thought. *That's good. It means Alec didn't kill those kinds of feelings forever.*

But then she thought, *I'm attracted to him. That's bad. He's like Alec, he hides things. I don't know the truth about him. I don't have the faintest idea of the truth.*

At about ten-thirty, Margie Prescott came in for a late breakfast. She worked the night shift at the pub and when she sat down, beckoned Shelby. Margie was a frank, friendly woman, inclined to speak her mind. Shelby went to her table and smiled. "The usual?"

"Yeah," said Margie. "Toast and two eggs over easy. But I wanted to tell you—I saw a guy last night at the pub who was real interested in you."

Oh, no, Shelby thought, with a wave of foreboding.

"Look," Margie said, "I don't want to pry. But the guy was drinking and all he wanted to talk about was you. His name's Dr. Alec Oliver. I thought I should let you know."

Shelby's muscles tensed, but she tried to seem unaffected. "Thanks, but I knew he was here."

"I stopped by the hotel on the way here," Margie said. "He's still in his room. Probably sleeping it off. Frankly, he doesn't hold his liquor very well."

Shelby felt bewildered. Alec never used to have more than one drink—ever. Why was he acting this way?

"Maybe I'm wrong," Margie said, "but I got the feeling he could have a mean streak. You want my pepper spray?"

"No," Shelby said numbly. "I can handle him."

"You sure?"

Shelby nodded. "Absolutely. I appreciate your concern. But I'd also appreciate it if you didn't discuss this with anybody else."

Margie said, "Gotcha. My lips are sealed."

Shelby hurried off to place the order, grateful the subject was dropped. Margie's heart was in the right place, she knew. But the message about Alec's behavior was disturbing

Yet why should she be surprised? She had been his lover, but she'd never really known him. She hadn't been able to imagine the things he was capable of doing.

Nick had promised help if she needed it. But she

couldn't take comfort in him, when she knew so little about him. He was the first man since Alec to make her feel like a woman, and it scared her.

In her first spare moment she took his card and shredded it.

She meant what she had told Margie. She would take care of herself.

AT THE DOUBLE BAR RANCH, Nick had laid his cards on the table with the skill he'd honed to perfection.

"Castle Enterprises is prepared to make you a one-time offer of nine thousand dollars an acre, in cash. That would be a total offer of forty-nine and a half million dollars."

Brock Munroe and his wife stared at him as if he had just announced that he was from outer space. They sat together on their living room sofa. Although Brock was a big, rumpled man, his wife was an exquisite little woman with her dark hair pulled back in a ballerina's bun.

She'd made the interior of their modest house an ode to style. She wore jeans and a simple cotton shirt, but on her, they looked as if they'd come straight out of *Vogue*.

An odd couple, Nick thought, and both seemed stunned at the mention of such a sum of money. Brock was the first to recover. He frowned and said, "You're bloody crazy."

"I'm not crazy," Nick said. "And I mean what I say. I could have the check for you by tonight. For forty-nine and a half million dollars."

Brock's lip curled sarcastically. "Very funny. Why don't you just round it off to fifty million? It'd be neater."

"I'm not allowed to go higher," Nick said. "And this is a one-time offer. You have until noon tomorrow to make up your mind."

"You can have my answer now," Brock said militantly. "And it's hell, no. My land's not for sale."

Amanda Munroe put a manicured hand on her husband's arm. "Brock—wait—don't be hasty. We need to talk about this."

"I just talked," Brock said, glaring at Nick. "My land's not for sale. Did you see a For Sale sign when you drove up?"

Nick said, "There's no sign. But you agreed to talk to me."

"I didn't know you were going to make some cockamamie offer like that," Brock said. "Who in the hell do you represent? Some drug dealer or something? Anybody with that much money has to be up to no good."

"Brock, maybe it's an oil sheik or tycoon," Amanda said, her hand tightening on his arm.

"Why would an oil sheik want to live here?" Brock demanded.

"Why wouldn't he go buy the King Ranch or some flashy place like that?"

"Mr. Belyle," Amanda said, "if you could just tell us who's making this offer…I mean, what is Castle Enterprises, exactly?"

"I'm not at liberty to say. But I represent a perfectly legitimate corporation. Domestic, not foreign."

"This is a crock of bull," Brock said contemptuously.

"I can write you a check right now, one hundred and fifty thousand dollars earnest money. I'll give it to you along with the copy of the sales contract."

He placed the contract, with the check clipped to it,

on the coffee table. Brock frowned harder, and Amanda looked more stunned.

Nick said, "If you accept this offer, you'll have until the end of June to vacate the premises."

"Are you deaf?" Brock retorted. "I'm not vacating the premises. This land is not for sale. At any price."

Amanda tugged at his arm for attention. "Brock, we need to discuss this in private. To dismiss it completely out of hand—"

"Indeed. You do need time to discuss it privately," Nick said, closing his briefcase. He rose.

"I'll see myself out. You can reach me at either of the two numbers on the back of my card. Castle Enterprises would appreciate it if you'd keep this matter confidential."

Brock Munroe started to say something, but his wife shushed him and gave him a beseeching look. Munroe looked as if he wanted to fling both the contract and the check in Nick's face, but he made no move. He sat, his brow like a thundercloud and his wife clinging to his arm.

Nick walked out the front door and to the Corvette. He imagined the Munroe household would not be an easy one for the next twenty-four hours.

Munroe had made it clear that he didn't want to sell. His wife, who obviously loved nice things, did.

Nick expected neither would give up easily. If he had sown the seeds of dissention in their marriage, so be it. But then he thought of Shelby, and he felt less cold-blooded. He even felt a twinge of guilt.

My God, he thought. *What's she doing to me?*

JUST BEFORE NOON, the phone rang at the Longhorn. Kasey, carrying a luncheon special, snatched it up with her free hand. She listened, frowned, and called to Shelby. "Shel, some guy wants to talk to you."

Apprehension ran through Shelby. She took the receiver and gritted her teeth when she heard Alec's voice.

"Shelby, I need to talk to you. I have to go into Austin today—there's a conference at UT, and I'm on a panel. But let me take you to supper when I get back."

"No," Shelby said. "I don't *want* to talk to you. Or see you."

Alec said, "I'm staying here a month to use the UT library. I gave my grad students take-home finals. A month is a long time. We can wipe out the past, make a new future—"

"No," she retorted. "We have no future. Don't call me anymore. Don't come here, either. I want *nothing* to do with you."

She slammed down the receiver. Alec couldn't be so egotistical that he believed she'd come running back to him. But she realized that it was exactly what he thought.

The blood drained from her face.

"Shel," Kasey said, "are you okay, hon?"

And Shelby, who had been raised to hate lies, lied. "I'm fine," she said. "Just fine."

ALEC RAN HIS HAND through his hair. His head ached like the devil. He had hell's worst hangover, and it was Shelby's fault.

He hadn't expected this treatment from her, of all people.

She'd been crazy in love with him; she'd idolized him. All that passion and adoration couldn't simply die; it was not possible.

No, he told himself. If she didn't love him, she'd be indifferent to him. But she wasn't and she protested too much. Hadn't some poet said frustrated love could disguise itself as false hate?

As for the dark-haired man she'd been with, Alec didn't know what the hell was going on there.

She'd been dancing by candlelight with the guy; she'd been *kissing* him. But that chunky barmaid had said the guy had just got into town that *day*. She'd also claimed Shelby had no romantic ties that anybody knew of.

Ha! Alec thought. She could have staged that candlelight smooch just for him—to make him jealous.

He found consolation in this flattering scenario. It stung to be rejected by Shelby—she who'd worshipped him as no other woman ever had. Well, she was still crazy for him and only pretending not to be, to save face.

He groaned, rose from the edge of the bed and went into the bathroom. He took two more aspirin and wondered how he could feel as bad as he did and still look so good.

As he studied himself, he decided he was far more handsome than the dark man, whose jaw was too square, who had that weird cleft in his chin, and whose nose was not nearly as chiseled as his own.

Besides, what sort of guy took a date to a diner and played honky-tonk music? He was probably some flashy salesman or flack who'd come to town and decided to put the move on the beautiful waitress.

Ah, thought Alec, lathering his jaw with cream to shave, indeed she *was* beautiful. The dark eyes and even darker hair, the lush mouth, the complexion that had a lovely, slightly golden cast.

From the first time he'd seen her, he'd wanted her in his bed, and he'd by God got her there. She was the only virgin he'd ever had. How shy she'd been. At first. How little she'd known.

But he'd taught her. Oh, how he'd taught her.

Now she was playing hard to get, that was all. But he'd got her before, and he'd get her again.

NEWS TRAVELED FAST IN Crystal Creek, even when it wasn't supposed to travel at all.

After Nick left the Munroe house, Brock Munroe called Martin Avery, asking for confidential advice. Martin was just finishing making a photocopy of the Harris contract.

The scene at the Harrises had confounded him. Now Munroe's information made his day seem twice as surreal.

"My God," said Martin, in disbelief. "He offered you *how* much? I can't believe this. Wait. Let me write down those figures. You've got a contract? Yes. Yes. I'd like to see it."

When Martin hung up, he was dazed. He did some quick math on his desk notepad.

Harris—2,500 acres @ $12,000 per $30,000,000
Munroe—5,500 acres @ $9,000 per $49,500,000
$79,500,000

Martin shook his head in disbelief. Who the hell was Nick Belyle, and what, in the name of all that was holy, was he trying to do?

Martin couldn't breach his lawyer/client confidentiality and tell anybody about this mystery—yet he had to ask people questions, or how could he advise his clients?

He ground his teeth and decided to phone Douglas Evans, who was not only mayor of Crystal Creek, but its leading realtor. Douglas seemed puzzled by the call but told him to come right over.

Martin hurriedly put on his suit jacket and left his office. "I don't know when I'll be back," he told his secretary, Tammi Cooper. "Cancel my appointments and then go home. Take the rest of the day off."

"But you said you needed me all day," she protested. "You said you'd pay me overtime for working on a Saturday afternoon."

"I'll pay you the overtime," Martin said. And he was out the door.

Tammi watched him leave in puzzlement. She was young, only twenty-two, brand-new to the job and a mere temporary replacement while Martin's secretary took maternity leave.

Tammi liked the pay, but she found most of the work dull. Still, it had its interesting moments—like today.

She knew Martin had been at Hole in the Wall, but she didn't know why although she'd *love* to. After all, she'd grown up at Hole in the Wall; her father had been foreman there.

Now Hole in the Wall was in trouble, and part of it was over a lawsuit that Martin was trying to help the Harrises settle. Martin had been acting funny since he'd come back from their place this morning—but why?

Then he'd got a phone call from Brock Munroe— Tammi knew, because she screened all Martin's calls. Now Martin had rushed off, his face pale and his expression so controlled he might have been wearing a mask. Had there been some kind of break in the Harris suit? And what could Brock have to do with it?

Tammi's curiosity rose. Not only would she love to know what was happening at Hole in the Wall, but so would her family. They all liked the Harrises and were concerned for them.

Tammi decided that she would just drift into Martin's

office and see if there were any little chores she could do—empty a waste basket, water a plant—just check things out in general before she left.

When she stepped inside, the first thing she noticed was that Martin had left papers in the tray of the copy machine. She picked them up to lay on his desk when she saw that the copies were a sales offer.

Her eyes widened—*a sales offer for Hole in the Wall!*

Yes! She saw the names: Scott and Valerie Harris—and the proposed buyer was listed as Castle Enterprises.

But when Tammi saw the amount of money offered, her jaw dropped and her heart almost stopped.

Thirty *million* dollars? Could it be possible?

Hands shaking, Tammi leafed through the pages—they were full of the complexities of real estate jargon, and none of it made much sense, but she understood the main thing: *Thirty million dollars.*

The shock of the sum made her knees weak. She sat down at Martin's desk to stare again at the numbers. No wonder Martin had been acting like he'd eaten locoweed!

Then she saw that the notepad, usually right beside the phone, was out of place. It was, in fact, right in front of her, so that she absolutely *couldn't* help reading it...

Harris—2,500 acres @ $12,000 per $30,000,000
Munroe—5,500 acres @ $9,000 per $49,500,000
$79,500,000

"Omigod," Tammi said. Her heart banged in her chest, and the numbers swam in her vision. Brock Munroe had been offered even *more* money—what was happening?

She glanced again at the contract. It had been pre-

sented by a "representative," a Nick Belyle. Wasn't that
the handsome stranger she'd seen yesterday at the Longhorn, giving Shelby Sprague the eye?

Great Googly-Moogly, what was going on?

She grabbed the phone and dialed her mother's number. "Mom," she said, "you won't believe this—listen—"

It did not occur to Tammi that she was doing anything
wrong. She was too stunned by excitement, too eager to
be the bearer of such astonishing news. She did not understand that she wasn't merely letting the cat out of the
bag. She was unleashing a tiger.

CHAPTER SIX

WHEN NICK REACHED THE Longhorn shortly after one o'clock, the news was not yet at flood stage. It was only a small river threatening to overflow its banks.

The café was still filled with people, but when Nick walked in the door, the only person he saw was Shelby.

She was leaning over a table, wiping it. She looked like a girl in a Vermeer painting, with the light pouring through the windows gilding her skin. Her dark hair gleamed and hung like an artfully arranged veil.

The line of her body was graceful, and he could see the intriguing curve of her breasts under her apron. The swell of her hips beneath her denim skirt was like erotic poetry to him.

I could look at you for the rest of my life, he thought. *And never get tired of it.*

She didn't look up, but she knew he was there. Somehow he was sure of this. It was as if their bodies sent signals of awareness to each other that went beyond the ordinary range of the senses.

He walked to her and said softly, "I told you I'd be back."

Shelby straightened and took a step back. It didn't matter. The magnetism still leaped between them.

She said, "So you're back. If you want food, sit down. If you don't, you should leave. We're busy, and I can't talk."

He sat down and stared up at her with a smile he hoped was charming. "Okay, I'm a customer. Talk to me."

"I'll get you a menu," she said and started away.

His hand shot out, gently grasping her wrist. "I don't need a menu. Just tell me what you'd recommend."

"I'd recommend that you take your hand off me."

He obeyed, but touching her left a pleasant fire coursing across his fingertips. "What would you say is the specialty of the house?"

She rubbed her wrist where he'd clasped it. Maybe she felt the same sensual vibration dancing over her flesh.

"The—the cheeseburger special is very popular."

He couldn't take his eyes off her, he kept drinking her in. She was getting flustered. He liked that. It meant she wasn't as indifferent to him as she pretended.

He said, "Maybe I'll just have a vanilla malt. Something smooth—"

He looked her body up and down "—and creamy—"

His eyes rested on her lips "—and sweet."

"A malt. Fine." She scribbled nervously on her pad. "Anything else?"

"I want something that melts in my mouth," he said. "Something that makes me tingle all over with pleasure. Something that excites all the senses, and that every taste makes me crazy for more."

"I think you want the elixir of the gods," she said. "We're fresh out."

"Then I'll just have to keep looking at you," he said. "Will you go out with me tonight? "

"No," she said. "One vanilla malt. That's all?"

"You love nature, don't you?" he asked.

She gave him a perplexed look. "What's that got to do with it?"

"You're worried about your precious Hill Country. You think I've got evil designs on it. Why don't you take me around, show me its beauties? Convert me?"

She hesitated, then said, "You ought to be able to see it on your own. Beauty is in the eye of the beholder."

"Sometimes the beholder has an untrained eye. Show me. I'm a quick learner. And motivated."

"Your desire to love the land is admirable," she said. "But it's not something I can teach you. It's either in your heart or it isn't."

"So love just—happens," he said. "Is that right? It just sort of—strikes you?"

"I don't know," she said, a fine line appearing between her brows. "I don't want to talk about it."

She turned on her heel and strode away. He watched her in admiration. He wanted to untie that apron, unbutton that blouse, unsnap that skirt. Layer by layer he undressed her and relished the process.

When she brought the malt to his table, he reached for the frosty glass. He brushed her fingers on purpose, and she flinched as if given an electric shock. The touch of her sent the same sort of potent current through him.

He was sexually excited by it, but also astonished. He realized that for the second time in his life, he was falling in love. And, just like the first time, it was with Shelby, the minister's oh-so-proper daughter.

SHELBY WENT ALMOST weak-kneed with relief when Nick at last left. When he was in the restaurant, his presence burned so brightly that the rest of reality dimmed in contrast.

This heightened awareness was exhilarating, but exhausting. She didn't want him to have this effect on her, yet she couldn't stop it. She had felt the same way when she'd had a crush on Nick years ago.

But that was puppy love. Now she was a grown woman and beyond such nonsense. She reminded herself that she'd once been dazzled by Alec, too.

She'd thought she'd found the real thing with him. But what she had felt had been only infatuation mixed with desire—and hero worship.

What she felt for Nick was different; it was more powerful, and more primal. She thought she'd suspended that kind of desire, but he'd awakened it.

She went to clear his table. Again he'd left a generous tip and his card with a message penned on the back: "If you change your mind or need help, call me. I figured you probably tore up my first card. Please keep this one. Love—Nick."

He'd written the numbers of his room phone and cell phone. She shook her head in exasperation. But she did not tear up the card.

Kasey sidled up to her. "You know," she said. "He really seems taken with you. And he's a hunk. You ought to give him a chance."

Shelby shook her head. "All he wants is a fling. I don't have flings."

One fling had been enough. It had nearly destroyed her.

APPROXIMATELY FIFTEEN minutes after Nick walked out of the Longhorn, rumors started seeping into the café.

Bubba Gibson had just sat down for coffee with Manny Hernandez, the local vet. Then Ken Slattery entered, his mouth set in a grim line.

Ken was foreman at the McKinney ranch. Shelby smiled at him as she set down the coffee mugs.

He nodded in greeting, but didn't smile back. He looked at the two seated men. "I just heard somebody's trying to buy Hole in the Wall for thirty million. And Brock Munroe's place for forty-nine and a half million."

Bubba, who had just taken a sip of ice water, nearly spewed it.

Manny looked both astonished and stricken. Shelby gasped.

Bubba wiped his chin with a napkin and sputtered, "Jehosaphat! Where'd you hear that? Hellfire, that's nearly eighty million smackoleons."

Ken's expression showed his deep concern. "It's true. I got the news from J.T. himself."

"Where'd *he* hear it?" Bubba demanded.

"Jerry Cooper," Ken said. "He and J.T. were talking cattle prices and Jerry got a call on his cell phone. His wife told him. Their daughter saw it at Martin's office."

Manny said, "Hole in the Wall's in trouble. They can't resist an offer like that." He shook his head as if dazed. His wife had worked at the dude ranch since it opened, and she loved it there.

"Resist?" Bubba retorted. "They'd be damned fools to resist."

"Who's offering that kind of money?" Manny asked. "What's he want with the land?"

"Some outfit called Castle Enterprises," Ken said. "J.T. tried to check it out on the Internet. He couldn't find anything. He called his stockbroker in Austin. The guy had never heard of them. J.T. thinks their agent is that stranger with the white Corvette."

Bubba shot Shelby a suspicious look. "That's the feller that keeps looking at you like you was an ice-cream sundae, and he wished he had two spoons. Is that who he works for?''

"Yes. He works for Castle Enterprises," she said, feeling sheepish.

"Well, what in thunder do they *do?*" Bubba almost bellowed. "What do they want here?"

"I don't know," Shelby said, yearning for escape. "I asked, but he said he couldn't discuss it."

"Then he's up to no good," Bubba said, banging his fist on the table. "I knowed it the first time I saw him."

Other people in the restaurant were now staring and listening. Manny looked gloomier than before. "Texas has some privately run prisons. I heard tell of another one being put in somewhere."

"I've heard that, too," Ken Slattery said, his face grave.

"They might make it into some sort of prison farm," Bubba muttered. "That Corvette boy could put thousands of felons right in our back yard."

"It might not be a prison," Slattery said. "Lynn's got an idea that somebody wants to put up a giant theme park."

"A theme park," Bubba said, even more aghast. "Hell's bells, then we'd be up to our keisters in tourists. It'd ruin the whole county. Where's that stranger? I want a word with him, by damn."

Ralph Wall, the druggist, charged in the door, his face florid with excitement. "Have you heard? Hole in the Wall's been sold for ninety million dollars—it's going to be turned into a rehab clinic for celebrities!"

"That's the last straw," Bubba said, smacking the tabletop. "I'll find that stranger and shake the truth out of him."

Everyone began to talk and ask questions at once. Ken

Slattery held up his hands in a plea for order, but nobody paid any attention. The river of rumor had swelled into a tumultuous sea.

SHORTLY AFTER FIVE o'clock, Shelby got a phone call. It was Nick. "Hi," he said in his velvety voice. "The news, I hear, has leaked."

"Leak is putting it mildly," she said. "It's spewing out like a broken pipeline."

"Somebody talked," he said. "I'd hoped they wouldn't."

Shelby blew a strand of hair out of her eyes in exasperation. The rumor had been traced to Tammi Cooper. Martin Avery, furious, had fired her; he was humiliated and Tammi was crushed. Whatever Nick was up to, he had already caused a whirlwind of trouble, and she knew she shouldn't get sucked into it.

"Why are you calling?" she asked. She hadn't thought it possible, but he was making her feel even more skittish than he usually did.

"I want to see you. But I don't think I should walk into the Longhorn now."

"A wise decision," she said. "Half the people who've been here want to lynch you. The other half want to sell you every inch of land they own, including their mothers' graves. And they all want to know what in heck you're up to. You've created a fine mess."

"Help me figure out how to fix it," he said. "What time do you get off?"

"I work an extra three hours on Saturdays. Till eight o'clock."

"Let me pick you up. We can go some place quiet and talk."

She conjured up a mental picture of him, the seductive

eyes, the innocent smile, the devilish cleft in his chin.
She remembered the feel of his mouth on hers, and that
familiar flutter tickled her stomach.

"I don't want to see you," she said, fighting to convince herself it was true. "I have to get back to work.
I'm going to hang up."

"Call if your mind changes," he said.

"It won't." *I will not go out with him*, she thought.
Will not, will not.

"We'll see about that," he said with a smile in his
voice.

HALF AN HOUR LATER, with the supper rush starting,
Shelby got a second phone call. It was Lynn McKinney.

"Shelby," she said, "Cal's home. We had a kind of
family council. Daddy says the talk is going crazy in
town. Is it true?"

"All too true," said Shelby.

"Nick Belyle made these incredibly high offers to the
Harrises and the Munroes. What are people saying?"
Lynn asked.

Shelby rubbed her forehead tiredly. "What *aren't* they
saying? Somebody wants to make one ranch out of it.
Somebody wants to cut it up into mini-ranches for rich
people. Or a housing development for not-so-rich people. Or a prison. Or a rehab center. Or a toxic waste
dump."

"Oh, Lawzy," said Lynn.

"What did Cal say?" Shelby asked. "J.T. said he
knew something about this outfit. What?"

Lynn's answer seemed to come reluctantly. "Right
now Castle Enterprises is a shell corporation. It could
stand for anything, be anything. At this point it's nothing
but a name and some legal papers."

Shelby frowned. "Then we don't know any more than before."

"Yes, we do," said Lynn. "The man behind the corporation is a millionaire named Brian Fabian. He's very mysterious. But Cal says he's a mover and a shaker. He's got controlling interest in dozens of corporations."

"What kinds?" asked Shelby, still puzzled.

"One, he's built a series of theme parks. But two, he's also deeply involved in the private prison business—which incidentally Cal thinks is a very *dirty* business."

"So it *could* be a theme park *or* a prison?" Shelby asked, finding both ideas repellent.

"Maybe," said Lynn. "But he also contracts for landfills and waste disposals. And he's a developer. He's built retirement communities, condos, low-cost housing, high-cost housing. You name it, he's in it."

Shelby's mind spiraled giddily. It was as if *any* of the rumors might be true. "Does Cal know what he wants here?"

"No," Lynn said. "But he found out that Nick Belyle is usually in charge of buying the land. He put a check on him, too."

Curiosity flooded Shelby. Against her will, she asked, "What did he find out?"

"He's out of Harvard, undergraduate and law degree. Before that, his past is hazy. He keeps to himself. Both his brothers work for Fabian, too. He's single, never married, and he's already got his first million. In Little Rock he was buying up land for Fabian to develop as trailer parks. He did the same thing in Arizona."

Shelby's mind pounced on an irrelevant detail. Nick was single, never married. He'd told the truth on that. But she said, "Trailer parks? Do you think he'll do that here?"

"Cal's trying to find out," said Lynn. "Daddy's half-sick about this. So are both my brothers. I am, too. Valerie called up in tears."

Shelby closed her eyes, hating the thought of Valerie weeping.

Lynn said, "She said it's driving her crazy and that she and Scott do nothing but argue. She'd give anything to know what this Fabian wants."

Shelby shut her eyes more tightly. She knew what was coming next.

Lynn said, "I heard that Nick Belyle was in the Longhorn for breakfast and lunch. That both times he had eyes only for you. Would you please, *please* consider talking to him again? If you could just try to find out what's happening, so we'd know—so Val could know. And then this nutty gossip could stop."

Shelby sighed. She felt like a lamb being sent to parley with the wolf king. But she said, "All right. I'll try."

"You're a doll," said Lynn.

I'm a fool, thought Shelby.

NICK WAS KEEPING A LOW profile.

It was best he be seen as little as possible, but he could not resist a chance to be with Shelby.

He told her that he'd pick her up in front of the Longhorn as soon as it closed. He'd take her over to Fredericksburg or someplace for supper, and then—well, who knew what might happen then?

He slowed the car when he saw her come out of the Longhorn, right on time, just as the other waitress put the Closed sign in the window.

Shelby stepped down the single concrete stair. She wore the same denim skirt she had earlier, the same white blouse, and sensible shoes. And she looked like a princess in disguise, trying to seem ordinary. He sucked in his breath in admiration that was tinged with lust.

Her glossy hair fell to her shoulders, and she held herself as gracefully as a dancer. But when she saw him, her expression looked wary, almost trapped. He pulled the car up to the curb, got out and opened the door for her. She slipped inside and he got back into the driver's seat.

"Hey, you!" somebody yelled from down the street. "You! Belyle—I got some questions for you—"

His answer was to gun the car and speed off into the thickening darkness. She said, "I'm surprised you've got enough nerve to show yourself in town."

"I'm a nervy guy. You're nervy yourself, being seen with me."

"Nobody's going to hurt me," she said. "You, I'm not so sure about."

"And I'm not so sure about you," he said. "What about your 'friend'?"

"He called from Austin," she said. "He got held up at the conference. He said he wanted to talk to me tonight, but I told him I'd be away."

"Who is he, anyway? He looks like a guy who models silk shirts for a living."

"He's a herpetologist," she said. "His specialities are newts and lizards."

"Seems fitting," Nick said. "So you're with me to escape from him?"

"Think of it that way if you want," she said. "Where are we going?"

"I heard about a German restaurant in Fredericksburg," he said. "Are you hungry?"

"Not especially," she said. "And I really don't want

to go clear to Fredericksburg. Can't we just go someplace close by and talk?''

"As long as it's a place with candlelight and champagne," he said.

"I don't need candlelight. Or champagne."

"I do. I like looking at you by candlelight. I want to
taste champagne and think that your mouth is tasting the
same thing—feeling the same thing, the chill and the
tang and the bubbles dancing on your tongue."

She sighed and leaned back against the headrest.
"You never quit, do you? Do these lines of yours actually *work* on anybody?''

"I don't know," he said. "I never talked this way to
anybody but you. You make me think things like that."

And that, heaven help him, was the absolute truth.

SHELBY FINALLY AGREED TO go to a steak house between Crystal Creek and Strobelville. It was called Mister Michael's, and few people from Crystal Creek went
there.

Mister Michael was an apostle of nouvelle cuisine,
and decorated his steaks with tiny orchids and his pork
chops with frangipani. He had his own greenhouse for
growing flowers and vegetables.

Nick asked for as private a table as possible, even a
private room, if available. Mr. Michael himself whisked
them to a charming little room in the back. It was intimate, with dark gold flocked wallpaper, a white linen
tablecloth and silver candlesticks with white tapers.

Mr. Michael lit the tapers, dimmed the overhead
lights, and bustled off to bring Nick's order for champagne.

"I'm not dressed for a place this fancy," Shelby said,

suddenly self-conscious of her denim skirt and plain blouse.

Nick smiled. "You're wearing candlelight and you wear it beautifully."

She sighed. "You talk fast, Nick. And you move fast. Now I know who you move for. It's Brian Fabian, isn't it? Which part of his organization do you represent?"

His back straightened and he blinked in surprise. "How do you know about Fabian?"

"Just because we're from a small town doesn't mean we're stupid."

He was clearly taken aback. "*What* do you know about him?"

She told him what Lynn had said about the privatized prisons, the tacky housing and the other questionable Fabian enterprises.

"You were a nice guy, Nick," she said. "How'd you get mixed up with a man like this?"

For the first time he looked uneasy. "He's not all bad. He runs an investment group, one of the best in the country. His business is to make money. He does nothing illegal. Not one thing."

"But not everything he does is savory, is it?" Shelby challenged.

They were interrupted by Mr. Michael who entered, poured the champagne, then left as quietly as a cat.

"To Crystal Creek," Nick said, touching his glass to Shelby's.

"To the well-being of Crystal Creek," she amended, then took a sip to the health of the town.

Then she set down the glass, crossed her arms on the table, and gazed at him. The candlelight flickered on his face, which was far more solemn than usual. "I asked you if Brian Fabian does some unsavory things."

"I suppose in some people's eyes he does."

"What about in your eyes?" she persisted. "Don't you dislike some of the stuff he's mixed up in?"

"I don't ask myself questions like that. I do my job. That's all."

She leaned forward. "And what's your reward for this unquestioning loyalty? Just—money?"

An expression of disgust crossed his face. "No. It's personal."

"He's an old friend, is that it?"

"I hardly know him," Nick said and took a large drink of champagne. "Let's change the subject, shall we?"

"No," she said stubbornly, "let's not. Why do you work for him?"

He set down the champagne flute. "The year after I got beat up in Beaumont—when you and I met—my family moved. We went to live with my aunt in Brooklyn. She sent us the money to come. My mom had no education. None. So she cleaned offices. Finally she got a job cleaning Fabian's private offices. He liked her."

"He liked her," Shelby repeated. "And so?"

"Look," Nick said almost truculently, "when he was younger, he was like me. A punk with no money. But he had a mother who worked her butt off for him. My mom reminded him of her. So he—took an interest in us. In my brothers and me. He helped put us through school. He hired us all."

She tilted her head. "He did this out of the goodness of his heart?"

"Yeah," Nick said. "That's about the only explanation, isn't it? I mean he certainly didn't have the hots for my mother. He liked young blond models, not middle-aged cleaning women."

"He did all this for you, but you hardly know him?"

"He keeps to himself. He's private."

"You mean like Howard Hughes, a recluse?"

"I mean I don't know. He keeps to himself."

"So you stay loyal to him out of, what, gratitude?"

"That word works as well as any. I got a good education, a good job. So did my brothers. My mother's taken care of. We owe it to him."

"And you do his work for him, even if it's dirty?"

One of his dark brows crooked into a frown. "Who says what I'm doing here is dirty work?"

"Can you tell me that it's clean?"

"I can't tell you anything," he said. "You know that. I'm sorry."

She shook her head in defeat. "I'm not up to more games. Take me home—please."

He stared at her unhappily. "The only reason you came tonight was to try to pry information out of me about Fabian. Right?"

"Right," she admitted, suddenly unhappy with herself.

"I'd like to set your mind at ease," he said. "All I can say is that Fabian will change Crystal Creek—that's true. But he won't ruin it. The place may even be better thanks to him."

"People don't want change," she told him.

"Life is full of changes, Shelby. It's *made* of them."

She knew this was true, but it gave no comfort. "Take me, home, please," she said. "I shouldn't have come. I wanted to help my friends, that's all."

The champagne was left almost untouched. He left a tip, paid the bill, and walked her back to the Corvette.

They rode back to Crystal Creek, making small talk to keep the smothering silence away. In some ways they'd changed a great deal in the last twelve years. In other ways they seemed not to have changed at all.

I like him, Shelby thought in consternation. *I could like him very much—but not with all the secrets he keeps.*

She thought of what Nick had said: Fabian would change the town, yet he might also better it.

The town had had its financial woes in the past. In the last decade it had been struck by a tornado that had left much of it in ruins. In some ways it had never fully recovered.

Taxes were too high, and though a benefactor had tried to set up a trust fund to aid the town, the money was mired in a lawsuit that threatened to be everlasting.

The town could use more commerce; it was still far from prosperous. But the wrong kind of business, the wrong kind of development could destroy its character, its uniqueness.

As if Nick could read her mind, he said, "If I could, I'd tell you more, Shelby."

"I understand," she said. But she was not sure she understood anything about him. Physically, he was irresistibly attractive. But morally he was ambiguous, frighteningly so. He seemed content to serve whatever cause he was paid to.

Silence, which they had fought, fell between them.

Shelby stayed lost in her own tumult of thoughts until they turned the corner that led to the Longhorn.

"Uh-oh," said Nick. "I was afraid this might happen."

With a start Shelby saw that the parking lot of the Longhorn motel was no longer nearly empty. Half a dozen cars and pickups were parked there, and men, mostly young, milled around as if waiting for something.

She recognized young cowboys and oil crew rough-necks. A few had beer bottles in their hands.

Shelby knew what they were waiting for: Nick. They wanted answers. Her mind flashed back to the first day she'd seen him, the day he'd been outnumbered and attacked, beaten and bloodstained.

Then, parked across the street under the streetlight, she saw Alec's blue Mustang, with Alec sitting at the wheel.

Alec was waiting, too. But not for Nick. For her.

CHAPTER SEVEN

"I DON'T THINK WE should walk into that," Nick said from between his teeth.

He swung out of the street, sped across the parking lot of the grocery store and exited the south side, out of the crowd's line of sight.

Nick drove fast and precisely, dodging from street to street, then down the highway going east. Shelby looked behind and saw one set of headlights following them. She had no idea whose car it was, but she was terrified. She knew some of the men in the crowd could be mean when they were liquored up.

Nick wheeled the Corvette down a side road. Shelby tugged at his sleeve. "What are you doing? Where are you going?"

"Trying to lose this guy tailing us," he said. "Then doubling back and going into Austin. We'll be safer in the city."

"B-but," she stammered, "what then?"

"We'll check into a hotel."

She recoiled. "I'm not spending the night with you."

"I'll get you your own room," he said out of the side of his mouth. "I won't violate your precious honor."

But as much as Nick zigzagged and sped, the car behind them hung on.

"Hell," he muttered. "I think it's your boyfriend."

"Alec?" she asked, horrified. "Are you sure?"

Nick glanced at the rearview mirror. "It's a Mustang, all right."

"Why would *he* follow us?" She felt more bewilderment than fear.

Finally, at the outskirts of Austin, Nick temporarily lost Alec by running a yellow light. Then he took a sharp left into the lot of the biggest motel in sight. He parked in the check-in lane, got out, opened her door and seized her hand. "Come on."

Alec was perhaps a quarter of a mile behind them. Had he seen them pull in? Shelby had no idea.

Nick led her to the desk. "Two rooms, next to each other," he said. "And make it snappy, please."

When he got the two card keys, he put his arm protectively around Shelby and led her to the bank of elevators. One's doors opened, and they stepped inside.

At that moment, Alec came in the door, his face pale with anger.

"Shelby," he said, "I've got to talk to you. Don't shack up with this bastard. You hardly know him. Shelby—I came back for you. This time we'll make it work. Dammit, Shelby—"

The bell captain, a large handsome man, clamped his hand on Alec's shoulder. "Not here, sir," he said. "You'll have to settle your differences someplace else."

"She's screwing him just to torture me!" Alec cried.

"Someplace else," the bellman said firmly, and began to propel Alec back outside.

Alec protested, "Do you know what I've given up for—"

The doors of the elevator shut, cutting off the sound of his voice.

"Oh, God," she said, sick with humiliation.

She put her face in her hands, but not to cry. She

wanted to shut out the image of Alec, white-faced and shouting.

Nick's arm tightened around her. "I'm going to stay with you awhile. I don't think you've seen the last of him."

Disgusted at the scene, she let her hands fall to her sides. "He doesn't know our room numbers. That man was taking him outside."

"He can get them a dozen ways. People can be bribed—and tricked. He can slip back in and be up here in no time. Security wouldn't even see him."

"But—" she objected "—I don't think he'd hurt me."

Nick put his hands on her shoulders. "He's already hurt you."

She flinched, remembering Alec's angry pleading. Nick leaned closer. "He's mad, and I don't want him near you. Now, please, get in your room and I'll go move the car. Don't open the door for anybody but me, okay?"

"All right." She sighed in resignation.

The room was lovely, almost opulent. It opened onto a small balcony, but she kept the doors shut, the drapes drawn. She sat on the satiny coverlet of the king-size bed. *What am I doing here?* she thought. *And why do I have to be here with Nick Belyle?*

But Alec had begun to frighten her. She had no choice.

ACROSS THE HIGHWAY, Alec stood in a cocktail lounge, staring out its front window. He could clearly see the hotel, and he watched as Nick strode out, moved the car and hurried back inside.

Alec's stomach shriveled into a small, poisonous ball.

He waited until he was sure Nick had time to get back to his room—the room he would use to have sex with Shelby.

When Alec had come into the lounge, he'd spotted a hard-faced waitress taking a cigarette break. She looked like she'd been around the block a few times and would cooperate without asking questions.

He'd paid her twenty dollars and told her to call the hotel, saying she wanted to know if her son, Nick Belyle, had checked in yet and how to phone his room.

Now the waitress appeared and handed him a scrap of paper with a two numbers scribbled on it. "Here, toots," she said. "He took two rooms. Have your jollies."

Alec didn't thank her. He stared for a moment at the numbers, 817 and 818, his anger rising. Did these fools think they were kidding anybody with the ruse of taking separate rooms?

Shelby was practically rubbing his nose in rejection. He couldn't believe it.

He went to the nearest payphone and dialed the hotel, punching in the extension number of the first room, 817. The phone rang and rang. It kept ringing. Nobody answered.

So you two are in the other room, he thought with rancor. *You're so pathetically transparent.*

SHELBY AND NICK LISTENED to the phone ringing next door in his room, and she had counted the rings: ten, as if the caller was obsessed.

The ringing stopped. There was a moment of silence. Then her own phone shrilled, jolting her heart.

"It's Alec, isn't it?" she said. She sat at the room's

ornate little desk drawing meaningless lines on a piece of hotel stationery.

Nick, standing by the window, nodded. He opened the drapes a bit and gazed out beyond the balcony rails. There was little to see. The room faced away from the highway, overlooking the lighted swimming pool and the ornamental gardens. The phone kept ringing.

"Should one of us answer it?" she asked.

"No," he said. "That would just encourage him." He went to the wall and yanked the cord from the jack, silencing the phone.

For a moment quiet ruled, and Shelby could hear the beat of her anxious heart. Then, muted but unmistakable, the phone began to ring again next-door in Nick's room.

He swore. "He's not going to pull this all night. I'll disconnect that one, too. I'll be right back."

He stormed from the room, and when she heard the other phone cut off in midring, she savored the stillness and gave a sigh of relief.

She moved to the door to let him back inside. "I'm sorry," she said. "This is my problem. You shouldn't have to deal with it."

He clasped her upper arms. His touch made her shiver, yet at the same time feel strangely safe.

"No," he said, firmly. "It's *our* problem. He wasn't the only one waiting at the Longhorn. I had my own welcoming committee."

She remembered the knot of men in the parking lot; they wouldn't have treated Nick gently if he hadn't given them the answers they wanted.

He said, "And there you would have been, with no Winnie the Pooh lunch box to save me."

Her heartbeat sped up and she was conscious of his

hands on her bare skin. "But why was Alec the only one who followed us?"

"I saw a police car coming around the far corner," Nick said. "You didn't notice?"

She shook her head. "Once I saw Alec, he was all I noticed."

Nick's thumbs began to stroke her arms softly, up and down. "I think somebody—maybe Albert—saw a crowd gathering and called the police. But Alec wasn't with the others. He was in his car on the street, and he saw us head-on."

He bent nearer, and his voice grew gentler. "Are you all right?"

"Yes," she said. But she didn't feel all right; she both wanted and feared Nick's nearness. "You shouldn't stay here tonight."

"Yes, I should," he said. "If you want nothing to happen between us, it won't. If you do, I'm a believer in safe sex. I mean that. You'd be taking no chances."

Sex is always a chance, she thought in dismay. He was about to kiss her, and she dared not let him.

She forced herself to break from him. She moved across the room so the king-size bed was like a barrier between them. "No. Go—please," she said. "I'm sorry for the trouble, and I'm grateful for your help. But go. Please."

He nodded, never taking his gaze from her, a gaze so intense it shook her heart and awoke feelings that she'd thought dead for years.

He said, "I'll go—if that's what you really want. But I'd like to ask you something."

She raised her chin. "Yes?"

"Which one of us are you more afraid of—Alec or me?"

The question paralyzed her. Across the empty bed, she stared at him. At last she murmured, "You."

"Why?" he demanded.

Because I care for you. And he means nothing to me.

She said, "Because you and I are on different sides."

"So are you and he, it seems."

"That's different," she rationalized. "He and I are in the past."

"But you and I aren't?"

She squared her shoulders and clenched her hands at her sides. "We're in the present, Nick. But there's no future."

He only nodded and smiled. "That loss is very great to me."

She feared it was to her, too, yet there was no remedy.

"If you need me," he said, "knock on the wall. I'm a light sleeper. I'll be there for you."

I'll be there for you. She knew he spoke the truth about that. He might hide why he was in Crystal Creek and how he might affect all of their lives, for good or evil—but he meant this promise to her.

She missed him the second he walked out the door.

AS SOON AS NICK CLOSED the door behind him, he wanted to go back to her. But he went to his room, unbuttoned his shirt halfway and stretched out on the bed, leaning against the headboard. He took his cell phone and dialed Fabian's most private number, the one for emergencies only.

Fabian sounded querulous when he answered. "What's wrong? Make it quick. I'm having supper with Miss Utah and Miss Delaware."

"Nice," Nick said. "I haven't had supper. I got chased out of town."

"You what?" Fabian practically yipped. "What the hell happened?"

"I left word with Armstead. The Harrises' lawyer's secretary leaked the news."

"I didn't *get* that word," Fabian snapped.

"Maybe you were too busy with your affairs in Utah and Delaware."

"Don't get smart. I could fire you in half a second. I *will* fire Armstead. It's his job to get news to me immediately."

Nick said, "This business is turning ugly, Brian. The land owners want to know what's going to happen to their property."

"It's none of their damn business."

"They've got deep emotional attachments to the land."

"That's their problem."

"The town wants to know, too. And this is going to affect them, every last one."

"Not my concern. Are you through?"

"No. Somebody found out you're behind Castle Enterprises, so the jig is up anyway. They're imagining the worst. Why can't I tell the truth?"

Fabian snarled, "I have rivals who'd cut my throat and dance in my blood if they had a chance to get the jump on me here. Furthermore—"

Nick heard someone in the hall, banging on a door. He was sure the door was Shelby's. He heard a voice shouting, and knew it was Alec's.

His pulse sped. "I've got to go—emergency."

"Hold on," Fabian retorted. "*Nobody* hangs up on—"

Nick hung up on him.

He raced to the door and flung it open. Alec, red-faced, was drawing back his foot to kick Shelby's door. As soon as he saw Nick, he took a step back instead.

Nick made his voice so soft and cool it was deadly. "Lizard boy, I've had enough of you. Get out and stay out, or I call security."

Alec's lip curled into a cruel twist. "So she's in there with you. And you've still got your clothes on? Why so slow? Maybe you're not stud enough for her."

Nick took a step toward him, but Shelby flung open her door. She faced Alec angrily. "Go away. You have no right to—to stalk me like this. I'll file a complaint. And it *won't* help your academic reputation, Alec."

"*You'll* complain?" Alec spat back. "*My* reputation? I came back to make an honest woman out of you, you little witch. You seduced me, you got pregnant so I'd divorce my wife and marry you. You ended up ruining my marriage—but I couldn't get you out of my head—"

Nick saw Shelby flinch. But sparks flared in her eyes. "You're twisting everything—" she began. "Get out of here before I—I—"

"You what?" sneered Alec.

Nick took another step forward, his fist doubled. But Alec was already backing down the hall toward the emergency stairs. He shook his finger in Nick's direction. "She's not good for much, buddy. But I'll give her this. She's a really great lay. And you, Shelby—I'll tell the world what a little slut you really are."

Nick lunged after him but Shelby clung to his arm, holding him back. Nick glared at the now-empty stairway door. "He can't go around yelling stuff like that. That's slander. You could sue his ass to hell and back."

Shelby tugged at his arm, drawing him inside. "Nick, calm down, please. Come in. I—I'll explain."

He looked at her questioningly.

She couldn't meet his eyes. "It's not slander. Most of it's true."

HE STARED AT HER, dumbstruck.

Shelby felt a mixture of fury, sickness and disgust. "Come in and sit down, please."

He followed her inside and threw himself into one of the matching armchairs as she bolted the door. "So what's this guy's problem with you, Shelby?"

She paced back and forth. She'd traded her work clothes for the hotel's thick terry robe and was barefoot. She shrugged and put her hand on the back of her neck. Her muscles ached with tension. "His wife must have finally thrown him out. I guess he decided he wanted me back. And now he's decided he doesn't."

"You and he were lovers." It was not a question, but a statement.

She willed back tears. "We were. Two years ago."

"And he was married?"

"I didn't know," she said in despair. "He lied. He said he was a widower, that he and his wife never had any children. That she wasn't able to."

Nick's face was unreadable. "He lied about the children, too?"

Shelby's muscles knotted more tightly. "He had two. And—and another on the way."

She'd never wanted to tell anyone. But now she poured the story out to Nick.

She had been twenty-two years old and had just graduated from a fine university with highest honors. She'd learned everything in her textbooks, but about men she was not merely ignorant, but foolish.

She'd grown up sheltered, always conscious that both her father and mother's positions meant that she must be modest and chaste. And she had been. She had wanted to be the perfect daughter.

"I was little Miss Priss," she said with self-contempt. "Remember that song, 'Look at me, I'm Sandra Dee'? That was me. 'Lousy with virginity.' Wouldn't go to bed till I was legally wed. People teased me. I didn't care. I thought I was in total control of my sexual feelings. I wasn't."

"Then you met him?" Nick said, crooking one eyebrow.

"Then I met him," Shelby said. "And I was in control of nothing."

She'd just ended a two-year platonic romance with an Irish exchange student; he went back to Dublin after she refused his proposal.

She signed up that summer for a graduate field trip, co-sponsored by a coalition of southwestern universities. The trip was to Oaxaca; the subject "Mammals and Reptiles of Southern Mexico."

One of the two professors was Alec. "I fell for him like a ton of bricks," Shelby said. "I was a total idiot."

The students had come from a dozen different schools. Alec was from the University of Nevada at Reno. The other professor, a woman in her fifties, came from Mexico City. None of them had known each other before.

All of the girls had crushes on Alec, who was thirty-five, handsome, worldly and brilliant. He let it be known his wife had recently died after a long and wrenching illness.

He implied that the illness had robbed them of any physical relationship. His late wife had been infertile, though he'd yearned deeply for a child. He hoped someday to be able to risk loving again.

Clearly this was a man who needed comforting, and

he chose Shelby to do just that. He told her he was as instantly attracted to her as she had been to him.

Alec had said they must keep the attraction secret. First, she was his student, and if word got back to his department, there might be repercussions.

Second, his wife's parents were still mourning; they could never accept that he had fallen in love with someone else only six months after his wife died. For their sake, too, the affair must be secret.

Shelby understood completely—or thought she did. She would slip out of her own tent at night and into his. She lost her virginity to him atop an old sleeping bag in the bleak Oaxacan desert and thought she was the luckiest woman in creation.

She lied, dissembled, pretended. She did things on the sly and on the sneak. At the time she found it deliriously exciting, and because she was in love, nothing really seemed wrong.

The field trip lasted four weeks; she was his mistress for the last two. She flattered herself that nobody knew what was going on, although they probably did. Alec kept saying how much he loved her and how he wanted to marry her.

When the field trip was over, the affair was not. It grew even more heated. Alec came to Austin as often as he could. He said Shelby shouldn't come to Reno because his late wife's parents might discover the relationship, and he wanted to spare them more pain.

"They're hurting so much, they can't understand how life can go on without her," he'd told her. "They'd never forgive me at this point. We have to be discreet. We have to wait."

She did not question anything he said. She sent all her love letters to his office instead of his home. She phoned him only at the university. Why *should* she question him? She loved him, and he loved her.

"I should have been suspicious," Shelby told Nick, her voice bitter. "I wasn't. I wasn't thinking at all. I didn't *want* to think."

He gave her a look that was sardonic, yet kind. "You're not the first woman this has happened to, you know."

She knew. But she fervently wished she hadn't been so swept away that all common sense was left behind. Talking about it left her with a taste like ashes in her mouth.

She said, "It gets worse. The field trip was in June. He came to see me three times in Austin in July. At the beginning of August, I suspected I was pregnant."

She paused and swallowed. "I was happy and scared at the same time. I thought I wanted his baby—I thought *he* wanted a baby. But I was afraid he'd think it was too soon to get married. I hoped he'd want to, though. I hoped wrong."

She paced the length of the room again, her eyes blurring with tears. "I mailed him a note. At the university, of course. He didn't even open it. He stuck it in a book, forgot about it, and took it home."

Nick sighed with disgust. "And the wife found it?"

She stopped pacing and looked in the mirror over the dresser, as if seeing something ruined there. "Yes. She found it. And he told her everything. She flew to Austin and came to my apartment. I had no idea she was coming. I'd had no idea she *existed*."

Shelby paused and bit her lower lip. "She said, 'Hello, *Miss* Sprague. I'm Alec's wife. If you think he's going to marry you, you're wrong. He'll never leave me. He likes my family's money too much. And he doesn't want your bastard baby. We have two fine sons, six and three. And I'm five months pregnant.'"

Shelby dropped her gaze and stared at the complicated pattern in the carpet. "I felt like something small and nasty and trapped. Like a worm pulled out of the dirt—naked, and speared on a hook. I'd committed adultery. I'd hurt a woman who'd never done me any wrong, put her children's happiness at risk. And then—"

Shelby squared her jaw. "And then she said, 'I've written you a check. It should cover your abortion expenses. There's also a note from Alec. It says goodbye.'"

She began pacing again, feeling Nick's eyes following her, wondering what he thought of her now. She said, "I was too numb with surprise to say anything. Too numb not to take the envelope when she pushed it at me."

Nick nodded, but said nothing.

Shelby shook her head and said, "She told me, 'You're not the first, you know.' Then she called me a whore. And she walked away. I stood there, like the fool I was."

She struggled to go on. "I went inside and opened the envelope. There was the check and the note from Alec."

"And what," Nick asked, an edge to his voice, "did Alec write?"

She still couldn't meet his eyes. "That he was sorry he'd been silly enough to jeopardize his marriage. That I shouldn't write him or expect to see him again. He loved his wife, and he hoped I'd use the check to do 'the right thing.'"

Nick said, "Don't tell me any more if you don't want to."

"I need to tell it," she said. "I've never said any of this aloud before. Not to my family, my friends, anyone."

She turned and paced again to the other end of the room, still gazing at the carpet. "I tore the check into pieces and burned it. At that point, I didn't know what I was going to do, what I'd tell people. It was the most horrible time of my life. I was glad my parents weren't alive to know the truth. But two days later I found out I *wasn't* pregnant."

"False pregnancy?" Nick asked.

"I guess," she said pensively. "It was for the best, of course—that there wasn't a baby. Then I applied for the job with Scott and Valerie, and hoped I'd never hear Alec's name again."

She couldn't help herself. She broke down in tears of shame, anger and frustration. Nick rose and came to her. He put his arms around her, pulled her close. "Don't cry over him. He's not worth it. Shh."

Shelby pulled back to look at him through her tears. "I was stupid to get mixed up with him. It was careless to chance getting pregnant."

He gripped her shoulders and stared into her eyes. "But *he* lied, you didn't. He was guilty, not you."

"No," Shelby said, twisting away, "his wife was right. The affair isn't the worst part. The worst part is I thought 'love' excused everything. The lies, the deceptions. And I wanted to please him in any way I could. I was shameless. I did some things I'd never even known people would do—"

Gently he put one hand over her mouth. "Shh," he whispered. He slipped his other arm around her waist.

"Don't say such things," he told her. "And don't

think such things about yourself. Is that why you haven't been with a man since?''

She nodded, too emotional to speak.

He let his hand glide from her mouth to cup her chin. He tilted her face upward. ''You don't trust your own judgment in love?''

''How could I?'' she asked, her voice broken.

''You should know you're wiser now,'' he said. ''You like me—I know that. But you don't trust me.''

''No,'' she said, the tears hot as they spilled down her cheeks. ''How could I do that, either?''

He stared into her eyes a long moment, his own full of conflict. He said, ''What if I told you the truth about Brian Fabian—and why he's so interested in Crystal Creek?''

''The truth,'' she said, as if she couldn't comprehend such an offer.

''Every bit of it,'' he said. ''Every secret thing I know.''

CHAPTER EIGHT

SHE BLINKED IN BEWILDERED surprise. "You can't tell me those things."

"Why not?" he asked.

"B-because I'd tell people. I'd feel morally bound to."

"I know that," he said. "I remember. You're the Lunch Box Kid."

"And you'd lose your job," she said with an uncomprehending shake of her head.

"I know that, too." His thumb grazed the side of her jaw, stroking.

"Your family might not forgive you," she said. "You said they owe Fabian almost everything. And so do you."

"I'll take my chances with my family," he told her. "I owe Fabian a lot. But I don't owe him my conscience. Or my heart."

"Why would you do such a thing?" she asked, her eyes troubled.

"For you," he said.

She exhaled in uncertainty and frustration. "I can't promise you anything in return."

"I didn't ask for anything," he said.

She hesitated, then drew away from him. "If I'm going to hear your corporate secrets, it'd probably be better if I didn't do it in your arms.''

He gave a smile. "See? I told you that you've learned from experience.''

She pointed to one of the two armchairs. "You sit there. I'll sit in the other one.''

He shrugged. "Fine. Let me get my briefcase. I'll show you the contracts. The plans. The whole ball of wax.''

She nodded, pulling her robe more tightly around her. Her face was pale and wary.

Nick knew, as he entered his own room, that Brian Fabian would consider him a traitor. He stared for a moment at his briefcase and wondered if he really was.

In a way, Fabian had bought him. And Nick had been paying him back all of his adult life. During those years and on Fabian's orders, he had done many things of which he was not proud and a few of which he was ashamed.

He was not proud of keeping Crystal Creek in ignorance and suspense. And he was weary of protecting Fabian's obsession with secrecy, his insatiable competitiveness and lust for profits.

He told himself that he wasn't betraying Fabian so much as reclaiming his own life. He hoped this was true.

Fabian had sent him to set up negotiations to buy the town's soul. In doing so, he had nearly sold his own.

He picked up the briefcase and went back to Shelby.

He sat in his chair, she in hers. He showed her the paper that gave him power of attorney for Castle Enterprises. He showed her copies of the contracts. Then he unfolded a large tricolored map of the dude ranch's property.

"If Fabian gets Hole in the Wall," Nick said, "he'll subdivide it into three sections."

With his pen he pointed at the smallest section the map, shaded green. "This would be made into a three-hundred-acre lake, a park and a golf course."

Her expression was of dismay. "A golf course? What about the wildlife? It'd change the whole ecology."

"It'll raise the value of the rest of the property," Nick said. "Fabian and his planners have it all figured." He pointed at a larger section, colored gold.

He said, "This thousand acres will be divided into four-acre lots for upscale houses."

She grimaced. "That'll be a thousand acres of range land gone. It'll change the environment, it'll change the town."

He leaned nearer to her. "Shelby, it can *help* the town. Two hundred and fifty new families with money to spend in Crystal Creek. And to pay taxes. If this town doesn't get an infusion of new blood, it's going to be gone. Remember that trouble two years ago?"

She nodded, but she didn't look appeased. "Yes. When they ran out of money for the middle school. I remember."

He pointed at the last area colored blue. "This thousand acres is an experiment."

"An experiment?" she echoed dubiously.

"Obviously this location isn't as prime as the gold area. But it'll be a prototype of a new kind of planned community. Lots will be almost an acre, a good size. Most of the Hole in the Wall buildings will stay, converted for community use. Buyers can choose from one of five house plans—"

She stood up suddenly, her fists clenched. "I hate it,"

she said with passion. "Cutting up beautiful land for a bunch of tacky houses—"

He stood, too, facing her across the coffee table. "They won't be tacky. Fabian wants it to be classy, clean, good-looking—"

"I still hate it," she said combatively. "He wants to turn Crystal Creek into a suburb. This is *ranch* country— it has its own history, its own traditions—and its own ecology."

His heart pounded, but he kept his voice calm. "People need homes. Austin's growing. This kind of thing is happening all over the Hill Country. It was bound to happen here, too."

"You're ripping up two and a half thousand acres," she accused. "You'll destroy beautiful country and turn it into—into putting greens and sand traps and *lawns*."

"Fabian wants to do everything possible to keep the atmosphere of this place the way it is."

"He'll *ruin* it. And bring thousands of people pouring in—outsiders."

"They're outsiders as long as the town decides to keep them outsiders," he said. "Other developers would divide the land into small ranches for people with big bucks. Fabian's doing something else here."

In truth, Nick believed in this part of Fabian's vision. He pointed at the map's blue area. "This part is for a more average family. Everybody wants part of the Texas dream. Should only the rich be able to afford it?"

This question stymied her for a moment. She opened her mouth, but nothing came out.

"Face it, Shelby," he said. "Crystal Creek hasn't grown for years. People are crowded in Austin, and all they want is a little more space, some fresh air, a safer place to bring up their kids.''

''Do they have to rape nature to do it?'' she challenged.

''Fabian doesn't want to rape this land. He wants to have a long, caring relationship with it.'' He looked her up and down. ''And you haven't asked about Brock Munroe's land.''

She crossed her arms and shot him a burning glance. ''What's Fabian got planned for that? A strip mine?''

''He'll take the fifteen hundred acres adjoining Hole in the Wall and make a nature preserve, to be owned in perpetuity by the people of Texas. It will never be touched. Ever.''

She looked dubious. ''I don't understand. What's in it for him?''

''Public favor—he hopes. So there you are. Somebody will come along and buy this land someday. Whoever does might not develop it with such thought. And he might not leave that fifteen hundred acres untouched.''

He could see her wavering, ever so slightly. She said, ''That land adjoining Hole in the Wall is all jagged hills and deep valleys and boulders. He couldn't build on it even if he wanted to.''

Nick felt a mocking smile tug at his mouth. ''You don't know Fabian. If he says, 'Build there,' they'll doze it flat, fill in the hollows and build. Don't look a gift horse in the mouth, Shelby. Fifteen hundred acres can be saved.''

She shook her head in perturbation. ''And the rest of Brock's land?''

''I can't tell you. I don't know myself yet. It depends how the first parts of the development go. Fabian will try to maintain standards, though. My guess is he'd split it into small ranches—fifty to one hundred and fifty acres apiece.''

She cocked her head in disapproval. ''The fat-cat weekend cowboys?''

''It could be worse,'' he told her. ''You know that.''

She sighed, and her breasts gave an interesting rise and fall under the robe. He wanted her. He wanted her so badly he'd laid all his secrets at her feet.

She ran her hand through her hair, rumpling its glossy fall. ''You know what I have to do now,'' she said. ''Don't you?''

''Yes,'' he said, wanting to draw her body near his, which ached for her. ''You're going to call the Harrises. And the Munroes.''

''Yes,'' she said. ''And after I do that, what will you do?''

''They have until noon to call me and accept or reject the offer. Maybe they'll sell. Maybe they won't. I inform Brian Fabian. Then turn in my resignation.''

Her dark eyes widened. ''Because you disobeyed his orders?''

''Yes. That, and it's time for me to move on to something else.''

''What?'' she breathed.

''I don't know,'' he said. ''I guess that depends on if you want me to stay around or not.''

Suddenly her face was stricken with conflict. ''I think you should go now. I have to make those calls. I—have to.''

''I know you do,'' he said. He walked to her, took her face between his hands and kissed her mouth, a light but lingering kiss that made his mind spin like a crazed top.

He broke the kiss while he was still able to do it. "If you want me, I'm next door," he said.

"I know," she said.

He put his maps and contracts back into his briefcase. She still had her arms crossed, more tightly than before. She kept her head down, as if she didn't want to meet his eyes again.

Shelby, he thought, *what's going on in that beautiful head? What else can I do to show you what I feel? How I feel? What else can I give?*

But she did not look at him, she did not give the faintest hint.

SHELBY CALLED VALERIE AND told her what she'd learned.

Valerie's voice was sad, but resigned. "If this Fabian's going to leave fifteen hundred acres untouched, that's better than I'd hoped for—even if it's on Brock's land. And what we've built here won't be torn down."

"You're going to sell?" Shelby asked, a lump in her throat.

"Scott says we have no choice. But knowing what's going to happen makes it easier. Maybe it's even better to think of it being used for homes for regular people and not just some millionaire's toy."

"Maybe," said Shelby, still unsure.

"Thanks," Valerie said, her voice quavering. "You're a true friend."

Shelby hung up and dialed the Munroes' number. Brock answered, sounding belligerent. Shelby explained Fabian's plan and told Brock she'd seen the maps.

Brock seemed relieved. "Maybe we could work out a compromise. I'd sell him those fifteen hundred acres for the preserve, but no more. Would he go for it?"

"You'll have to ask him yourself, Brock. I don't want to be the go-between."

"It's a glimmer of hope," he said. "Amanda and I have been going round and round about this. It'd be a welcome compromise. Thanks, Shelby, you done good, hon. You're one heck of a spy."

I didn't spy, she thought. *He told me of his own volition. He didn't have to.*

Brock said, "He's a bastard to put us in this spot. I don't like the idea of this durned development at all. But God knows I need the money. Still, I resent him coming in here the way he did, like a damned hired gun."

He was doing his job, thought Shelby.

She told Brock goodbye, hung up, and unplugged the phone again. She wondered if Alec was still out there somewhere in the night watching and waiting for another chance to lash out at her.

Alec, she thought. *He's used me and lied to me and shamed me, and now that I won't run back into his arms, he's trying to make me into his whipping girl.*

She truly didn't believe he'd left his wife. She'd probably divorced him, finally tired of his lies and sick games.

When Shelby wouldn't take him back, he'd hurled abuse at her. But Nick wouldn't believe it; he had defended her, and more important, he'd told her not to condemn herself.

With a jolt she realized she'd been letting Alec hold her prisoner for the past two years. She'd punished herself by not letting herself care for any other man and by suppressing all sexual desire.

By letting Alec dominate her thoughts and actions, she'd let him keep possession of her. Until now, he'd held her as his hostage.

I don't want him to be the only man who's ever possessed my body. I want to exorcise him. I want to be free again.

She rose from the chair, pulled the ties of her robe tighter, and left her room. She knocked on Nick's door. "Nick," she said, "it's me. Are you still awake?"

The door swung open. His face looked stark, almost haggard.

She thought she scented smoke. "What's that smell?" she asked. "What are you doing?"

"I was out on the balcony. Burning my business cards," he said. "And I guess my bridges with them."

Looking past him, she could see the balcony doors were open. On the little wrought iron table was an ornamental pottery dish. Beside it were splayed perhaps two dozen of his expensive business cards. On the dish was a pile of ash and a scattering of burned matches.

"Can I come in?" she asked.

Something flickered like blue fire in his eyes. He held the door wider for her. She entered. He looked at her. She looked at him.

He said, "You come bearing messages from the Harrises? Or the Munroes? Or both?"

"I bear no messages," she said. "They can bear their own."

He smiled self-deprecatingly. "I hope you don't come bearing grudges."

"No," she said. "Nick, remember what you said about hearts being set free?"

His smile grew more crooked. "I guess I'm not a very good poet."

"If a poet helps you see things a new way, he's a good one."

"I don't know what you mean," he said.

She stepped nearer to him and put her arms around his neck. "Set my heart free, Nick," she breathed, lifting her face to his. "Make love to me?"

His hands grasped her waist and tightened, pulling her closer. "What is this? I wouldn't want you to do this out of a sense of—of—"

She stopped his words with a kiss.

And what a kiss it was. Behind her closed eyes she saw comets and whirling constellations. Her blood turned to liquid fire that ran hotly through her veins.

His mouth felt every bit as sensual and expert as it looked. His lips possessed hers, pretended to free them, retook them, and then took them more completely.

Their tongues thrust and parried, first in flirtation, then in mutual, frenzied seduction. He groaned, she gasped, their breaths mingled.

His body pressed against hers, and she strained to fit closer still to the heat, power and hard muscle of him. With another helpless groan, he broke the kiss and his mouth moved to her jaw, her throat.

His lips explored the silky skin above her collarbone as one hand pushed aside her robe and the other tugged to unknot her belt. As the cloth fell from her shoulder, she first felt the rush of coolness of the air on her naked flesh, then the warmth and urgency of his mouth.

He pulled away from her, breathing roughly, his eyes

sweeping up and down her nakedness like blue fire. "You," he said from between his teeth, "are so beautiful.

"So beautiful," he repeated. He took her hand and pressed it against the erection that bulged beneath his jeans. Her fingers clasped it, feeling the heat and power of it straining beneath the denim.

He gazed at her breasts, cupping one in each hand. "So beautiful," he whispered the third time. His fingers stroked each sensitive nipple, making them harden and ache for more.

"Oh," she moaned softly, feeling helpless and aggressive at the same time. She unsnapped his jeans and struggled to drag down the zipper.

At last it was undone, and she took the thickness and power of his maleness in her hand, stroking it, teasing it to even greater tension.

"I've dreamed of this," he said raggedly. His head dipped and his mouth closed over one of the nipples his hands had excited to exquisite desire. He nibbled and kissed and sucked, his tongue flickering like moist flame and sending heat coursing through her.

His mouth moved to tantalize and arouse her other breast, then began to play between the two, making her faint with need for him. The innermost part of her loins pulsed with want.

Then his fingers were there, playing near her most excitable spot, circling and taunting with fluttering massage that made her feminine center pulse. "I can't stand it anymore," she said, trying to draw away.

"I can't either," he said in a growl. "Unbutton my shirt—please."

With shaking fingers she did. He had a hard-muscled

chest with curling dark hair. He ripped off his shirt, shucked off his jeans and kicked them out of the way.

His wallet was on the bedside table. He fumbled in it drew out a condom. "Help me with this," he said. Somehow, half-crazy with desire, they stretched it over his erect penis.

"Now," he said hoarsely, and they groped toward the bed, tumbling into it.

"Oh, yes," she answered. "Now. Now. Now."

THEY MADE LOVE TWO more times that night. The next morning, Shelby awoke in happy languor beside him. He had said he loved her.

She propped herself on her elbow and stared at him, drinking in his rumpled black hair, his long lashes dark against his tanned skin. She was tempted to lay her finger on the cleft in his chin, to wake him with a kiss.

But his cell phone rang and he was awake instantly. He sat up with a moan and a swear word. "I hate Alexander Graham Bell," he grumbled. "But I love you."

He kissed her naked shoulder and answered the phone.

"I am not allowed to respond to a counter-offer on price," he said. He listened intently. "That's right," he said. He listened again.

She marveled at how intent and businesslike he could be, naked, unshaven, a forelock of dark hair hanging over his forehead.

"I'll see you at ten o'clock," he said and hung up. He turned to Shelby and put his arms around her. "Maybe there's time for a quickie," he said in a seductive voice.

But his phone rang again. "Maybe not," said Shelby. He swore, but answered it. When he hung up, his expression was of distaste. "Things are happening. I've got to get back to Crystal Creek."

Shelby glanced at the clock and grimaced. "So do I. The Longhorn opens at eleven for the after-church crowd."

He looked at her with a wry thoughtfulness. "Will you feel like a scarlet woman?"

"No," she said, and kissed him on his cleft. "I'll feel like a whole woman. Finally."

ON THE WAY TO Crystal Creek, Nick explained to Shelby that the Harrises had agreed to all terms. Brock Munroe had not. He would agree to sell only the land that would be used as the nature preserve.

Brock had asked for a higher price, but Nick was not allowed to grant one. Brock, with some misgivings, had accepted this.

Shelby looked at the land on either side of the highway and thought, with mixed feelings, of so much of this beautiful country going to Brian Fabian.

Nick said, "I know you have your doubts about Fabian. Trust me, Shelby, land has to change ownership some time in Crystal Creek. It could fall into worse hands than his."

"I hope your faith is justified," she said worriedly.

"I think it is. His in me, though, will be shot. Well, so be it."

"Nick," she said, turning to him, "what will you do? If you're not working for Fabian?"

"I don't know. I've been a rolling stone for years. Maybe I should stick around here and gather some moss. You like this country, don't you?"

"I love it," she said with feeling.

"Maybe I'll open up a law office in Crystal Creek. There are going to be legal questions coming up about the development. And I know the business. If Fabian does try to get away with anything, I'm the guy who knows how to stop him. I know all his tricks. He taught me himself."

"You'd stay in Crystal Creek?" she said.

"Maybe I'll buy one of Fabian's lots." He grinned. "Organize a home owners' association. Try to get you elected the chairperson of environmental concerns."

"You're joking, but it's a job that'll need doing," she said.

"I'm not joking," he answered. "I mean every word of it. I just don't want to stick around Crystal Creek *today*."

She felt a wave of disappointment. "Where will you go?"

"Las Vegas," he said. "If you come with me."

"Las Vegas? *Why?*"

"Because I figure it's the fastest place in the world that a man and a woman can get married. And I want to marry you, if you're of a mind to have me."

They had reached Crystal Creek now. The Longhorn restaurant and motel were in sight. She said, "I can't just run off and marry you—it's too reckless. We haven't known each other long enough."

"Twelve years isn't long enough?" he asked.

"Well—all of those years we were mostly apart," she pointed out.

"Not here, sugar." He pointed at his heart. "The first time I saw you again, I knew you'd been with me all that time. I just didn't know how much."

"You're a very slick talker," she said. "You know that?"

"When you're a lawyer, that kind of helps," he returned. "So will you run off to Las Vegas and marry me?"

"I can't decide a question that big that fast," she protested.

"Okay," he said. "I'll be back from this contract business sometime after one. You can decide then."

"Nick!" she scolded.

He pulled up in the motel parking lot. "Honey," he told her, "when I say I want to marry you, I want you to know I mean it."

She looked at him and thought, *He does mean it. Wonder of wonders. He really does.*

He helped her out of the car, walked her to her door and kissed her. "See you the afternoon," he said.

"HMM," KASEY SAID WHEN Shelby came in. "Where were you last night? Albert said some roughnecks were gathered in the parking lot. He called the police. But that you never showed up. Neither of you."

"Albert talks too much," Shelby said, her face growing hot. She refused to say more. But she kept catching Kasey giving her a cryptic smile that said, *So you're human, after all, eh, kid? Good for you.*

The crowd descended in full force on the Longhorn, and as before, everyone was abuzz about why Nick Belyle was so eager to buy property.

But this time the Harrises and the Munroes must have stayed mum about their affairs. People chattered and guessed and gossiped, not knowing that even as they talked, papers were being signed.

More than one person cast suspicious looks at Shelby, as if to say, *Ah, that one knows more than she lets on, she does.* And a few of the bolder ones, like Gloria Wall and Shirley Ditmars, actually asked her.

"That's the Harrises' and Munroes' business, not mine," Shelby would reply coolly. The crowd kept her on the run, and she was glad. It gave her no time to brood.

She knew that she couldn't run off with Nick to Las Vegas—it was too rash, their relationship still too new. She'd thrown caution to the wind with Alec; she wouldn't make the same mistake twice.

Of Alec, she hardly thought at all. It was as if finally the door of her cage had opened, freeing her to fly away from the guilt of the past. She was able to love again, and it was Nick she loved.

Alec had hurt her, but she had healed, and he could not hurt her again.

IT WAS ONE-THIRTY WHEN Nick walked into the Longhorn. The crowd was still thick, but he saw Shelby as immediately as if she were the only person there.

He walked to his usual small table and sat down. She came to him right away. "How did it go?"

"The Harrises—fine. Scott seems philosophical about it. Valerie cried—a little. She said to tell you she'd be fine."

Shelby's face saddened for her friend. "And the Munroes?"

"He was kind of truculent. She was kind of sulky—I think she wanted him to sell it all. But they seem like they'll be fine."

He looked into her eyes. "I went over to the hotel

and faxed copies of everything to Fabian. I'll send the real copies by courier tomorrow. I phoned him, told him that I'd let his secret get out, and I was resigning.''

Her brow furrowed in concern. "What did he say?"

"He called me an ungrateful sonovabitch and said he'd see I never worked in the investment field again. I said, 'Fine.' I thanked him for everything he'd done for me, and then I hung up.''

Her eyes searched his face. "And how do you feel?"

"A little sad," he said. "A little regretful. But mostly—I feel free." He smiled. "It's a good feeling."

She smiled back. "Yes," she said. "It is."

He said, "So are you going to marry me?"

She shook her head. "It's too fast, too soon. Let's take our time and make sure we've got it right.''

He said, "I know we've got it right. So, in your heart, do you. Would you object if I bought you a ring?"

She gave him the sidelong look that always drove him a little crazy with wanting her. "Well…I suppose that…if…"

The door burst open, and Alec stepped in, his face flushed with anger. "I've been waiting to get you two together in public. How do you like her now, Belyle? Good in bed, isn't she? Did she tell you how she had to take money from me for—"

Nick was across the room. He seized Alec by the front of his shirt and slammed him against the nearest wall so hard that the framed pictures leaped and thumped back into place, but crooked.

"You're a coward, Oliver. A coward and a liar. Stop stalking this woman. If you say another word about her, I'll rip your face off and feed it to the coyotes."

"Let go," Alec ordered. "Get your hands off me. I'll

find out who your boss is. I'll report you for assault, you bastard, and your career will be over.''

Nick slammed him against the wall again, so hard the pictures jounced twice this time. ''You're about an hour late, lizard wizard. Now tell the truth. Did you leave your wife? Or did she throw you out?''

Alec's face paled. His boldness melted like snow in the sunlight. ''She filed for divorce.''

Nick shook him. ''Now apologize to the lady. And tell all these nice people you've been lying about her.''

True fright shone in Alec's eyes. ''I—I'm sorry. I lied about her. I—I won't bother her again. Just let me go, all right?''

Nick opened the door and shoved him through it. ''Get the hell out,'' he ordered. ''And don't come back.''

Alec ran for his car, which was parked across the street. He climbed inside and switched on the engine and started to pull away from the curb.

But he paused and screamed, ''I'll sue you for assault, you bastard! I will! You'd better know a damned good lawyer.''

''Matter of fact, I do,'' Nick muttered, watching the Mustang screech down the street.

The customers in the restaurant sat in stunned silence for a moment. Nick turned toward Shelby. She looked stricken, but she was not crying. Her head was high. He went to her and put his arm around her.

A big man stood up at one of the tables. It was Sheriff Buddy Jackson in full uniform. ''Folks, that's the man I heard was drunk over at the pub a couple nights ago. Now he comes in and maligns a girl that's not got a mean bone in her body.''

"He maligned the woman I love," Nick said. "The woman I aim to marry."

Jackson nodded and stroked his salt-and-pepper mustache. "Now, I don't believe I saw any assault in here today. Nope. Sure didn't. Didn't see anything like an assault. Did anyone else?"

The diners looked at each other cautiously. Finally, they all began to shake their heads no.

"Glad to hear it," said Buddy and sat down to finish his roast beef.

Gloria Wall leaned over to whisper something to Shirley Jean Ditmars. Other voices began to buzz softly. Shelby still held her head high, but she trembled slightly.

Nick knew he had to defuse the gossip and get her out of there. He dug into his pocket and pulled out his money clip. He called out to Kasey and said, "I know you'll excuse her early today. Here's a little gratuity for any inconvenience it causes you." He laid three hundred-dollar bills on the counter.

"The truth is," he said, "she and I have a date to drive to Austin and shop for an engagement ring. So wish us luck—we're on our way."

He swept Shelby up in his arms and carried her out the door. She still wore her apron and had her order pad clutched in one hand.

"Are you crazy?" she protested as he carried her down the sidewalk and to the parking lot. "What will people think?"

"They'll think I'm the luckiest man in Texas," he said. "And they're right."

He set her on her feet and opened the car door. "Well, get in," he said. "We have shopping to do."

He got in beside her. His face became serious. "I

thought you should get out of there. You didn't need to listen to them whisper and mumble.

"Besides," he said, "I thought a dramatic exit might give them something different to talk about. Now," he said, "will you let me buy you a ring? Please?"

She smiled. "You're something," she said. "You know that?"

"Does that mean yes?" he asked.

She thought a moment. "That means yes."

He put the car in gear. "Who'd have thought it?" he mused.

"What?" she asked, putting her hand on his thigh.

"That a guy like me gets the minister's perfect daughter."

"I'm far from perfect," she said.

"I'll be the judge of that," he said and kissed her. "Austin, here we come. We've got diamonds to buy. Great big ones."

He paused and cast her an amused glance. "By the way—don't I owe you a slip and a lunch box, too? I wonder if they make platinum lunch boxes."

Dear Reader,

I was delighted to venture back with all of you to the fictional town of Crystal Creek. After all, what's not to love? Cowboys, pickup trucks, spicy Tex-Mex and down-home country cooking. Not to mention friendly people, extended families and a sense of community and caring.

Of course, I have a special reason for going back there so often—my family lived in Austin for eighteen years. All three of my children went to school there, and my husband and I, native Midwesterners, became Texans at heart. And that's the thing about Texas. The people there welcome you with open arms and make you feel right at home. Even blue-blooded Yankees like Claire Page.

Claire has come to Crystal Creek to seek some respite from the turmoil she caused back in Boston by leaving her fiancé at the altar. What she doesn't plan on finding in the charming community is a second chance at love.

I hope you enjoy this story as much as I enjoyed writing it.

Best wishes,

Cathy Gillen Thacker

Made for Lovin' You
Cathy Gillen Thacker

CHAPTER ONE

"DUCHESS, SWEETHEART, please don't do this to me," Claire Page said in her most persuasive voice as she lay on her stomach and peered into the one-foot break in the white latticework that edged the bottom of the porch.

Liquid dark brown eyes stared back at Claire.

Claire sighed and tried again as her golden retriever backed even farther beneath the guest cottage on the McKinneys' Double C Ranch. "I know you didn't enjoy the plane ride here."

Her cousin Cynthia's husband, J. T. McKinney, was a fabulous pilot, his private plane cozy and as comfortable as could be. But it had also been her dog's very first time flying. And Duchess did not look ready to forgive Claire for the unscheduled but very necessary journey out of Boston.

Claire grimaced as the rough Texas grass tickled her nose. "I know the turbulence we encountered scared you to death and that it's hotter than blazes here." An understatement, if there ever was one. It was one hundred and five degrees in the shade, and it was only June! Who knew what the weeks ahead might hold, as they got deeper into their very first Texas summer. "But you can't stay under the porch forever," Claire stated firmly, tapping the ground with the flat of her palm, in the hand signal learned eight months ago in puppy obedience classes. "You have to come out. Now, Duchess." Duchess merely whined and backed even farther away from Claire.

Claire sighed, and let her head fall in defeat. Now what was she supposed to do, she wondered, crawl beneath the porch to physically, pull out her misbehaving dog, or continue to lie here like an idiot, coaxing her?

Without warning, a shadow loomed over her. The commanding footsteps were accompanied by the sound of a throat clearing, and a husky male voice. "I wouldn't do that if I were you," the witness to her highly embarrassing predicament said.

"What?" Claire shot back, still stubbornly holding her position, even as she turned her head slightly to get a knee-down look at the person talking to her. The last thing she wanted was an encounter with one of the cowboys that worked on the ranch. And from the scuffed state of the dark brown boots and the worn hem of the jeans, she could tell that this was no city slicker looming over her. But rather, was a tall, strong and capable-looking cowboy.

Which was, Claire thought, exactly what she didn't need. An encounter with a Marlboro Man who thought she needed rescuing.

"Don't put your face down in the grass that way," the interloper continued in his soft, compelling Texas drawl. "Fire ants, you know."

Claire tensed even more. "What are they?" she asked hurriedly, lifting her head off the ground.

"Ants that sting—usually in a group if they feel threatened. You can get a couple dozen bites in a matter of seconds, if you disrupt one of their nests. And the welts burn like fire—hence the name."

That, she didn't need. Hadn't she already suffered enough pain and humiliation the past few weeks?

In a much more cooperative frame of mind, Claire popped up, to a sitting position. With the help of the cowboy's gallantly outstretched hand, she struggled to her feet.

"We haven't met." The tall sexy cowboy kept a hold on her right hand, as she planted her low-heeled sandals in the grass. He stared down at her in a way that was just friendly and amiable enough to make her heart skip a beat. "I'm Dusty Turner," he told her with a cordiality that would have impressed even Claire's proper New England family.

Claire's hand tingled where their palms touched. His hand was so much warmer and rougher than hers. His bittersweet chocolate eyes so much more direct. She swallowed hard around the lump in her throat. "Claire Page."

"I know." The cowboy's sexy grin widened. He released his grip on her hand as he surveyed her from head to toe, taking in her rumpled clothing and slightly worse-for-wear state. "Cynthia's cousin from Boston."

"Right again," Although her newly honed sense of self-preservation was telling her to run for her life— before she became overwhelmed with the undeniable charisma of his presence—Claire thought it would be rude to tear her eyes from his ruggedly handsome face.

Oblivious to the licentious nature of her thoughts, his thin sensual lips curved in a knowing smile. "J.T. said you'd be staying here."

Until I lick my wounds. And get over the humiliation I left behind. "That's the plan," Claire announced cheerfully, doing her best to pretend her life was not in ruin.

"I also know you want to be given wide berth."

"They told you that?" Usually, J.T. and Cynthia were much more circumspect than that.

He shrugged his broad shoulders affably. "Everyone in Crystal Creek knows they went up to Boston to attend your fancy wedding."

"Only it didn't happen," Claire reflected, recalling even now how perplexed and horrified everyone—including Cynthia and J.T.'s nine-year-old daughter, Jennifer—had been as Claire had dashed, red-faced and sobbing, back down the aisle before the ceremony was completed.

"Right. So they came back, with you in tow," Dusty continued summing up the situation matter-of-factly.

Claire's exodus to Texas had been Cynthia and J.T.'s idea, seconded by the rest of the Page family. Claire knew what they were all hoping—that somehow she would do as her cousin Cynthia had a decade earlier, and find the love of her life right here in Texas. But Claire had no such agenda for herself. All she wanted to do was put the debacle of her near-wedding behind her. And avoid answering any more of the questions being put to her. She sighed, discouraged to find she had brought the scandal of her actions with her to Crystal Creek, instead of leaving them behind her, as she had hoped. "My humiliation is now complete."

Again, Dusty flashed her a sweet-as-molasses smile. "There's nothing wrong with calling off something that obviously would have been a mistake."

Claire lifted her chin to look deep into his eyes. "How do you know my marriage to Dennis Elliott would have been a mistake?" she demanded, aware that there was nothing she disliked more than a guy who thought he knew it all, when he really understood nothing.

"Because if it wasn't, you would've married him," Dusty answered practically, before nodding at the porch. "That your dog under there?"

Now, onto the other reason for her embarrassment. Claire sighed again, ''Yes.''

He bent to study the break in the seam of the latticework. ''Need some help getting her out from under there?''

''No,'' Claire stated decisively. If there was one thing this whole situation had taught her, it was that she had to stand on her own two feet, and not run to anyone else to take care of life's calamities for her. It was up to her and her alone, Claire told herself sternly, to make herself happy. She didn't need some sexy Texas cowboy to help her out.

Dusty lifted his brow in a very skeptical fashion.

''I can do it,'' Claire insisted.

''Oh, I can see that,'' he drawled, rolling his eyes, and tossing his Stetson up onto the porch.

''Really. I don't need your help,'' Claire said.

''It's no problem.'' Dusty ran his hands through the wavy layers of his dark brown hair, before striding closer to the porch. ''I promise.''

''But it would be for me.'' Claire moved quickly to cut him off at the pass.

Dusty did a double take. ''Beg your pardon?''

She moved between Dusty and the jagged break in the latticework. ''I've decided I am going to stand on my own two feet, for a change,'' she announced, putting both her hands on her hips.

''Wouldn't dream of stopping you from doing that,'' he replied, just as emphatically as he prepared to move her aside, with or without her cooperation.

''So that means,'' Claire continued defiantly as she dug in her heels and refused to respond to the light but insistent pressure of his hand on her left elbow, ''I can't act like a damsel in distress and allow you or any other man to solve my problems for me."

He dropped his hand. Blew out a long, exasperated breath. "What if I just come to your rescue instead?" he asked chivalrously.

Claire offered a tight, but unrelenting, smile. "Same thing," she said.

He took his time, studying her hair, her face, her lips, before returning his gaze oh so deliberately to her eyes. "Not necessarily, you being a Yankee in Texas, and all that."

Taking offense at the humor-filled presumption in his low drawl, Claire squared her shoulders for battle. "Duchess is my dog," she stated flatly, once again. "I can handle her. So if you'll just be on your way." Claire made shooing motions with both hands.

"All right," Dusty relented with obvious reluctance. Once again, he looked deep into her eyes. "But if you change your mind," he said.

Claire held up a staying hand, deliberately cutting off whatever else he had to say, and promised in a low, equally determined voice, "I won't."

DUSTY PICKED UP HIS HAT, placed it back on his head, and walked off, shaking his head all the while. Women. Particularly pretty women. And Claire Page was nothing if not drop-dead beautiful in that patrician New England way that made even the most unsociable cowboy stop and stare. Her chin-length platinum-blond hair was cut to frame her elegant oval face. And the perfection didn't end there. Her long-lashed eyes were the blue of the Texas sky, her cheekbones elegantly high, her skin flawless and ivory. She couldn't have been more than five-six, which made her a good eight inches shorter than he was, but she more than made up for that with her lithe, slender body and abundant curves. Damn, she was sexy, he thought as he gave her one last look, even if she wasn't the most neighborly woman he had ever met.

"What is Claire doing?" Sandy Russell asked as Dusty joined her in the yard, outside the barn. J.T.'s eighteen-year-old granddaughter was often at the ranch, to visit family and help with the horses. Today, the high school senior, who was currently thinking about becoming a vet herself one day, was there to help Dusty vaccinate some of the colts and fillies that had been born during the spring.

Dusty reached into the back of his dark green pickup truck, and opened his leather veterinary bag. "Her dog's run under the porch and won't come out."

"Why didn't you get Duchess out for her?" Sandy asked as she leaned against the side of the pickup in typical tomboy fashion, arms folded in front of her, one ankle crossed over the other.

Dusty looked over at the ponytailed teen, who had a reputation for stubbornness every bit as strong as her stepmother's. Once Sandy's or her stepmom's mind was made up about something, the saying went, it stayed made. That made for a lot of friction between the two when they didn't see eye to eye. Fortunately, Lynn and Sandy were brought together in an equally strong way by their love of horses and their penchant for hard physical work.

"Because Claire doesn't want the help," Dusty said. And Dusty made it a policy not to go where he wasn't wanted or needed, even when, as in this case, he was all too ready and willing to lend a hand. In preparation for the day's activities, he began lining up the medicine and syringes on the flatbed of the truck, so everything would be in easy reach.

"It doesn't look like Claire's being very successful." Sandy squinted at the attractive blond city slicker lying in the grass. "In fact, I think Duchess has gone even further beneath the porch, than she was a minute ago," Sandy said, as she dropped down on her haunches to get a better look.

No surprise there, Dusty thought, with another impatient shake of his head. Figuring the less audience Claire and her recalcitrant pup had, he turned back to Sandy. "Why don't you get a bridle out of the barn, and bring the first filly out into the yard so I can take a look at her," Dusty suggested.

Sandy beamed. "Sure thing."

While Sandy trotted off, her messy ponytail bobbing on the back of her head, Dusty couldn't help but hazard a glance back at the guest cottage. To his surprise, Claire was no longer simply lying beside the uneven break in the latticework. She was scooting forward on her tummy, ready to work her way in, too.

Dusty didn't know what had happened to the decorative wood trim beneath the porch. He did know a break like that hadn't happened on its own. Which meant something—other than Claire's dog—had probably busted up the white skirt. And the scent of that destructive something was likely what Duchess was after.

He wasn't so worried about Duchess. She was a dog, and likely had the instinct to keep herself safe, if whatever had done the damage was still in there.

City slicker and visiting socialite Claire Page was another matter. She obviously didn't have the sense God gave a goose.

Swearing silently and vigorously to himself, Dusty

dropped what he was doing and headed for the guest house, his long strides tearing away the grass. "Don't go in there!" he yelled to Claire.

Claire backed out just far enough to cast him a disparaging look over her shoulder. "Don't tell me what to do!" she shouted, then dropping back on her tummy and elbows, prepared to work her way right back in.

Her head disappeared. So did her shoulders.

As he knelt beside Claire, Dusty heard a thumping sound and suddenly caught a glimpse of what Duchess was after. Aware there was no time to lose, he grabbed hold of Claire's legs, just above the ankles, and prepared to save her whether she liked it or not.

CHAPTER TWO

ONE MINUTE CLAIRE WAS head and shoulders beneath the porch, the next she was lying on the grass, just outside of it. Her heart pounding, Claire whipped her head around and stared up at Dusty Turner in stunned indignation. "What the heck do you think you're doing?" she demanded, wondering where he got off tugging her out from beneath the porch that way.

He stepped over her as if she were nothing more than a nuisance. "Move."

"What?" she demanded, even more shocked at the raw command in his low tone.

He scowled a dire warning. "I said move!"

Before Claire could do more than draw a quick insulted breath, he bent over her waist, wrapped his hands around her middle, and behaving as if she weighed no more than a feather pillow, lifted her up. Dropping her down on the grass he crawled forward, not stopping until he had disappeared completely beneath the porch. "Come here, girl," Dusty ordered Duchess, and there was no mistaking the quiet urgency in his voice. "You don't want to mess with that," Dusty continued soothing in a quiet, confidence inspiring tone.

Mess with what? Claire wondered, craning her neck to see, as Dusty disappeared into the shadows.

Moving closer to the latticework, Claire peered beneath the cottage. She couldn't see much. It was too dark in the crawl space. But she could hear something. Thump, thump, thump, followed by a low growl from Duchess's throat.

Too late, Claire realized what Duchess and Dusty had already picked up on—there was danger there. She moved even closer, putting her face directly against the wood skirt edging the porch. Through the latticework, she could make out Dusty, lying flat, in the center of the crawl space. Duchess was just ahead of him. Backed into a corner was one of the ugliest wild animals she had ever seen. A good two and a half feet long, it looked like it weighed about twenty-five pounds. It had the face of a rodent and was covered with quills. The porcupine's back was bristling and arched toward Duchess, as it banged its tail back and forth in warning.

Duchess emitted a low growl in return, and crawled even closer. Quills flew like poison darts from the porcupine's back.

"So much for the dignified approach," Dusty muttered, grabbing Claire's golden retriever by her hips and hind legs. "Duchess, you're coming with me whether you like it or not."

Duchess yelped in surprise. Seconds later, Dusty had pulled her out from under the porch. Grabbing all four of Duchess's legs, he picked up the sixty-five pound dog and brought her over to Claire. "Get her up on the porch, safely out of harm's way, and hang on to her. I'll be right back."

He leapt up and made a dash for the green pickup truck parked next to the barn. A scant minute later, he was back, a gun in his hand.

Claire gasped and held a wiggling, impossibly excited and whining Duchess all the tighter. "You aren't going to shoot it!'' she said in dismay. She wanted it gone, not dead.

Dusty stuck a dart in the end of the gun. He knelt down before the hole in the latticework. ''Don't worry. The only thing this is going to hurt is its pride.''

TEN MINUTES LATER, Dusty had the well-sedated porcupine in a cage on the back of his pickup truck.

''What are you going to do with it?'' Claire asked, glad the situation was over.

Dusty strode toward her, his steps long and languid. As he came closer, Claire noted his eyes were alight with a distinctly sexual, distinctly masculine appreciation of her. ''I'm going to take it over to the vet clinic and have it tested for rabies.''

''You think it was sick?'' Claire asked uneasily.

Dusty shrugged and came up to sit beside Claire and her pup on the top of the porch steps. He had washed his face and hands in the outdoor spigot, but his blue denim work shirt and snug-fitting jeans were streaked with dirt, as was her outfit.

''Let's put it this way,'' Dusty said. ''Male porcupines are known to venture out of their home territory during mating season, but that doesn't start until September. So, this fella could have gotten lost, or he could've just been looking for more salt—porcupines need a lot of salt in their diets—and ended up under the porch.''

Trying hard not to notice how much she appreciated Dusty's sturdy male presence and inherently chivalrous nature, Claire stroked her hand down Duchess's back. ''There's salt under the porch?''

Dusty sat forward slightly, clasped hands dangling between his spread knees. ''There's wood glue and paint, both of which have adequate salt sources in them, and which you can see he was already nibbling on. Hence, the break in the latticework happened, near as I can tell, sometime during the night. Porcupines are mainly nocturnal, so he was probably under there just sleeping off the binge. That is until Duchess here got wind of his scent.''

Another shiver ran through Claire as she shifted instinctively closer to Dusty. "What would have happened if Duchess had gotten close to him?" she asked. She was embarrassed by her need for protection, but unable to deny it, all the same.

Dusty reached over and petted Duchess, too, caressing her thick golden fur with long, gentle strokes. "She might have caught a quill.''

Claire gasped at the thought of that—those quills had looked dangerous—and pressed her free hand to her chest. "Is it poisonous?''

"No," Dusty said, frowning, as he continued to lavish affection on her pet, "but as you can guess it would hurt like the dickens, and if Duchess had caught one in the eye, it could have blinded her.''

"Oh my goodness.''

Dusty slanted her a reproachful sidelong glance. "As they say, you're not in Boston anymore," he chastised Claire sternly. "You need to keep a better eye on your dog. Probably keep her on a leash.''

Claire tensed at the censure in his voice. Obviously, he thought he could have done a lot better managing Duchess from the get-go. Not sure why that should irritate her, yet knowing it did anyway, she snapped, "Thank you for the advice.''

He regarded her quietly. "Let me guess." He dropped his hand back to his muscular thigh. "You'd already thought of that.''

"Obviously." As she watched how lovingly attentive Dusty's touch was as he stroked and caressed her beloved dog, she knew his treatment of a woman would be even more gentle and loving. Claire swallowed and pushed the unwelcome thought away as a pulse beat of silence stretched between them.

Sandy Russell came forward. "Are we still going to vaccinate the horses today, Dusty?"

Dusty rubbed his jaw with his hand as he took a moment to consider. "It's getting kind of late, and I've got to take this porcupine into Crystal Creek, so—maybe we better do it in the morning, and do them all then." He picked up his Stetson from where he had left it, on the porch, and put it back on his head. "Nine o'clock all right with you?" he asked.

"Sure." Sandy headed off, her cowgirl boots eating up the ground, both hands shoved in the back pockets of her jeans.

"We better be going back inside, too," Claire said stiffly. She started to move away, then remembering her manners, turned back to him once again. "Thank you for saving my dog," she said politely, wishing he hadn't made her feel like such a fool and an incompetent pet owner all in one fell swoop.

But Dusty merely grinned and touched his hand to the brim of his hat. "No problem, ma'm," he reassured her with a wink and a sexy smile. "No problem at all."

"THAT MUST HAVE BEEN something," Cynthia said to Claire as Claire stood in the kitchen of the Double C ranch house.

Cynthia was making a curry feast for dinner, with all the fixings—a meal she was rightly famous for—and the kitchen smelled deliciously of roasting spices and beef.

"I don't know when we've seen a porcupine around here," Cynthia continued as she finished cooking up the chapati—an unleavened bread much like a tortilla—on the griddle.

"Not very often, that's for sure, Mommy!" nine-year-old Jennifer said, as she plucked a piece of warm chapati from the linen-lined basket.

Cynthia smiled at her and J.T.'s daughter. "Do me a favor, would you please, honey? And go and tell Daddy that dinner will be ready soon. He's in his study."

Because it was Lettie Mae's day off, Claire helped Cynthia carry everything into the formal dining room, where the table had already been set. "I thought you said it was going to be just us this evening," Claire said. There were five places, not four, set.

"We have another guest coming," Cynthia said, as she placed everything in the center of the big table.

Claire felt herself tense as she continued pouring ice water from the pitcher into the glasses already on the table. "Male or female?"

"Male. Now, Claire," Cynthia warned, almost too innocently, "don't jump to conclusions."

"So this isn't a fix-up?" Claire pressed.

Cynthia hesitated—a fraction of a second too long.

"I thought you understood—after what I went through with Dennis Elliott—the way he kept things from me and ran away from his personal responsibilities—that I couldn't be involved with anyone else. Not even on a very superficial, fixed-up level," Claire said. The last thing she needed was to yet again get entangled with a man who didn't share her values.

"I understand you don't want to be serious about anyone for a while," Cynthia said firmly, "but that doesn't mean you can't have a social life or make new friends."

"Just out of curiosity, is this new friend you want me to meet male or female?" Claire asked.

The look on her cousin's face was all the answer she needed.

"Okay," Claire said, turning around on her heel, "I'm out of here."

"So soon?" a low male voice said, from directly behind Claire. "And here I thought we were going to get to know each other better."

Claire knew that voice. It was like velvet. Caressing her senses. Drawing her in. The only thing was, she did not want to be drawn in. Not at all. Not that it wouldn't be easy to forget one failed romance by immediately starting another one—it would. But it wouldn't be wise. And Claire was determined to be very wise this time.

She turned, and found herself staring into Dusty Turner's eyes. Like her, he had obviously showered and changed clothes before dinner. His white western shirt was nicely ironed, and so were his jeans. He had left off the Stetson this time. And his wavy dark brown hair was brushed away from his temples and off his brow.

"I would make introductions, but it seems you've already met Dr. Turner," Cynthia said.

Claire turned her gaze back to Dusty's closely shaven jaw. "Dr.?" she echoed stupidly, doing her best not to inhale the tantalizing woodsy fragrance of his cologne. She supposed if she hadn't been so busy noticing how handsome and sexy the rugged cowboy was, she would have figured that much out on her own. Instead, she had assumed he was a hired hand who worked on the Double C, and left it at that.

"Claire's a doctor, too, although she's a pediatrician." Cynthia smiled and continued bringing Claire up to speed with a veteran hostess's zeal as Dusty eyed her with unchecked interest. "Dusty's a veterinarian. He's gone into partnership with Manny Hernandez, at the veterinary clinic in town. He was living out at the Hole in the Wall dude ranch until recently."

"I got evicted, along with all the other residents of the Hole in the Wall," Dusty explained. "Castle Enterprises bought four thousand acres of prime ranch land. They've already invested upwards of seventy-five million dollars. Fifteen hundred acres—Brock Munroe's property—is going to be a nature preserve. But the rest of it—the old dude ranch—is going to be subdivided into three sections."

Cynthia sighed. "I have to hand it to Brian Fabian— he doesn't waste any time. He had surveyors out there the day they closed on the ranch, three weeks ago. The week after that, his company hired a local outfit to begin clearing some of the land for a three-hundred-acre man-made lake, a park and a golf course."

"It sounds like Castle Enterprises plans to drastically change the landscape," Claire sympathized.

"Not to mention play havoc with the natural ecology by chasing out all manner of wildlife," Dusty added.

"As you can imagine, Brian Fabian and his company haven't been particularly well-received by the town," Cynthia explained, "or our family."

Claire understood that. The McKinneys wouldn't want anything done to the land that would impact J.T.'s Double C Ranch, his daughter Lynn Russell's thoroughbred horse ranch, or his son Tyler's vineyard, all of which were in the area.

"It's not just the ranchers who are up in arms about the changes Brian Fabian is making," J. T. McKinney said gruffly, as he and his nine-year-old daughter Jennifer joined them in the dining room. "A lot of people are out of work and or a place to live, now that they've closed the Hole in the Wall.''

"Fortunately, for me, J.T. and Cynthia were kind enough to allow me to bunk in the old stone house, that belonged to J.T.'s grandfather, Hank Travis, while I look for another more permanent place,'' Dusty explained.

"I'm sure you saw the stone house,'' Cynthia said.

"It's real close to the guest house,'' Jennifer piped up.

Yes, Claire noted, it had been. About fifty yards, if her guess was correct.

Dusty flashed her a sexy grin. His hand placed gallantly beneath her elbow, he guided her to her seat at the table. "Like it or not,'' he leaned down and murmured seductively in her ear, "you and I are going to be neighbors.''

Claire sighed.

And she'd thought—erroneously, it now seemed—that her days of man trouble were over.

CHAPTER THREE

"IF YOU WOULDN'T MIND, Cynthia and I've got a few questions to ask you about that article you dropped off the other day, about the latest genetic engineering techniques for cattle," J. T. McKinney told Dusty as dinner came to an end, and nine-year-old Jennifer—who'd just been excused from the table, scampered off.

"Be happy to answer them," Dusty smiled. "But we wouldn't want to bore Claire."

"Actually," Claire said as she rose from the table, too, "I think I'd like to call it a night. It's been a long day. And I still need to feed and walk Duchess before I put her down for the night. But thank you for the lovely dinner, and for putting me up here at the ranch."

"Our pleasure." J.T. smiled at Claire warmly.

Assuring the others she'd show herself out, Claire headed for the front door while the other three headed for J.T.'s study. On the porch, Jennifer was curled up on the white wicker settee, a beautiful Persian cat in her lap.

"Hey, Claire, want to see my new kitten?" Jennifer asked enthusiastically.

"Sure." Smiling, Claire sat down beside Jennifer. As always, she was most comfortable around kids—maybe because they were always so open and honest. Claire stroked a hand over the kitten's gray fur as she admired her pretty face. "What's her name?"

"Pokey. 'Cause she likes to poke around stuff." Jennifer patted the white fur on her kitten's tummy, then looked back up at Claire. "Do you have a kitten, too?"

Claire settled back against the floral cushions on the wicker settee, and crossed her legs at the knee. "I'm more of a dog person myself. We always had dogs, growing up. So when I finished my residency and wanted a pet, I got a puppy for myself. But your mom—well, she was always really fond of cats."

Jennifer beamed. "She still has one, you know."

"Tiffany?" Claire recalled Cynthia's beloved tabby, who had moved to Texas along with her mistress, upon Cynthia's marriage to J. T. McKinney, nearly a decade before.

Jennifer nodded, then continued with customary effusiveness, "Tiffany likes me and Daddy and Mommy a lot, but she mostly hides from other people. And anyway, Tiffany's getting too old to want to play much, so Mommy and Daddy gave me Pokey." Jennifer beamed proudly, adding, "On the condition that I take care of her all by myself."

"And have you?"

"Oh, yes."

"That's great." Claire smiled. She gave Pokey a final pat on the head and started to rise.

Jennifer squinted her head at Claire, at that moment looking very much like her blunt-to-a-fault rancher father instead of her very proper and citified mother. Claire could tell by the way Jennifer was looking at her, that the little girl had something on her mind.

"Is there something you want to ask me?" Claire said.

Jennifer nodded. "Except—" she hesitated again.

"What?" Claire prodded.

"I'm afraid you'll be mad if I do."

"I doubt that." Claire's work as a pediatrician had taught her to answer children's questions as they came up, rather than let them fester. She sat back down, prepared to talk with Jennifer until Jennifer was no longer troubled by whatever was on her mind. "Go ahead," she prodded when Jennifer was still silent. "Shoot."

"Well, I want to know how come you didn't get married, when you were supposed to," she said after a moment.

Claire knew her sudden bolting had upset and baffled everyone at her wedding.

"Did you say no, you wouldn't marry Mr. Elliott, 'cause he was a cat person and you were a dog person?" Jennifer asked curiously.

Claire only wished the difficulty had been that easy to resolve—or forgive. She sighed, not sure how to explain it so a child would understand. "It was a lot more complicated than that, honey," she said gently, figuring the less the impressionable Jennifer knew about this subject, the better.

Jennifer frowned, sighed, and looking all the more embarrassed and perplexed, cuddled Pokey all the closer to her chest. "My mom said it's none of our business why you said, 'On second thought, I don't' instead of 'I do' and ran back down the aisle. Mommy says just to let you relax."

"That sounds like a plan to me," a low male voice said behind them.

Claire turned, saw Dusty lingering to the left of them, next to the asters and chrysanthemums. The look in his eyes said he had overheard a lot more than Claire wished.

"I was thinking I might take a look at your dog,"

Dusty interjected, as he continued closing the distance between them.

"Why?" As he neared her, Claire found she was inexplicably on edge.

Dusty stood with his legs apart and stuck his hands in the belt loops on either side of his fly. "I didn't have a chance to examine her as thoroughly as I would have liked earlier. I just want to make sure she wasn't hurt in her tangle with the porcupine. Unless," he tilted his head slightly to the side, "you'd prefer to simply take your chances."

"Of course not." Claire stood, giving Dusty a look that let him know she wasn't buying his lame excuse for a single second. He simply wanted to spend time with her, and was using her dog as an excuse. But, deciding the very talkative Jennifer didn't need to witness anything further that was being said between them, Claire merely smiled and said, "I'll see you later, Jennifer."

Jennifer cheerfully returned Claire's wave. "Bye. Come back over soon. And next time bring Duchess. 'Cause I like dogs, too."

"This isn't necessary," Claire told Dusty stiffly, as soon as they were out of earshot.

Dusty fell into step beside her. "What?"

Claire turned her head slightly to the side and looked down her nose at him. "You. Chasing after me."

Dusty looked her up and down as the corners of his mouth curled up. "Is that what you think I'm doing?" he asked as they headed for the guest cottage.

"Aren't you?" Claire countered impatiently as her high-heeled sandals clicked on the decorative stone walkway. She wished she had worn something other than the pale pink sheath, with the modest V neck, front and back. If she had, his eyes might not keep returning to look her over.

"And I thought that porcupine was a might prickly," he drawled, as his glance dropped even lower.

Flushing with awareness, despite her desire to remain perfectly cool, she informed him sternly, "I'm not interested in starting a relationship with anyone at the moment."

"I have no interest in being fixed up with a potential mate either," he said firmly as they reached the cottage steps. "Even by someone as well-meaning as your cousin Cynthia."

"Good, because I'm on the rebound," Claire continued.

"Been there, too," Dusty said softly.

Claire couldn't imagine him running from anything the way she just had. And still was. "Who dumped who?" she asked lightly, attempting to inject a little humor into the conversation.

"No one," he told her solemnly. "My wife died."

Claire's eyes widened in surprise as their gazes met and held. "I'm so sorry," Claire said quietly, after a moment, her heart going out to him for the loss he had suffered.

"How recently did it happen?" Claire asked gently.

"Two years ago."

"And you're still not over it," Claire guessed, as she looked deep into his eyes.

Dusty shrugged as he held his hands in front of him, palm up. "I'm not sure you ever get over a broken heart," he replied honestly. "But you do learn how to go on and start living your life again." He looked at her meaningfully. "You will, too."

The last thing Claire wanted from anyone, never mind

Dusty, was a lesson on how to go on with her life. She pivoted away from him, hands knotted at her sides, and started up the steps, to the porch. "Thanks for the pep talk, but again, I don't need it or want it."

He swept ahead of her to get the door. "Fiesty little thing, aren't you?" he said as he pushed it open.

"That's Dr. Fiesty to you," Claire said.

He erupted in laughter, shook his head, and looked into the cozy living room. "Where's that pet of yours?" he demanded cheerfully. "I want to give her a thorough going-over."

Thorough was right, Claire thought, a good forty minutes later. First, Dusty had gone off to get his vet bag, while Claire brought Duchess out of the bedroom, where she had been kept. Returning, he had paused to make friends with Duchess. Then he had suggested they go ahead and let Duchess eat her evening meal, and then of course, Duchess'd had to be walked right away, so she could stretch her legs and get her rowdiness out. By the time they had gotten back to the guest cottage, it was nearly dark, so Claire had ended up inviting Dusty inside. And it was only then that he got down to business, asked Claire a whole host of questions, like what heartworm medication Duchess was on, and what immunizations the pup'd had, and examined Duchess head to toe.

"What are you looking for?" Claire couldn't help but admire both his professionalism and his gentleness with her pet.

"First, any sign of rabies, and you'll be glad to know there are none. Then any signs of injury from a porcupine quill that I might have missed earlier—again, I didn't find any. And last but not least, ticks and flea bites."

"Ticks!" Claire shuddered. It seemed the Double C was fraught with peril she hadn't expected.

"You're on a ranch. It's summer. You're going to need to worry about both ticks and fleas, which is why," Dusty explained as he pulled a blue plastic packet from his vet bag, "that I suggest we go ahead and put some of this on Duchess tonight."

He handed her the applicator, his warm, capable hands brushing hers as he did so. "What is it?" Claire asked, disturbed to find she was tingling from even that slight touch. Which made her wonder, what it would be like if he kissed her.

Not, she amended quickly and sternly to herself, that she would ever find out.

Oblivious to the licentious nature of her thoughts, Dusty tugged on a pair of surgical gloves. "It's a flea and tick repellent. You put the medicine on the coat, right here at the back of her neck, where she can't get at it or lick it, and work it into the skin."

Claire handed the tube back to him. He then snipped off the bottle-shaped top. She held Duchess by the collar, stroking her head to keep her calm while Dusty moved behind Duchess to apply the cream. "It's oily."

"Yeah." Dusty rubbed it into Duchess's skin with a soothing motion. "And it'll look like that—kind of greasy—for a day or two, then it'll be absorbed into the body and it will protect her from brown dog ticks, American dog ticks, lone star ticks, and deer ticks—which are the major carriers of Lyme disease."

Claire frowned, aware she was beginning to get worried, Dusty or no Dusty living nearby. "I had no idea I'd be putting Duchess in danger by bringing her here," she murmured, watching Dusty rip off his gloves, throw them away, and wash his hands. All she had wanted to do was flee the mess she had made of her life back in Boston.

Dusty came back to Claire. He clamped a reassuring hand on her shoulder, his little finger brushing the bare skin of her arm. "Duchess isn't in danger," he said gently, looking down at Claire in a way that seemed both protective and a tad more intimate than the situation called for. "But there are potential problems and pitfalls you will encounter here in Texas that you might not have in Boston. And I want you to be aware of them."

"Well, thank you," Claire said. Even though she didn't need it, it was nice having Dusty looking out for both of them.

CLAIRE COULDN'T SAY WHY she felt bereft after Dusty had left and ambled on over to the stone house where he was staying. She only knew that she did. And she knew that it was foolish. She wasn't looking for a romantic entanglement with anyone right now. Never mind a stubborn, sexy cowboy cum vet who was far too nosy for his own good. But she fell asleep dreaming about him, nevertheless, and woke up not being able to wait to run into him again.

And she did—during breakfast at the main house.

He came in, just as Claire was finishing her coffee. He looked ruggedly sexy in jeans, a light blue plaid shirt and boots. His dark brown hair was brushed neatly away from his face, his jaw was freshly shaven. He smelled like mint toothpaste, shampoo, soap and woodsy cologne. He flashed Claire a smile, and her heart turned over in her chest. Flushing, she smiled back and did her best to appear completely unaffected.

"What'll it be today, Doc?" Lettie Mae Reese asked,

looking—if possible—even more fond of Dusty than the rest of the McKinney clan.

"The usual," Dusty winked at the dark-skinned housekeeper.

Lettie Mae winked right back at him. "You and your huevos rancheros," she teased, before bustling back into the kitchen to comply.

"Cynthia and I want to go ahead with the approach you suggested, for our new crossbreeding experiment," J.T. told Dusty. Noticing her confusion, J.T. then turned to Claire and explained, "We're going to let the computers choose which specific cows we crossbreed, to see if we can get a better hybrid."

Cynthia nodded, her enthusiasm for the venture plain. "Usually, we just decide to cross a Brangus with a long-horn, for instance, but now we're going to match 'em up not only breed by breed, but cow by cow, to see if we can't produce a super breed of cattle that is both lean and disease resistant."

"The approach is a little cutting edge for me, but Cynthia has convinced me that it's the way to go, from a business perspective," J.T. said.

"Sounds fascinating," Claire said. And right on the money. Which wasn't surprising, given Cynthia's acumen as an investment banker, and J.T.'s ranch knowledge.

"Great," Dusty enthused as he sipped his orange juice. "I'll talk to the genetic engineers at Texas A and M this morning and tell them to get going on it right away."

"Speaking of plans," Cynthia said, as Lettie Mae returned with a plate of hot, delicious food and set it in front of Dusty. "How is the house hunting coming?"

Dusty thanked Lettie Mae, then cut into the traditional

ranch eggs with gusto, forking up a bite of fried egg and crispy corn tortilla, covered with a spicy red tomato gravy. "Pickings are slim but I'm going to look at a few more properties later in the week." Dusty glanced at Claire. "I've got a terrific realtor, if you decide to settle here, too."

Claire frowned, as she spread jam on a fluffy buttermilk biscuit. "Why would I want to do that?" she asked cooly.

"I don't know." Dusty shrugged his broad shoulders amiably, not the least bit put off by the chill in her attitude. "Maybe because Crystal Creek, Texas, is the greatest place in the world to live, and the town is in desperate need of a pediatrician."

Claire regarded him steadily—she had expected this kind of cheerleading from her cousin, but not him. "I'm part of a group practice in Boston." In fact, she had her life all set now that she had completed her residency.

"Exactly." Dusty regarded her with exaggerated sympathy. Finished with one egg, he cut into the other. "The operative words being *in Boston.*"

Claire rolled her eyes, while Cynthia and J.T. exchanged intrigued looks across the breakfast table. Ignoring the subtle mental matchmaking going on, Claire continued grilling Dusty—it was her way of keeping the focus of the conversation away from her. "Have you lived here your whole life?"

"I only wish." Dusty sat back in his chair and drank his juice with the same gusto he had devoured his breakfast. "But no, I hail from Houston. And lovely a city as that is, I'd never go back. Not in a million years." He waggled his eyebrows at her. "Stay here long enough and you might feel the same way."

"I doubt that," Claire said stiffly as she took a sip of

her coffee. In the kitchen, the phone began to ring. "For starters, Texas is way too hot for me."

Lettie Mae Reese came back in, portable phone in hand. "Claire? Dr. Nate Purdy would like to speak to you."

CHAPTER FOUR

"AGAIN, I'M REALLY thankful. I hate to bother you on your vacation, but we're really shorthanded and I've got a dozen kids that need to be seen this morning and no way to work them in," Nate Purdy told Claire a short while later as he led her into his private office, away from the ringing phones and bustling activity. Office hours weren't set to start for another thirty minutes, but already the clinic was swamped.

"Have you thought about bringing in another physician?" Claire asked Nate as he handed her a white coat to use. She put the long jacket on, adjusting the collar, then put a stethoscope around her neck. The truth was, she was kind of glad to have something to do in a medical sense.

"We're looking for a pediatrician." Nate paused. "I don't suppose you'd be interested in applying for the job."

Claire shook her head. "Already have one, back in Boston. But thanks, anyway."

She spent the morning seeing pediatric patients with a wide variety of complaints. Her last patient was Hank Russell, Lynn McKinney Russell's son. The nine-year-old boy had broken out in hives and couldn't seem to stop scratching and fidgeting even for one second, even while Claire examined him.

"I don't want another shot," he said crossly.

"I think we can go with liquid antihistamine and some topical ointment," Claire said, getting both items out of the medicine cabinet, above the sink. "It won't work as fast as a shot in getting rid of the hives, but it'll get the job done," she said as she poured the grape-flavored medicine into a little plastic cup, and gave it to Hank to drink.

"He's had shots the last two times he's been in here," the pregnant Lynn explained, pressing a hand to the small of her back as she eased into a chair.

Claire studied the notes on Hank's chart. Although not life-threatening, the hives were uncomfortable and unsightly. She'd like to be able to prevent them in the future. "This is the third time he's broken out in hives in the last month," Claire murmured, noting the red weals seemed to be concentrated on his arms, hands, legs, and face—anywhere his skin was not covered by his t-shirt, shorts, socks and sneakers. "Any idea what might be causing the allergic reaction?" Thus far, his rash appeared to be contact—not systemic—allergy. Which meant it had likely been something Hank touched or brushed against, rather than inhaled or ingested.

Lynn shook her head. "Nate gave me a list of things to watch out for—eggs, shellfish, nuts, fruit—in case it turns out to be a food allergy. He hasn't had any of those things since all this started."

"What was Hank doing before he broke out in a rash?" Claire asked. "Has there been any common denominator to the outbreak of hives that you can think of?"

"Like what?" Lynn frowned and rubbed her sternum, as if she were having some heartburn.

"Like has he been outdoors?" She relaxed against the counter and folded her arms in front of her.

Lynn smiled fondly at her son. "He's always outdoors. Especially now that we have a new Lab puppy."

"Rover is really cute," Hank piped up enthusiastically.

"I bet." Claire smiled at Hank before turning back to his mom. "Any chance Hank is allergic to the dog?"

"No. We've had dogs forever, and he's never had a problem. And I can think of plenty of times when he has played with the puppy recently and not gotten a rash."

"Okay." Claire made a note of that on the chart. She looked back at Lynn and continued her sleuthing. "What about soaps and perfumes and household cleaners, anything with chemicals in it. Are you using anything new? Washing with a new laundry detergent or brand of soap?"

"No. Everything is just the same as it has always been. Except for the land-clearing going on at the dude ranch."

"That's probably created a lot of stress for your family," Claire sympathized.

"No kidding." Lynn sighed.

"My sister Sandy really hates those bulldozers," Hank said. "She thinks they're ruining the land."

"We've tried to calm Sandy down," Lynn said. "But we haven't had much luck—all we usually do is end up arguing with her about it." At Claire's inquisitive look, Lynn explained, "Sandy and her friends wanted to do a sit-in or chain themselves to some trees, to try and physically block the dozing, and we wouldn't allow it."

"There was lots of yelling that day," Hank recounted seriously.

"I wouldn't call it yelling," Lynn corrected her son, before admitting to Claire, "but our voices were probably loud. We didn't want Sandy or her friends getting into any kind of trouble and she resented us for stifling her free speech as she put it. Anyway, the development has remained an emotional subject at our home, as you might well imagine.''

Claire nodded. She was beginning to see that. Not just in the Russell household but the community at large. There didn't seem to be a person in Crystal Creek who didn't have strong feelings about Brian Fabian and Castle Enterprises.

Claire looked at Hank curiously, watching for any signs of distress. ''Does it upset you when they talk about the changes going on at the property right next to yours?'' she asked gently.

''Sometimes,'' Hank admitted with a shrug. ''But then I usually go out and play with my new puppy and give Rover a bath or something and feel better.''

Claire looked at Lynn, who was rubbing her lower back again, as if it ached. ''Any chance this might be stress-related?''

''I don't know,'' Lynn paused. ''I suppose it's possible. To tell you the truth, we've all been feeling the stress. I've been having backaches and heartburn, and I know both are from the tension—wondering how what's going on over there is going to impact us, and my thoroughbred horse business.''

Claire smiled reassuringly. ''I know it's hard right now, but maybe you could all try and relax a little, not let Brian Fabian or his company's activities get to you quite so much because if Hank's rash is stress-related that might take care of it, and prevent future outbreaks.''

''And if it's not?'' Lynn asked.

''Then we'll have to keep up our detective work until we find what the culprit is, so I want you to call me if he breaks out in hives again. Doesn't matter what time it is, day or night," Claire kindly emphasized. "I want to know."

"I HEARD YOU'RE WORKING at the clinic," Dusty drawled.

Claire looked up from her spot at the Longhorn Coffee Shop. It was 2:00 p.m., and she just now had time for lunch. Dusty looked as ravenous as she was. "Just mornings, to help out with their patient load until they can find another partner and I head back to Boston. They've got a lot of kids that need to be seen and not enough staff."

"You don't mind sacrificing your vacation?" Dusty asked curiously.

Claire shrugged. "It'd be hard to relax knowing there are kids here in need of medical attention."

"I see your point about that. I'd probably feel the same way. Mind if I join you?" He slid into the booth opposite her.

Thrilled to see him again, even if she wasn't about to let him know it, Claire eyed him with barely checked amusement. "Can I stop you?" she asked dryly.

"Probably not," he told her cheerfully.

Dusty paused to exchange warm greetings with Nora, the proprietress. He placed his order without even looking at the laminated menu of Texas specialties before handing it back. "Chicken fried steak, mashed potatoes, green beans and a large iced tea, thanks."

"Coming right up," Nora said as she bustled off.

Dusty turned back to Claire. He stretched his long legs out beneath the table, next to hers, and propped his forearms on the edge of the table. "So, how was it?"

Finding her throat suddenly parched, Claire sipped her

mint-flavored iced tea. "Surprisingly fun and interesting." She'd been under the impression the pace—professionally—in a small town would be slower and less challenging. Instead, it seemed to be even more demanding than the big-city practice she had joined back in Boston.

Dusty continued to look at her as if she were the most fascinating woman on earth. "I heard Nate and his partners were thrilled with the job you did. They'd like you to stay on permanently. Can't say as I blame 'em," Dusty drawled, tilting his head to one side. "You would make a fine addition to the community. Cynthia and J.T. both say so. And soon," he continued, his dark eyes sparkling warmly, "everyone else who gets to know you will say so, too."

"If I didn't know better, I'd think you were lobbying for Nate," Claire teased, trying not to read too much into Dusty's praise, as Nora made their way back to the booth, a white stoneware plate in each hand.

"Or maybe just me," Dusty drawled as they were served their food.

Nora winked and having caught the tail end of their conversation, said, "Honey, he'll have you talked into staying in no time."

"No," Claire said firmly, reminding herself sternly she had already decided that as charming as Dusty was, as attracted to him as she was, she was not going to have a rebound romance with him, "he won't." They could be friends, but that was it.

"If you say so." Nora shot Claire a disbelieving grin and headed back to the grill.

"Keep this up and you're going to have people thinking there is something between us," Claire warned.

"Isn't there?" Dusty shot right back.

FOR A MOMENT, CLAIRE was too shocked—and too irritated with him—to reply. Which was just as well,
Dusty thought, since it gave him plenty of opportunity
to study his luncheon companion. She had looked beautiful at breakfast with her hair all perfectly in place, and
her lipstick on. And she looked great now, with her silky
blond hair curving forward against her chin and wispy
tendrils popping up all over the place. Her lipstick was
long gone, and she had rolled her long sleeves up above
her elbows, in deference to the heat outside. Her cheeks
were flushed a soft pink—and the longer she talked to
him, the pinker they got. Which told him one thing—
she was as aware of him, as he was of her. And that was
something that was not going to change. No, Dusty
thought, that was something that was only going to get
more pronounced over time. And there wasn't a darn
thing either of them could do about it, either. Chemistry
like that just happened. It was magic. And it was something that shouldn't be run away from, no matter what
unfortunate romantic circumstances had led them both
to flee to Crystal Creek.

"What could we possibly have between us?" Claire
asked finally.

Dusty shrugged and tried not to scare her away.
"We're both newcomers to Crystal Creek, relatively
speaking anyway."

"Yes, but I'm not staying," Claire emphasized flatly
as she bit into a meat loaf spiced with salsa, green and
jalapeño peppers and onion.

"That's what I thought when I arrived here two years
ago," Dusty took a bite of his own chicken-fried steak.
As expected, the breaded beef was fried to perfection,
coated with a peppery white-cream gravy, and so tender
and good it practically melted on his tongue. "And look

at me now, I'm a partner in a successful large-and-small animal vet practice getting ready to buy a house.''

"Congratulations.'' Claire sprinkled salt and pepper on her mashed potatoes. "But what's going on with me has nothing to do with what's been going on with you.''

Dusty merely grinned. "Really.''

Claire glared at him. "Really.''

Dusty sat back and took a long draught of tea. "You don't like it here?''

"Actually, I love it. The countryside is beautiful, the Tex-Mex cuisine out of this world, and the lack of traffic and the laid-back pace of the small town is very relaxing.''

About that, Dusty concurred. The community of seven-thousand residents was postcard pretty, with its rolling hills and tree-lined streets. The people were friendly. Crime almost nonexistent. "So what's waiting for you back in Boston, besides gossip and scandal surrounding your wedding that wasn't?'' Was she secretly waiting to get back together with the guy she had run away from at the altar, Dusty wondered uneasily. The last thing he wanted to do was get involved with a woman who was still hung up on someone else.

But, to his relief, Claire didn't really look as if she were homesick at all. She seemed to be enjoying where she was.

"Okay, you got me there.'' Claire dragged her fork through her fried okra, making restless zigzag motions. "I admit, coming here soon after the debacle was really just a way to get away from all the brouhaha, but like it or not—'' she paused and looked at Dusty seriously "—I'm going to have to face the music sometime. Putting it off won't make it any easier. And it won't make me any stronger.''

"You're interested in that." Dusty found it an admirable ambition.

"Yes," Claire said, shooting him a defiant look from beneath her thick blond lashes.

"Why?" Dusty asked curiously, liking the intimate turn their lunch conversation had taken.

"Because—if you must know," Claire admitted reluctantly, her cheeks pinkening all the more, "I've never been on my own emotionally. And having realized this, I am determined to be as strong and independent in my personal life as I am in my professional life."

Finished with his meal, Dusty sat back and folded his arms in front of him. "Spoken like a true Texan." He gave her a wink, meant to further lift her mood as he teased, "Maybe you do belong here after all."

But to Dusty's disappointment, Claire refused to smile. Her soft bow-shaped lips remained clamped together in a defiant line. "I'm serious about this, Dusty," she said, as she looked him square in the eye. "This whole wedding that nearly was but wasn't has made me realize that I've been too dependent on others for my whole life."

Needing—wanting—to understand more about her, Dusty sobered, too. "What do you mean?" he asked quietly.

Claire turned her hands, palm up. "I was sheltered by my parents when I was growing up, in much the same way my cousin Cynthia was. When they died, my older brother and his wife took over. And they sort of kept tabs on me and encouraged me through medical school and pediatric residency. Then about a year ago, they both took jobs in Seattle, and I found myself alone for the first time in my life."

"Is that when you took up with your ex-fiancé?"

Claire nodded and drew a deep, bolstering breath as she continued her confession. "The point is, when I look back now, I realize that I panicked at the idea of being alone, and ended up getting engaged to a man without really knowing him. The whole experience of almost marrying the wrong person has made me realize that I need to learn how to be alone and get along without depending on anyone to come to my rescue, the way you did with the porcupine yesterday. So I made this decision to come to Texas briefly—at Cynthia and J.T.'s invitation—to lick my wounds and pull myself together. And then I'm going to go back to Boston and resume my life and this time, for the first time, I am truly going to stand on my own two feet."

Dusty liked her plan. With one exception. The part that had her leaving Crystal Creek. "I respect your right to make your own decisions," he told Claire seriously.

"Thank you." Claire released a sigh of relief.

"But I have to tell you," Dusty continued frankly, "I think you're going overboard with this independent bit." He saw her blue eyes flash indignantly and put up a hand before she could interrupt. "Not that I haven't done the exact same thing myself. I have. My need to shut out the rest of the world, and along with it, the possibility of any and all future hurt, was what brought me to Crystal Creek two years ago."

The stubborn tilt of Claire's chin softened, just a little. "Then you should understand how I feel," she replied quietly.

"I do." When it looked like she might bolt before he could finish, Dusty leaned across the table and took both her hands in his. "But you need to understand something, too. I'm a healer by profession. I can't and won't walk away from any living thing in pain or obvious trouble. If you need a friend, someone to talk to, a shoulder to cry on, I'm here for you," he finished firmly.

Claire wrested her hands from his light, staying grip. "I'm all done crying," she told him cantankerously.

"Good." Dusty smiled. The last thing he wanted was her shedding tears over some other guy—or anything, for that matter. "But the offer still stands," he told her just as stubbornly. "And in the meantime, you could do something for me in return for helping you out with your pup, and testing that porcupine for rabies—it was negative, by the way."

"Good." Momentarily distracted, Claire peered at Dusty thoughtfully. "What are you going to do with the porcupine?"

"A game warden picked him up this morning. He's already been set free—far away from the Double C."

Claire's lips slid into a pout as she studied him suspiciously. "And this means I owe you?" she demanded.

"Not really," Dusty allowed, glad the conversation was back on less contentious ground, "but I could use the help." Seeing he had her interest—if not her cooperation—he plunged on. "As I think you heard last night, I'm trying to buy a house for myself, and sizing up real estate is not exactly my forte. Frankly, I'm not all that domestic."

Claire rolled her eyes. She sat back again, beginning to relax. "Really."

"Yeah. You never would have guessed, I'm sure," Dusty quipped back. "Anyway, although I'm not currently looking for a romantic involvement with anyone, I do plan to get married someday and I want a house that a woman will be happy with."

Claire began to get his drift. "You want me to give you the female perspective," she guessed.

Dusty shrugged his shoulder amiably. "You do seem pretty particular in your likes and dislikes. I figure if I could please you, I could probably please any woman." And for reasons he couldn't quite figure out, he wanted to please just her. Even knowing that if it were up to her nothing of any significance would ever develop between them. Dusty wasn't usually the kind of guy who pursued lost causes. He didn't like to waste time or energy when it could be put to better use. But something about Claire intrigued him, in a way no woman had ever intrigued him before.

Claire hestitated, thinking, weighing her options. Trying, Dusty decided, to determine what his real motives were.

"There are only two properties," Dusty rushed to assure her, before she could think of a concrete reason to back out. "It wouldn't take much time."

"I guess I do owe you," Claire ruminated, at length.

"Then you'll do it?" Dusty's hopes rose.

Claire nodded, her expression more businesslike than Dusty would have cared to see, but she was cooperating just the same, and for that he was happy.

"Just name the time and place," she said.

CHAPTER FIVE

"So, you're going out to look at houses with Dusty tonight?" Cynthia asked Claire later that afternoon. She was in the kitchen, frosting cupcakes with Jennifer, while Lettie Mae, the family maid, who was getting on in years and could no longer work from sunup to sundown without a break, took her daily afternoon rest.

Claire put her handbag aside and sat down with them at the big table in the center of the room. "We have an appointment with the realtor at six." She accepted the glass of mint tea that Cynthia handed her with a smile and softly murmured thanks. "Which means neither Dusty nor I will be here this evening for dinner. I hope that's all right."

"It's fine. I'm glad the two of you are getting along so well," Cynthia returned enthusiastically, as she handed Claire a chocolate cupcake, too.

"Even so, you shouldn't read anything into it," Claire cautioned, as she peeled the pastel paper baking cup off the bottom of the treat. "I'm just doing a favor for a very casual friend."

"I understand." Cynthia's eyes sparkled merrily.

The back door slammed. Cynthia's eighteen-year-old step-granddaughter Sandy Russell stomped in. "Have you seen how many trees they've cut down over at the Hole in the Wall dude ranch?" she demanded, upset, as she paced back and forth. "It's a crime, I'm telling you, what they are doing to the native Texas landscape over there, to make way for that lake. All of the bluebonnets and the desert marigolds are gone. They've chopped down dozens of cedar and juniper trees, too! That's probably why we had a porcupine under the guest house porch. Poor thing probably had its home destroyed and was scared all the way over here. Something ought to be done to stop it!''

Cynthia held up a staying hand. ''Honey, your grandfather and I and your parents have been over this with you. Castle Enterprises now owns that land. They have every right to put a lake on the property.''

''Even if we hate the idea?'' Sandy asked dispiritedly as she slumped into a chair.

The back door shut again—a lot more quietly this time. Dusty walked in. He looked at the tears welling in Sandy's eyes, then shot a questioningly look at Claire.

''Sandy's upset about the land clearing and bulldozing over at the old Hole in the Wall dude ranch,'' Claire explained.

Dusty shook his head in mutual regret. ''A shame to see all those good riding trails go, isn't it?'' Dusty commiserated gently.

Sandy wiped the excess moisture from the corners of her eyes, sniffed, and said in abject misery, ''Not to mention the nature camp we all went to as kids and the reserve that had all the exotic animals.''

Claire tried to soothe Sandy, too. ''Maybe that could be set up somewhere else,'' she said.

''They've been purchased by a private collector, and will be moved soon,'' Dusty reported matter-of-factly. ''Unfortunately, the public won't be able to enjoy them any longer.''

"Now do you see what I mean?" Sandy cut in, her high voice quavering. "You see how unfair this is?"

"What about the rest of the dude ranch?" Claire asked. "Is anything going to be salvaged?"

Cynthia nodded. "They're keeping the tennis courts and the pool open, and the lodge can still be rented out for parties and weddings but it's only for community residents."

"So we won't be able to go there anymore unless we're a guest of someone who lives in one of the houses that will be built there," Sandy complained tearfully.

"And that's a shame, isn't it?" Dusty said comfortingly. "Because we all loved the dude ranch. Me especially, because I lived there until it was bought out by Brian Fabian. But that's just the way these things go," he stated with an accepting shrug of his broad shoulders. "And we have to deal with it. Move on."

Sandy sniffed and folded her arms in front of her tightly. "What if we don't want to move on?" she asked unhappily. "What if we still want to try and stop it somehow?"

"Honey, that just isn't possible," Cynthia said firmly.

"Well, I don't want to live next to a lake and a golf course and a stupid old subdivision." Sandy pouted.

Silence fell in the kitchen. No one seemed to know what to say, since everyone pretty much felt the same way.

Claire, seeing a way she could be of help to both the disgruntled teen and the McKinney-Russell family as a whole, said, "There's something else we need to think about here." Claire stood and carried her glass over to the sink. She threw her empty cupcake wrapper in the trash. "Sandy, do you mind if the two of us go somewhere and talk? Would that be okay with everyone else?''

They all looked as surprised as Sandy by the invitation, but consent was quickly given by all concerned, nevertheless.

Claire thanked Cynthia for the tea and cupcakes, and took Sandy out the back door. ''There's nothing you can say that's going to make me feel any better about this,'' Sandy declared heatedly as she and Claire walked over to the guest cottage.

''How about we do something to make someone else feel better then?'' Claire said as she let herself into the house. Duchess, who had been cooped up most of the day, was so happy to see Claire and Sandy that she wagged her tail so hard she fell over.

Sandy smiled at the golden retriever's antics, despite her blue mood.

Ah, the healing power of animals, Claire thought.

''Mind if we take Duchess on a walk with us?'' Claire said.

Sandy managed a watery smile for the happy pup, despite her suspicious attitude about the talk to come. ''Not at all.''

Claire snapped a leash on Duchess and the two set off. ''I saw your mother and little brother today, over at Nate Purdy's office. Your mom was going to bring you in one day, so the two of us could talk, too.''

Abruptly, Sandy's expression turned to one of concern. ''What about?'' she asked anxiously.

''Your little brother, Hank.''

Sandy stepped carefully over the rocky terrain where the waters of the Claro River splashed over limestone ledges. ''Yeah, he's been breaking out in hives, ever since they started construction on the property next door.''

Claire paused so Duchess could sniff the base of some cedar trees, select a spot, and do what needed to be done. ''Actually, the medical records show your little brother's illness dating a little farther back than that—since all these changes have been going on around town.''

''You think there's some connection?'' Sandy asked curiously, as they moved into the woods that lined the river.

''It's possible it's a reaction to the stress. It wouldn't be the first time someone has broken out in a rash because they were worried or upset.'' Claire paused beside a twisted mesquite tree, as she said seriously, ''Then again, it could be something else—something your little brother is coming into contact with that is causing his allergic reactions. We just don't know yet. But your mom told me she's been pretty tense lately over all the hubbub, and she's been having backaches and heartburn, as a result.'' Neither of which were any fun. Claire had advised Lynn to talk to Nate before she left, and Nate had prescribed a mild antacid for the pregnant Lynn to take that wouldn't harm her baby. He had recommended she use either hot or cold compresses for her backaches.

Sandy froze in her tracks. ''My mom and the baby— they're okay, aren't they?''

''Yes,'' Claire said, as Duchess stuck her nose in a strand of bright orange Indian paintbrush wildflowers, ''but this tension and worry is not healthy for anyone in your family. So if there is anything you can do to make things more harmonious in your household, I think you might want to seriously consider doing just that.''

Sandy stuck her hands in the pockets of her jeans as they took off again. She slanted Claire a contemplative glance. "You're saying I should back off with my protests, is that it?"

Claire looked the teen straight in the eye and said bluntly but gently, "I'm saying there is something to serenity. To having the courage to change the things that you can and to accept the things that you can't change."

"Like the demolition of the dude ranch to make way for a lake, park and golf course," Sandy guessed with a disillusioned sigh.

BY THE TIME CLAIRE AND Sandy returned with Duchess from their walk, J.T. was waiting for her on the front porch of the guest cottage.

Dusty shot Sandy an empathetic look. "Feeling better?" he asked.

Sandy nodded. "Claire made me see I need to take my protests down a notch, at least around the house."

"Seems like a wise choice." Dusty nodded his approval.

"Yeah, well, it's the only one I've got. I'll see you guys." Sandy hopped into her car, and drove off.

"I'm impressed," Dusty told Claire as she and Duchess joined him on the porch. "You were obviously really good with her."

"Thanks." Claire led the way inside. "So were you, by the way." She knelt to take off Duchess's leash. "Although, for the record, I didn't change Sandy's mind about the development, but I hope I got through about her behavior around the house."

"Even so, that's something else we have in common," Dusty said as Claire got out Duchess's food and water dishes.

"What?" Claire filled both dishes and, because the

guest cottage had no kitchen, set them on the ceramic tile floor in the bathroom.

He lounged against the bathroom counter, radiating all the take-charge masculinity of a Texas cowboy and the gentle healing power of a vet. It was a potent combination, made even more devastating by his handsome, sensual presence, and the way he kept pursuing her.

"We're both good with kids."

At his comment, all sorts of romantic thoughts and fantasies came to mind. Claire pushed them away defiantly. Unless she got hold of herself, who knew what might happen between them? The very last thing she needed to be thinking about was what it would be like to have his baby. Or to make a baby with him. "It's no big deal," Claire made light of his observation resolutely. She met and held his eyes. "That's easy, if you like kids."

"I agree." He looked down at her and gave her an affable smile. "But not everyone is cut out to be a good parent, or in our case, friend and or mentor to them."

But Dusty was, Claire couldn't help but think. He had the same kind and sure way of dealing with them as he did with animals.

Claire settled Duchess in her roomy travel crate with her sleeping mat and chew toys. Satisfied Duchess was taken care of, Claire turned to Dusty. "Ready to go look at those houses?"

Dusty nodded and still regarding her thoughtfully, extended a hand toward the door. "After you."

"WE'RE NOT MEETING a realtor?" Claire said in surprise after they had parked in front of a house with a For Sale in front.

Dusty stepped out of his pickup truck, reached for his

hat, and settled it square on his head. "One of the benefits of a small town. I'm trusted enough just to be given the keys to both properties." He circled around to help her—rather unnecessarily, she thought—step down from the cab. After all, it wasn't as if they were on an actual date or anything.

"You're not afraid to be alone with me, are you?" he asked, keeping his hands on her waist a fraction of a second too long.

"Don't be silly." Claire stepped away from the tantalizing warmth of his grip. "I know you're going to behave yourself."

He smiled at her in that exceedingly confident, all-male way. "I'm not sure whether to take that as a compliment or an insult."

The last thing she wanted to do was flirt with him. She was too attracted to him as it was. "Take it as neither," Claire ordered grouchily, turning her glance away. "And let's just get down to business."

"Yes, ma'm." Dusty touched a finger to the brim of his hat, bowing to her command, but his lazy cheerfulness remained undaunted.

Ignoring him, Claire rushed on ahead.

The first house was a ranch-style home. Built in the early seventies, it sported a very basic floor plan— kitchen, dining and living room on one side of the house, three bedrooms and a single tiny bath with cramped outdated, fixtures on the other.

"I would say this is definitely a fixer-upper," Claire said, as they toured the house together, room by depressingly small room.

"Which explains why it's been on the market for the last six months, with barely a nibble," Dusty said, ducking his head as he moved through a doorway. He pivoted slowly, as he surveyed the master bedroom from all angles. "The price is right though. The owners just dropped it again."

Claire looked at the closet, which was tiny and old-fashioned. Unfortunately, there was no way to expand it without further diminishing the size of the eight-by-ten master suite. Frowning, Claire stepped back out into the hall. "Well, you could knock out a wall here and combine two of the bedrooms into a master bedroom and bath. Or you could build an addition onto the back of the house that has a master suite as well as a family room and powder room. New paint and carpet would also help."

Dusty furrowed his brow. "That sounds like a lot of work, though. And I'm not sure I want to live in a construction zone."

"Can't say I blame you there."

Deciding that one just wouldn't do, they moved on to the next property.

"This is more like it," Claire said, as they got out of the car and headed up the walk. "At least from the outside." It was a two-story limestone house, built in the traditional Texas farmhouse style, with a steeply pitched roof and equal number of windows on either side of the centrally located front door. Inside, the floor plan was just as basic. Living room and dining at the front of the house, on either side of the entryway, family room, kitchen, breakfast room, and laundry room at the rear of the house. Front and back stairs connected to the second floor, where there were four bedrooms and two baths.

"Definitely family friendly," Claire said, as she looked around approvingly.

Dusty paced out the large master bedroom, then walked back down the hall. He considered her for a moment, then leaned closer, bringing the tantalizing woodsy scent of his cologne with him. "You don't think it's too big?"

"For a bachelor, maybe," Claire conceded, trying not to think about how much she wished she had met him some other time, some other way, when she wasn't on the rebound and determined to stand on her own emotionally, at long last. "But," Claire continued, still looking deep into Dusty's dark brown eyes, "if you plan to marry and have kids one day—"

"I do," he interrupted her, his interest in her as clear and pronounced as his interest in the future.

Claire shrugged and doing her best to ignore how good it felt to be here with him like this, continued cheering him on. "Then I would definitely say this is the place. I mean, there's still work to be done. Some of this wallpaper is downright ugly. And the entire house needs new carpet, or possibly wood floors. Those are very popular now and easy to maintain."

"Then that settles it," Dusty said easily. "I'll put a bid on it tomorrow."

Claire turned back to him. She loved the place. But it was a big decision. In his case, she suspected, a life-altering one. "Are you sure?" she asked him warily as she lingered in the master bedroom doorway. She wanted him to be happy. She didn't want to be the key to his happiness, or even any small part of it. It was too much responsibility. Too much to hope for after the way she had just crashed and burned back in Boston.

"Oh, yes, I'm sure," Dusty replied as a sexy smile tugged at the corners of his lips.

As he continued to study her warmly, her breath caught in her throat, her heart beat wildly, and her head tipped back all the more. "What are you thinking?" she whispered, even as she struggled against the unexpect-edly erotic sensations already coursing through her. If he brought on this much of a reaction with just a smile and a look, what would happen if he actually touched his lips to hers? Claire wondered in alarm.

"About how much I want to do this," Dusty mur-mured back as he joined her in the portal. His dark eyes gleaming triumphantly, he wrapped his arms about her and brought her body flush against the taller, stronger length of his.

CHAPTER SIX

"TELL ME YOU'RE NOT going to kiss me," Claire breathed, her back against the wooden doorframe.

"I'll tell you no such thing." Dusty framed her face with the callused roughness of his hand and scored his thumb across the softness of her lower lip. "Because I am going to kiss you, Claire," he promised, as he tightened the arm anchored around her waist, dipped his head, and brushed her lips with his own. "Right here," he murmured in a low sexy voice that stirred her senses. "Right now."

His lips captured hers, longing swept through her with disabling force, and suddenly Claire was right where she wanted to be, doing exactly what she wanted to do. His mouth slanted across hers in a fierce, burning kiss that urged her to answer his passion. Aware nothing had ever felt so good or so right, Claire moaned low in her throat and moved closer yet. Standing on tiptoe, she wreathed her arms about his neck and pressed her breasts against his chest. The desire he felt for her clear, he pressed his manhood against her, hot and hard through the soft denim fabric of his jeans. Her excitement mounted, fueled by the rasp of their breathing in the empty house, the forbidden nature of the embrace. She moaned as he tilted his head, deliberately increasing the depth and the torridness of the kiss. And then his hands were moving beneath the hem of her blouse, molding her breasts through the thin lace of her bra. Claire tangled her fingers in his hair and caught his head in her hands. A melting warmth raced through her, and she deepened the kiss even more, as he circled the aching crowns and teased her nipples into tight buds of awareness. And still it wasn't enough, Claire thought, as she tilted her head back and arched against him, letting the wonderful eroticism of his touch flow over her in warm waves.

She wanted to make love with him, here, now. Even though she knew they couldn't.

Dusty had never meant this to be anything more than a simple kiss. But the moment he had Claire in his arms everything had changed. Oh, he had known her mouth would be soft and delicate. He hadn't counted on her being so quick to respond to him. And once he had felt her surrender, there had been no stopping with just one kiss. He'd had to hold her, touch her, do everything he could to make her see they were meant to be together, that she was meant to be his woman. And his alone. Even if it wasn't the time—or the place—for them to make love. Even if they were going to have to wait to take this to a higher plane.

Reluctantly, Dusty ended the kiss. And then swiftly, they were back to reality. The passionate adoration in Claire's sky-blue eyes was quickly replaced by confusion. She stared at him, wide-eyed, aroused. Pressing a hand to her lips, she told him in a low shaken voice, "I promised myself I wasn't going to let anything like this happen."

Dusty knew that, just as he knew that the advent of love and or passion was something you just couldn't plan. And somewhere deep inside Claire he was pretty sure she knew that. "Some promises are meant to be broken," Dusty replied, just as firmly. And furthermore,

GET 2 BOOKS FREE!

GET 2

HOW TO GET YOUR
2 FREE BOOKS AND FREE GIFT!

1. Peel off the MIRA sticker on the front cover. Place it in the space provided at right. This automatically entitles you to receive two free books and an exciting surprise gift.

2. Send back this card and you'll get 2 "The Best of the Best™" novels. These books have a combined cover price of $11.98 or more in the U.S. and $13.98 or more in Canada, but they are yours to keep absolutely FREE!

3. There's <u>no</u> catch. You're under <u>no</u> obligation to buy anything. We charge nothing – ZERO – for your first shipment. And you don't have to make any minimum number of purchases – not even one!

4. We call this line "The Best of the Best" because each month you'll receive the best books by some of today's most popular authors. These authors show up time and time again on all the major bestseller lists and their books sell out as soon as they hit the stores. You'll like the convenience of getting them delivered to your home at our special discount prices . . . and you'll love your *Heart to Heart* subscriber newsletter featuring author news, horoscopes, recipes, book reviews and much more!

5. We hope that after receiving your free books you'll want to remain a subscriber. But the choice is yours – to continue or cancel, anytime at all! So why not take us up on our invitation, with no risk of any kind. You'll be glad you did!

6. And remember…we'll send you a surprise gift ABSOLUTELY FREE just for giving "The Best of the Best" a try.

SPECIAL FREE GIFT!

We'll send you a fabulous surprise gift, absolutely FREE, simply for accepting our no-risk offer!

Visit us online at
www.mirabooks.com

® and TM are trademarks of
Harlequin Enterprises Limited.

BOOKS FREE!

Hurry!

Return this card promptly to GET 2 FREE BOOKS & A FREE GIFT!

Affix peel-off MIRA sticker here

YES! Please send me the 2 FREE "The Best of the Best" novels and FREE gift for which I qualify. I understand that I am under no obligation to purchase anything further, as explained on the back and on the opposite page.

385 MDL DNHR

185 MDL DNHS

FIRST NAME	LAST NAME

ADDRESS

APT.#	CITY

STATE/PROV.	ZIP/POSTAL CODE

DETACH AND MAIL CARD TODAY! ▼

(P-BB3-02) ©1998 MIRA BOOKS

The Best of the Best™ — Here's How it Works:

Accepting your 2 free books and gift places you under no obligation to buy anything. You may keep the books and gift and return the shipping statement marked "cancel." If you do not cancel, about a month later we will send you 4 additional novels and bill you just $4.49 each in the U.S., or $4.99 each in Canada, plus 25¢ shipping & handling per book and applicable taxes if any.* That's the complete price and — compared to cover prices of $5.99 or more each in the U.S. and $6.99 or more each in Canada — it's quite a bargain! You may cancel at any time, but if you choose to continue, every month we'll send you 4 more books, which you may either purchase at the discount price or return to us and cancel your subscription.

*Terms and prices subject to change without notice. Sales tax applicable in N.Y. Canadian residents will be charged applicable provincial taxes and GST.

he wasn't about to apologize for acting on his feelings. Nor should she.

"Not this promise!" Claire declared. She brushed by him and stalked through the hall, down the stairs, and out the front door.

Dusty knew the attraction she felt for him, both physical and emotional, was counter to all her original plans and promises to herself. It wasn't, however, the great catastrophe she was making it out to be. He locked up then sauntered down the walk after her. By the time he reached the pickup, she was already sitting in the cab. "Look, I know you think we crossed the line here tonight," he said as he climbed behind the wheel, and shut the door after him.

"And then some," Claire said stonily, staring straight ahead.

"But I can't bring myself to regret it, either," Dusty told Claire firmly, as he fit his key in the ignition. *It had been too special. No woman had ever made him feel like that.*

Finally, Claire turned to look at him. She studied him warily. "I thought you weren't looking to get involved with anyone," Claire snapped in a low, voice.

Dusty wanted nothing more than to haul Claire right back in his arms and kiss some sense into her. But given the fact that they had an audience of about six kids, right across the street, he decided against it. This time words—not actions—would have to convey his feelings. "I said I wasn't looking to be matched up with a woman by other people, even those as well-meaning as Cynthia and J.T.," Dusty corrected with a beleaguered sigh. The color in her face, the new fire in her eyes, made him grin. "Finding you—" Dusty said softly as he paused and shook his head, and looked deep into Claire's eyes. "The way I look at it, I've done *that* all on my own."

"WHAT'D YOU DO TO GET Claire so mad at you?" Jennifer asked Dusty Saturday morning, as he headed outside after breakfast.

He paused and got down to Jennifer's level. As usual, she was spending time with her kitten, Pokey, outside on the porch. Pokey was eating her breakfast of cat food and a small saucer of milk while Jennifer simultaneously petted and watched over her. "What makes you think Claire is mad at me?" Dusty asked curiously, although he knew darn well that was the case. He just hadn't figured anyone else on the ranch would notice.

"The way she was looking at you, when you came in to the house this morning," Jennifer explained. "That's the way I look at boys when they stand too close to me at recess or something."

That pretty much described it, Dusty thought. She had been most ladylike in her goodbye the night before. As icy as a Boston winter, too.

"Were you standing too close to Claire?" Jennifer continued curiously, as she tugged on the end of one of her long blond braids.

Dusty thought about the kiss he and Claire had shared. She had responded to him as passionately as he had responded to her. She just didn't want to admit it, because admitting it would be surrendering to something beyond her control. Something uncharted. Exciting. Dangerous. They could get their hearts broken here, if they weren't careful. They could also find more happiness than either of them had ever dreamed about. Dusty was counting on the latter.

Aware Jennifer was waiting for him to answer her, Dusty said, "It was something like that, I guess."

Jennifer sighed loudly. "Claire's still kind of upset because her wedding got called off, isn't she?" Jennifer guessed.

"Maybe," Dusty conceded. But what that had to do with him, he didn't know. Unless Claire was going to turn into the kind of woman who hated all men, after a bad experience with one. And whatever had happened between Claire and Dennis Elliott had to have caused her momentous pain. Otherwise, he was willing to bet Claire would not have humiliated herself and her family by running back down the aisle. And she certainly wouldn't be acting so scared and hurt now, with him. He supposed he was just going to have to give her some time.

Jennifer scooped Pokey up and put her on her lap. "Mommy says Claire's had a rough time and we need to give her her space."

"It sounds like good advice," Dusty said. Advice he should have followed before kissing Claire last night. He wondered what she had planned for today. As far as he knew, she wasn't scheduled to work at the clinic over the weekend.

Jennifer looked up as the door on the guest cottage slammed. "Uh-oh. Duchess is loose again."

Dusty followed the little girl's glance. Claire's golden retriever was indeed without a collar, or a leash. And she was running full-out for the pasture where the long-horns were kept. That was no laughing matter. One good kick from one of those cows could put Duchess in a world of hurt. And Claire was clearly not going to be able to outrun her four-footed friend.

Swearing silently, Dusty jumped up and raced after

the frisky pup. He bypassed Claire and caught up with Duchess just as she managed to wiggle between the bottom and middle slats on the fence. Lickety split, she was all the way in the pasture.

"Duchess!" Claire called frantically as she caught up with them both. "I mean it! Come back here right now!" she ordered her dog.

"It's going to take more than that," Dusty said. He grabbed the dangling leash and collar—which were still attached together—out of Claire's hand, and vaulted over top of the fence. Once on the other side, he stopped and let out a loud, commanding whistle.

The longhorns ignored him, but Duchess stopped, looked and listened.

Dusty whistled again and patted his thighs. "Duchess, come!" he ordered authoritatively.

To her credit, Duchess thought about it—she really did. But in the end, curiosity—and Mother Nature—won out. Bypassing the longhorns closest to her, she headed straight for the steaming pile of solid waste, and stopped, dropped, and rolled. Over and over again.

"OH I DON'T BELIEVE IT!" Claire cupped a hand to her mouth and nose as Dusty led a still dung-covered Duchess across the pasture. Her mission accomplished, the pup was trotting happily at Dusty's side. "What on earth would cause Duchess to do that?" Claire demanded, vigorously fanning the air in front of her nose.

"That's one of the great mysteries on earth," Dusty said, as he led Duchess around to Claire, who was—understandably—keeping her distance for the moment, from both Dusty and her dog. "Scientists think there is some chemical in the dung that attracts dogs, probably because it repels bugs and anything else the dog might consider annoying. Anyway, if a dog is anywhere near a fresh pile—and again it has to be fresh, they don't want anything to do with the old stuff—the dog will do exactly what Duchess just did. Which is why true ranch dogs usually sleep in the barn instead of the house. If they have free rein to get near the cattle, it's impossible to keep them out of the dung.''

Claire shook her head at Duchess, then looked back up at Dusty. "Now what?" she demanded.

Dusty shrugged, glad to see that thanks to the mischief-minded Duchess, Claire was no longer angry with him about the kiss. Or at least, he amended silently, she wasn't thinking about it at the moment. Which gave him an opportunity to get on her good side. It was an opening he didn't intend to miss.

"It's your dog," he drawled.

Claire lifted her brow and made a face at him. "Yes, and you're the vet."

Which didn't quite make it his problem. Unless, of course, he were feeling generous and wanted it to be. Dusty didn't have to think about it too long. He decided to come to her rescue once again. "Well, obviously Duchess needs a bath," he said. "And a good one."

Claire bit into her lower lip and continued to keep her distance from her stinky dog.

"Does your vet clinic also do grooming?" she asked.

The stench coming off Duchess was so bad it was all Dusty could do not to hold his nose. He frowned and looked down at the golden retriever, who was lying on the ground, panting and out of breath from her misadventure.

Dusty shook his head. "Not this kind, no. Besides how would you get her there? You can't put her in a car this way and I refuse to let any animal ride in the back of a pickup, it's too dangerous. We're going to have to wash her down out here in the yard.''

Claire blinked. ''We?'' she echoed weakly.

No way was she laying this all on him. Especially after making such a show about remaining strong and independent. ''I assumed you wanted help. But if you don't—'' Dusty was prepared to back off. Pronto.

''Uh, no. If you…uh insist… I won't refuse,'' Claire said, color sweeping her cheeks.

''Somehow, I figured that,'' Dusty said dryly. He looked Claire straight in the eye. She might not realize it yet, but for this, she owed him another kiss. One without the inner angst this time. ''Well, don't just stand there,'' he commanded impatiently. This was not the way he had planned to spend his only other Saturday off that month. ''Go put on some old clothes, grab some manner of dog soap or shampoo, and let's get going on this.''

CLAIRE KNEW SHE WAS taking advantage of Dusty by asking him to help her with Duchess, after the way she had behaved the previous evening when he had dropped her back at the guest cottage. But she couldn't help it. She wanted to be with him. And she liked being rescued by him.

It was old-fashioned, of course. And completely inappropriate for her to be leaning on a man this way for whom she planned to have no intimate relationship with. And maybe, she could somehow repay his kindness.

It was worth a try anyway.

And anything, Claire noted silently, was worth it if she could restore some amiability to their relationship. When she finished dressing, she grabbed some of her own shampoo and conditioner, and rushed out to join him.

"Thought you might appreciate these," Dusty said, as Claire met him back in the yard.

"Thanks," Claire said, as she accepted the surgical gloves he handed her. She was happy to see he'd had the foresight to tether Duchess's leash to a tree, for her bath. Claire tugged on her gloves. "I knew there had to be some perks associated with knowing a vet."

"Glad to see I'm appreciated." Dusty turned the water on at the spigot and dragged the garden hose over to where Claire was standing with her dog.

"How come you don't have any pets?" Claire asked, as they started by having Dusty stand behind Duchess and hose the worst of the mess off, while Claire stood in front of her pet and held Duchess's head in her hands, petting and soothing her all the while, so she'd stay still. Claire looked up at Dusty. "Most of the vets I know have a veritable zoo living with them. I would have figured you for a major dog person."

"Actually, I am," Dusty admitted, as he put the hose down and picked up a bottle of Claire's jasmine-scented shampoo. "And up until recently, I had two dogs," Dusty said, as he poured shampoo onto his palm and began lathering up Duchess's fur. "Ace, a black Lab that had been with me since puppyhood. He was my tenth birthday present, and he went everywhere with me, including college. And then I had Susie-Q, a St. Bernard who became mine when I married Jill. In fact," Dusty smiled fondly, as he related, "that's how Jill and I met. She brought her St. Bernard puppy over to the clinic for her vaccinations and puppy checkups at the student-run clinic at Texas A and M when I was in vet school. She used to tease that she didn't know who I fell in love with first, her or Susie-Q."

"Which was it?" Claire asked, as she worked shampoo down Duchess's chest, tummy and front legs.

"Well, let's put it this way." Dusty paused to spread shampoo through Duchess's long, fluffy tail. "I never met a puppy I wasn't ready to adopt. But Jill was something special."

"Tell me about her," Claire urged quietly, admiring the love she heard in Dusty's voice. Obviously, he had cared deeply about his late wife, and it appeared his love had been returned.

A distant look came into Dusty's eyes as he recited the facts as if by rote. "Jill was an elementary school-teacher. She taught second grade. And she was sweet, kind, beautiful, smart, all the things you'd want in a life."

And, Claire thought, a part of him missed her to this day. She swallowed around the knot in her throat, aware the pain she had suffered had been nothing compared to the sorrow he had endured. After all, she had never really loved Dennis Elliott, she knew that now. Dusty had given his late wife his whole heart. "What happened?" she asked quietly.

Dusty looked down as he began to rinse the soap from Duchess's coat and gave the task more than necessary attention. "She had an aneurysm."

The husky catch in Dusty's voice brought an answering sorrow to Claire's heart. She didn't know if it would help him to talk about this with her, but it might, so…she had to ask. "The doctors weren't able to help?"

Dusty shrugged and continued what he was doing, working blindly as he rinsed the soap from Duchess's now-clean-and-fragrant-smelling coat, as he looked Claire straight in the eye and continued with obvious regret, "They didn't know about it until she got a blinding headache one day at school. That by itself wasn't anything out of the ordinary. Jill suffered from seasonal allergies and had a tendency to get migraine headaches when pollen counts were high and the cedar was in full bloom. Anyway, she called me after classes let out for the day, and asked me to come and get her. She didn't feel up to driving home in Houston's rush hour traffic. I left right away—I knew it had to be bad if she called and asked for my help, but by the time I got to the school, the aneurysm had already burst. We took her to the hospital. She was there for several days. But in the end there was nothing the doctors could do to bring her back, so we—her parents and me—had to let her go."

Claire could only imagine the horror. "Was she the only family you had?"

"By then, yeah." Finished, Dusty set down the hose. He smiled fondly at Claire's pet as Duchess shook herself vigorously, flinging water every which way. "Except for Ace and Susie-Q," Dusty amended as he ripped off his rubber gloves. "I'd lost my own parents a couple years before. Anyway, it was a pretty rough time," he concluded as he walked over to turn the water off.

Claire could only imagine the suffering he had been through. She knelt beside Duchess and realizing how lucky she was to not have endured anything like what Dusty had, in the loss of his wife. She took off her gloves and began drying Duchess with a towel. "Were your dogs sad, too?" she wondered out loud.

"Oh, yeah." Dusty also picked up a towel, and knelt on Duchess's other side. "Both of them really missed Jill," he said as he worked the cotton terry cloth through Duchess's coat with soothing circular strokes. "Susie-Q in particular. She used to lie by the front door for hours, just waiting for Jill to come home. Every time a car door slammed she'd jump up and run to the windows and look out. When she'd see it wasn't Jill, she'd lie back down again, the saddest expression in her dark eyes.'' Dusty paused to swallow as they finished and stepped back. ''That was one of the reasons I moved to Crystal Creek in the first place. I thought a change of scene might help us all.''

Claire handed Duchess a rawhide chew bone—her reward for being so cooperative during her bath.

''And did it help?'' Claire asked.

Dusty made a seesawing motion with his hands as he and Claire took Duchess up onto the porch of the guest house, and tied the end of her leash to one of the round white columns that supported the roof. Mindful of their damp, dirty clothes, they sat down together, at the top of the porch steps.

Dusty frowned as he answered her question. ''Not as much as I'd hoped,'' he said, his thigh brushing hers, as he settled next to her, even closer. He took her hand in both of his, surrounding it with warmth. ''Suzie-Q kept looking for Jill. Ace was still pretty sad, too. I knew it was just going to take time to heal and that's when Suzie-Q got hit with cancer. There wasn't anything that could be done—the tumor was too close to her heart. I kept her as comfortable as I could, but she died about two months later.''

''Oh, Dusty,'' Claire's heart went out to him and she tightened her grip on his hand. ''That must have been really hard, for you and Ace.''

''It was.'' Dusty met her commiserating glance with a wan smile. ''Anyway, for the next year it was just me and Ace and life gradually started going back to normal.

I wasn't exactly happy but I wasn't sad all the time, either. And neither was Ace. So we sort of went back to the bachelor ways and had good times again. You know, sort of lived life as the spirit moved us.''

Claire could imagine how that would have been in a rough and tumble way. "Just you and your dog," she said.

"Yes." Dusty reflected a moment, and then gradually his happiness faded and his eyes filled with sadness once again. He fixed his gaze on a distant point. "There toward the end, Ace's arthritis got really bad, especially in his hips." He paused, shook his head. "I knew from the way he moved and his age—he was nearly eighteen—that he didn't have long. Anyway, one morning I woke up and found he had slipped away peacefully, in his sleep."

Claire gulped around the knot of emotion in her throat and did her best to keep her composure. "And that's when you decided not to get another dog," she guessed. Just as he had decided, for a while, not to love.

Dusty released a hefty sigh, for a moment looking as if he had the weight of the world on his broad shoulders. "I figured a wife and two dogs was all the loss a guy could reasonably be expected to take in two years." He looked over at her, caught sight of the single tear rolling down her cheek.

"Hey." He touched his thumb to her cheek, wiping the salty moisture away. "I didn't mean to make you cry."

The tears came in earnest then. Embarrassed, Claire ducked her head. "It's just so sad," she mumbled in a choked voice, turning her head toward his chest.

"Yeah, it was." Dusty took her all the way into his arms, not caring that they were in full view of anyone who might walk by or look out a window as he comforted her. "But there's some good news in all this," he told her in a tender voice. He waited until she looked at him before he continued. "Being around you and Duchess has made me want a dog of my own again."

"Just a dog?" Claire teased, moving back and away.

"And a woman," Dusty acknowledged as he took her wrist playfully in hand, and tugged her close again. "One very sexy, Bostonian in particular."

Their gazes locked and for a second, Claire couldn't think or breathe. Claire wasn't sure what to make of such a bold declaration. She only knew his pursuit of her was very exciting, in a thrilling way. It was making her want to toss out all those promises she had made to herself, about being strong and independent, and living life strictly on her own for a while.

Dusty traced the back of her wrist with his fingertips, then circled it lightly with his hand. "Like it or not, Claire, I'm coming all the way back to life again," he stated softly, looking deep into her eyes. "And it's all because of you."

CHAPTER SEVEN

DUSTY GAVE CLAIRE THE rest of the day to think about what a gentleman he had been. Around dinnertime Saturday evening, he ambled over to the swimming pool to see her. "The way I see it," Dusty told Claire the moment she stopped swimming laps and looked up, "you owe me."

Claire swam lithely over to the edge of the deep end. Once there, she stayed chin deep in the water, treading water and clinging to the edge with her hands.

"For what?" Claire demanded wryly, sinking down low enough to blow bubbles across the surface of the water.

Trying not to think about how pretty she looked, with drops of water clinging to her lips and the blush of summer sun across her face, Dusty knelt down on the hot cement in front of her. If he weren't so certain he would have been intruding on her privacy, he would have gone back to the old stone house, put on his swimming trunks, come back and gotten into the water with her. As it was, he was stuck—in jeans, boots and a long-sleeved shirt— in the shimmering one-hundred-and-five-degree heat. Claire, however, looked quite comfortable in the cool water of the pool.

"Rescuing your dog, not once but twice, and then bathing her," Dusty replied. "Given what she had been rolling in," Dusty stressed with a stern look as he remembered the stinky mess, "you and I both know that was above and beyond, *way* above and beyond, the call of duty."

"True." Claire folded her arms on the ledge in front of her and continued to tread water like she hadn't a care in the world. Whereas Dusty had all his hopes pinned on the evening ahead.

"So what do you say?" Dusty continued boldly, hoping like hell he was not going to be shot down before he even got out of the gate. "Will you go with me to Manny Hernandez's birthday party tonight?"

A thoughtful look on her face, Claire swam down to the shallow end and walked up the curved steps to the cement. "He's your partner, right?"

"Yes." Dusty picked up her beach towel, and doing his best to keep his eyes only on her face and not on her body, handed it to her. He was only partially successful—the sleek supple curves of her slender frame, and the wet clinging fabric of her dark blue maillot, drew him like a magnet. He had suspected Claire was beautifully toned, head to toe, her skin silky soft and perfect. Now, he knew it for a fact.

Knowing he'd score no points with Claire by revealing his ardor for her at this stage of the game, Dusty swallowed, and did his best to keep his mind strictly on the subject at hand—tonight's festivities in Crystal Creek. "Manny's wife, Tracey, is throwing the party for him, and she told me if I didn't show up with a date of my own this time she would provide me with one," Dusty said, his mouth and throat going dry as he watched Claire towel off with careless efficiency, her breasts jiggling softly all the while.

Dusty adjusted his stance to cover the growing snugness at the front of his jeans. "So you see, you'd really be doing me a favor if you decided to ride along with me,'' he said casually, hoping like hell she didn't drop her glance to his lower half. "And it would give a proper Boston lady like you a chance to see a genuine Texas dance hall, in all its Saturday night, shoot-'em-up glory,'' he said, concluding his sales pitch cheerfully.

Apparently oblivious to the lustful direction of his thoughts, Claire dropped the towel and picked up a white robe that covered her from neck to knees. She slipped it over her head and shimmied it down the rest of her body, past the dip of her waist, the curve of her hips, the slender perfection of her thighs.

Only when the cloth was perfectly adjusted on her lithe form, did she look up at him again. "Is it really going to be that rough and tumble a place?'' she asked, slicking her wet blond hair back away from her face with the flat of her hand.

"I don't know,'' he teased, as she slid her bare, sexy feet into a pair of sandals, the same dark blue hue as her swimsuit. "I expect to find out you're going to have to go along with me. And, if you're unhappy, you can catch a ride home later with Cynthia and J.T., 'cause they're going to the party, too.''

"I know.'' Claire picked up a wide-toothed comb, a half-read romance novel and a bottle of sunscreen. She bit her bottom lip with the edge of her pearly white teeth. "They already asked me to ride along.''

Disappointment shimmered through Dusty, as he guessed, "And you refused?''

Claire lifted her slender shoulders in an elegant little shrug before meeting his eyes once again. "I wasn't sure I wanted to go,'' she said softly, an interested light in her sky-blue eyes.

"And now?" Dusty inquired, his hopes rising once again.

Claire's lips curved in a pretty smile that was part invitation, part warning not to make another pass at her. "Like you said," she retorted dryly, her voice telling him there was no possibility of further physical intimacy between them. "I owe you."

CLAIRE WASN'T SURE WHAT she should wear to a real Texas dance hall, but she did know it should be something western. The only thing she had in her closet that fit that description was a pair of red cowgirl boots that had been given to her by Cynthia upon her arrival at the Double C. And a pretty blue, rose and cream dress, with cap sleeves and a full, swirling skirt that clung to her slender waist and ended just above her knees. She topped it off with a vanilla-colored lady Stetson that pulled the whole ensemble together in a reckless, sexy sort of way most unlike Dr. Claire Page from Boston.

So who was she really? Claire asked, as she surveyed herself in the mirror. Line-dancing Texas woman? Or buttoned-up Boston pediatrician? And why, she wondered, all the more pensively as the doorbell sounded, did she have to choose? Why couldn't she be both? And get everything there was to get out of life? Here. To-night.

Her heart pounding with anticipation of the evening ahead, she grabbed her bag and headed out to the porch, where Dusty was patiently waiting. Their eyes met. And in that moment, she knew it was going to be a life-altering night.

In an effort to disguise her true feelings, she made a funny face at him as his gaze swept her raptly from head to toe, and found—if she guessed correctly—absolutely nothing lacking. "You don't have to say it," she bantered lightly, pretending to misunderstand his interest in her attire. "I know I'm wearing the colors of an American flag."

"Not to mention the Lone Star colors," he said, with a teasing wink. "But not to worry," he murmured softly in her ear as he stepped forward to gallantly take her arm. "You look very fetching."

So did he, Claire thought wistfully. The black jeans and black-and-red western shirt molded the muscled contours of his body in a pleasing fashion, while the black Stetson tugged low across his brow gave him a slightly dangerous look. She knew this wasn't a date. Wasn't anything like it. But it felt like one. It felt as if she were well on her way to becoming his woman, whether she planned for that to happen or not.

"Thanks," she said softly, as they moved toward his pickup truck, their steps meshing as naturally and effortlessly as their breaths.

The yard was as quiet as one would expect on a Saturday night. The air was hot and still and scented with the flowers that surrounded the house, the sun just starting to go down in the western sky. And Claire was so aware of Dusty she could barely breathe.

She turned toward him, waiting for him to either unlock or open the passenger door. His eyes connected with hers and held. He smiled down at her lazily, and then, as if unable to resist teasing her about her outfit one last time, squinted at her hat, dress and boots. "And not to mention patriotic, in a very Texas way, even for a Yankee."

Claire rolled her eyes, even as the hot blush of awareness rose in her cheeks. "You can stop complimenting me anytime," she drawled right back.

Dusty shook his head, and instead of opening her door as she had hoped, he backed her up against the side of his just-washed truck. He braced his hands flat against the metal on either side of her. His eyes shone with an ardent light. ''Not before I do this,'' he told her in a quiet, self-assured tone, caging her body with his taller, stronger one. Then his head was lowering slowly, deliberately toward hers.

Claire saw the kiss coming. Knew she should turn her head to the side, away. Instead, she rose up on tiptoe. And then Dusty's lips were on hers in the way she had been fantasizing about, making her spirits soar, her heart pound and her knees weak. She moaned—first in protest, then in surrender as he used his lips and tongue to maximum advantage, conjuring up need and passion, heat and tenderness. Overwhelmed by the hot, minty taste of him, she threaded her hands through his hair, pressed her breasts against his chest, and brought him closer yet. She kissed the voluptuously soft corners of his mouth, swept his mouth with her tongue, then let him take charge and kiss her more deeply, intimately still. Holding her tightly, he continued his mesmerizing, sexy kisses until desire swept through her in hot, urgent waves, and she arched against him, no longer caring what common sense dictated, only caring that this moment—this connection between them—never end.

When he finally lifted his head, and looked down at her, Claire was trembling so badly she could barely stand on her own. And she knew if she let anything else happen, so much as a single kiss or caress, they would never make it to the party. There might not be any future for them, but there would certainly be no going back and undoing anything, either.

Was she ready to take such a big step?

Was he?

Steadied by the difficult reality of the situation they'd found themselves in, she dropped her hands from the hard swell of his biceps, stepped back. As much as he still wanted her, and she wanted him, she knew she couldn't do anything without thinking it through a little more, because she couldn't afford, wouldn't let herself make, another mistake.

Pretending, for argument's sake, that what had just happened had been all on his side, she turned back to him stubbornly and demanded grumpily, "What was that for?"

Dusty flashed her another irresistible smile. "Couldn't help myself," he drawled, reaching behind her to open the door for her at long last. His heated gaze returned to her face, and lingered so long he had her tingling hotly all over again. "You looking so fetching and all."

She frowned as he helped her inside the cab. "I thought we agreed we weren't going to do that," she reminded him firmly, trying not to think how vitally alive she felt whenever she was near him. How very much a woman.

"No," he corrected mildly, leaning over to help her with her safety belt, too. "*You* said we weren't going to do that. I never said that."

Claire's heart pounded all the harder as she searched his eyes for any clue as to what the evening ahead of them held. "Meaning you are going to kiss me again?" she ascertained.

Dusty smiled back at her tenderly, and promised in a low husky voice, "You bet, darlin'. Every chance I get."

Claire tried. She really tried to be ticked off at Dusty, for kissing her the way he had back at the Double C.

But every time she worked up a full head of steam, he did something sweet or charming or funny or just darn nice.

"Admit it," Dusty said, several hours later when they were enjoying the birthday party for Manny and dancing together at Zack's. "You find me very attractive."

"Modest, too," Claire quipped, aware she was not just enjoying Dusty's company, which she had secretly expected to all along, but the honky-tonk atmosphere of the dance hall.

It had been decorated festively, in honor of Manny Hernandez's birthday, and closed to the general public for the night. A buffet of favorite Texas foods had been set out on the long wooden bar. There were long-necked bottles of beer, wine from Tyler and Ruth McKinney's vineyard, a magnificent four-tiered chocolate birthday cake from the German bakery, and hand-churned vanilla bean ice cream to go with it. A country and western band played favorite tunes. Everyone in attendance was in a celebratory mood.

Dusty's dark brown eyes sparkled with mischief. "For the record, I find you mighty pleasant to look at and be with, too. That is," he amended with a wince, "when you're not stepping on my foot."

Claire looked down and found the toe of her boot had indeed landed on the toe of his. "Sorry." She hadn't quite gotten the hang of two-stepping yet. Most of the time she had it right, but if the tempo of the tune was too fast, she would eventually flub up. As she had just done.

"That's okay." Dusty used his arm that was wrapped around her waist, as leverage, to bring her nearer still. Still regarding her intently, he waggled his eyebrows at her in a teasing manner. "I like it when you can't get close enough to me."

Determined to outmaneuver him, Claire wedged as much distance between their torsos as she could, given his right arm was still locked about her back, bringing her in contact with him from waist to shoulder, his other hand clasping her hand warmly.

Unfortunately, her victory was short-lived. And she knew it even before she accidentally bumped into the person behind her.

"Careful," Dusty warned as he swept his glance down their bodies, focusing particularly on the halves below the waist, where they were clearly not touching. He leaned down to whisper in her ear, "Or you're really going to have people looking at us. And trying to do the same thing. You know, dance with their—" he paused, drew back far enough to look at her and cough discreetly "—'ahems' sticking out. They'll probably even want to give the dance a funny new name."

Seeing his point and noting he was right—they were getting a few interested stares from the other party guests, given the way their bodies were angled, Claire frowned and scooted her lower half in. Using the arm clamped about her back as leverage, Dusty dropped the flat of his palm to her waist and brought her even closer, until they were once again touching in one long electrified line and she was practically dancing on his toes again. "That's better." He regarded her with a satisfied grin.

Better for what? Claire wondered, as her pulse raced all the harder. Showing her how very much she desired him and he desired her? Claire tilted her head back and studied him with the same frankness he was regarding her. "You're going to be trouble with a capital *T*, aren't you?" she said softly.

Dusty shrugged his broad shoulders modestly and searched her eyes. "I'd like to think so, if it's the heart kind of trouble. The kind of trouble that turns your life upside down and makes you reconsider all sorts of things."

Like marriage? Claire wondered.

Or passion.

Or vacation fling.

He hadn't said.

She wouldn't ask.

After all, once burned, twice shy.

Aware Dusty was still waiting for her reaction, Claire paused, bit her lip. And kept dancing with him, nice and slow, even after the music had ended, and the other guests were moving apart and clapping for the band. "The only thing is, I'm not sure I'm in the market for that kind of trouble, Dusty," Claire said softly, honestly.

Once again, he wasn't discouraged by her lack of outright enthusiasm. Dusty moved forward, as the next song began, and pressed his lips against her ear. "Just give it a chance. Let whatever happens happen," Dusty advised her tenderly.

BUT, UNFORTUNATELY DUSTY noted with dismay as the evening wore on, Claire wasn't about to let that happen. Instead of getting closer to him, she became more remote. Cautious. And quiet. Oh, she let him dance with her, all right, without trying to pull away anymore, and she laughed at all his jokes, but she offered up nothing of herself. And by night's end he had, to his frustration, gotten no closer to her than he had been when the evening had begun. And that feeling of stymied frustration intensified when she left him to go talk to her cousin. Alone. Just as the birthday party wound to an end around midnight.

"Well, thanks for the lovely evening, but I'm catching a ride home with Cynthia and J.T.," Claire told Dusty, when she had returned to his side.

Too stunned by Claire's decision for words, Dusty blinked in surprise, while beside Claire, Cynthia McKinney looked at Dusty in what could only be described as acute disappointment. Her husband, J. T. McKinney, looked at Dusty as if wondering what in tarnation Dusty had done to screw this perfect evening up. And the truth was, Dusty didn't know.

Or maybe he did.

Deciding reluctantly not to make a scene, or give the good folks of Crystal Creek anything more to talk about than he and Claire already had that evening by dancing and flirting with each other all evening long, Dusty tipped his hat at Claire. Then smiled and said, "Sure. Good night, y'all. I'll see you tomorrow back at the ranch."

His spirits falling faster than a bucket down a well, he watched them all walk out together.

"What just happened?" Manny asked, as he walked over to stand shoulder to shoulder with Dusty. Happy as could be, ever since he had married Tracey Hernandez, Manny wanted everyone—including and especially his business partner—to be as contented as he was. He tipped back his hat and looked over at Dusty. "What did I miss?"

"I think it was a shut-out," Hutch said dryly, as he joined them.

A former AAA ballplayer, who once played for a Boston farm team, and now owned a bar and chili parlor,

Malcolm "Hutch" Hutchinson had a more worldly view than many of the residents of Crystal Creek. "Come on over to the bar. I'll buy you a drink. One for the road."

Finding he needed the companionship of other guys in the wake of his unexpected defeat, Dusty readily accepted the offer. "But make it coffee. I'm driving," Dusty warned.

"Me, too." Hutch slapped him on the back.

They settled down, steaming mugs of java in hand. "So what's going on with the two of you?" Hutch said, reaching down the length of the polished wood bar to bring some of the food their way, "If you don't mind my asking, that is."

Dusty took a crisp tortilla chip from the big terra-cotta bowl, and broke it in half, mostly for want of something to do, since he wasn't really hungry. "I want to date her. But she insists she isn't ready."

Hutch dipped a tortilla chip into what remained of the seven-layer dip. "She came with you tonight, didn't she?" he pointed out, with the same sort of candor that made his down-home chili parlor such a popular place to hang out, have a beer and talk, and philosophize about life.

"Only because I sort of cajoled her into it," Dusty said, as he loaded a chip with the mixture of refried beans, guacamole, sour cream, grated cheddar, olives, tomatoes and green onions. In retrospect, however, given how their evening together had just ended, Dusty thought he might have been better off to have just let Claire refuse him, and let that be that.

"Which is why you think she left you high and dry just now and went home with her kinfolk," Hutch guessed, as he got out another handful of chips and loaded them up, too. "Because she didn't really want to be here with you in the first place."

Dusty sighed and took a sip of coffee, and wished he had ordered a soda, because the java really didn't go with the dip at all. "Maybe I should have seen this coming," he said.

Hutch demolished several more chips and dip. Dusty noted Hutch didn't seem to mind the peculiar combination of food and drink. "Now I don't follow you," Hutch said lazily.

Dusty shrugged and tried out his theory on the compassionate ex-ballplayer and former ladies' man. Hutch was well-known for his shrewd people instincts. He usually sized people up correctly from the get-go. So if Hutch felt Claire was just leading him on a merry chase...consciously or not...

"Maybe that's just the kind of hot and cold gal Claire is," Dusty speculated casually, though not really believing it, then waited for Hutch's notoriously frank reaction. "Wanting to be with a guy one moment, not wanting anything to do with him the next." Dusty had met up with a few of those in the past. He'd steered clear of them. With Claire that didn't seem to be possible though. He wanted to be with her all the time, and when he wasn't with her, like now, he was thinking about her. Dusty had thought—hoped—Claire was feeling the same way. Been so besotted with her that he couldn't see things the way they really were? The only thing Dusty knew for sure was that he had never in his life wanted a woman as badly as he wanted Claire.

But Hutch was already shaking his head. "No. I don't think that's the case with Claire, not at all."

Dusty waited to hear more and Hutch continued, "My wife, Betsy, has taught me a thing or two about women and what they really want and need. And let me tell you, it isn't always obvious. From where we both were sitting tonight, that Claire Page is plumb crazy about you.''

Dusty raised a skeptical brow. As much as he wanted to believe that, there was evidence to the contrary. Dusty frowned. ''Then why,'' he asked Hutch dryly, ''am I sitting here with you while Claire Page is driving home with J.T. and Cynthia right now?''

''Might have something to do with that rich guy she was set to marry,'' Hutch supposed as he quaffed the rest of his coffee and held out his cup for another refill from the bartender. ''Betsy comes from a very proper, very wealthy family, too. People like that, who are always guarding their money, thinking about it, worrying about it, trying to keep others from stealing it, don't always behave in the way you or I or other ordinary folk might. In fact, most of the time rich folk like that put other people, their feelings, their welfare, dead last over just about everything else. So their reputations don't get ruined and their bank accounts stay intact and growing.''

''But there's nothing about Claire to hurt anyone's reputation,'' Dusty said. ''And as for money, the Page family is very well off in their own right. At least, that's the buzz around town.'' Cynthia Page McKinney hadn't wanted for anything, before her marriage. And J. T. McKinney was wealthy in his own right, in both land and money. Claire's branch of the family was said to be very wealthy, too.

''So maybe it was strictly something that other fella did,'' Hutch guessed. ''Either to Claire directly or someone else that got her so turned off.''

As much as Dusty did not want to admit it, he knew Hutch had a point. Maybe, like him, she would recover over time. The question was, could he wait two years—

the same period it had taken him—for that to happen? Dusty had no answer for that. He took a deep breath, wanting every ounce of wisdom a much-traveled and life-experienced man like Hutch could impart. "So what are you saying?" Dusty asked cautiously.

"Just that Claire might have had had some very good reasons for saying 'I don't' to that fella of hers up in Boston instead of 'I do.' And furthermore," Hutch reasoned practically, looking at Dusty man-to-man, "I think Claire should be admired for keeping those reasons to herself. After all," Hutch theorized with his trademark compassion and understanding, "discretion is the better part of valor. What good would it do to wound others the way Claire has so clearly been hurt?"

CHAPTER EIGHT

J.T.'s DAUGHTER, Lynn Russell, arrived back at the Double C Ranch at the same time that Cynthia, J.T. and Claire drove up. Since it was nearly midnight, and they had just seen her and her husband, Sam, in town at the party for Manny Hernandez, everyone—including Claire—was surprised to see the pregnant Lynn out at that time of night.

"What's up?" J.T. asked his thirty-five-year-old daughter, as they all got out of the cars.

"I was going to ask you the same thing," Lynn replied in bewilderment. "What's the emergency here tonight?"

"I don't think there is an emergency," Cynthia cut in, looking just as puzzled as her stepdaughter and her husband.

"Well, Allie, our oldest daughter," Lynn explained to Claire, "said she and Sandy and Hank were all watching a movie. Around ten-thirty Sandy got a phone call. When Sandy hung up, she told Allie her help was needed out at the ranch, and that we—" Lynn pointed to herself and Sam "—were not to worry if she didn't get home until very late, that she would be home as soon as her mission was accomplished. So naturally, we assumed you had a mare about to give birth or something, and that one of the hired hands had asked Sandy to come over and help out."

"I didn't call Sandy, but I'll check with the foreman."
J.T. strode off toward the stables to investigate.

Another set of headlights swept the drive. A green
pickup truck pulled up beside the other two cars. Dusty
got out. "Something happening to one of the horses?"
he asked Lynn—who, in addition to being a wife and
mother, was a ranch owner, and one of the state's pre-
miere horse breeders.

Quickly, Sam Russell brought Dusty up to speed.

J.T. strode back to join them. "Sandy's not here and
no one here called her." He looked at both Sam and
Lynn. "Any chance she might be out with friends?"

"I don't know," Lynn hedged. But it was clear from
the look on her face, Claire noted, that Lynn thought it
was a distinct possibility.

Sam frowned. "Obviously, our daughter is up to
something. Guess we better try and find out what it is."

J.T. and Hank took their cars and fanned out to scout
the usual teen haunts while Cynthia and Lynn went inside the Double C ranch house to start making calls to
all of Sandy's friends. Dusty and Claire were left outside. "I know this isn't our problem," Claire said.

Dusty nodded agreeably as he met her eyes. "I feel
like we should do something to help, too."

"But what?" Claire sighed in frustration. "We don't
know where Sandy might be."

Dusty turned to Claire, a speculative look in his dark
brown eyes. "Don't we?"

"YOU WERE RIGHT," Claire breathed in satisfaction a
half an hour later, as the two of them parked at the entrance to the old Hole in the Wall dude ranch. "That is
Sandy's car, over by those trees."

Dusty looked as disappointed as Claire felt in their

young friend. "All I knew was that she was likely up to mischief of some sort with her friends," Dusty said, perfectly willing to give credit where it was due.

The two of them emerged quietly and walked forward, first with the body of the vehicle between them, then side by side. He slid a steadying hand beneath her elbow as they trod over the rough ground. His touch was warm and comforting and Claire leaned into his support gratefully.

"You were the one who connected her current cause—stopping the construction of the lake on the old dude ranch—with tonight's disappearance," Dusty continued with a shake of his head. "And voilà, here she is."

"As well as half a dozen other kids, from the looks of it," Claire said, looking over the collection of empty vehicles. "The question is where on the property are they, and what exactly are they doing?"

Dusty swore as they heard the sound of a bulldozer starting up, in the distance. "There's our answer. Come on," he said, rushing back to his truck, Claire by his side. They jumped in the cab. He started his engine and off they went, bumping over the newly leveled ground, horn blaring, emergency lights flashing. One by one, the bulldozers came to a stop. Dusty put his truck in park, cut the engine. He left his headlights on and climbed out of his truck. Claire followed his lead as he signaled for all the kids on the bulldozers to do the same. One by one, they cut their engines and joined him on the ground, in the beam of the headlights from his truck.

"Give me one good reason why I shouldn't call the sheriff on all of you," Dusty began grimly.

Sandy Russell ducked her head sheepishly, as did the other eighteen-year-olds—like Rory Jones who also

worked part-time summer job at the Double C Ranch—
in the group. "We're doing a public service here," Rory
Jones said defiantly.

"Yeah," one of the other boys piped up in their defense. "We're saving the ecology."

Dusty's scowl deepened. "By stealing bulldozers and
other heavy equipment?" he countered in stark disapproval.

"We weren't stealing it exactly," Rory said.

"We were just going to hide it from them," Sandy
said. "So they couldn't finish stripping the land and dig-
ging the man-made lake."

"Yeah, we figured if we caused them enough grief
they might decide to take the hint and build their
crummy lake and golf course somewhere else," Rory
said.

"I sincerely doubt that would have worked," Claire
said wearily.

"I don't care how noble your motives were, your actions were dead wrong," Dusty said firmly, as two more
pickup trucks pulled up beside his, one after another.
Two men in their mid-twenties got out. Dusty introduced
both to Claire as Chuck Cooper and Barry Armbruster,
the two men who owned the construction company hired
to clear and flatten the land per Brian Fabian's and Castle Enterprises's instruction. Shortly thereafter, a sheriff's car pulled up as well.

A big man with a salt-and-pepper mustache got out.
The name tag pinned next to his silver badge said Sheriff
Buddy Jackson. Claire noted the county sheriff looked
just as unhappy with the situation as all the other adults.
"What in tarnation is going on here?" Wayne Jackson
demanded.

Briefly, Dusty and Claire explained.

Wayne looked at Sandy. "Your grandpa J.T. would have your hide if he knew you were doing something like this, bringing shame to the McKinney name."

Sandy bristled. "Somebody has to stand up to Castle Enterprises!"

"Well, this isn't the way to do it," Sheriff Jackson shot back, even more sternly. "And I expect your kinfolk are going to tell you that, too, just as soon as they get ahold of you."

Sandy folded her arms against her body and continued to sulk.

Sheriff Jackson gave the kids another look—that warned them not to even think about running off before he finished dealing with them, then motioned all the adults to one side. "So what do you think?" Wayne Jackson asked the owners of the purloined construction equipment. "Do you want me to take them in and book them?"

Chuck and Barry exchanged glances. Whatever they were thinking, both seemed to be in agreement. Finally, Chuck said gruffly, "Look, Barry and I both know what it is to be young and do something foolish."

"We don't, however, think the kids should get off scot-free for something like this, that's why we called you, Sheriff, when we saw what those kids were up to," Barry said sternly.

"What if they did some sort of community service as their punishment instead?" Claire suggested.

"Or better yet, put in time helping you fellas out here," Dusty said.

Chuck and Barry agreed those were both fine suggestions, and together, a perfect solution for a thorny problem. They worked out an agreement with the county sheriff on the spot, and then the sheriff went back with the other adults to talk to the kids. "Okay, here's the deal for all you young whippersnappers," Sheriff Jackson said. "All your parents are going to be called and told about this. And then you kids are going to make up what you've done here, to Mr. Cooper and Mr. Armbruster and their construction company by helping them clear the land. Any questions?" Sheriff Jackson sternly regarded all the kids. They shook their heads no. "Didn't think so," Wayne Jackson said.

"Well that worked out well," Claire said in relief, as she and Dusty got back in their pickup truck and drove away. Although she knew most, if not all, of the kids would be facing disciplinary measures at home, as well.

"The kids are lucky all the adults around here are so understanding," Dusty said. "In the big city, they'd probably be facing a misdemeanor."

Claire slanted Dusty a curious glance, aware more than ever how easy it was to be with him, no matter what circumstances they found themselves in. He seemed to enjoy being with her just as much. "Is that a plug for life in a small town?" Claire asked with a smile.

He shrugged his broad shoulders amiably, and gave her a teasing look. "You can take it however you like," he drawled.

And, Claire thought, as she studied the optimistic expression on his handsome face, there was no doubt about it—Dusty wanted her to stay on in Crystal Creek permanently, marry and settle down with him.

Three days ago, the idea would have been ludicrous.

Now…it didn't seem so unappealing.

And that was crazy.

She couldn't move here on a whim. Even if she loved the friendly, caring people and the laid-back atmosphere of small-town, Texas life. And she certainly couldn't move here on the rebound—no matter how much she felt at home here, or was tempted to stay—just so she could be close enough to Dusty to be able to see him and talk to him and be with him every day. Because if she did that, she'd be rearranging her life and leaning on a man instead of doing what she'd originally set out to do, which was to prove she could be independent.

Aware she was headed into dangerous territory, Claire took a deep breath, and tried to steer her thoughts away from the mixture of desire and admiration she felt for Dusty, and back to the problem facing the community. "What else do you think might happen regarding the town's opposition to the proposed subdivisions and all the changes going on over at the Hole in the Wall?" she asked curiously.

Dusty made a seesawing motion with one hand. Claire had only to look at his expression to realize his view was a little more cosmopolitan than that of the residents who had spent their entire lives in Crystal Creek, and wanted the city and countryside to stay pretty much the way it always had been. "People are already starting to calm down," he said, as they reached a stop sign. He turned to her and tugged playfully on a lock of her hair. "Besides, change can be good, you know." He smiled, his double meaning as clear as the starry Texas night above. "You just need to have an open mind."

BACK-TO-BACK EMERGENCIES kept Dusty busy all of Sunday and late into that night. By the time he got back to the ranch, the lights at the guest house were out. Another call before dawn had him leaving the Double C before Claire was even out of bed. But Monday evening as he finally headed home from town after a long, grueling day and a brief but important stop at his realtor's office, he was ready to have some quality time with Claire.

Unfortunately, when he pulled up into the drive, he saw a rental car parked next to the guest house.

Frowning, he grabbed the papers he wanted to show Claire and got out of his pickup truck. Jennifer bounded off the porch of the big house, and came toward him, her kitten Pokey cradled in her arms. "Hi, Dusty," she said.

"Hello, pumpkin." Dusty ruffled Jennifer's hair, which earned him her cute, scrunched-up-nose look. "What's going on around here?" He figured if anyone would know who Claire's company was, it was likely to be Jennifer.

"Mr. Elliott called my mom and asked if he could come by to tell Claire he was sorry, so my mom said he could, because as far as she was concerned he did owe Claire an apology for the stuff that happened on the day they were supposed to get married. But she also said if Claire wanted Mr. Elliott to go, he had to go."

And he was still here, Dusty noted grimly.

"How long has Mr. Elliott been here?" Dusty asked.

Jennifer shrugged and let out a disappointed sigh. "I'm not really sure. I know he's been in there a while."

Which meant what? Dusty wondered uneasily. Could the two of them actually be getting back together? And how long, before he found out?

INSIDE THE GUEST HOUSE, Claire stared at Dennis in a mixture of consternation and anger. "Where do you get off even proposing something like that to me?" she demanded angrily. She had told him, before she left Boston, that she never wanted to see or hear from him again. Instead of accepting that, however, he'd hired a private investigator to track her down, and then insisted on seeing her. Claire had reluctantly agreed, but only to give them both the closure they needed to get on with their lives. Unfortunately, her former fiancé didn't seem to want to do that.

"Look," Dennis said, his handsome face twisting into a mask of complete exasperation, "I did what you wanted me to do. I took care of the boy!"

Claire flung up her hands and paced the small living room restlessly. "But only because your lawyer and public relations people advised you to do so," she pointed out in disgust, wondering what it was she had ever seen in him. Surface charm and professional success only took a person so far.

Dennis scowled and reminded her, "You wanted me to be honest with you."

"Yes, I did," Claire bit out angrily. "And the facts are, if you hadn't settled the boy's mother would have sued the pants off of you, dominated the news with the juicy details of her grievances against you, and sent your company's stock tumbling."

Unable to argue with her about that, Dennis continued his defense of his actions matter-of-factly. "The boy and his mother will never have any financial worries for the rest of that kid's life."

The boy.

Not my son.

How could he be so cold and unfeeling about his own flesh and blood? Claire wondered.

And how could she not have seen it?

Where had her judgment—her good sense—been?

"So as far as I'm concerned," Dennis continued, "it's case closed."

"And that's really the bottom line for you, isn't it,

Dennis?'' Claire said, so sad and angry she didn't know if she would ever recover from the disillusionment she had suffered at the hands of her ex-fiancé. She stared him down. ''You feel you have done what is required of you, and that's it. That's all. Subject closed.''

GOOD MANNERS AND HIS desire to let the situation play out the way it was supposed to play out, required that Dusty let Claire entertain her ex-fiancé in private. But the moment Dennis Elliott stormed out the guest cottage door, slammed into his rental car, and drove off in a huff, all thoughts of propriety went right out the window. Dusty left the porch of the stone house, where he had been going over those papers he had wanted Claire to see, and headed straight for the guest cottage.

He thought, given the rude way her ex-fiancé had left, that Claire might be upset. And he was right. Tears were streaming down her face as she yanked open the door and regarded him with more unhappiness than anyone should ever have to feel. ''What?'' she asked tiredly.

''Mind if I give you a hug?'' Dusty said.

And without waiting for her to reply, he did.

CHAPTER NINE

CLAIRE TOLD HERSELF SHE should definitely not be allowing this to happen. The last thing she needed was another emotional entanglement destined to bring her nothing but heartbreak but when Dusty wrapped his arms around her and held her close, she couldn't turn away. She loved his warmth and his strength, his kindness and caring. But that did not mean, she thought, as she felt the passion stir deep inside her, she should begin a love affair with him. And if he held her this way much longer, she knew in her heart that was exactly what would end up happening. The attraction between them was that strong.

Tensing, she splayed her arms across his chest and pulled away, demanding irritably, "What do you think you're doing?"

Dusty ignored her signals and continued to cradle her protectively, one arm anchored firmly about her waist, the other hand moving up to cup her chin. "I'm giving you a much needed embrace," he said, gently caressing her face her cheek with the pad of his thumb. He paused to search her eyes. "Or are you going to stand there and tell me you don't want a friend to talk to right now."

Claire released an exasperated sigh. Leave it to Dusty to figure out what she needed before even she knew. "I hate it when you're right when I wish you were wrong," she said, tongue in cheek.

"I know." Dusty flashed her a crooked grin, all the sympathy she ever could have wanted in his eyes. "So are you going to invite me inside or what?"

Claire took his hand in hers, and led him inside the guest cottage. Duchess ran to greet him, and the two enjoyed a joyful reunion, before Duchess settled down with her chew toy once again.

"So, I guess you and your ex-fiancé haven't been able to work things out yet," Dusty said as he settled on the plump overstuffed cushions of the sofa.

Claire went to the small refrigerator, tucked beneath the small guest bar in the corner, and brought out two cans of diet soda. She set them on the black marble countertop, then reached for the crystal glasses in the cupboard above it. "We're never going to work things out," she said.

His expression concerned, Dusty watched Claire add ice to their beverages. "Sure about that?" he asked casually.

Claire had only to look into Dusty's eyes to know that he would stop pursuing her—right this instant—if she told him she had even the slightest hope of patching things up with Dennis. She splashed soda into both glasses. "He's not the man I thought he was."

Dusty stood and walked over to stand beside her. His dark eyes radiated both worry and compassion, as he prodded, "And you know that because—?"

Claire swallowed, aware it hurt to even speak the truth. And once again, she wondered how she could ever have made such a terrible mistake. "He has a four-month-old son that he refuses to even acknowledge, never mind love."

DUSTY STARED AT CLAIRE IN shock. Their hands brushed as she handed him his glass of diet soda. "You're kidding.'' This wasn't what he had expected at all, but it certainly explained the mixture of disillusionment and anger he saw in Claire's eyes whenever the subject of her near-marriage or her ex-fiancé came up.

Claire sighed, and taking Dusty by the arm, led him back to the sofa once again. She curled up on one end of it, he sat down in the middle.

"I only wish I was kidding,'' she said, her expression both hurt and resigned.

Dusty didn't know how any man could turn his back on his own child. Unless the man had no character at all. He reached over and took Claire's hand in his. "When did you find out?''

Claire sighed and meshed her fingers tightly with his. "On my wedding day. I was in the anteroom and the music had just started playing when a very sweet and very vulnerable-looking young woman slipped into the room. She told me she was a flight attendant from Chicago. She'd had an affair with Dennis. He'd gotten her pregnant and then broken up with her because of it. She thought he would change his mind about being part of their baby's life once the child was born, but that despite repeated pleas from her, he had refused to even see the child. She thought I should know the truth about Dennis before I married him and she wanted my help in convincing him to do right by the boy.

"I didn't want to believe her,'' Claire continued, "not without proof. But there was something in her eyes that made me realize I had to get to the bottom of whatever was going on. So I asked her why she had waited until then to talk to me.''

"And she said?'' Dennis prodded.

"That Dennis had been stringing her along. Promising

her he would go to Chicago to see her and the baby and do right by them, he just needed more time to adjust to the idea of being a dad. And she had believed him—until she found out from someone in his office that he was getting married. She knew then that he had lied to her. She figured he was lying to me, too. Which was right, because even though Dennis and I were engaged, he hadn't told me any of it,'' Claire concluded sadly.

''You must have been pretty upset and confused,'' Dusty said sympathetically.

''To put it lightly.''

''So what'd you do?''

''I went to the room where Dennis was waiting and confronted him.'' Claire shook her head sadly, recalling. ''Dennis told me we would straighten it all out later. That as far as he was concerned the baby boy could be anyone's child. It wasn't necessarily his.''

''Did you believe him?''

Claire frowned. ''I wasn't sure but I knew Dennis had definitely slept with her in the months before he and I started dating. And then simultaneously denied her pleas for help and tried to keep me from finding out about it— the guilt about that was written all over his face.'' Claire sighed and swept a weary hand through her hair as she continued recounting that horrible day. ''Meanwhile, the music was playing. All the guests were waiting.''

''And you had a split second to decide whether to go ahead with the wedding or call it all off,'' Dusty surmised.

Claire nodded. ''All I knew for certain at that point was that I didn't want to let everyone down. So, I let myself be pressured into going ahead with the wedding as scheduled.''

Dusty's heart went out to Claire—he could well imagine what an impossible situation she had found herself in. ''And then in the end couldn't go through with your vows,'' Dusty said.

Claire nodded grimly. ''The whole time we were standing in front of the priest, I was thinking about the look in that young woman's eyes, and the guilt in Dennis's. I knew that I couldn't pledge my love to a man like that. Never mind spend the rest of my life with him! So when it came time for me to say, 'I do,' I said, 'On second thought I don't.' And ran back down the aisle and out of the church.''

Dusty shook his head in silent commiseration. ''I don't blame you.'' Claire deserved much, much better.

Claire pressed her soft, bow-shaped lips together and released a rueful sigh. ''Well, then you're about the only one,'' she said wryly, alluding to the social scandal she had left in Boston.

Sensing she needed comfort now more than ever, Dusty rubbed his thumb across the satiny underside of her wrist. ''No one else knows the truth. Do they?''

Claire drew a deep breath and averted her eyes. ''I haven't told anyone but you and Cynthia and my brother and his wife.''

Dusty took a moment to reflect on that revelation. ''Why not?'' he asked quietly. Was he just in the right place at the right time? Or was there something more—something special—happening between them, that wasn't going to disappear even if Claire did eventually leave Crystal Creek and go back to Massachusetts, as she had originally planned?

Claire turned toward him once again, her breasts accidentally brushing against his arm. Her sky-blue eyes were troubled as she explained the reasons behind her silence. ''It's a very touchy situation. Dennis is a very well-known businessman in Boston, and we're both from socially prominent families. If word were to get out about the real story behind our failed engagement, the papers and scandal sheets would go crazy with it. I knew if I told the rest of my friends and extended family, they'd feel they had to defend me to the gossips, and I didn't want reporters hearing about it through the grapevine, and going after the baby and his mother.'' She sighed, shook her head. ''Dennis's deliberate cruelty was hard enough to bear, privately, without having to deal with a public scandal, too.''

So instead, Dusty thought, Claire had let her own reputation be torn to shreds. Dusty frowned as his thoughts turned to her ex-fiancé once again. ''Is he ever going to do right by the boy?''

Claire shrugged and recounted unhappily, ''He just settled a large sum of money on the child—that's what he came here to tell me. But he only did that because she threatened to sue him if he didn't consent to a DNA test. So he did. And then, once the results were in, well, he had to come through or face a paternity suit.''

Dusty shook his head in silent admonition. ''Prince of a guy.''

''Really,'' Claire agreed bitterly. She raked a hand through the satiny strands of her light blond hair and released a tremulous breath. ''And to think I almost married him.''

''The important thing is, you didn't,'' Dusty said firmly, very glad that Claire had escaped a life of misery with the guy. Aware it was all he could do to keep from pulling her over onto his lap, kissing her soundly, and stamping her as his, he continued bluntly, ''And now, if you don't want to, you don't ever have to see him again.''

"I will if I go back to Boston. We know a lot of the same people." She'd run away from the situation temporarily but she couldn't keep running forever. Sooner or later, she'd have to return.

"Is that how the two of you got involved in the first place?" Dusty asked curiously.

Claire nodded, recalling without wanting to how Dennis had literally swept her off her feet. "He's five years older than me. Very charming. Successful. Driven. He really appreciated and supported my dedication to my career. And he didn't seem to mind the long hours I worked. Looking back, I realize the time we did spend together was all kind of superficial. We went to a lot of exciting, elegant and romantic places and we made a striking couple. But we didn't spend a lot of time talking about the things that mattered most—like our values."

"How long did you date before becoming engaged?" Dennis asked gently.

"Just three months."

"You think that was too short a time," he guessed.

"Now, yes. Don't you?"

Dennis shrugged. "I think it all depends. If you love someone and know you want to spend the rest of your life with them, then you ought to be able to get married whenever, wherever, you want."

That was just it, Claire thought, troubled. How did you know it was right, or that he was the one? She felt a deep attraction for Dusty. He seemed like a wonderful man. Caring, compassionate, principled. But what if he too had secrets? What if there were things he wasn't sharing with her? She didn't want to make the same mistake twice.

Claire sipped her diet soda and shot him a curious glance. Determined to shift the conversation back to less intimate territory, she asked, "What were those papers you brought in with you?"

Dusty got up and went to the console table next to the door. "I was going to show you the contract I signed on that two-story house." He picked up the papers and brought them back to the sofa, for her perusal.

Claire studied them with delight. "You bought it?"

"I'm going to," Dusty confided happily, very glad she had helped him pick it out, "just as soon as the inspections and deed search are complete."

"Good for you."

"That's actually why I came over." Dusty took her hand in his. "I was going to ask you to go to dinner with me and celebrate. So tell me." He searched her pretty blue eyes hopefully. "Are you up for it?"

"Absolutely," Claire said, as the phone began to ring. Motioning for Dusty to wait, Claire picked up the receiver, said hello, and then listened intently. "Oh my," she said sympathetically. "Well, tell him I'll be right there." When she hung up, she said, "That was Lynn Russell. Hank's broken out in hives again. I'm going to have to go borrow one of the cars so I can go over and see him."

Admiring her dedication to her patients as well as how easily she switched gears—not every physician wouldn't have minded having their time off disrupted that way—Dusty held the door for her, and said, "I could drive you to the Russell ranch."

Claire's face lit up. "You wouldn't mind?"

"No problem," Dusty assured her. He was glad for the excuse to spend time with her. "Guess it pays to have a pediatrician in the family," he teased as they walked to his pickup truck.

"Actually, I'd do this for any of my patients," Claire

admitted cheerfully. "I'm one of the few old-fashioned enough to enjoy making house calls."

Dusty wasn't surprised by that—he had known Claire was special the moment he laid eyes on her. That they'd turn out to have such great chemistry and were becoming, not just potential lovers, but such great friends, was an added bonus.

Claire was quiet on the drive over. "Are you worried about Hank?" Dusty asked.

"Stymied and frustrated is more like it," Claire admitted, a rueful smile curving her soft lips. She shot a glance at Dusty. "I hate not being able to help a kid right away, but sometimes it's a while before we docs can pinpoint the source of an allergy."

"Which is another reason you're going over there in person," Dusty guessed.

"I want to look over his home environment, see if I can pick up any clues."

As before, Hank's face, arms and legs were covered with red wheals. "So what were you doing when you started itching again?" Claire asked, as soon as she had finished examining him and given him another dose of the liquid antihistamine.

"Dunno. Just playing," Hank said. Without waiting for further questions, he ran off to play with his golden Lab puppy, Rover.

"Don't look at me," Sandy said lifting her hands in an exaggerated gesture of surrender. "I haven't talked about anything upsetting or stressful at home since you and I had our talk," she said.

"Glad to hear that," Claire said. But that didn't negate what had happened the night before. Sandy had gone missing and then been caught by the police. "We had our talk with Sandy in the car on the way home," Lynn explained.

Reminded, Sandy's expression turned sullen—but accepting. She sighed loudly and told Claire, "Mom and Dad made it clear that I've got to cool it with the protests or I'll be grounded indefinitely. And since my social life my senior year is too important to miss, I'm going to do what they've wanted me to do for weeks now, which is to leave the wrangling to the people who get paid to wage such fights—the lawyers."

Good idea, Claire thought. She looked back at Lynn and Sam. "So there were no slammed doors or emotional arguments at home last night or this morning?"

Sandy and her parents all shook their heads. And it was clear from the looks on their faces that peace had finally come to the McKinney-Russell household once again.

Yet Hank had suffered another case of hives.

"When did the hives start?" Claire asked.

"I noticed them half an hour ago, right after Hank and I finished taking Rover for a walk," Sam said.

Claire's eyes fell on the damp towels and a bottle of puppy shampoo next to the hose. "Did Rover have a bath today?"

"Well yes he did, around noon."

"Did Hank help you?"

"Yes. He always helps. He loves to lather up the dogs."

"Do you use this shampoo on all your dogs?" Claire noted an aging black Lab and a collie, curled up on the porch.

"No. For our two older dogs, we use a flea and tick shampoo on them. But those would be too harsh for Rover. So we use this." Lynn brought the white bottle with the yellow cap to Claire. "It's formulated just for puppies, and has a no-more-tears formula to protect their eyes."

"Fresh new fragrance," Claire noted, reading the label out loud. "Which means it's got perfume in it." She looked back at Lynn and Sam. "The other three times that Hank broke out in a rash—had he helped give Rover a bath with this shampoo on those days?"

Lynn thought back. "Actually, you know what? He had!"

Claire smiled. "Then I think we've found our culprit."

"Good job," Dusty said, on the way home.

"Thanks." Claire smiled. She was glad Dusty had come with her.

"We still on for tonight?" Dusty asked hopefully.

Claire smiled. "Absolutely." She wouldn't miss it for the world.

CHAPTER TEN

"THANKS FOR LETTING Duchess be Jennifer's dog, just for tonight," Cynthia told Claire an hour later, as Claire carried in Duchess's sheepskin-covered dog bed and several chew toys into the big house, and up to Jennifer's bedroom on the second floor.

"No problem," Claire said. She figured the "sleepover" would be good for both child and pet.

"It's just that Jennifer wants a Lab puppy just like Hank's," Cynthia continued, as she helped Claire get everything situated, then went back across the lawn to get Duchess, who was still waiting, not quite patiently, at the guest cottage.

"And you prefer she stick with just Pokey for now," Claire noted, as she let Duchess out of her crate, and snapped on a leash.

Cynthia nodded, and said, "Cats are much easier to take care of than dogs."

"You're right about that," Claire said. You didn't have to walk a cat in the rain. With a cat, all you had to do was make sure the litter box was clean. And Jennifer already had the responsibility of caring for one pet. "Plus, puppies are a lot of work, at least initially. They have to be housebroken and trained."

"I know," Cynthia said wryly as she followed with the travel crate. "Which is why I'm hoping the overnight with Duchess will allow Jennifer to get her fill of dogs for a while.''

Claire smiled as she let Duchess sniff around the bushes. ''And if it doesn't and just increases her lust for a dog instead?''

Cynthia shrugged as J.T. and Jennifer came out of the barns and strode across the yard to help. ''Then Duchess may soon have a canine friend living right here in the big house,'' Cynthia told Claire cheerfully. ''And we may find ourselves attending puppy obedience classes every week right along with Lynn and Hank and Rover. But let's not get ahead of ourselves. By morning, Jennifer may well have decided that she's more cat person than puppy person, at least for the moment.''

''Could happen.'' Claire smiled as she handed over Duchess's leash to Jennifer. J.T. took charge of the Duchess's sleeping crate.

''In any case, it's hard to tell who is happier with the evening's arrangement,'' Claire drawled. Duchess looked delighted to have a new friend to romp with. Jennifer was equally besotted. ''And this works out great for me, too,'' Claire continued, ''since I'm planning to be out all evening.''

''I'm glad you're going out to dinner with Dusty tonight,'' Cynthia said, as she and Claire lingered on the guest house porch.

Claire looked over at the stone house, and saw Dusty was walking out to meet her, right on time. He was wearing khaki slacks and a light blue sport shirt, instead of the usual work jeans. The thought he had dressed up just for her made her heartbeat skyrocket.

Pretending an insouciance she couldn't begin to feel, given the fact she was about to go on her first real date with Dusty, Claire turned back to her cousin. ''You saw

Dennis was here.'' She guessed at the reason behind Cynthia's concern.

Cynthia nodded grimly. "I heard Dennis arrive. And I heard him leave.'' Her eyes softened sympathetically. "The day of the wedding, I must admit, I wasn't sure you were doing the right thing in calling it all off. But once you told me what happened, I knew there was no way you could marry him. Just as I knew you had to see him one more time to finally close that chapter of your life and move on.''

"It did help,'' Claire admitted. "It made me realize that I was never really in love with him, just the image he presented. At heart he was pretty shallow and superficial.''

"Unlike, say, Dusty Turner,'' Cynthia guessed.

There went her cousin again, matchmaking. "Right,'' Claire said, smiling.

"Does that mean you and Dusty are getting along better?'' Cynthia asked hopefully.

"I think it's safe to say we're friends,'' Claire replied honestly, warning herself to go slow where a sexy man like Dusty was concerned.

HENCE, IT WASN'T A SURPRISE, as she and Dusty sat together enjoying the sunset at The Oasis, a popular restaurant on Lake Travis, that the talk between them turned intimate once again.

"So why did you become a vet?'' Claire asked, as she dipped a crisp tortilla chip into a bowl of hot *chile con queso*. The melted cheese was loaded with green chiles, jalapeño peppers and sweet red tomatoes, and it was so spicy and good it practically melted on her tongue. She had realized on the way to the restaurant that there was still so much she didn't know about Dusty, and wanted—needed—to know.

Dusty took a sip of his margarita and helped himself to some chips and *queso,* too. "My Dad was a vet. I used to help him out at his vet clinic in Houston." Dusty smiled, recollecting. "Of course, he was strictly a house-pet doc. He didn't do any large animals or farm work."

"But you do both, don't you?" Claire asked. She didn't know what she was enjoying more—sitting out-side overlooking the lake on such a beautiful summer evening at sunset. Or the company.

Dusty nodded in answer to her question. "As well as exotic animals. Whereas my partner Manny Hernandez likes to do primarily large-animal work—horses, cattle and the like."

Claire smiled, noting the way the light blue of his shirt looked against the healthy suntanned hue of his skin. He had shaved again, before they went out, and as he looked at her, his dark brown eyes glowed with affection. Just being near him like this made Claire tingle from head to toe. "That must work out well," she said, doing her best to quell her skittering pulse.

"It does." Dusty smiled again, looking even sexier.

Finding it was beginning to get a little chilly on the rocky hillside high above the lake, now that the sun was going down, Claire untied the thin cotton sweater from around her neck. "What attracted you to the profes-sion?"

Dusty leaned over to help her shrug into the lacy white cardigan. He then moved his chair close to hers, and turned it, so they were both overlooking the rainbow hues of the sunset. "I'm a healer by nature," he said, his knee nudging hers, as they settled more comfortably in their chairs. "I just like taking care of things that are hurting, making 'em feel better."

"You could have gone into medicine to do that," Claire teased, as she took a sip of her margarita. "And been a people doctor, right alongside me."

Dusty inclined his head to the side, admitting with a rakish grin, "I thought about it."

"And?" Claire prodded. Why, suddenly, was she feeling so wild and free? Like she had her whole life— her future—ahead of her? And that total happiness was just within her grasp.

Dusty shrugged and took her hand in his, lightly caressing the back of it, generating tiny sensations of heat and pleasure. To Claire's satisfaction, he looked like he was having fun tonight, too. "I decided I liked animals better. What about you?" He slanted her an interested glance, leisurely taking in her windswept blond hair and pretty pastel yellow sheath, before returning—deliberately—to her eyes. "How did you get involved in medicine?"

Claire looked into his eyes and saw all the understanding and respect she ever could have wanted there. "I loved science," she said simply. "It was my favorite subject in school. And my parents wanted me to do something prestigious. Medicine seemed like a perfect fit, for my interest and their ambition."

He studied her, his grip on her hand gentling even more. "There's more to this story than you're telling, isn't there?"

Claire didn't know how Dusty did it—he always saw through to the heart of her.

"You can tell me," he persisted tenderly. "I'm really good with secrets.

"I really want to know," he persisted as they both continued sipping their margaritas.

"It'll sound sappy." And overemotional. Claire didn't like being thought of as sappy. She wanted to be sophisticated like the rest of the Page family.

She turned her gaze to the horizon, and saw the blue of the Texas sky was swiftly turning dark.

"Why don't you let me be the judge of that?" he asked softly.

Again, this was something that Claire had never told anyone for fear of sounding ridiculous. She didn't know quite how Dusty was doing it, but he was helping her to open up. To share parts of herself that she had never shared with anyone. That alone was nothing short of a miracle. To find that he understood her…applauded her…was connected to her in some mysterious but elemental way…just made it so much the better. Claire had wanted to be close to someone, really close, for as long as she could recall. Dusty seemed to be offering her that. As much as she needed to protect herself from risking anything, and or being hurt again, she couldn't turn away. She drew a deep, bolstering breath, and launched into her tale.

"Well, as I said, my parents favored medicine from the get-go, but I wasn't really sure that was what I wanted. It meant seven more years of training, four in medical school, and three in residency, and that seemed like an awfully long time. I had just about decided that I should do something easier like clinical research or even pharmaceutical company sales and distribution, when we got hit with this really bad blizzard." Claire flushed self-consciously, aware they were about to get to the hokey part, but the encouragement in his eyes prodded her to continue.

"Anyway, I was driving home from the university to my off-campus apartment, and there was a wreck on the interstate. I saw a young kid thrown from the vehicle in front of me. He landed in a snowbank on the side of the road, and that's probably what saved his life in the end, but his injuries were significant and it was truly horrifying just the same. I pulled my car over and got out to help."

Claire swallowed, recalling the mixture of terror and compassion she had felt that night. She looked up at Dusty and was sure he understood exactly what she was talking about, and more important, had felt the same emotions at one time or another himself. She took a deep breath and continued her story.

"I stayed with that little boy until the ambulance arrived, just doing all the first aid stuff and comforting and reassuring him, and he held my hand the whole time." Even though it had happened years ago, Claire could never think about that night without tearing up.

She wiped the moisture from the corners of her eyes and looked at Dusty steadily. "That was the first time in my entire life I felt as if my life meant something, like I had some purpose for being here on earth, but at the same time I was extremely leery of it." She paused, drew a deep breath. "I knew med school involved incredible sacrifice. And frankly," Claire frowned self-deprecatingly, honest enough to admit, "I'd led such a pampered existence up to that point, I wasn't at all certain I was up to it. But I applied anyway, got accepted, and once I was in, everything that happened just seemed to reinforce the feeling that medicine was where I belonged. And I've never regretted it since."

"Why pediatrics, and not some other medical specialty?'' Dusty asked quietly, his dark eyes radiating both approval and understanding.

Claire shrugged, not sure she could explain that. "I have an affinity with children. I'm drawn to them. I understand them. They respond to me. I just love being around them," she said simply.

Something in his face changed. For a moment, he went absolutely still, as if dealing with a few demons of his own. "You want kids of your own someday, then?" he asked warily, after a moment.

Claire couldn't say why exactly—she just knew her answer was crucial to her future with Dusty. "Oh, yes," Claire said enthusiastically, easily able to imagine herself with three or four children of her own. "Absolutely."

Dusty relaxed his broad shoulders slightly and his mood turned even more guarded. "Just don't wait too long," he advised her curtly.

Now, Claire knew there were problems from his past that haunted him, too. "Why do you say that?" she asked, just as quietly.

"Nothing." He shook his head, looking irritated with himself for having spoken out on such an intimate, personal subject. "I shouldn't have said anything. It's none of my business. Or anyone else's but yours, for that matter."

Claire leaned forward and took one of his warm, callused hands in both of hers. "Come on, cowboy," she urged playfully. She wasn't about to let him clam up when she had just bared her soul to him. She wanted the two of them to be as close as they could be, and that meant knowing what was in his heart. "It's your turn to explain yourself and tell me some deep, dark intimate secret." She let her gaze rove the ruggedly handsome features of his face and gave him a coaxing look, before prodding him gently. "Now why did you give me that particular piece of advice?"

For a second, Claire thought he wasn't going to answer her.

Then he gave her a lopsided smile, sat back in his chair, and continued ruefully, "I guess it's my one big regret about my marriage," he told her in a low, brooding tone. "I let my wife talk me into putting off having a family—she wanted everything to be perfect before we brought a child into this world—and then it was too late. Our time had passed us by."

Claire saw the hurt in Dusty's eyes, the disappointment. No wonder he wasn't much for waiting for the right time to have a romance. Waiting hadn't gotten him anywhere before. "I'm sorry," she said softly, honestly, her heart going out to him.

Dusty lifted his hands in a what-the-heck gesture that let her know he had put the past behind him, and despite his sadness and the regrets he would always harbor about what might have—should have—been, was looking only to the future to guarantee him his happiness now. "It just wasn't meant to be," he told her.

He had accepted that.

He wanted her to do the same.

DUSTY AND CLAIRE WERE quiet as they drove back to the Double C, both lost in thought.

"So much for sharing secrets," Claire teased as they got out of the car, and Dusty walked her to the door of the guest house. It was well after midnight, and it looked like everyone else had gone to bed hours before. "It's left us with nothing to say to each other." They had talked nonstop the rest of the evening. The conversation just hadn't been as intimate. It was as if Dusty had put up a wall around his heart, in the same way she had put up a wall around herself, directly after her near-wedding.

Claire didn't want any walls between them.

"Oh, I wouldn't say that," Dusty disagreed amiably, as he and Claire let themselves inside the guest house. They were greeted by silence, instead of an exuberant Duchess, as per usual. He turned to her, a wickedly mischievous smile on his face. "As it happens, I've got plenty to say to you," he drawled.

Something in the look he gave her had her heart pounding. Claire swallowed around the sudden tension in her throat. "Such as?"

Dusty closed the distance between them in three long strides. He wrapped her in his arms and brought her against him, length to length. "Like I want you to stay here, Claire," he murmured in a low, husky tone that seemed to come straight from his heart. "I don't want you to go back to Boston at all."

"Oh, Dusty," Claire murmured, knowing this wasn't in the "no deep or emotional involvement agenda" she had fashioned for herself at all. And then it was too late. His head was lowering, his lips were on hers, and the world around her ground to a halt. There was nothing but the two of them. Just this moment. This kiss.

CHAPTER ELEVEN

CLAIRE HAD PROMISED herself she wouldn't do this—wouldn't throw herself recklessly into a love affair with Dusty—but the taste of him, so hot and wickedly male, set off a firestorm of need deep within her. She surged against him, fitting her softness to his hardness, and their bodies melded in an instant of pleasure. Then the yearning to be close, to be appreciated for the woman she was, the woman she wanted to be, took over once again, making her tremble and tense, and bit by bit, Claire felt the last of her inhibitions melt away. Her lips parted and she drew his tongue more intimately into her mouth, stroking it, learning what he liked, even as he expertly pleasured her. Lower still, she could feel the hard length of his body, pressing against hers. And still they kissed, slowly and lingeringly, deeply and passionately, until her heartbeat hammered in her throat and she was so aroused she could barely think.

Dusty drew back, breathing raggedly, gallant to the last. "Tell me to leave," he said hoarsely.

Claire shook her head. She knew she was acting on impulse, that she might regret it later, but right now, she couldn't turn away from the closeness and intimacy he offered. She had never felt this desirable before, never even dreamed it possible. "I want you to stay," she whispered, her spirits soaring ever higher. She wanted him to show her how people should love each other. And to prove it, took him by the hand and led him into the other room, to her bed.

Eyes darkening passionately, he watched her toe off her shoes, reach beneath the hem of her dress, and peel off her stockings, then took her back into his arms. "This will change everything," he warned her hoarsely.

Claire knew, but she wanted to yield to him and the need that drove them both. "It's already changed," she told him softly. Because she loved him, she thought as the scent of his cologne filled her senses. Even though she knew it wasn't what she had planned or even the time for it to happen, she loved him.

Claire's come-hither look and throaty whisper was all Dusty needed to propel him to make her his woman, once and for all. He kissed her again, sweeping her mouth with his tongue, delving deep in a rhythm of penetration and retreat, until there was no doubt at all—for either of them—about what he wanted, or what was coming next. She clung to him, kissing him back, then trembled as he dispensed with her lacy white cardigan. Unzipped the back of her dress and eased it off. Clad in two tiny pieces of transparent ecru lace, she was every bit as beautiful and sexy as he'd thought. Heart pounding, he rained kisses down her neck, across the satiny skin of her collarbone, to the uppermost swell of her breasts. He threaded his hands through her hair, and tipped her face back up to his, kissing her as ardently as if the chance would never come again, before dropping once again to the flushed pink curves of her breasts and taut rosy nipples. Aware he had never wanted a woman the way he wanted Claire, he finished undressing them both, then guided her gently to the bed. His tongue teased her lips apart, and then plunged into her mouth, again and again, before going lower still. Flattening one hand against the small of her spine, he stroked the dewy softness, moved up, in, then touched and caressed her breasts, rubbing his thumbs over the tender crests. "You're so beautiful," he murmured, kissing his way up her thigh, to her tummy, then down again.

His own body throbbing, he loved her, discovered her, until she was trembling from head to toe, arching her back, moaning soft and low in her throat, and tangling her hands in his hair. Unable to get enough of her, he plunged his tongue inside her, tasted her sweet wet heat. Her head fell back. "Dusty," she whispered, shuddering again.

He held her until the aftershocks passed, then parting her knees with his, settled between them. He kissed her again, until she gave him back everything he had ever wanted, until the pleasure was sharp, stunning. Then lifted her against him, and surged inside. With an exultant cry, she closed around the hot, hard length of him. The soft silky curves of her breasts and her tightly budding nipples pressed against his chest. "Don't hold back," she pleaded, urging him to go deeper, harder still. Until their hearts thundered in unison and there was no doubting they needed this…needed each other…and then together, they were soaring ever higher and vaulting into a shuddering pleasure unlike anything they had ever known.

HOURS LATER, DUSTY AND Claire lay wrapped in each other's arms, their bodies still humming from the last in a string of climaxes. Dusty had no idea how many times they'd made love. He just knew the powerful chemistry between them came along once in a lifetime—twice, if you were lucky. He realized Claire was nervous about the fact they'd deepened their relationship irrevocably by making love. He understood why. He hadn't expected everything to happen so fast between them, but he didn't regret for one moment that it had. He and Claire were meant for each other. He knew it and he thought somewhere deep in her heart, despite the quick way they had gotten together, that she knew it, too. Unfortunately, as the cold light of morning approached, he could feel her beginning to distance herself from him, heart and soul.

Wanting to prevent that, he curved his arm around her, and coaxed her closer still. "This was nice," he murmured contentedly, a wave of strictly male satisfaction roaring through him.

"Yes, it was nice," Claire agreed readily, her slender body tensing—somewhat predictably, Dusty thought—within the protective caging of his. "But—" Claire flushed and sat up, bringing the sheet with her.

"But what?" Dusty sat up, too, a warning sounding in his head. He couldn't believe Claire was going to try and deny the import of what had happened between them, but as he looked at her face he knew that was exactly what was happening.

"But we can't get carried away and read too much into this one night, Dusty." A deeply conflicted expression on her pretty face, Claire climbed out of the bed. The first light of dawn filtering in through the shades on the bedroom window, she perched on the edge of the mattress, a distance away from him. Her blue eyes held an ocean of regret as she looked at him. "We barely know each other."

Dusty took her rejection like a sucker punch to the gut. He had been around the block long enough to know a maybe-we-should-reconsider-this speech coming when he saw one. "I know enough to realize I love you," Dusty said quietly as he stood, and took her in his arms.

He swore inwardly—he wasn't going to let her walk away from what they'd found. Not without a fight.

Claire swallowed and splayed both her hands across his chest. She looked deep into his eyes and said sincerely, "I made a promise to myself, Dusty, that I would stand on my own two feet for a while and not make any rash decisions."

Dusty pushed aside his hurt that Claire was not as happy about their lovemaking as he was. Knowing, however, that she wasn't trying to play any games with him, merely get her thinking straight, enabled him to be very gentle with her. Wishing he could just kiss the troubled look in her eyes away, he said softly, "This was fast, I'll grant you that. But I wouldn't call it rash. Because that would mean it was reckless and wrong." *And damn it all, it just wasn't.*

Claire clamped her lips together stubbornly and pushed away from Dusty. She went to the closet and grabbed a yellow satin robe, slipped it on. "I still want to rewind the clock a bit, Dusty."

This didn't sound good, Dusty thought, as he shrugged on his low-slung black briefs. "And do what?"

To his disappointment, she did not look at him directly as she ran a brush through the sexy disarray of her hair, restoring order to the silky light blond strands. "Take the time I had initially planned to recover from everything that has happened to me." As she caught his glance, the color in her fair cheeks deepened.

"With Dennis," Dusty ascertained grimly as he reached for his slacks and shrugged those on, too.

"Right."

Dusty couldn't believe she was punishing him for something he hadn't done. He was silent a moment, studying the grim set of her lips. "How much time?" he asked, his mood tense but hopeful.

Claire swallowed, and stood her ground. "A year," she said.

She might as well have sentenced him to a life without love. Because it damn well amounted to the same thing, Dusty thought resentfully. The silence between them grew even more strained. He strode closer and stood with his arms folded in front of him, thighs braced apart. "So you're punishing me because of the way he hurt you," Dusty ascertained.

Claire glared at Dusty contentiously. "I'm being practical," she shot back, just as hotly, "and I'm doing that for both of us. I really need to stand on my own two feet. I don't want to make the same mistake again, and besides, it's way too soon for me to be getting involved with anyone."

The corners of Dusty's lips turned up ruefully. "The horse is kind of out of the barn on that one, don't you think?" he drawled. Unable to help himself, Dusty took her into his arms again. He kissed the nape of her neck. Her cheek. Her lips.

She released a trembling sigh that spoke volumes about the tumult inside her. "Dusty—" she whispered shakily.

"You love me, too, Claire," he whispered persuasively, running his hands through the silk of her hair. "You wouldn't have been in bed with me just now, making love to me, if you didn't."

Claire didn't deny that. She was not the kind of woman who slept around, and she never had been. If her heart wasn't involved, her body wasn't, either. Nevertheless, Claire knew she had to be sensible here. She wanted Dusty to be realistic, too. Claire took a deep breath and forced herself to push him away once again. "I still want to wait," Claire said firmly.

"Until everything is perfect," Dusty guessed unhappily, a muscle working in his jaw.

Her tension building, Claire drew on all her courage and attempted to be as fair as she could about this. "Look," she suggested calmly, "maybe if we just concentrate on being friends for a while, get to know each other the old fashioned way, by writing and calling each other, things will eventually work out." *We'll feel more certain. We won't be in a situation where we are risking quite so much.*

Dusty stared at her as if she were little more than a stranger. "And you want us to do this for a year?" he asked incredulously.

Claire thought about the original promise she had made to herself. How she had wanted to stand on her own, and be truly independent for the first and only time in her life, so that she would know without a doubt she could do it, that she didn't need to lean on anyone emotionally to get by. "Yes," she said firmly.

Dusty's dark brown eyes gleamed with a mixture of disillusionment and disappointment. "I don't think so, Claire," he said stiffly.

Claire watched in a panic as he snatched up his shirt and put it on. She swallowed around the growing tightness of her throat. "How about half a year then?" she countered quickly, figuring that was a pretty big concession on her part.

To her surprise, Dusty didn't budge. "No," he said tightly.

"So what are you telling me, then," she asked, aware she was suddenly feeling like she was the one losing absolutely everything, "that you don't want an old-fashioned, long distance romance?"

Dusty released a short, impatient breath as he buttoned up his shirt. "I'm telling you that I don't want anything to do with an arrangement that is arbitrarily punishing us both! So you made a mistake in picking the wrong guy to walk down the aisle with?" he stated angrily as he tucked the hem of his shirt into the waistband of his slacks. "So what?" He stormed closer, every inch of him vibrating with emotion. "Neither you nor I were looking for love when you came to the ranch, but we found it, anyway."

"Did we? Or is it just infatuation?" Claire shot back, just as emotionally. "And how can we really tell what this is unless we take some time to examine our feelings and really put it to the test?" He was asking her to move much too fast, just like Dennis had. And this time, she just couldn't do it. She had been swept off her feet, then pressured to make the situation permanent once—she didn't care what Dusty wanted, she wasn't going to make the same mistake again.

"Look," Dusty said, his exasperation with her clear, "if it were up to me, I would ask you to move here to Texas and be with me today. Or let me move to Boston and be with you—today. But I'm willing to stay here and let you go back to Boston, and to take it slow and easy, maybe with only phone calls or letters at first, if you would be more comfortable with me courting you that way *initially*," he stressed. "But in return," he continued stubbornly, "I want something from you, too. Some willingness to meet me halfway, and spend time with me in person and make love with me when we do see each other. Because I'm not going to get in the kind of situation I was in before."

He was talking about his marriage now. His pain. "What do you mean?" Claire asked warily.

Dusty's expression hardened. "I know what it's like to incessantly put off for tomorrow what should be enjoyed today, because the overall situation isn't as perfect as we'd like it. And I have to tell you," he confided sternly, "I'm not willing to live that way again, always dreaming about the future, but never enjoying the present. I want kids. I want to be married—to you. I want to go to sleep every night in your arms and wake up the same way, and I want to love you the way you deserve to be loved, Claire, with all my heart and soul."

Claire wanted that too. So much, in fact, that it terrified her. She hadn't felt anywhere near this passion for Dennis. She shook her head miserably, moved away. "You're asking too much, Dusty." She held up both hands to keep him from taking her in his arms. "It's too fast." She had never been this happy before and she was terrified it wouldn't last.

"Fine." Dusty tugged on his boots, stood and stalked out the bedroom door.

Her heart pounding, Claire followed him into the living room. "Where are you going?"

"I played the waiting game before and watched my chance for happiness slip away because Jill would never budge from what she wanted or meet me halfway. This seems like the same thing to me," he told her gruffly.

The tears she had been holding back slipped down her face. "It's all I can give. Don't you understand? Dennis pressured me into marrying him before I was really ready to make that decision. I don't want to make the same mistake again." She wanted her relationship with Dusty to last—the only way she saw that happening was if they gave it a solid foundation of friendship first.

"It's not enough, Claire." He looked at her one more time, shook his head in grim disappointment, before yanking open the door. "You know where to find me if you change your mind."

"I MOVED TO THE LONGHORN Motel temporarily, so if you need to reach me for an emergency, that's where I'll be," Dusty said later the following day.

Manny looked up from the paperwork on his desk. It was the part of their veterinary practice they hated the most, and both Manny and Dusty usually waited until the last possible moment every month to complete it. "I thought you were staying at the stone house on the Double C."

Dusty handed Manny his half of the necessary book-work, then popped open the lid on his can of soda. "I was."

Manny tossed down his pen and leaned back in his chair. Curiosity shimmered in his dark eyes. "J.T. and Cynthia kick you out?"

Dusty lingered in the doorway and drank thirstily from his can. "No. I just figured it might be more convenient to be in town, while I'm waiting to close on my house." This way, he and Claire wouldn't have to keep crossing paths. She could enjoy the rest of her vacation at the ranch before returning to Boston as planned.

Manny sized him up shrewdly. "Bull. You've got the look of a man who has woman trouble, if I've ever seen one."

"Well, you're right about that." Finding he needed to talk to someone, Dusty shut the door behind him and sank down into a chair in front of Manny's desk. Briefly, he explained what had happened while Manny listened attentively. "Anyway, I figured moving out would be the gentlemanly thing to do," Dusty finished.

Manny nodded thoughtfully, then asked, "Have you ever worked with homing pigeons?"

Dusty shook his head.

"To get them to come back to you, first you have to let them go."

But for how long, Dusty wondered. How long?

"HOW DOES IT FEEL TO BE back in the saddle again, so to speak?" Cynthia asked Claire over the phone.

Terrible, Claire thought, as she reached down to pet Duchess, who was curled up at her feet. She'd been back in Boston for a full two weeks. She and Dusty had stopped seeing each other nearly a month ago. She was standing on her own, all right, living life as independently as possible. Unfortunately, the satisfaction she felt about that did not begin to outweigh the loneliness she felt deep inside. And she sensed it never would, no matter how much time passed.

Aware her cousin was waiting for her to answer, she said, "Life has returned to normal. I see patients, go to the hospital, the gym to work out." *Then come home and eat a frozen dinner or a salad and go straight to bed and stare at the ceiling and think about what I might be doing if only I'd allowed myself to take a chance and stay in Texas with the first man, the only man, I've ever fallen head over heels in love with.*

Jennifer, who was also on the line in this three-way, gals-only call, said, "Don't you miss Dusty? I bet Dusty misses you 'cause he sure has been awfully sad."

"Okay, Jennifer, that's enough for now," Cynthia told her daughter kindly but firmly. "I think it's time you checked on Pokey and made sure Pokey has enough water in her dish.''

There was another pause as Jennifer dashed off, sneakers clattering on the wood floor, then Cynthia got back on the line. "Sorry about that. I'm trying to teach Jennifer about discretion being the better part of valor, but so far her curiosity and concern for you outweighs any disapproval I might voice."

"That's okay," Claire replied, doing her best to keep from sounding as depressed as she felt. "She brought up a subject I wanted to touch on, anyway." Claire gripped the phone tightly, wishing she didn't already feel that she had given up the best thing that had ever happened to her. "How is Dusty?" Claire asked nervously.

Cynthia paused again, then said finally, "Well, to tell you the absolute truth, I have seen him a lot happier. But J.T. and I understand why the two of you are keeping your distance, that it's a difficult situation."

"In other words, Dusty is still upset with me," Claire said with a sigh, lamenting the fact that although she had sent Dusty several letters and an e-mail or two, he hadn't responded to any of it. Making it clear he was not going to agree to a relationship of any kind conducted strictly on her terms, with no concessions made to his wants or needs, which were to see her and make love to her as often as possible.

"I think deep down Dusty knows this is what you want and need right now, even if he isn't likely to come right out and admit it," Cynthia said kindly. "Give him time, Claire. Maybe he'll come around."

But what if he doesn't? Claire thought miserably. *What then?*

CHAPTER TWELVE

"SO YOU'RE REALLY TAKING a vacation," Manny Hernandez said.

Dusty grinned as he picked up his duffel. He had never been more certain in his life that he was doing the right thing. "Boston, Massachusetts, here I come."

"Well don't worry about anything here," Manny reassured. "I know what you have to do there is even more important."

Wasn't that the understatement of the year, Dusty thought, as he slapped his hat on his head and shouldered his way out the door. It was a risk, of course, going there to see Claire—uninvited and unannounced—when she had said she didn't want him courting her in person, but Dusty knew this was a risk he just had to take. There were some things too important to leave to fate.... And he sure as heck didn't want Claire forgetting him, or what they'd shared.

Dusty was nearly at the door of his truck, when a dog came running around the corner of the building at full clip. As the golden retriever reached him, it bounded up off the ground, put both paws on his chest, and licked him enthusiastically beneath the chin. "Duchess!" Dusty said, amazed, as he knelt and stroked his hands over the dog's face, neck and shoulders. "What are you doing here?"

"I think the better question is," her owner said, as

she rounded the corner right behind her pet, "what am I doing here?"

Dusty blinked, not sure he was seeing right. He gave Duchess a final pat on the head and stood. "Claire?"

The corners of her soft lips turned up as she strode toward him resolutely. "Looks like I got here just in time to keep you from going on your trip," she noted happily.

His heartbeat picked up as he studied the feisty determination on her pretty face. He hoped like heck this meant what he thought it did. But after what she'd already put him through, he didn't want to jump to conclusions. "You heard?" he retorted, deciding to hear what she had to say first, before he told her what was on his mind.

Claire nodded solemnly as her eyes meshed with his. "An hour ago, shortly after I arrived. And you didn't ask me what I was doing here yet."

Damn, but she looked good, Dusty thought. Aware it was all he could do to keep his hands to himself, he tossed his duffel in the back of his pickup. "So what brought you back to Crystal Creek?" he asked warily.

"I'm moving here," Claire announced matter-of-factly as she leaned against the back of his truck.

Happiness began to unfurl deep inside him. "You are?"

Claire nodded in obvious satisfaction. "Yep. As of today, I'm an official Crystal Creek resident. I'm joining Nate Purdy's medical practice."

Dusty regarded Claire seriously, glad she was joining their community, but still not sure what that meant for the two of them. Had she come here simply to tell him that, or was there something more? Hoping she hadn't come to Texas just to escape the gossip in Boston, he said even more circumspectly, "Nate and his partners must be pleased."

"They are," she conceded, just as solemnly, studying his face. Gazing deep into his eyes, she sashayed closer in a drift of jasmine perfume. "But what about you?" she continued probing softly as she splayed her hands across the front of his shirt. "How do you feel about it?"

Dusty paused, aware a lot seemed to be riding on his answer. Without warning, there was a lump in his throat the size of a walnut, and a growing heat in his chest. "I guess that depends on why you've come back," he told her huskily, after a moment, looking down into her face. "If it's to be here, and still be out of my reach—well I can't think of a better way to torture me to death than that."

"I have no intention of torturing you, except maybe with love," Claire said softly. The next thing Dusty knew she had closed the distance between them entirely and wreathed her arms about his neck. As she went up on tiptoe, he wrapped his arms around her, too. Their lips met in an explosion of heat and tenderness, and then they were kissing as sweetly and lovingly as if they had never been apart at all. "I've missed you," Claire whispered shakily, when they finally came up for air.

"I missed you, too," Dusty murmured back tenderly, unashamed to admit. "So much." He raked his hands through her hair and then, unable to help himself, kissed her again, even more passionately.

"It seems the total independence I was looking for was highly overrated," Claire told him in a low trembling voice. "There's a difference between standing on your own two feet, which I still plan to do, and pushing everyone who loves you away, which I don't plan to do any longer."

Dusty tightened his grip on her protectively, drawing her closer yet. "Thank heaven for that." He smoothed the hair from her face, and paused to look deep into her eyes. "But you weren't the only one who was wrong, Claire," he admitted in a low, rusty-sounding voice. "I shouldn't have pushed you to go faster than you were comfortable going. I'm not a patient man by nature, but I can be that for you if it is what you need."

Claire snuggled against him, abruptly looking as contented and hopeful about the future as he felt. "What I need is you, Dusty, because the love we've found is too precious to throw away."

"I couldn't agree more," Dusty said, and to prove it to her, kissed her passionately once again. "So where are you staying?" Dusty asked eventually.

Claire linked both her hands in his. "I leased a house here in town. I thought it might be more convenient, for a lot of things." The least of which was loving Dusty, Claire amended silently. "You?"

"I just closed on my house day before yesterday." Dusty went to the cab of his truck and opened the door. He motioned for Duchess to get in, and she jumped up, tail wagging merrily, and hopped into the storage area behind the seat. Dusty turned to Claire and gallantly offered her a hand up into the cab. He leaned over to help her with her safety harness.

"Want to see it now that I've moved in?"

Claire smiled up at him. It felt so good, so right, to be back in Crystal Creek with him. "I was hoping you'd ask," she said cheerfully.

"I was hoping you'd say yes." Dusty grinned. His hands braced on either side of her, he leaned over to kiss her once again, until Claire knew everything was going to be all right. Not just for today, but forever.

Dear Reader,

Crystal Creek has seemed like a magical place to me ever since I leaned how it was created. Editor Marsha Zinberg and several authors—including Bethany Campbell, who leads off this collection—gathered in the Texas Hill Country and let their imaginations run wild. What fun! Okay, I was sort of jealous. A teensy bit full of envy. Pea-green, to be honest.

So when I was invited to be a part of the Crystal Creek crowd at last, I felt as if I'd been asked to join an exclusive sorority. I would be allowed to play! It wasn't long before I discovered why everyone connected with the project remembers it so fondly. And why it was definitely time to go back. I'm thrilled to be able to add a few more residents and another story to the tapestry that is Crystal Creek.

Warmly,

Vicki Lewis Thompson

She Used To Be Mine

Vicki Lewis Thompson

CHAPTER ONE

TEAGUE SLOAN, JR. WAS coming back to Crystal Creek today on a traitor's mission.

Kendra had half expected that to be the main topic of conversation in Curly Sue's Beauty Parlor this morning. But so far nobody had said a word, not Sue Clements, who owned the shop, not Angie Dunbar, the other stylist, not even Mary Gibson, who probably had come in for a manicure to give Kendra moral support.

Ever since Kendra had met Mary three years ago, the older woman had been like a mother to her, and she of all people would understand how upsetting Teague's return would be, especially considering the job he'd come to do. But as Kendra wiped the old polish off Mary's nails with a cotton ball, Mary talked about the weather instead of Teague.

"It's warm for June," Mary said.

"It is," Kendra agreed as she breathed the sharp, yet familiar, scent of polish remover. Working usually calmed her, and she really needed calming today. "How are your tomatoes doing?"

"I'll be picking them next week, sure as the world." Mary proceeded to talk about her garden, as if Teague Sloan didn't exist, as if the Hole in the Wall dude ranch hadn't been sold, as if their whole world hadn't turned topsy-turvy in the past six months.

Unfortunately neither the gardening discussion nor the

familiar routine of reshaping a client's nails eased Kendra's anxiety. Sue and her client Carolyn Trent were talking about the merits of hardwood floors versus tile, and Angie's client Lettie Mae Reese, a maid out at the Double C, was adding her opinion of which was easiest to maintain.

Kendra suspected they were deliberately avoiding the topic of Teague on her account. But from her perspective, the air in the beauty parlor was thick with what wasn't being said. Last week some rich guy named Jack Bennett from the Dallas area had bought all the exotic grazing animals that had roamed over Hole in the Wall acreage in its heyday. He'd hired the very same Dallas trucking company Teague worked for now to transport the animals, and Teague, the low-down dirty rat, had volunteered for the job.

It would be one thing if he'd been told to do it and had no choice, but no, he'd *volunteered*. He'd admitted as much on the phone to his friend Boomer, a wrangler out at the Double C, who had spread it around Zack's Saturday night, which meant by Monday it was all over town.

Well, Kendra had always known Teague had solid brass ones, and this just proved it. People's lives had been changed forever when the dude ranch had started having financial problems and Scott and Valerie Harris had been forced to lay people off, including her and Teague. Now that the ranch was finally sold, the entire town was up in arms because of the changes that threatened Crystal Creek's future.

Land was already being cleared for a subdivision with the cutesy name of Bluebonnet Meadows, although the homes would be on one-acre lots and plenty expensive. Because of the development in progress, the animals had to be moved, but that was no reason Teague had to personally help dismantle the ranch. He acted like he had no loyalty to the place where he'd worked as a wrangler all those years, the place where he'd met Kendra, the place where they'd fallen in love.

Or at least she had fallen. She wasn't so sure about Teague. In the back of her mind she wondered if he'd volunteered to transport the animals because of her, though. Maybe he thought four months without the great Teague Sloan would have her begging him to take her back to Dallas with him.

Not likely. After all the effort she'd put into creating a niche for herself at Curly Sue's, she wasn't about to leave, not even if he got down on his knees and begged. *Like he ever would.*

No, he'd probably strut around town and expect her to run after him, pleading to be taken back. That is, if he still cared about her and hadn't found another girlfriend in Dallas. Despite being the most bullheaded man she'd ever met, he could also be very sweet. Add to that his soulful brown eyes, a mischievous grin and tight buns, and you had a guy that naturally attracted women.

Kendra didn't spend much time thinking about that. She knew a lot about self-preservation, and thoughts like that had to be banished immediately.

Ever since she'd heard about Teague's impending arrival, she'd tried to prepare herself. But when the black eighteen-wheeler rumbled past the beauty parlor on its way out to the Hole in the Wall, she lost her cool and knocked over a bottle of Radical Red nail polish. Fortunately, she didn't get any on Mary.

"I'll bet you're strung tight as barbed wire, knowing he'll be in town." Mary pitched her voice low in an obvious attempt to keep the conversation private.

As if anything could be private in this salon, or even in the town of Crystal Creek. But no one would ever hear Kendra complain. She loved small-town living with a passion, gossip and all. She was never leaving. Never.

"I'm more worried than anything." She grabbed a tissue and wiped the tiny pool of red from her laminated manicurist's table. Then she picked up Mary's right hand and began applying Radical Red to each nail. The shade had been a hard sell for Mary, who was so conservative she refused to color her graying hair. But Kendra liked shaking up her clients a little.

"Worried?" Mary asked. "About seeing him, you mean?"

"No. If I should run into him, I can handle that." Or so she was telling herself. "It's just that I was hoping that Suzette would have her baby by now, but she hasn't. I called over to Hole in the Wall before I came in this morning and she's not in labor yet, although it could be any time. I'm afraid Teague's going to stick to the schedule and put her on the truck with the other animals, whether she's given birth or not."

The heartless jerk would probably do something like that. He also knew that Suzette was special to her, but he'd already shown that sheltering her feelings wasn't his top priority. Nothing mattered but his stupid pride.

"That wouldn't be right," Mary said. "Suzette shouldn't leave until she's had that baby."

Kendra gave Mary a grateful look as she released her right hand and reached for her left. She could always count on Mary to take her side. "No, she shouldn't."

Sue, a shapely woman with hair the color of ripe rhubarb, had never been shy about adding her two cents. She gestured toward Kendra with the curling iron she was using on Carolyn Trent's blond hair. "Honey, I really think you should talk to him about that."

"I'm not sure I'm the one to talk to him." Kendra thought about the horrific argument they'd had before he left. Teague might think she was deliberately trying to cause problems for him if she asked him to hold up on loading the animals.

"I think you are exactly the one to talk to him," said Carolyn, turning her head so abruptly that she nearly got a curling iron in the eye. "You've bonded with that creature. What do you call it again?"

"A gerenuk." Kendra smiled at Carolyn, owner of the Circle T Ranch and an all-around nice lady. Carolyn was scheduled for her weekly manicure right after Mary.

Several months ago Carolyn was of the opinion that a ranch woman didn't need to have her nails done, but Kendra had won her over with the help of Cynthia McKinney. In fact, Kendra owed much of her success to careful plotting by Cynthia, aided and abetted by a few other local women who'd been clients when Kendra worked at Hole in the Wall. But Cynthia had been the key player. Apparently if the wife of J. T. McKinney thought getting a manicure from Kendra was the thing to do, others in town followed suit.

Kendra knew she was lucky that Cynthia had taken up her cause. When the beauty salon at the dude ranch closed, the hair stylists had all left the area, knowing they couldn't compete with Curly Sue's for the local business. They'd counseled her to do the same, convinced that Crystal Creek couldn't support a full-time manicurist. Without Cynthia McKinney converting half the town's female population, it probably wouldn't have.

"Gerenuk," Sue repeated. "I love that name. It sounds like something that should be Luke Skywalker's

pet. And the way you trained her to stand on her hind
legs and give you a kiss—I've never seen anything like
it. You deserve to see Suzette's baby born.''

"I just want to make sure it *is* born. But I'm afraid
of getting into a power struggle with Teague about it.''
Kendra finished stroking the bright polish over Mary's
nails and reached for the bottle of clear top coat, rolling
it upside down between her palms. Befriending Suzette
was the closest she'd ever come to having an animal of
her own. She was grateful that after she'd moved away
from Hole in the Wall, Scott and Valerie had let her
keep visiting the long-necked little antelope.

Now that the animals were finally being relocated,
Scott and Valerie would be leaving the dude ranch, too.
Although Kendra hated the thought that she might never
see Suzette again, she was more concerned about Suzette
going into labor during the trip to Dallas. A crowded
livestock trailer was not the place to give birth. Anything
could happen.

"It won't be a power struggle if you talk nice and
don't lose your temper," piped up Lettie Mae from the
salon's other chair, where Angie was rolling her hair
onto pink curlers. Lettie Mae had a standing appointment
on Wednesdays for her wash and set. She said she was
"working up to" getting a manicure.

"I don't know if I could keep my temper if I cared
about something as much as you care about that antelope," Angie said. Tall and slender, she had a long mane
of permed hair and a big dose of the crusader in her
personality. She popped Lettie Mae under the dryer and
walked over to join the conversation. "None of this
would be happening if you'd done what I wanted and
let us take up a collection to buy her for you.''

Kendra shook her head. "Absolutely not. With all the

people who were put out of work when Hole in the Wall closed up, it wouldn't be right to collect money so I could buy a pet antelope.''

"We couldn't be talking about that much money." Angie propped a slim hip against the edge of Sue's workstation.

"Guess again," Kendra said. "She's more valuable than any of the other exotics out there, and Scott said Jack Bennett could hardly wait to get her. Besides, I don't have anywhere to keep her or her baby.''

"I told you that you could bring her out to the Flying Horse," Mary said. "Bubba said so, too. After herding ostriches all these years, he sees nothing unusual about boarding a gerenuk or two.''

"I know, and I really appreciate that you two would do that.'' Kendra began applying the clear coat to Mary's nails. "But without Suzette, Bennett might not want the rest of the animals, and Scott needs to move them off the property in the next few days.''

"I hate the idea that Scott and Valerie sold that place," Mary said. "I still think they should have taken Bubba's suggestion and converted Hole in the Wall to an ostrich ranch.''

Kendra didn't point out to her that converting Hole in the Wall to an ostrich-raising operation wouldn't have helped either Teague's situation or hers. It might have helped the town, though, because then Scott and Valerie would still own the land instead of the mysterious developer, Brian Fabian.

"How's Bubba's arthritis these days?" Carolyn asked.

"He has good days and bad days. But we're managing.''

Kendra suspected that Mary was putting up a good

front. Kendra knew better than anyone that the Gibsons were struggling to keep up with the ostrich operation, and many thought the Gibsons might give in to the temptation to sell out, just like Scott and Valerie had. If Teague hadn't been such a stubborn fool, that would be less likely.

Bubba and Mary had offered to make him foreman of the Flying Horse Ranch when he'd lost his wrangler's position at Hole in the Wall. They'd had special plans beyond that, too. They'd expected Teague and Kendra to get married, live on the Flying Horse and eventually go into partnership with the Gibsons.

Kendra had been so thrilled with the prospect that she couldn't see straight. But Teague, son and namesake of the late, great rodeo star Teague Sloan, had turned them down. He'd been nice to their face, saying that he was ready to relocate and all, but privately he'd told Kendra that his daddy would spin in his grave if his son became an ostrich boy. He'd rather drive a truck for an outfit in Dallas than stoop so low.

Of course he'd expected her to leap at the chance to move to Dallas with him. He'd been amazed she'd refused. She'd been amazed he could ask. He knew the helter-skelter life she'd led as a kid being dragged around the country by her mother and whoever was her mother's boyfriend-of-the-month.

Teague also knew that after landing the manicurist job at the salon at Hole in the Wall, Kendra had put down roots at last. In her opinion Teague would have a much easier time herding ostriches than she would have leaving the first place that had ever felt like home.

Not only that, Mary and Bubba had generously provided them with a chance to build a future. Kendra couldn't see how driving a truck would do a thing for

Teague's future, considering that all he'd ever wanted was to live and work on a ranch. Cattle or ostriches, he'd still be on a ranch. She understood that he idolized his father, but the rodeo star had left his son with some ridiculous prejudices about the role of a cowboy.

"Why don't you ask Dusty Turner to help you convince Teague to delay until Suzette has her baby?" Sue asked.

"Great idea," Carolyn said. "Get a vet into the picture. That'll help you hold on to your temper and make it less about you and Teague and more about Suzette's welfare. I can't believe this Jack Bennett person would want to take a chance with Suzette, once he knows the circumstances."

"You're right." Kendra couldn't believe she hadn't thought of that. "I should call Dusty right now. I've been wanting to congratulate him on his engagement to Claire, anyway."

"If he's able to leave the clinic," Sue said, "the two of you could drive out to Hole in the Wall immediately. It'll take Teague a while to round up those animals, so you have time before he starts loading."

"But I have Carolyn's manicure to do."

"I'll reschedule," Carolyn said quickly. "This is a heck of a lot more important than a glossy set of nails." She smiled at Kendra. "Although, to my surprise, I have come to appreciate a glossy set of nails."

TEAGUE'S GUT CHURNED AS he drove the familiar road to Hole in the Wall. When he'd volunteered for this job it had seemed like the perfect excuse to see Kendra again. He hadn't planned out how to engineer a meeting with her, but he'd figured something would come to him once he was on the scene.

Now he was on the scene, and he'd cruised right past Curly Sue's without stopping. It would have been the best time to go in and talk to her, because once he had the animals loaded he'd have to stay with the truck. Well, damn. He was a yellow-bellied coward, is what he was.

He was also afraid a woman like Kendra Lynn Burton wouldn't want to have a thing to do with a guy who had thrown away a chance to be with her. She'd also thrown away the chance to be with him, but for the first time he was beginning to understand why she was attached to Crystal Creek like a burr to a saddle blanket.

For six months he'd been telling himself that the town wasn't all that special. Yet he'd seen a lot of country driving for the Dickerson Line, seen a lot of cities and towns. Going through Crystal Creek just now, he had to admit it was very special.

He'd forgotten how much he used to enjoy roaming the streets talking to people, shopping for a new Stetson at Ralph's Hat Emporium, and then dropping into the Longhorn Coffee Shop for a piece of homemade pecan pie. He couldn't duplicate that experience in a giant shopping mall, that was for sure.

He'd missed Zack's, where the music was loud enough to dance to and soft enough to carry on a conversation. He'd missed being a ten-minute horseback ride from some of the best trout fishing in the state. But mostly he'd missed Kendra.

He should have stopped at Curly Sue's. He'd taken this route knowing Kendra would probably be there working this morning. With the way news traveled in this town, his phone call to Boomer had been reported at Zack's Saturday night and had spread from there.

Kendra would know it was his rig going past the beauty shop window.

The black Freightliner had been washed and detailed for this occasion. The stock trailer he was hauling wasn't particularly glamorous, but the truck was a beauty and he'd wanted Kendra to be properly impressed. He didn't mind impressing the rest of the town, either, but Kendra was his main target.

Now he'd blown his chance to talk to her first thing. He'd planned to park the rig beside the Longhorn for the night, but since he couldn't go far from the truck, all he could do was call her from his cell phone and ask her to meet him at the coffee shop. She might not respond to a phone call as well as seeing him in person. She might tell him where he could put that cell phone.

Teague sighed, disgusted with himself. He couldn't very well turn around and drive back. That would look dumb. So he had no choice but to keep going, while memories of Kendra came at him right and left.

He passed the one-screen movie theater and remembered going to the show to see that candy movie she'd lusted after, *Chocolat*. Afterward she'd strolled down the sidewalk hand-in-hand with him, her blond hair bouncing against her shoulders while she licked away at the double-fudge brownie ice cream cone he'd bought her at Wall's Drugstore. How she loved her chocolate.

"Crystal Creek is the best place on Earth," she'd said that night.

He'd agreed with her then, because he'd had her and a job he loved. Now he didn't have either.

After he finally made it out of town and was headed toward Hole in the Wall, he drove by a dirt road that wound back into the hills and past a large granite outcropping. Right beyond that outcropping used to be his and Kendra's favorite spot for making love. They used to park under the stars, spread a blanket in the back of his pickup and in no time be in paradise. Nothing in the world had ever felt so right to him as being deep inside Kendra.

When he'd left Crystal Creek he hadn't meant to stay faithful to her, though. He'd been so damned mad at her that he'd thoroughly intended to be *un*faithful, and the sooner, the better. It hadn't worked out. He'd been on exactly three dates with three different women, and in each case the night had ended with him kissing them on the cheek and apologizing for his lack of enthusiasm.

Kendra had to agree to come to Dallas with him. She just had to. But he'd been a darn sight more optimistic before driving through town and being reminded of how much she loved the place, apparently more than she loved him. Now there was a depressing thought.

About a quarter mile before the main entrance to Hole in the Wall, he came upon a huge billboard with "Blue-bonnet Meadows" plastered across it. Underneath the lettering was a picture of a laughing and very citified-looking family—a father, mother and two little blond kids. Teague had known about the development and had thought he didn't care one way or the other. Turned out he didn't like the idea one damned bit.

Once they cleared the land for a housing development there would be precious few meadows and damned few bluebonnets left. He'd missed the wildflower season this spring. Now some of the fields he'd ridden through with Kendra by his side would never be the same. They'd be full of roads, houses and families.

He had nothing against families. Someday he might even have one of his own. But when that day came, he wanted to be surrounded by open country. He shuddered at the thought of all the people moving into what used to be uninhabited range.

As he turned into the ranch entrance, off to his left were clouds of dust where the 'dozers were working, carving roads and easements for the electricity. He drove a ways more and saw a neat semicircle of five model homes going up. Work trucks were scattered around and guys wearing hard hats climbed over the structures. The sound of nail guns and power saws shattered what used to be a peaceful countryside.

Teague took note of all the activity and wondered if the Crystal Creek that Kendra loved so much was doomed. She might be giving him up for something that was about to disappear. Maybe he'd tell her that. If he saw her. *When* he saw her.

The lodge still looked the same, though, and the guest cottages, corrals and outbuildings. A collection of cow-hide chairs still sat along the veranda, but they were all empty.

That was the biggest difference, Teague realized. This place used to be humming, with folks gathered on the veranda, others out in the corrals mounting up for a trail ride, kids splashing in the pool out back. Now, when he cut the engine of the big semi, there was silence except for the distant rumble of the 'dozers and the muted staccato noise from the model-home construction site.

A feeling of longing for what had been hit him so hard that his throat tightened. Angry at himself for getting emotional, he cleared his throat and stepped down from the cab.

Scott must have heard him pull in because he came out the door and down the steps to meet him. "Hey, Teague." He extended his hand. "It's good to see you."

"Same here." Teague gripped his former employer's

hand. He'd always liked Scott, even if he was a lawyer who liked to play at cowboying. Anybody looking at Scott would swear he was a cowboy, with his pearl-buttoned shirt, boot-cut jeans and a Stetson covering his blond hair. "I saw a few changes on the way in," Teague said.

"Yeah." Scott grimaced. "Progress."

"Must be tough to see it, though."

"It is." Scott sighed and tipped back his Stetson. "We might have been able to hold on to the place, too, except for the lawsuit. We never really recovered from that."

"You know what I think about that lawsuit. I've never had much use for lawyers, present company excepted." Teague couldn't believe some idiot had claimed to know how to ride, managed to fall off and do permanent injury to his back, and then been able to successfully sue Hole in the Wall for damages. Teague had been the wrangler bringing up the rear of that trail ride, and he'd seen the sorry way the guy sat a horse. That greenhorn never should have left the corral.

Scott grinned. "I don't consider myself a lawyer anymore."

"Then what are you aiming to do after you leave here?" Teague had an idea that some of the money from the sale of Hole in the Wall had gone to paying legal fees and other accumulated debts.

"We've bought a bed-and-breakfast in Prescott, Arizona," Valerie said, coming down the steps to join her husband. "How are you, Teague?"

"I'm fine, ma'am." Teague touched the brim of his hat. "Arizona, huh?"

"We found a big old Victorian that's gorgeous but needs a little fixing up." Valerie ran a hand through her auburn hair and smiled at Scott. "We're going to see how much of it we can do ourselves. It should be fun."

"If we don't kill each other in the process." Scott chuckled and put an arm around Valerie's waist.

"I'll bet you'll do just fine." Teague was happy that they'd found a new challenge. He should have known the two of them wouldn't be crying in their beer over this. They were perfect for each other, and he felt a twinge of envy looking at them, so secure in their love, no matter what fate dished out. He'd thought he had that with Kendra, but their love hadn't weathered a change in circumstances worth a damn.

"I guess we need to get those animals rounded up and loaded," Scott said. "Before Earl left a week ago he brought them up to the south pasture, away from the bulldozer activity. We still have a couple of horses in the barn, so between the two of us, if you'll tell me what to do, we should be able to get them into the truck."

"But it's almost lunchtime," Valerie said. "Let's go have something to eat first."

Scott glanced at her. "Sounds good to me, if Teague can spare the time."

"I'm in no big rush," Teague said. "I'm sticking around town until morning, anyway. Mr. Bennett wants to take delivery in the daylight."

"Then let's rustle up some food," Valerie said. "I'm trying to clean out the refrigerator, so no telling what you'll get, but—"

"Isn't that Dusty Turner's pickup?" Scott said, interrupting.

"I think it is," Valerie said.

Teague turned to look down the road, and sure enough, a dark green pickup with a customized shell over the truck bed was coming toward them. He vaguely remembered that Dusty Turner was the vet who'd gone into partnership with Manny Hernandez a while back.

The pickup pulled up behind the eighteen-wheeler and a tall cowboy climbed out from behind the wheel. But it wasn't Dusty Turner who commanded Teague's total attention.

The passenger door opened and Kendra, looking like an angel sent from heaven, hopped to the ground. Sunglasses covered her blue eyes, but the rest of her was right there for him to see—low-rider jeans that showed off her tiny waist, and a tight little pink T-shirt that defined breasts he'd been dreaming about for four solid months. The shirt's cropped hem left about two inches of creamy skin exposed, just enough to stampede Teague's hormones.

He gulped, unable to think of a single snappy thing to say.

"Hello, Teague," she said softly.

CHAPTER TWO

KENDRA WAS PROUD OF herself for getting those two words out, because when she looked at Teague she forgot to breathe. She'd hoped that in his absence she'd glamorized her mental picture of him, but no such luck. If anything he'd become more of a hottie than she remembered.

Maybe he looked better because he was standing near that big black truck. The truck definitely added to his macho image. Surely his shoulders hadn't been that broad and his hips that narrow four months ago. Then again, maybe he'd been working out in a fancy Dallas gym since she'd last seen him.

But if his body seemed more toned, his face was achingly familiar, shadowed as usual under his favorite black Stetson, the one she'd helped him pick out at the Hat Emporium. Oh, that face. She'd trailed kisses along those strong cheekbones, stroked her finger down that straight nose.

He had on sunglasses, which she'd expect him to use in order to drive that big ol' truck, but they were different from his old pair. These reminded her of what a race car driver might wear—wraparound, yellow lenses, expensive. Sexy.

He was still clean-shaven. She'd wondered several times if he'd grown a mustache or a beard after he left just to spite her. A face like his didn't need adornment, in her opinion, and she hadn't wanted whisker burn when they kissed.

And how they'd kissed. He had a mouth built for it, especially when she regularly treated his lower lip with ointment to keep it from getting chapped in the sun and wind. Even rubbing lip balm on Teague had been a sensuous experience. Apparently nobody had been taking care of that chore, because his lower lip was a little bit chapped.

More dazed by this meeting than she wanted to be, Kendra watched Dusty shake hands with Teague and Scott.

The vet tipped his hat in Valerie's direction. "Good to see you, Val."

"We were about to raid the refrigerator for lunch," Valerie said. "Care to join us?"

"Thanks, but I have to get back to the office pretty soon. Kendra and I drove out to take a quick look at Suzette and see how she's coming along."

Teague grew more alert. "She hasn't had her baby yet?"

The mention of Suzette snapped Kendra from her fog and reminded her why they were here. Suzette and her unborn baby needed a champion, and she intended to be that champion. "Not yet," she said. "But it could be any moment, right, Val?"

"I think so," Valerie said. "Of course, I've never been up close and personal for an antelope birth, much less a gerenuk, but I'm assuming it's not a whole lot different from horses."

"When was the last time you checked on her?" Dusty asked.

Valerie glanced at her watch. "About three hours ago. I took a walk out there while Scott was talking to the

Bluebonnet Meadows people about how soon they could come in and start...converting the lodge to a club-house.''

It seemed obvious that Valerie hated the thought of her home becoming a clubhouse. No wonder she'd left during that discussion, Kendra thought. If the development folks wanted to move into the lodge ASAP, then time was running out for Suzette.

She turned to Scott. ''What did you tell the developers?''

He glanced at his wife. ''I said we'd need at least until the weekend to finish packing.''

''He knew he'd better say that or I'd drown him in the horse trough,'' Valerie said. ''We still have tons to do, and that's not even taking into consideration Suzette's baby.''

So Scott had bought some time, Kendra thought with a sigh of relief. Now she needed Teague's cooperation, but she had to remember to include the vet in her request as everyone at the beauty parlor had coached her. ''Teague, Dusty and I think it would be best if you waited to transport the animals until after Suzette's given birth and we know the baby's all right.''

Teague's jaw tightened. ''Look, I know how you feel about Suzette, but Jack Bennett's paid a lot of money for these animals, and he calls the shots. My company guaranteed delivery tomorrow.''

''No, you *don't* know how I feel about her.'' A warm flush of anger loosened her tongue. ''But never mind that, since I'm sure you don't care, anyway.''

''Yes, I do. But—''

''The point is,'' Kendra barreled on, ''did your company guarantee delivery of live animals? Because if you take Suzette in that truck and she goes into labor, she might end up dead, which might not bother *you,* but—''

''I understand the gerenuk is particularly valuable,'' Dusty said smoothly, interrupting Kendra. ''Bennett might appreciate you taking extra care with her.''

Dusty's measured tone brought Kendra up short. She'd just done exactly what she'd lectured herself not to do. She'd lost her temper. And from the set of Teague's jaw, so had he.

Scott held up both hands. ''Time out. We might be debating a nonissue, here. Somebody could simply walk down to the pasture and see if Suzette's had her baby since Val last checked on her.''

''Spoken like a lawyer,'' Valerie said with a laugh.

''An ex-lawyer,'' Scott said.

''I'll go,'' Kendra said immediately.

''So will I.'' Dusty started back toward his pickup. ''I'll get my bag, in case anything needs to be done.''

''She might not let you near her,'' Valerie warned. ''Kendra's the only one she really trusts, and I'm not sure even Kendra will be tolerated when Suzette goes into labor. Remember she started life in the wild. None of those animals are completely tame, not even Suzette.''

Dusty opened the pickup's door and pulled out his medical bag from behind the seat. ''I'll give it a try, anyway.''

''Then I'll go inside and start some lunch,'' Valerie said. ''Anybody who can stay and eat with us is welcome.''

''I'd love to.'' Dusty closed the door. ''The thing is, I have surgery in less than an hour. But if Kendra could get a ride back to town, then she—''

''I'd better leave with you.'' Kendra had asked Sue to reschedule all her appointments for the day because she hadn't known what would happen out at Hole in the Wall. Still, she didn't want to spend any more time with Teague than necessary, and if she went back to the shop she might get some walk-ins this afternoon.

"If you want to stay, I could run you into town after lunch," Scott said. "Val's given me a list of errands as long as Suzette's neck."

"Yes, stay," Valerie said. "The more people I have around, the less I'll think about leaving on Monday."

Loyalty to her former employer made Kendra hesitate. Three years ago Valerie had taken a chance on her, a complete unknown who'd called all the way from Philadelphia asking for the manicurist's job. Valerie had said later that she'd been able to tell from Kendra's voice how much she yearned for a place like Crystal Creek. Valerie understood that rootless feeling—she'd been adrift once herself.

"Okay, I'll stay. And thanks," Kendra said.

"Great," Scott said. "The more the merrier. I'll help Val with lunch while you go out to the pasture. Teague, I'll bet you're parched after the drive. How about a cold beer?"

Kendra hoped that Teague would take Scott up on the offer and go inside. The less time she spent in his company, the better.

"Thanks. Maybe later," Teague said. "Right now I think I'll tag along with Dusty and Kendra. I might be able to help. Next to Kendra, I'm the one who knows Suzette the best."

Well, damn. Kendra grimaced. She couldn't imagine why he'd want to come with them, but she didn't dare tell him not to. Angering him more might hurt her cause. "Then let's go see the expectant mommy," she said with as much courtesy as she could muster.

SCOTT FOLLOWED HIS WIFE into the house. "You laid that guilt trip on Kendra on purpose."

Valerie glanced back at him and grinned. "Worked, didn't it?"

"Like a charm. But I don't think a potluck lunch will be enough to bring those two back together. Kendra's ready to slice and dice that ol' boy."

"I don't blame her." Valerie walked into the spacious kitchen and over to the commercial refrigerator. "All he had to do was agree to wrangle ostriches, and they could have lived happily ever after at the Flying Horse." She opened the door and scowled at the contents. "You know, this is going to be a hodgepodge meal."

"We'll make it work. Just start pulling stuff out and I'll help you figure out what to do with it."

Valerie sighed. "Okay." As she talked, she piled containers of food on the counter. "Anyway, I think it was a promising sign that Teague wanted to go down to the pasture with Kendra and Dusty. He might be wondering if Dusty's a rival, which would be very good, psychologically."

"You don't think he knows that Dusty's engaged to Claire?" Scott opened plastic lids and peered at the contents of the containers.

"He's been in Dallas for several months, and the way he was looking at Dusty, I don't think he has the faintest idea the guy's engaged, which is fine with me. A supposed rival might make Teague reconsider his original decision. He could do that ostrich thing."

"Maybe, but then again, maybe not. Have you seen the box he keeps with all the champion buckles from his dad's rodeo career?"

Valerie closed the refrigerator door and turned to him.

"No, I haven't, but what does a box of buckles have to do with anything?"

"I was down at the bunkhouse one night when he got them out for the guys to admire, and I have to admit, the man deserves respect for what he accomplished. But he had strong opinions—"

"Prejudices," Valerie said.

"Don't let Teague hear you say that. He promised his daddy he'd keep the cowboy tradition alive in the Sloan family, and he takes that promise very seriously."

"But Teague's driving a truck! That's not being a cowboy."

Scott laughed. "It's closer than you might think. Besides, he sees the truck driving as temporary. Locking himself into wrangling ostriches on the Flying Horse would be permanent. He thinks that would be breaking a deathbed promise."

Valerie let out a gusty sigh. "Were we ever that dumb?"

"Dumber. Or have you forgotten that I didn't want to get involved with you because you were such a good manager for my ranch?"

Valerie laughed. "True."

Abandoning his examination of the leftovers, Scott walked over to his wife, wrapped his arms around her and rested his cheek against her hair. "I know you identify with Kendra and her struggle to get settled. But she's a tough little gal. She'll survive, and if she and Teague belong together, they'll work it out."

"I'd love to know they've worked it out before we leave for Arizona."

"Judging from the way they were spitting at each other a while ago, that's a tall order."

TEAGUE DIDN'T KNOW Dusty Turner all that well, but he'd taken an instant dislike to the vet. Last Teague had heard, Dusty was single, and he seemed entirely too friendly with Kendra, giving her a ride out here today and being so doggoned willing to check on the gerenuk for her. Then Dusty positioned himself between Teague and Kendra for the walk down to the pasture.

Kendra and Dusty had themselves a nice little chat as they all trudged through dry, ankle-high grass on the way to the gate. Kendra described how she'd spent nearly four months taming Suzette, and Dusty hung on her every word. Neither of them paid Teague a never-mind.

Damn it all, he'd been afraid that Kendra would be upset about losing Suzette, but he'd hoped that she'd feel better knowing he was the one transporting the animals to Dallas. He'd planned to take special care of Suzette and her baby, which he thought for sure would be born by now. Matter of fact, he'd thought Suzette and her baby would be a drawing card to help bring Kendra to Dallas.

The way Teague had it figured, he'd get in good with Jack Bennett and explain how Kendra had trained the antelope to put her feet on Kendra's shoulders and give her a kiss. She'd have started right in on the baby, too, knowing her. Bennett might ask Kendra to come out and put on a show when Bennett was entertaining some of his rich friends. That way, Kendra could keep up her contact with the gerenuk and Teague would be a hero.

Unfortunately, Suzette's baby was late and Teague was so far from being a hero it was pitiful. Dusty Turner, with his medical bag and special skills to help with the birth, was the hero. Teague had become the big bad man who wanted to take Suzette away forever.

He decided to move on ahead and open the gate. Gates and corrals were his territory. No telling if Turner would have the good sense to close it after himself.

"Thanks," Turner said.

Kendra didn't thank him. Far from it. Her glance clearly challenged his right to be along on this trip.

"I didn't know she hadn't had the baby," he said. "If I'd known, maybe I could've—"

"You didn't bother to find out, either." Kendra walked away, her nose in the air.

She had him there. Cussing to himself, he latched the gate and started after them. He'd been so intent on how Kendra would react to seeing him again that he'd pushed Suzette to the back of his mind. He hadn't wanted any complications, so he'd told himself there wouldn't be any. Instead he'd pictured Kendra dying for a second chance to move to Dallas with him. He'd planned to generously give her that second chance.

From the moment the three people stepped into the pasture, the exotic antelope sprinkled around the pasture clustered according to breed and faced the gate. Teague had never quite understood the appeal of having animals which weren't native to Texas hanging out around the ranch. But their curving horns and unique coloration had fascinated Scott and a good many of the guests who used to ride out, cameras ready, to take pictures.

"Which one's Suzette?" Turner asked.

"I don't see her." Kendra tucked her hands in her hip pockets and gazed around the pasture.

Oh, God, Teague remembered that stance of hers—breasts thrust forward, fingers sliding in her back pockets, pockets that curved so gently around her bottom. She'd been standing like that on the front porch of the lodge the first time he'd noticed her, and he'd never wanted anyone else since that moment.

She'd been working in the ranch's beauty salon for several weeks before they'd met, because she had a small room at the lodge and he'd slept and ate down at the bunkhouse. He'd had no call to go into the salon, so they'd completely missed each other until she happened to be standing on the porch when he'd arrived to check with Scott about one of the horses.

At first she hadn't wanted to date someone at work because she was afraid of messing up her good deal at the ranch. She'd explained that settling down in this little Texas town was her cherished dream. When she was a kid, her mother had taken up with one urban slimeball after another, and Kendra had gone to eleven different schools in as many cities. After graduation she'd enrolled in beauty college as a way to get away from her mother's drifter lifestyle.

Although she'd stayed in Philadelphia because that's where she'd trained, she'd told him she hated big cities. When a client who'd vacationed at Hole in the Wall mentioned that the ranch needed a manicurist, she'd leaped at the chance. She'd come to the ranch a pure greenhorn hungry to learn how to be a ranch girl.

Teague had used that hunger as an excuse to be with her. He'd taught her how to ride, how to dance the Texas two-step, even how to string barbed wire. Never in his life had he been so patient waiting for a woman to give him the green light.

When she still balked, even though he could tell she wanted him as much as he wanted her, he'd gone straight to Scott and Valerie and asked permission to date Kendra. Scott had slapped him on the back and told him to go for it. Valerie had warned him not to break Kendra's heart.

He'd have to say that if anybody had done any breaking of hearts, it had been Kendra breaking his. She'd been the only woman he'd ever bought an engagement ring for, and she'd turned him down, saying that she couldn't take it with strings attached, like promising to move to Dallas. To his way of thinking, if a woman loved a man she shouldn't care where they lived, so long as they could be together.

He understood why she'd needed the steadiness of Crystal Creek at first, but she had him now. Or she could have him, if she'd stop being so stubborn. He still had the ring safely stored in the wooden box where he kept his dad's buckles. That box went everywhere with him, so he had it in the truck right this minute.

"There she is." Kendra pointed to a scrub oak at the edge of the pasture.

Teague looked, and sure enough, there was Suzette lying under the tiny bit of shade cast by the tree, her reddish-brown coat blending in with the dried grass and dirt underneath. Most of the leaves had been chewed off the tree by the grazing animals, but a few remained, and Suzette was taking advantage of the cover.

He would have recognized her by her exceptionally long neck, but even more by her lack of horns. All the other animals in the pasture—blackbuck antelope, wild Corsican rams, East African oryx and axis deer—had horns. Serious horns, even on the females. Rounding them up would be tricky, which was one of the reasons he'd volunteered.

The male gerenuk, father of the baby soon to be born, had sported a wicked-looking set of seventeen-inch horns. He'd never been friendly like Suzette, although

Kendra had tried to tame him, too, and had named him Sultan. Then, right before Teague left for Dallas, Sultan had died from some sort of stomach trouble. Knowing Kendra's tender heart, Teague guessed she'd have spent extra time with Suzette after that, keeping her company because she was the only gerenuk left on the ranch.

"I can't tell if she's alone or not," Kendra said. "Let me walk over there first."

Teague couldn't argue, but he wasn't crazy about being stuck here with Turner.

"She really cares about that antelope," Turner said.

As if Teague needed to be told. "Somebody should have notified Jack Bennett about this situation." He sounded cranky, which he most certainly was. None of this was his fault, yet he had the impression Kendra was blaming him, anyway.

"Val and Scott have had a lot to think about."

Teague knew that, too, and didn't appreciate being reminded. He really didn't like standing here with Turner while they both watched Kendra make her way slowly toward the gerenuk. Kendra looked so damned good, with her hair shining in the sun and her outfit showing off her dynamite figure. Anything could be going through Turner's mind.

Teague tried to think of ways to establish his position with Kendra. "Did she tell you I'm the one who taught her to ride?"

"I don't think she mentioned that."

"Oh, yeah," Teague said. "We've ridden all over this ranch. We used to spend hours exploring." From the corner of his eye he could see that Turner was still concentrating on Kendra.

"I know she's good with animals," Turner said. "I was thinking of asking if she wanted to spend one day a week at the clinic, helping out. The extra money might allow her to buy that house she wants a little sooner.''

''I guess it would.'' *A house?* Teague didn't want to let on that he knew nothing about Kendra planning to buy a house. And he sure as hell didn't want her working with Turner. That could spell disaster.

When Kendra drew within about ten feet of the scrub oak, Suzette got up and moved away.

''There's no baby,'' Turner said.

Teague was getting sick of being told the obvious. ''Nope. Didn't think there would be,'' he added. In reality he'd had no clue, but he wanted to sound knowledgeable.

''Oh?'' Turner glanced at him for the first time. ''And that would be because…?''

''Uh…because of the way she was lying there.''

''Hmm.''

Teague figured the vet wasn't buying it, so he elaborated. ''You know, sort of thoughtful.''

''Thoughtful?''

''Exactly. I know this animal. If she'd had the baby, she would have looked more intense.'' Teague didn't know how much longer he could sling this bull with a straight face.

''If you say so.'' Turner went back to watching Kendra.

She pulled something out of her pocket and held it out toward Suzette.

''She brought carrots,'' Turner said.

''Just like I taught her,'' Teague added.

Suzette kept retreating, despite the carrot.

''Well, if she won't let Kendra near her then I don't stand a chance,'' Turner said. He sighed and glanced at his watch. "Which makes me pretty much useless for the time being."

"Pretty much," Teague said cheerfully. He considered the vet useless, period. He couldn't understand why Turner's partner Manny Hernandez couldn't have come out with Kendra instead. Hernandez had more experience. Plus he was married. "Where's Manny?" he asked.

"Out of town this week," Turner said. "And like I said, I have a surgery coming up soon. So I'm afraid I'd better start back."

"Yep, you should." Teague hadn't heard such good news since they'd headed out to the pasture. "I'll tell Kendra you had to leave. She'll understand."

"Sure she will. She's great."

Teague clenched his jaw. "I know that."

Turner studied him a moment. "Do you?" Before Teague could answer, the vet turned and walked away.

CHAPTER THREE

KENDRA TALKED SOFTLY TO Suzette and held out one of the small carrots she'd brought her. "Come on, sweetie," she crooned. "I know you're feeling nervous. You've never had a baby before, and you're the only gerenuk in this pasture. But it's me, Kendra. I won't hurt you or that precious little one you're carrying."

Suzette gazed at her with enormous brown eyes, her long ears twitching in all directions as she tried to gauge potential danger. This gerenuk was on the small side according to the research Kendra had done in the library. Although Suzette was about the height of a Great Dane, she was more delicately made and weighed about sixty pounds when she wasn't pregnant. Her enlarged belly made her slim legs and neck look spindly and out of proportion.

She and Sultan had come from the semidesert of East Africa, so they should have thrived in the climate of the Hill Country. But unlike the other exotic animals Scott had imported, the gerenuk hadn't produced any babies until now. Kendra liked to think that Suzette had finally gotten pregnant because with Kendra's help she'd started to feel at home on this ranch. And now she would be moved again.

After taking a tentative step in Kendra's direction, Suzette paused and stared at the gate. Kendra decided the two men standing there were making the gerenuk even more nervous. Thinking she'd motion them farther away, she turned in time to see Dusty unfasten the gate and step outside the pasture.

Shoot, he'd probably decided to leave for his scheduled surgery, now that he could tell Suzette hadn't had her baby. She wished Dusty could stay a little longer, though. She didn't want to be out here alone with Teague.

Suzette watched until Dusty was several yards from the pasture. Then she minced closer to Kendra, craned her neck and took the carrot.

"So it was Dusty who spooked you," Kendra said.

Munching her treat, Suzette sidled closer.

"Gonna let me pet you?" Kendra slowly extended her hand toward Suzette's neck. When the gerenuk didn't back away, she risked a light touch. At last Suzette allowed herself to be stroked.

She'd been skittish for the past two weeks, as if instinct told her to be careful now that she was about to give birth. Once she'd grown heavy with her pregnancy, Kendra had stopped asking her to perform the trick she'd learned. Standing on her hind legs didn't seem like a good idea. Now that Suzette would be leaving the ranch, she'd probably forget that particular trick.

The gerenuk stopped chewing and looked beyond Kendra.

Footsteps crunched in the grass, and Kendra didn't have to look around to know that Teague was approaching. She pitched her voice low. "You're going to scare her."

His voice was equally quiet and steady. "No, I'm not. She remembers me."

So do I. Kendra's hand trembled as she continued stroking Suzette's neck. Oh, she remembered everything, like the sound of his voice, low and intimate the way it had been just now, the way it had been when he'd made love to her. She remembered his scent, which teased her the closer he came. She even remembered the rhythm of his footsteps.

He walked slowly to Suzette's other side.

The gerenuk turned her head and sniffed the hand he held out. Then she licked it thoroughly.

Teague chuckled. ''I'll bet she's after the salt. I was eating a bag of tortilla chips on the way here.''

Kendra chose not to glance over at him. Hearing him chuckle like that was bad enough. Thinking of all the bags of tortilla chips they'd shared while sitting under the stars drinking a long-neck and dreaming about the future made her heart ache.

''Guess I'll take a look at the situation with this little gal,'' he said. ''I'm no vet, but I think I can tell how close she is.''

Kendra watched as Teague talked reassuringly to Suzette while he moved toward her rump.

Then he crouched down and studied the gerenuk's backside. ''No sign of anything going on yet.''

''But it'll be soon.'' Kendra didn't want him to decide it was safe to load Suzette into the trailer.

''Maybe.'' He looked directly at Kendra. ''I've missed you.''

Her pulse raced. ''I would have thought by now you'd have a bunch of girlfriends in Dallas.''

He meandered back to his original position and began stroking Suzette's neck. ''I won't lie to you. I damn sure tried to do that. I couldn't seem to get interested in anybody.''

Now her heart was pounding really hard. ''That's too bad,'' she said, not meaning a word.

"Is it?" His voice was deceptively soft. "Have you found somebody?"

She hesitated, wondering if she should make up a new lover. It would serve him right.

"Dusty?" he asked.

"Dusty?" She was caught by surprise. "Dusty Turner?"

"Is there another Dusty around town?"

"No. Only that one." She realized that he didn't know Dusty was engaged. Maybe she wouldn't tell him yet. "But I'm not dating him." She hadn't thought about dating anyone since Teague left, but he didn't need to know that.

"Then who?"

Her cheeks warmed. She was a lousy liar, especially when it came to Teague. "I'm...not dating anyone special."

"But you're dating?"

"Um..."

Even though his sunglasses disguised the look in his eyes, she could see the lines of tension around his mouth and knew he was tortured by the thought of her with someone else. No matter how angry she was about his stubbornness, she couldn't put him through that kind of hell.

"I'm not dating," she said quietly. "I haven't even tried."

His shoulders relaxed. "That's good to hear."

"Why?" She wondered if she dared hope that he'd changed his mind about Mary and Bubba's offer.

"Kendra...what if I could get you a job working for Jack Bennett?"

She stared at him in confusion. "What on earth are you talking about?"

"You're good with animals. Even Dusty said that. You've trained Suzette to do that trick. Maybe you could do the same thing with her baby, and even some of the other exotics that Bennett has on his ranch. And then—"

"Teague Sloan, you're talking nonsense and you know it." Now she understood, and she wasn't happy about the direction of this conversation. "In the first place, I'm a manicurist, not an animal trainer, and in the second place, you could get me a hundred jobs, but it wouldn't make any difference. I'm not moving to Dallas!"

Suzette bolted and trotted several yards away.

"Now you've scared her, yelling like that," Teague said.

Kendra clenched her hands at her sides and fought her disappointment. Nothing had changed. Teague wasn't here to announce that wrangling ostriches didn't sound so bad, after all. "I wasn't yelling," she said. "I was making a point, a point that you seem to want to ignore."

"You bet I want to ignore it." He tugged his hat lower over his eyes. "You might as well come right out and say you don't love me."

"Me?" Her chest grew tight. "How about you? If you loved *me,* then you'd be happy to give ostriches a try so that we could settle down here in Crystal Creek. But no, you won't even consider it, even though you know that living here is the one thing in the world that I…" She paused and tried to get control of her emotions. She didn't want to cry in front of him. Dammit, she wouldn't cry and give him the satisfaction.

"See? Did you hear yourself? You said that settling down here was the one thing in the world you wanted.

Obviously marrying me ranks a very poor second on your list.''

"Why should I be the one to give up everything?''

"Kendra, this is only a *place*. You can make new friends in Dallas. Hell, we could live in one of the suburbs, and it would be just like a small town. It's not like you were born here, for God's sake!''

She took a shaky breath. ''I do feel like I was born here. I know good and well I wasn't, but it feels like that. And I want my children to be born here.''

His mouth thinned. ''I notice you didn't say *our* children.''

"Oh, Teague.'' She swallowed a lump of pure misery. In happier times they'd spent hours working out the details of their future life. They'd planned to rent one of the cottages at Hole in the Wall in the beginning, while they saved money. They'd dreamed of Scott and Valerie selling them a few acres eventually. Surely they would have agreed to that, which would have allowed Kendra and Teague to build a little place where they could have raised their children and still have been close to their jobs. The whole plan was in shambles, now.

Teague's voice took on a pleading tone. ''If you'd only give Dallas a try.''

"That's what my mother used to say all the time. *Give Chicago a try. Give Minneapolis a try. Give Cincinnati a try.* I did, Teague. I gave all of them a try, and I never felt at home. Not until I came to Crystal Creek.''

"But you'd have *me* in Dallas!''

She gazed at him, hating the pain they were causing each other. ''If you'd chosen anyone else, that would be enough. I think you picked the wrong girl.''

He stared at her in silence for several long seconds. Then he sighed. ''Maybe so.''

God, that hurt, to have him agree with her. She had to look away from him or risk breaking down. Her glance went to Suzette. Once again, the situation with Teague had pushed Suzette's problem into the background.

Kendra forced herself to put aside her own concerns and focus on the little gerenuk. "It's obvious we're not going to work this out between us, but I hope you can at least help Suzette."

"I plan to."

"You do?" She hadn't expected him to agree that quickly. "How?"

"While I was watching you try to coax her over to you, I—" He paused and cleared his throat. "I decided to call Bennett and see if I can convince him to wait on that delivery."

She controlled the impulse to hug him. "I appreciate that. I really appreciate that, Teague."

"It's the right thing to do." A muscle twitched in his jaw. "I knew that before, but I hadn't figured out how to handle it if he won't wait."

"And how will you?"

"I'll call my boss at the trucking company and tell him he'll need to find another driver for this job. That will delay things, and it might be long enough."

This was the compassionate man she'd fallen in love with, and the warmth of that love washed over her. Teague was a good guy. She'd always known that, even when he made her furious. "But…but you might get fired."

He shrugged. "So I'll get another job."

And she knew exactly the job she wanted him to take if that happened. "Teague, if Mary and Bubba's offer is still open, would you—"

"No."

"Just like that? No?" She couldn't believe Teague could be so noble and loving one minute and so frustratingly stubborn the next. She could cheerfully wring his neck.

"That's right. I'm still not interested in being the foreman at the Flying Horse." He stuck his thumbs through his belt loops, as if for emphasis. "I'm a cowboy, Kendra."

Yes, she would love to wring his neck. "Bubba's a cowboy, too!"

"Not anymore, he's not. He's an ostrich boy. Look, we've been through this a million times. I don't see the percentage in wrangling ostriches. It's plain unnatural."

"And that's what I'm talking about!" Oh, he was maddening, standing there looking so gorgeous, yet refusing to be reasonable. "You expect me to give up living in Crystal Creek, but you won't consider taking a job on an ostrich ranch. Is that fair?"

"I don't know if it's fair or not, but I can't see myself changing my mind." He gazed at her in silence for a moment. "Maybe you picked the wrong guy."

Oh, damn, here they were back at this same place, the point of no return. She swallowed. "Maybe I did."

Teague sighed. "Well, since we're not getting anywhere with this discussion, we might as well go back to the lodge so I can call Bennett. Val and Scott probably have lunch ready by now."

"I imagine they do." Food sounded like a terrible idea, but Kendra knew there was no point in standing out in this pasture any longer. The sooner Teague called Bennett, the sooner she'd know whether or not Suzette had been given a reprieve.

Teague started walking toward the gate, and she followed.

After three steps he stopped and turned back.

She nearly ran into him.

He faced her, his jaw clenched. "The hell of it is, I still want you so much I can barely stand it."

She gulped. "You do?"

"Yeah, I do." Slowly he took off his sunglasses.

Those chocolate-brown eyes of his were a potent weapon, and she figured he knew it. Her heart thudded heavily under his scrutiny. "That's…inconvenient."

"You don't know the half of it." He reached over and lifted her sunglasses to rest on the top of her head. Then he drew in a sharp breath. "There. That look in your eyes—that's what I've dreamed about night after night. Then I wake up, and I'm hard as granite."

She certainly remembered being the lucky recipient of that response. Her body grew moist from the memory. God, he smelled so good. She used to love to bury her nose against his neck and breathe deep. She wanted to do that now.

His gaze roamed over her. "And you're in the same fix, aren't you?"

She wondered if she dared try to deny it.

"I don't even have to ask." He drew closer. "That tight little shirt gives everything away." His voice dropped to a murmur. "You still want me, Kendra." Holding her gaze, he cupped her breast and rubbed his thumb over her taut nipple. "Don't you?"

Her heart thundered as she looked into his dark, sexy eyes. She held back the moan of pleasure his touch always coaxed from her. "Whether or not I still want you doesn't matter."

"Guess not." He tipped back his hat and hooked the

earpiece of his sunglasses inside his belt, all signals that he intended to get even more personal with her.

She should step away, but she couldn't make herself do that. She remained right where she was and allowed him to slide his other hand beneath her hair and cup the back of her neck.

After that, she couldn't seem to stop herself from putting her arms around him. As always, he felt so solid, so *right*. From the beginning, she'd known that Crystal Creek was her destiny. It had been the same the first time she'd kissed Teague. She'd never expected to have to choose between them.

She shivered as he caressed her moist skin, damp from the heat and the tension of having him so close. Kneading her tight muscles with his fingers and the heel of his hand, he continued to cup her breast and brush his thumb over her aching nipple. She fought not to close her eyes and lean into his caress. For months she'd tried to convince herself she didn't need him, didn't need this. But she did.

Her breathing grew shallow. "Wanting each other… makes everything worse."

"Guess so." He had the intense look in his eyes that always meant a kiss was on the way.

Her gaze drifted to his lips. "Kissing me isn't going to change my mind."

"I know." His mouth curved in a slow smile. "At least it didn't four months ago. Neither did making love to you until you couldn't see straight. You're a tough cookie."

"I know what I want."

He combed his fingers up through her hair and cradled the back of her head. "Right now you want me to take you to bed." He squeezed her breast gently, stoking the fire.

It was an expression he'd used many times before, even though they'd never shared a bed. She hadn't felt right making love in her room at the lodge, and he'd lived in the bunkhouse. Renting a motel room had seemed kind of tacky, so they'd made do with the back of his pickup. Even now, a bed wouldn't be necessary. He could lay her down in the dry grass and have whatever he wanted from her.

She met his gaze, trying to maintain her cool. "Maybe I do, but I'll get over it."

"Yeah." He tipped her head back and aligned his body with hers, letting her feel how aroused he was. "That's what I keep telling myself, too."

At last she closed her eyes in surrender. "Okay, Teague. If you're going to kiss me, then do it."

"Why should I?"

Her eyes snapped open again. "What?"

He gazed down at her, his mouth hovering very close, his breath feathering her lips. "It won't get me anywhere, and we'll both end up more frustrated than ever."

She didn't think she could be much more frustrated. "You are the most infuriating man I know."

"That's something, anyway."

"Teague..." She stopped just short of begging.

"Aw, hell. You know I will. I can't resist you." Swiftly and surely his mouth covered hers.

The moan she'd been trying to control escaped as she wrapped him tight in her arms. She abandoned herself to his kiss, to the remembered flavor of his mouth and the bold thrust of his tongue. He was rough with her, and she with him. Anger and frustration blended with the hot taste of lust to override any hint of tenderness.

He released her breast and grasped her bottom, lifting her to her tiptoes and fitting her snugly against the bulge in his jeans.

Wrenching his mouth from hers, he pushed his hips hard against hers. "Remember?" he said, panting. "Remember how it was?"

"Yes." She was drugged with wanting him.

His voice rasped harshly. "How could you give that up?"

"How could *you?*"

"I don't know. God, I don't know." He captured her mouth again, but with more gentleness this time.

Slowly his lips moved against hers, telling her without words how he'd missed her, how he loved her, still. Tears gathered beneath her eyelids. She needed him so. More than she'd ever imagined. And he needed her, too.

But there seemed to be no answer for them.

Reluctantly she drew away from his kiss and eased out of his arms. "We…we should go back to the lodge."

He gazed at her, hands on his hips, chest heaving. "Yeah. This is crazy." He continued to stare at her. "You look very kissed."

She touched her mouth. In her agitation over seeing Teague again, she'd climbed out of Dusty's pickup and forgotten the purse lying beside her on the seat. She hoped he'd noticed it and left it with Val and Scott.

"I like it when you look like that," he said softly. "I used to imagine how great it would be to wake up beside you in the morning and make love to you when you were still all warm and sleepy."

Misery settled in her chest. "Saying things like that won't help."

"What will help? Is there anything I can do to get

you off my mind? Because if you have a suggestion, I'd love to hear it.''

If she had any suggestions, she would have taken them herself, so that she could forget about him. But at least she hadn't deliberately tried to see him again. "If you're trying to forget me, why did you volunteer for this job of moving the animals?''

He rubbed the back of his neck. "I thought…I thought you might have reconsidered.''

"I haven't.''

"So I see.'' He settled his hat more firmly on his head and put his sunglasses on. "By the way, no matter what happens with Bennett, I'll be staying here overnight, parked by the Longhorn. I'll be sleeping in the cab of my truck.''

Sexual tension curled in her stomach. "So what?''

"Just thought I'd mention it.''

"Why, so we could have one more night together, for old time's sake?'' Even as her heart scorned the idea, her body didn't. Her body thought it was a terrific concept. "What's the point in that?''

"We've never made love on a bed. There's a real comfy one in the cab of that truck.'' With that, Teague turned and walked toward the pasture gate.

"Isn't that just like a man,'' she called after him. "Wanting to ignore all the issues so he can focus on sex!''

Teague shrugged and glanced back over his shoulder. "Just keeping you informed of the possibilities.'' Then he continued on toward the gate. After unlatching it, he held it open and glanced back at her. "Coming?''

If she'd had something to throw at him, she would have. Instead she simply glared at him as she started toward the gate. How dare he offer her a night of sex, when it looked as if that would be all they'd ever share? That was so crass, so decadent, so...tempting.

Between now and tonight she'd have a good talk with herself and make sure she didn't stoop to the level of pleasure for pleasure's sake. So what if she hadn't ever made love to him on a real mattress? So what if rolling around with Teague on the bed inside that macho black truck sounded like the most exciting thing she'd ever done in her life?

He was a stubborn, opinionated man, and she had to get him out of her system. If she intended to have any success with that, then visiting his truck tonight would be going in exactly the wrong direction.

"I can tell you're thinking about it," he murmured as she whisked past him and out the gate.

"I'm thinking that you have a lot of nerve, even suggesting such a thing."

"You're right, I do have a lot of nerve." He latched the gate and caught up with her. "The question is, how much nerve do you have?"

CHAPTER FOUR

TEAGUE KNEW HE WAS A fool to hope that making love to Kendra tonight would swing the decision in his favor. She might not even take the bait and show up at his truck. The way she was striding along beside him, her nose in the air and those trendy sunglasses making her look like a movie star, anyone would suppose she found the idea of joining him in the cab of the eighteen-wheeler unthinkable.

But he was also recalling how she'd kissed him, as if he was a chocolate truffle and she'd stayed off sweets for a year. Speaking of truffles, he'd brought her some of those, too, from a big-deal candy store in Dallas. He didn't kid himself that she'd change her mind about the city because she liked the truffles, but they couldn't hurt his cause, either.

If only she could understand that Dallas and apartment living were temporary, and eventually they'd live in a rural area near a little town like Crystal Creek. Maybe not exactly like it, but close enough.

"What's this I hear about you wanting to buy a house?" he asked.

Her gaze whipped around to meet his. "Who told you that?"

"Turner. He's thinking of hiring you one day a week at the clinic, if you want to earn some extra money so you can get the house sooner." Turner had probably figured out that if she bought a house she wouldn't be going to Dallas with Teague.

Kendra faced forward again and kept walking. "Hmm."

He waited to see if she'd say anything more, but she didn't. No doubt she was keeping quiet just to be ornery because she knew he wanted more information. What a difficult woman. He should have his head examined for continuing to try and lasso her.

But then again, his head wasn't the part of his anatomy directing the operation most of the time. "Would you work for Turner?"

"I might."

He didn't like the sound of that. Maybe she wasn't looking at Turner as a potential date right now, but give that vet a chance and he'd convince her otherwise. Any man with eyes would want Kendra. And the vet had the added advantage of already being settled in Crystal Creek.

"What sort of house are you thinking to buy?" he asked.

"I don't know yet. I have to see what I can afford."

"One in Bluebonnet Meadows?"

She made a face. "Not likely. Way too rich for my blood. Besides, I hate what they're doing to Hole in the Wall land."

"Well, there's one thing we can agree on."

She was silent until they reached the steps leading up to the porch. Then she put her foot on the bottom step and turned to look at him. "Bubba and Mary have been approached about selling the Flying Horse."

He pulled up short and stared at her. "You're kidding." The idea of Bubba and Mary selling out made him queasy.

"There's this guy, Brian Fabian, who wants all the land he can get around here. Hole in the Wall was only the beginning. Shelby converted the first guy he sent out here, Nick Belyle, the one who arranged the sale of Hole in the Wall. But now—"

"Nick Belyle. Is that the guy Shelby hooked up with? Boomer said something about her getting married soon."

"That's him, and he used to work for Fabian. Shelby got him to see that Fabian's plan to buy up a bunch of land could ruin Crystal Creek, so he resigned from Castle Enterprises and decided to live here. With Shelby."

Teague could hardly miss the challenge in her voice. This Nick character had done what Teague was supposed to do—give in to the woman in his life and relocate to Crystal Creek. "Well, I'm happy for Shelby, then," he said. "She was always real pleasant to me back when we all worked here."

"The wedding's next month. She asked me if she should invite you, but I said I didn't know if you'd want to come."

"Of course I'll come."

"I'll tell her, then. It'll be a wonderful wedding. She's so happy now that Nick's in her life." Kendra's gaze left no doubt as to the point of this conversation.

Teague sighed. Every time he turned around some other guy had taken on the role of a hero, making him look like the goat. He searched for a fly in the ointment. "I'll bet the folks around here aren't crazy about Nick, though, if he helped set up the sale of Hole in the Wall."

"At first people were suspicious of him, but now that they know for sure which side he's on, they're accepting him. And goodness knows Crystal Creek can use his legal skills since we have this Fabian guy to contend with. He didn't let Nick's resignation stop him. He seems to have lots of money, and like I said, we think he's going to send another representative to talk to Bubba and Mary about the Flying Horse.''

Teague's uneasiness returned. ''Do you think they'd sell to him?''

''I hope not.'' She thrust her chin forward in a very belligerent way. ''But you know it's getting tough for them to run the place.''

He knew that she'd aimed that comment right at him. ''If you're trying to make me feel guilty—''

''They were your friends. I thought you'd want to know what's going on.''

''They still are my friends.''

''Are you going to see them while you're here?''

He'd thought about that and knew he should, but the truth was, talking with Bubba and Mary made him uncomfortable. They'd expected him to snap up their offer, and he'd seen the disappointment in their eyes when he'd turned them down. No matter how nicely he'd refused, they still could have taken it as an insult to them and their ostrich business. They probably had taken it as an insult.

''So you aren't planning to see them,'' Kendra said.

''I don't know how much time I'll have.''

''Right.'' She turned and started up the steps.

''Kendra, dammit! Every Sloan for six generations has worked with cattle. Coming from up north like you do, you can't know what that means to me, but I wish you'd at least try to understand. I'd be sacrificing a way of life.''

She stepped up to the porch and turned around. ''I do understand. More than you know. I wish you could get a job wrangling horses and cattle, but men like Brian Fabian and his developments are going to make that less and less likely. So while you're trying to hold on to a way of life that's disappearing, you're going to lose a lot of other things in the process.''

''Maybe so, and as long as you brought up the point, have you taken a good look at your precious Crystal Creek? Once Bluebonnet Meadows is built up, what's going to happen to your folksy little town? Before long you'll see strip malls and traffic jams. Is it worth giving up a lifetime of us being together for a place that may be totally different in five years?''

Her sweet little mouth tightened into a straight line.

''Got you there, haven't I?''

''Crystal Creek is *not* going to end up like that,'' she said, ''because the people in this town, people who care about the future of this area, will make sure of it. Me, included.'' Then she stalked inside.

And Dusty Turner would be among those people, Teague thought sourly. The vet definitely had the inside track now that he was an official resident and businessman. Turner would wear the white hat, while Teague, who'd left town, would be assigned the black hat. Damn.

KENDRA FOUND HER PURSE on a table by the front door and grabbed it.

''Are y'all coming in for lunch?'' Scott called from the kitchen.

''Yes,'' Kendra called back. ''Sorry we took so long. I'll be right there after I wash up.'' She ducked down the hallway to her left and into the bathroom so she could repair her makeup.

She did look kissed. She examined the evidence in the mirror while washing and drying her hands at the pedestal sink. The mirror also reflected a bathroom paneled in oak and outfitted with reproduction antique fixtures.

Like everything else in the lodge, it was loaded with class. She tried to imagine the lodge as a clubhouse and shuddered.

Well, that whole encounter with Teague had certainly been a disaster. No matter how resolved she was, she couldn't seem to hang on to her temper where he was concerned. Or her lust. She needed to be friendly. That's all. Just friendly. He deserved that much because he was about to put his job on the line in order to keep Suzette and her baby safe.

She didn't have to worry that he'd go back on that promise just because they'd had words. Once Teague agreed to something, he stuck to it, but Kendra thought she should show a little more gratitude. Yet she had trouble being grateful to a man who stubbornly refused to see her point of view and then dangled a night of sex in front of her as if that was a whole separate issue.

Her boss Sue maintained that men could compartmentalize better than women. Sue would probably say that there was nothing surprising about Teague wanting to have sex tonight even though they might never see each other again. He wouldn't understand wasting the opportunity when they were so obviously turned on by each other.

However, if Kendra went to his truck tonight—not saying that she would, but *if* she did, she'd be going with an agenda. Teague had been doing without for the past four months. He'd admitted that nobody else held any interest for him, which was very good news. And outstanding ammunition.

She didn't approve of women who used sex to get their way. She really didn't. But Teague had been the one who'd issued the invitation to join him in the truck tonight. Whatever happened would be rightly his own fault.

Because she knew firsthand that Teague was a highly sexed man, he'd be a regular powder keg by now. If they had a wonderful time in the cab of his truck, he might find it very difficult to continue living in Dallas. He also might be jobless, which would make moving back here and taking the foreman's job at the Flying Horse that much more appealing.

She almost wished he would lose his job over this incident with Suzette. On the other hand, if Bennett refused to give Teague an extra few days to deliver the animals, that would show that Bennett was not a kind man, which would be bad for Suzette and her baby. What a mess this had turned into. Every way she turned were hazards.

After combing her hair and reapplying her lipstick, she took her purse back to the table by the front door before going into the large kitchen, where she knew Val and Scott would have organized lunch. The big pine table was set for four, with bowls and platters of food that would feed ten, easily. Kendra counted two kinds of pasta salad, a large bowl of coleslaw, another of potato salad, a platter of cold fried chicken and a plate of sliced deli meat. While Scott put ice in tall glasses, Val stirred a pitcher of tea.

Teague, a cell phone to his ear, leaned against the open back door looking out onto the deserted grounds. He'd hung his hat beside Scott's on the pegged rack beside the door.

Kendra realized he was talking to Bennett, so she took her cue from Val and Scott and remained quiet.

"Very soon," Teague said. "But this is Mother Nature we're talking about. She won't be rushed. It's just that I would hate for the gerenuk to go into labor during the trip. You could lose both mother and baby.''

Kendra exchanged a look with Val, who held up crossed fingers. Bennett had to agree to wait or Kendra wouldn't feel the least bit good about Suzette's new home.

''That's great,'' Teague said.

A collective sigh told Kendra that they'd all been holding their breath.

Teague turned, looked over at her and stuck his thumb in the air.

She smiled at him, finding that gratitude she'd had trouble locating moments earlier.

Teague finished his call to Bennett and made another to his boss, who was obviously telling him to do whatever he needed to keep Bennett happy.

Kendra allowed herself to bask in the satisfaction of achieving her goal. Suzette had been her main concern from the beginning, and now the gerenuk was out of danger. Teague had been willing to sacrifice his job for that goal, too. She didn't want to forget that, no matter how obnoxious he became. Of course because she was prepared for him to be a pain in the behind, during lunch he turned on the charm, as if determined to keep her off-balance.

''If you have some spare lumber around, I'd like to build a crate to hold Suzette and her baby and keep them separated from the rest of the animals,'' he announced after he'd sat down and served himself a generous portion of food.

''I'm sure there's some in the barn,'' Scott said. ''Help yourself. While I'm in town I'll pick up a couple of sets of hinges and a latch so you can put a door on the thing. A crate is a good idea.''

"Yes, it is," Kendra said. Teague was piling on the good will, and she was a sucker for that.

He turned to Val. "And if you have a couple of old blankets, or a scrap of carpeting for the floor..."

"Absolutely," Val said. "I'm so glad you and Kendra are taking care of Suzette. I knew we had a problem, but I've been so frantic I didn't have time to think about it. I kept hoping she'd deliver that baby and solve everything."

"Maybe tonight," Teague said.

Kendra swore that he winked at her as he said it. The rascal. She'd dished herself lightly and wondered if she'd be able to finish what was on her plate. All she could think about was whether she should visit the truck tonight. She wanted to. Just watching him across the table was getting her worked up. But if she made love to him tonight and he still wouldn't move back to Crystal Creek...that would be horrible.

"I could build the crate this afternoon, then," Teague said.

"Good," Val said. "Because I think Suzette will have that baby tonight. Call it a hunch, but I'll take bets on it."

Teague dug into a mound of coleslaw. "I believe in hunches. I think tonight's the night."

This time Kendra was sure he winked at her.

"Listen, I know you truckers sleep in your cabs," Val said, "but you're welcome to stay in one of the guest rooms for as many nights as you're here."

Teague chewed and swallowed a bite of chicken. There seemed to be nothing wrong with *his* appetite. "That's right hospitable of you, but I couldn't put you to the trouble." He flicked a glance at Kendra. "I know how busy you are packing up and all."

"Don't feel too sorry for him, Val," Scott said. "When I walked Dusty out to his pickup, we both wandered over for a peek into that cab."

Val laughed. "I'll bet you did. Guys and their trucks."

"This is way more than just a truck," Scott said. "Plush situation you've got there, Teague. Refrigerator, big bed, microwave, TV. I'm sure you don't suffer in that cozy little setup."

Kendra sure didn't need to hear that whole description. She pretended to be very busy eating, but heat flashed through her as she considered the real reason Teague wanted to stay in his truck tonight.

"Well, Teague can at least use the shower in here and help us eat some of this food," Val said.

Teague dabbed at his mouth with a napkin. "I appreciate the offer, but I'm sure I'd get in your way. I'll leave the trailer here, if that's okay, but I'd feel more comfortable taking the rig into town and parking by the Longhorn. They're expecting me, and I promised Boomer we'd get together for a meal at the coffee shop tonight."

Kendra realized something else about this arrangement of his. The Longhorn was within walking distance of the little duplex she rented. Although he'd never visited her place, he'd probably found out from Boomer where she lived. He'd wanted to make sure that temptation was well within her reach. She wouldn't even have to leave her car parked by the Longhorn and draw unwanted gossip. A secret rendezvous with a sexy man in a big, macho truck. Teague knew her well enough to construct a scene she'd find almost impossible to resist.

Val surveyed the heavily laden table. "Well, Teague, I can see you're bound and determined to be independent, and I admit I'll be very busy the next couple of days, so I appreciate your consideration. But I'm afraid most of this food will end up going to waste.''

"That's for sure." Scott pushed aside his plate. "I've stuffed in all I can hold and we've barely made a dent."

"I'm full, too," Kendra said.

"Not me." Teague polished off the last of his potato salad. "I worked up a heck of an appetite driving down here." He smiled at Kendra, a dangerous sparkle in his brown eyes. "Would you please pass me that chicken? I'm one hungry cowboy."

She knew exactly what he was hungry for. He'd rolled into town complete with his own luxurious bedroom. He looked so darned sure of himself that he deserved to be stood up tonight.

Scott put his napkin beside his plate and turned to his wife. "If you don't mind, I think I'll get started running those errands." He glanced at Kendra. "That is, if you're ready to go."

"I am, but I don't want to stick Val with the dishes."

"I'll do the dishes," Teague said. "I promise I won't let her near them. You folks go ahead and take care of whatever you need to."

"Thanks." Scott pushed back his chair. "But I still wish you'd let us feed you dinner. You could ask Boomer to come out here."

Teague laughed. "Now there's a cowboy who could clean out your refrigerator. But, seriously, I want to spend some time in the coffee shop and see some of the old gang, not just Boomer. If Shelby's working tonight, that'll give me a chance to wish her the best on her upcoming marriage." He paused. "Are you guys okay with this Nick person, by the way?"

Scott nodded. "Yeah, Nick's turned out to be okay.

He helped guide us through a couple of tricky complications when we bought the B and B in Arizona.''

"I'm glad to hear it." Teague took a swallow of his iced tea. "And thanks again for the offer of dinner, but I really do have some folks to see tonight. I'll probably hang around the coffee shop until they close up. Then it's off to bed with this ol' boy. It'll be a full day."

Kendra had been in the process of leaving the table as he threw out his last comment, and she almost knocked over her chair. He'd just told her when to arrive at the door of his shiny black bedroom! His ego was nearly as huge as his truck.

Her cheeks grew hot as she wondered if Scott and Valerie had picked up on the message. Apparently not, because they'd started talking about the errands Scott was supposed to run.

She glanced at Teague, who was eyeing her with interest. "After all that work you'll be doing today, you deserve a good long rest," she said. "I do hope nobody disturbs you."

He shrugged, keeping his gaze locked with hers. "Crystal Creek's usually pretty quiet after ten o'clock, but if it happens, it happens."

Kendra lowered her voice. "Don't count on it."

Teague grinned at her, cocky as ever.

"Ready, Kendra?" Scott asked.

"You bet. Bye, Val. You'll call me if anything happens with Suzette?"

"Sure thing."

Kendra allowed her attention to shift briefly to Teague. "I'll probably see you again before you leave," she said. "I'd like to be here when you load up the animals."

His gaze flickered.

Good. He's not so all-fired sure of himself now.

"Don't worry. I'll wait for you," he said.

His statement could easily apply to the loading of the animals, but Kendra didn't think that's what he'd meant at all. He'd wait for her tonight. She still didn't know what she was going to do. Teague didn't know what she'd do, either, and that was the important thing.

BY THE TIME TEAGUE pulled away from the lodge late that afternoon, he'd taken Valerie up on the offer of a hot shower, and he felt refreshed and ready for whatever the night held. He'd worked up a good sweat creating a sturdy traveling crate for Suzette and her baby, and he'd also walked out to visit the gerenuk one more time. From his experience with horses he'd say she was showing all the signs of going into labor in the next few hours.

If she'd been a more domestic animal, Scott and Valerie would have moved her into the barn, but she still had wild instincts, and the pregnancy had brought them out even more. Being closed into a stall in the barn might stress her more than it would help. Scott and Valerie agreed with him that having humans hovering around wasn't a good idea, either. They'd have to leave her in the open pasture and trust that all would go well.

Teague hoped to hell Suzette gave birth successfully. Taking her away from Kendra would be hard enough. If anything happened to the little antelope, Kendra would be a total mess.

In Teague's estimation Kendra needed a dog—a good sturdy dog. The gerenuk had given her a taste of caring for an animal, but Suzette was too delicate and nervous to make a really good pet. Teague didn't want to encourage the dog idea right now, though, because his apartment didn't allow animals. Someday he'd return to his true calling, and by then he hoped to have saved enough to buy a little piece of land with room for a couple of horses, a dog or two, maybe even some chickens.

That was the plan he'd laid out for Kendra, but apparently it was too long-range for her, and he hadn't promised the land would be located near Crystal Creek, either. If what she'd said about this Brian Fabian joker was true, regular folks wouldn't be able to afford land around here after Fabian had driven the price through the roof.

Teague kept the air-conditioning on all the way to the Longhorn. By ten o'clock the temperature should have cooled enough that he wouldn't need air-conditioning while he slept. Or didn't sleep. His groin tightened beneath the denim of his freshly washed jeans. She was keeping him guessing. He'd prefer knowing for sure that she'd be there tonight at ten.

Hell, he'd prefer having her accept his ring, quit her job at Curly Sue's and head back to Dallas with him. They seemed a long way from that happening, but if he could once get her naked and in his arms, he thought his chances would improve considerably.

He pulled into a space reserved for truckers next to the Longhorn Motel and shut down the truck's diesel engine. The coffee shop directly across the parking lot looked the same, its red-and-white-striped awnings still cheerful and familiar. Teague wondered if fast food was in Crystal Creek's future and if that would be tough on the Longhorn.

Probably not. The Longhorn was a gathering spot, the exact opposite of a restaurant where most orders were packed up to go. Real conversations took place at those oil-cloth covered tables, fueled by coffee served in ceramic mugs instead of disposable cups. The Longhorn and Zack's had been the main hangouts for Teague and his friends.

Boomer had suggested meeting at Zack's instead, but Teague would be expected to drink a beer or two, maybe three or four, if he spent the evening at Zack's. Because of what he hoped would be happening later on, he didn't want the beer, but he also didn't relish explaining the situation to Boomer. Some things were best kept private.

And thanks to a blackout curtain that hung between the front of the cab and the bedroom area in the back, he and Kendra could be very private. The curtains were tied back now, and he swivelled his seat to glance once more at the sleeping area.

He'd fixed it up real nice, with soft sheets and plump pillows. A single red rose was staying fresh in the refrigerator, and he'd lay that on the pillow later, along with the gold box of truffles currently chilling. A guy who didn't know Kendra well might have stuck a bottle of wine in there, too.

Kendra wasn't much of a wine drinker. Once in a while she liked to share a long-neck with him, and he had a couple of her favorite brand, just in case. But they'd discovered that sex was more fun without the liquor, so they'd made a standing rule that whenever they planned to make love, neither of them would drink alcohol. Teague was planning on making lots of love.

He'd also brought a couple of Alan Jackson CDs she liked, and the speakers in the Freightliner were primo, but they might not spend much time listening to music, either. He'd stored up enough wanting to fuel an entire night of making love. Tonight he was ready to go for a new record in how many times he could do the deed.

But the number of times wasn't the main element, he reminded himself. Quality counted more than quantity.

If he focused on that quality, he might very well be able to take that ring out of the wooden box tucked under his seat. The ring belonged on Kendra's finger, and he was determined to get it there. He'd love her so hard she wouldn't be able to say anything but yes.

CHAPTER FIVE

KENDRA WAS BUSIER THAT afternoon than she'd expected to be, so she had no time to tell Sue and Angie about the situation with Teague and the gerenuk. Bluebonnet Meadows had chartered a bus to bring prospective buyers to the site, and after giving them a sales pitch they'd turned them loose on the town for the rest of the day.

For some reason many of the women decided to get manicures. Although Kendra worked steadily until the bus left at five, she couldn't begin to fit everyone in. Apparently all the embellishments she'd learned as a manicurist in Philadelphia had impressed the city women, because she'd handed out more cards in three hours than she'd given away in four months of working at Curly Sue's.

The rush of business hadn't spilled over to Sue and Angie, but that wasn't surprising. Not many women would get their hair done in a strange beauty parlor on a whim, but a manicure took less time and wasn't such a risk.

Angie had to leave right after she finished with her last client, but Sue hung around to sweep the floor and straighten the shop. Kendra also suspected Sue wanted to hear about Teague, which suited Kendra perfectly. She needed someone to dish with, and Sue was more into that kind of down-to-earth girl talk.

Angie might have brought up feminist principles and the question of being treated like a casual sex object. Kendra didn't want to get bogged down in principles, and she didn't really believe Teague thought of her as a casual sex object. But she needed to decide if taking him up on his invitation would put her ahead of the game or way behind.

"That busload of city folks sure turned into a bonanza for you." Sue swept locks of black hair from her last cut into a dustpan and dumped them into the trash.

Kendra finished counting her tips and tucked the money in her purse. It was a sizable amount. "It felt lopsided. I wish some of them had decided to get their hair done, too."

"I'm not worried. They had plenty of time to observe how we do hair, and most of them took cards from me and Angie. They'll give us a try once they move here. It beats driving all the way in to Austin. I've been so busy hating the idea of a bunch of houses out there that I clean forgot they'd be filled with potential customers."

"I know." Kendra tightened the cap on a bottle of polish. "And I know we can all use the money—"

"You're not just whistling Dixie."

"But this afternoon reminded me of the chain where I worked in Philly, and how we were supposed to run people through like they were on a conveyor belt. It was nearly impossible to get to know your customers, because you were so worried about getting on to the next one. They kept track of our speed, and the slow manicurists were fired. I make less money now, but I enjoy my job a heck of a lot more."

Sue laughed. "Honey, you don't *ever* have to worry about me keeping track of your speed. These walk-ins were a total surprise today. If the time comes when you want to say no more walk-ins, that's cool.''

Kendra glanced around the somewhat cluttered, but homey shop. To be honest, she liked it much better than the upscale salon at the ranch. This was no unisex beauty parlor. The flowered wallpaper and stacks of tabloids beside the hair dryers branded it as an all-female establishment. In Crystal Creek the men went to Jake's Barber Shop and the women went to Curly Sue's. The Hole in the Wall had changed a few of those patterns, but when it closed, things returned to normal.

"Sue, would you ever expand this place?" she asked.

Sue took off the green smock she'd been wearing while giving a perm and sat down on her stylist's chair. "I never considered it until today." She swivelled her chair to face Kendra. "But if we had that kind of traffic on a regular basis, we couldn't handle it with only the three of us." She paused. "Okay, what's that sad look for?"

"I like it this way."

"You may like it, but it's gonna take you a gazillion years to afford a little house, and that's not mentioning that old car you're driving, which may give out any day now."

"Puff has plenty of miles left." Kendra knew she'd kept the car too long, but aside from the expense of buying a new one, she hated to think of getting rid of the car she'd had since she was sixteen. She'd named the car after Puff the Magic Dragon, and Teague used to say magic was the only thing keeping it going.

"As for me," Sue continued, "I wouldn't mind buying this building instead of throwing away money on rent. I know Angie wouldn't turn down more business, either. She needs a steady cash flow in order to save the whales and the California redwoods and the three-toed squirrel.''

Kendra smiled. They both teased Angie, but they respected her idealism and had often donated to her causes.

''You can't stop progress, kid,'' Sue said. ''But even if I expanded, you'll never see anybody putting on airs at Curly Sue's. This wild hair color of mine is about as uptown as we're going to get. This is a good, honest place to get your hair done, and that didn't change when we added you as a manicurist. You may be a northern gal, but once we fix your accent you'll pass for a native.''

Kendra laughed and wondered if she ever would sound like everybody else in town. People had told her that her vowels were starting to stretch out, and more than once she'd caught herself saying *y'all*. ''I wouldn't mind passing for a native.''

''That's good, because we're all ready to adopt you. So, I'm dying to know, what happened out at Hole in the Wall?''

Kendra filled her in on Suzette's current condition and Teague's phone call to Jack Bennett.

Sue nodded. ''Very nice work. So can you tell if Teague's still hell-bent on living in Dallas and working for this trucking company?''

''Apparently so.''

''Kendra, your cheeks are as pink as the roses in that wallpaper over yonder. I have to assume there's more to this story than you're telling me.''

''He doesn't have another girlfriend.''

''Good for him. It's nice to know there are still guys out there with some sense of commitment.'' She narrowed her eyes. ''Did he convince you to move to Dallas?''

''No, but I think that's his goal. Did you see his truck go past here this morning?''

''Yes, ma'am, I saw that honkin' big rig. Looked like a deluxe model to me.''

''It is, and he, um—'' Kendra paused to clear her throat. ''He wants me to spend the night with him in that truck.''

''Color me *so* not surprised. Are you gonna?''

''Well, if I thought I could turn the tables and change *his* mind…''

Sue grinned. ''Excellent.''

''I don't know, Sue. I didn't have any luck before, and he still acts like wrangling ostriches would betray his cowboy heritage.''

''Yeah, well, he probably has to talk like that, to hold on to his manly pride.'' Sue climbed out of the chair. ''Hop in. Let's increase your odds.''

''How are you going to do that?'' Even though she was doubtful, Kendra got up and went over to Sue's station.

''You're a perfect candidate for the Goldilocks Special.''

Kendra started to laugh. ''The *what?*''

''Drives guys wild. I'll fix your hair in big fat sausage curls, so you look as innocent as Goldilocks. Don't wear much makeup, either, and dress in some girlish outfit, like that denim jumper you have, with maybe that T-shirt of yours that has little flowers embroidered on it.''

Kendra gazed at her with skepticism as she climbed into the chair. ''How is that image going to help?''

''Contrast, honey. Delicious contrast. Underneath, you'll have on those sexy undies you ordered from Frederick's of Hollywood and never had the chance to wear.

Naughty and nice in one package. I'm telling you, Teague will be wrangling ostriches in no time."

AS LUCK WOULD HAVE IT, Bubba and Mary Gibson came into the Longhorn for pie and coffee while Teague was sitting there with Boomer and a couple of other cowboys from the Double C. Realizing he had no choice, Teague excused himself from his buddies and walked over to the booth where Bubba and Mary were settled in scanning their menus through their reading glasses.

Teague wondered why they were bothering with menus. By now they knew the danged thing by heart. Then he realized they might be using the menus to have something to do because they'd seen him on the far side of the room and didn't want to be caught staring. He hated this awkwardness, but he didn't know what to do about it.

They both looked tired, and Teague felt guilty all over again. Mary had dressed up for the occasion in a flowered skirt and white eyelet blouse. Bubba was sporting his turquoise as usual. He had a custom hatband worth a small fortune in stones, plus an impressive ring. Tonight he'd added a bolo tie with a handsome piece of turquoise the size of a hen's egg.

As he approached the booth, Teague became convinced this was no chance meeting. They'd come into town in hopes they might run into him. It was even slightly possible that Nora, the coffee shop owner, had called them when he'd walked in and ordered dinner. Kendra wasn't the only person in town who wanted him to take the foreman's job at the Flying Horse, obviously.

People might be worried that the Gibsons would sell out unless they got some help, and there would go another chunk of prime rangeland to that Brian Fabian guy.

To make matters even more complicated, Bubba wasn't all that easy to work for. Teague got along fine with him, maybe because Bubba reminded him of his father. Bubba wasn't about to take on any cowboy that came down the pike. He'd settled on Teague, and only Teague would do.

Teague walked up to the booth and touched his fingers to the brim of his hat. "Evenin' folks. How y'all doing?"

They both looked up in a good imitation of surprise.

"Why, Teague Sloan, how nice to see you," Mary said with a big smile. "Kendra said you were in town."

"Yes, ma'am. For a little while."

"Saw your rig outside," Bubba said. "You got a Cummins engine in that thing?"

"Sure do," Teague said. "She glides over these hills smooth as warm syrup on a stack of griddle cakes."

"Humph." Bubba adjusted his bolo tie. "Wouldn't catch me being cooped up in one a' them damned cabs for hours on end. There's a bunch of idiots on the road nowadays."

Teague figured that Bubba included him in that description. "Yes, sir, there are at that. I try to steer clear of them."

Mary took off her reading glasses. "How long are you here for, Teague?"

Teague noticed a startling thing. Mary Gibson's fingernails were red as a stoplight. Kendra's doing, no doubt. On an impulse he decided to tease Mary a little and see if they could still joke around like they used to. "Well, ma'am, I thought I'd spend another three or four minutes at your table, and then move on to the next. I'm really in demand."

Mary laughed.

Bubba didn't. He peered at Teague over the top of his reading glasses. "I got an offer on the Flying Horse."

"So I heard."

"Pretty damned good offer." There was a challenging light in Bubba's eyes. "The place is worth more'n I thought."

"But he's not taking the offer," Mary said quickly. "We don't want to sell."

"It goes without saying that we don't *want* to," Bubba said. "Plus, the way I got it figured, there's more money where that offer came from. You catch my meaning, son?"

Teague did know. Bubba was holding out for more. And if more came along, that could be the end for the Flying Horse. Unless, of course, Teague could see his way clear to wrangle ostriches.

Mary's gaze was wistful. "How are you enjoying Dallas?"

"It's fine, ma'am." It wasn't, but his living conditions were only temporary, and he was hardly in Dallas much, anyway. Most of the time he was in the cab of his truck. And Bubba was right—that cab could get very confining. Still, it had to be better than chasing after a pile of feathers on stilts.

But he had a disturbing thought, now that Bubba had pointed out how much time he spent in the truck. If Kendra came to Dallas with him, he'd be leaving her alone in that big city a good part of the time. Somehow he'd neglected to consider that unpleasant detail. She couldn't come with him on the road because at this stage they'd need her to work.

Bubba pushed back his hat and scowled at Teague. "Tell me this. Are you fixin' to stick around until that little antelope has her baby? Because Kendra has her heart set on seein' that happen, y'know.''

''I know.'' Teague was glad he had something good to report. ''And I'll be staying. My boss told me to hang tight until that happened. The company wants to make sure Mr. Bennett is happy.''

''Do you know Bennett?'' Bubba asked.

''No, can't say as I do.''

''I thought you might have made his acquaintance, 'cause of your daddy. I saw in a magazine a while back that Bennett's setting up his own personal rodeo museum.''

''I didn't know that.'' For weeks Teague had been in his own world daydreaming about Kendra, so he'd probably missed all kinds of news about the Dallas area. ''I'll be sure to ask him about it.''

''You do that. Your daddy was one helluva bull rider. Bennett should have some mention of him in that there museum.'' Bubba adjusted his bolo tie again. He looked as if he'd had about enough of wearing it. ''Collecting all those animals and starting a museum from scratch—the guy must have more money than he knows what to do with.''

''A lot of people seem to have that problem lately,'' Teague said.

''Money isn't everything,'' Mary said quietly.

''No, ma'am, it isn't.'' Teague decided he'd better say his goodbyes while he had at least a couple of points on Bubba's scoreboard. ''Well, it's good to see you both again. I'd better get on back to my table.''

''Come out to the ranch if you have time,'' Mary said.

''Thank you ma'am. I'll surely do that if I can.'' Touching the brim of his hat again, he turned and walked back over to his friends.

Boomer, a string bean of a cowboy, grinned at Teague as he slid back into the booth. "Did you tell them you're ready to start punching ostriches?"

"No, but I told them all of you were thinking to change professions just anytime now. He's expecting you at the Flying Horse next week."

Henry, another of the Double C wranglers, glanced over at Bubba and Mary. "If I thought I could get along with that old codger, I'd give it a shot. I mean, he was ready to cut you in on the operation after a while, right?"

Teague nodded. "Yeah, but—"

"But nothing," Henry said. "That place of his is worth a nice piece of change. So what if you have to chase some danged birds around?"

Teague picked up his coffee mug. "Not interested."

"You are one stubborn cuss, Teague Sloan," Boomer said.

Teague sipped his coffee. "So I've been told."

TWO HOURS LATER Teague lay sprawled on his ninety-six-inch-wide mattress watching some late-night talk show he didn't give a damn about. He kept the volume down so that he'd hear a knock on the door of the cab. The CD was cued if that knock came. Condoms were stashed in a small drawer within reach of the bed. It was fifteen past ten, and he was getting worried that she wouldn't arrive after all.

Worry seemed to be his middle name these days. A half hour ago he'd been worried that he'd never get his buddies out of his truck. They'd insisted on checking it out, and he'd had to work like crazy to keep them from opening the refrigerator and finding the rose and the chocolate. He'd never hear the end of it if they knew he'd become such a romantic.

They'd turned on the TV, tested the sound system, and even suggested he take them all for a ride so they could evaluate the suspension he'd been bragging about. He'd talked his way out of that by claiming that he might be coming down with the flu.

Well, it wasn't a complete lie. He was achy. Achy and hot from not making love to Kendra for weeks on end. He couldn't imagine how he'd survive if she didn't show up tonight. Truth be told, he wouldn't be worth a plugged nickel. He needed her so much that he—

Was that a knock? Heart pounding, he grabbed the remote and turned off the TV. There it was again, the sweet, sweet sound of someone tapping against the side panel of the driver's door. She was here! Gulping for air, he banged his knee on the driver's seat as he fumbled his way to the front of the cab.

He wondered if she'd worn one of his favorite outfits, like the nearly see-through blouse he liked, and that pair of black velvet pants that fit her like a second skin. She really made him drool with that combo. Or maybe she'd have on that slinky red dress of hers, the one that showed so much cleavage it drove him wild. Of course, he was already wild, but he wouldn't mind seeing her in something totally hot. He turned the driver's seat around, out of the way, and peered out the window.

There she stood in the glow from the parking lot lights, and she looked…like an innocent young girl. He blinked, not quite sure what to make of the curls and the loose-fitting denim jumper. Had she come here to *talk?* God, he hoped not. Well, maybe they could talk eventually, but first…first they had other business to attend to.

At least she was here. He took a deep breath and opened the door. "Hi," he said, trying to sound casual. His voice squeaked.

She gazed up at him, her hands in the pockets of her jumper. "This truck is enormous."

Maybe that's why she looked so childlike to him. She was dwarfed by the truck. "Yeah, it is," he said. Brilliant comeback. Frantically he tried to remember all the smooth dialogue he'd practiced in his head. But mesmerized by her angel's eyes, he couldn't think of a single line.

"And shiny," she said. "Was it just washed?"

"Um, yeah."

"You always did like to keep your vehicle clean."

He remembered several occasions when they'd washed his pickup and her old car together, soaking each other with the hose, teasing and kissing and fondling—working each other up for the night ahead when they'd take his pickup out under the stars.

But tonight was different. Tonight they had a real bed, and his goal was to get her into the truck and into that bed. "Would you...like to see the inside?"

"Okay."

He leaned down and held out his hand to help her up the steep steps. As soon as she put her hand in his, the second he touched her warm skin, he was hard as a rock. He clenched his jaw, determined to show a little finesse. No way was he going to tackle her and throw her on the bed.

The bed. He'd forgotten to get out the truffles and the rose. "Um, could you wait here a minute?"

She looked confused. "You mean here on the step?"

"Yeah. Just...hold on to that mirror bracket there if you feel unstable."

"I don't feel unstable, but I don't really want to hang around outside your—"

"Just for a second." He released her hand and banged into the driver's seat again as he started toward the back of the cab. He'd meant to dim the lights, too. And start the sound system. Damn. He'd never actually tried to seduce her before. They'd just sort of…come together.

But tonight was so important. If tonight went well, then maybe she'd let go of her obsession with Crystal Creek and replace it with her obsession for him. He hit the power button for the sound system and jerked open the door of the small compact refrigerator. He'd wrapped the bottom of the rose stem in wet paper towels like the florist had told him, and the rose still looked pretty good.

He was so tense he was shaking, but he managed to grab the rose and the box of chocolates. Sticking the chocolates under his arm, he was fumbling with the wet paper towels when she spoke.

She was right behind him. "Teague, what in heaven's name are you doing?"

Startled, he spun around, dropped the chocolates on the floor and smacked her in the face with the rose and the wet paper towels.

CHAPTER SIX

KENDRA DECIDED THAT following orders was not a good way to begin an evening in which she hoped to overcome Teague's stubbornness. Standing on the step outside his truck waiting for him to do something-or-other wasn't her idea of how a take-charge woman behaved.

Maybe he'd been misled by this Goldilocks Special that Sue had insisted was such a great idea. Despite the sweetness of the outfit and hairstyle, Kendra had never been the kind of cooperative girl who did exactly as she was told. So she ignored his instructions and climbed in the truck.

What a scrumptious sight greeted her. Behind the two swivel seats in the front of the cab, it was wall-to-wall mattress. The blue plaid blanket tucked around it looked soft, and even the walls were upholstered in gray velour. It seemed that every available surface in that cubby would be plush and giving, perfectly suited to what she had in mind.

Alan Jackson sang to her from speakers hidden somewhere in the padded walls. Teague had remembered he was her favorite, and that was a good sign. She noticed curtains on either side of the sleeping area. They were pulled back now, but once drawn, they'd close out the world. She could hardly wait.

Excitement surged through her, leaving her very hot and more than a little damp between her thighs. Her anticipation grew as she looked at the well-muscled cow-boy bending over the refrigerator tucked between the seats and the bed. He had an outstanding set of buns, and she'd missed having them around to ogle on a daily basis. If all went well tonight, that situation would be remedied soon.

She spoke his name, but he was so intent on his job that he apparently didn't hear her over the music. He pulled a couple of things out of the refrigerator, but she couldn't see what they were. As he turned toward the bed, she edged between the seats for a better view.

Finally she couldn't stand the suspense any longer. Coming right up behind him so that he'd hear her this time, she asked him what he was up to. From his reaction, she must have scared the daylights out of him. Something soft and wet caught her across the face and she cried out in surprise.

"Dammit, Kendra! You shouldn't sneak up on a person like that."

"I was just curious!" She wiped the moisture from her cheeks and looked down to see what he'd been hold-ing that had whipped across her face when he turned around. "Is that a rose?"

"Yeah." He held it up, showing off the flower in one hand and several damp paper towels dangling from the other. "Or it was." The impact had snapped the bloom at the base where it joined the stem, so the rose was hanging its plump little head, no longer erect.

But Kendra's brief glance had also taken in the area below Teague's belt, and he didn't have the same prob-lem as the rose. Thinking of what lay beneath that soft denim made her consider pushing him back onto the bed and getting down to business.

But he'd brought her a rose, and that deserved some

ceremony. She took it from him and propped up its soft head with her thumb so she could bury her nose in the petals for a long appreciative sniff. Then she gazed up at him. "Thank you. You've never brought me flowers before."

"I know that." He sounded impatient. Then his voice gentled. "And I should have. I've been thinking about our time together, and I realized I dropped the ball on a lot of things. I should have given you little presents and sent you love notes and flowers. So what if the other guys at Hole in the Wall would have teased me about it? I shouldn't have let that stop me, but I did."

She was incredibly touched. "I didn't miss those things. All I ever wanted was you."

His expression softened. "Don't tell me you wouldn't have liked it, though. You should see your face, just because I got you this busted rose."

"Bringing it now is perfect. But when we were on the ranch, we tried not to call too much attention to ourselves, remember? We didn't want to act foolish and make Scott and Val regret letting us date. We were so afraid of losing our jobs." She smiled sadly. "And then we lost them anyway."

His eyes mirrored her sorrow. "That was the happiest time of my life, working at the ranch during the day and being with you every night."

"Me, too." She caressed the rose petals as she gazed into his eyes. "I didn't need presents."

"Maybe you didn't *need* them, but I should have been more considerate. I brought you chocolates from Dallas, too. I've always known how you love them, but I never got you a box of those, either." His glance swept over the floor. "You'd better watch where you step. There's truffles everywhere."

"Truffles?" She dropped to her knees and sure enough, very expensive chocolates were scattered on the carpet, along with an elegant gold box. She was amazed that her rough and tough cowboy had walked into one of those fancy stores and paid the kind of price they asked for a box like this. She started to pick up one of the pieces.

Teague crouched down next to her. "Don't eat them."

"But they're *truffles*. Maybe we could wash them off."

"Nope." He took the candy from her. Picking up the box, he collected the pieces he could reach and tossed them inside. "Boomer and the guys were in here walking on the carpet with their boots, and you can imagine what's on the bottom of those boots. I should've told them to take them off. I'm sorry the candy's all ruined. I'll get you more."

"You don't need to do that."

"Yes, I do." He looked so disappointed that his plans hadn't worked out. "You need something special."

Her heart contracted as she realized how much he cared about her. "Then kiss me."

His gaze met hers, and the flash of heat made his dark eyes glow.

That was the look she could live on. His eyes were richer, more decadent and tempting than any chocolate in the world. She began to tremble as she imagined how good their lovemaking would be tonight, after all this time. They had a real bed, a private place where no one could see or interrupt. They'd never known that kind of luxury.

He put down the box, cupped her elbows and pulled her to her feet. But as he started to lean toward her, he stopped, released her and stepped back. "Okay, I need to know if I start kissing you, if you're gonna...make me stop.''

Her mind was so filled with thoughts of her and Teague naked together with hours to explore the possibilities that she struggled to understand what he meant. "Stop?''

"You know. Kissing is okay, but then the rest is off-limits.''

She was thinking pretty much limitless sex right now. For the first time they could really let themselves go. "Why would you think that?''

"I was afraid you'd...come here to talk. Just talk.''

"Why?''

He glanced at her outfit. "Your hair...and your dress...they seemed...''

Now she got it. "Innocent?''

He nodded.

"You don't like this look?'' Sue's Goldilocks Special seemed to be causing more trouble than it was worth.

"It depends on what you're trying to tell me. If it means I'm supposed to keep my hands off you, then I have to say I hate it.'' He swallowed. "But I wouldn't force myself on you. It's only that if I kiss you, I might have some trouble holding back, because it's been a real long time, and I—''

"This outfit and hairstyle is supposed to turn you on.'' Knowing he'd have tried to keep himself in check made him even more adorable.

"It is?''

"You're supposed to get a picture of this sweet, innocent girl on the outside....'' She paused and clasped the rose in both hands and looked up at him from beneath her lashes. "But then when you take the outfit off—'' She stuck the rose between her teeth and struck a flamenco dancer's pose.

''So I'll be taking it off?''

She took the rose from between her teeth and laid it across the headrest of the passenger seat beside her. ''I was hoping you would.''

''Hot damn. How about right now?'' He started gathering the skirt in both hands so he could pull the jumper over her head.

She loved knowing he was desperate. So was she, but she was enjoying her power and couldn't resist teasing him. ''Before you kiss me?''

He let go of the dress and groaned. ''I told myself over and over not to rush. And here I am rushing. I—''

''Let's rush.'' Relenting, she grabbed the hem of her jumper and whisked it over her head. The T-shirt followed, sailing into the front of the cab. She stood before him in her Frederick's of Hollywood bra and panties, itty-bitty scraps of black lace that made her feel very naughty.

She'd never thought of buying something this revealing when they were going together. It had seemed like wasted effort when they made love in the dark in the back of a truck and sometimes left most of their clothes on, in case someone should come along and discover them there. After he'd left for Dallas, she'd ordered the underwear as a morale booster and then had tucked it away because she'd felt silly wearing it with no one to see her.

The way Teague was looking at her, she didn't feel the least bit silly.

His gaze was riveted to her body. ''That's…I've never seen you wear…something like that.''

''I know.'' His expression of lust was all she'd hoped

for. "You said you should have brought me flowers and candy. Well, maybe I should have worn sexier underwear, even though we made love in the dark. You might have liked touching satin and lace instead of plain cotton."

He shook his head. "I always thought you were plenty sexy."

"Yes," she said softly. "But you should see your face now. Maybe I took you for granted, too."

"Okay, maybe it does really turn me on to look at you like this. I've never really been able to, and I'm only human. That...that outfit's incredible."

"Thank you." She kicked off her shoes and walked around the scattered chocolates to get to the bed. "Care to take it for a test drive?"

He groaned. "Absolutely." The poor guy seemed to be having trouble breathing. "After I do this."

Keeping his attention glued to her, he reached for the swag holding one side of the curtains. He fumbled for it, released the curtain and jerked it across the opening.

She lay against the pillows, heart pounding. "Do you realize we've never seen each other completely naked?"

"I guess...." He swallowed. "I guess that's right." Continuing to stare at her, he walked over to the other curtain. Truffles crunched under his boots, but he didn't seem to notice. "We're gonna fix that real quick." He drew the other curtain to meet the first, and they were cocooned, invisible to the world.

"I'm not complaining. Making love to you was fantastic. But I—" She hesitated, wondering how much courage she had.

"What?" His gaze was intense as he started toward her, unbuttoning his shirt on the way.

"Stay...stay there."

He paused and frowned. "Please don't tell me you're not gonna let me—"

"I'm gonna let you," she said. "I'm gonna let you do anything in the world you want. But first—" She took a shaky breath. "First I want you to stand there and undress for me. Let me watch you take off your clothes."

A tremor passed through him, and his voice was strained with excitement. "Wow. I didn't know you thought like that, Kendra."

"Do you mind?"

"Heck, no, I don't mind!" He fumbled as he finished unbuttoning his shirt and took it off. "If you're feeling like some…some adventure, then I…I might have some ideas, too."

"You might?" Every one of her nerve endings vibrated in anticipation of what Teague might consider adventurous.

"If you won't be shocked."

She began to quiver. "I don't think you'll shock me." Drive her insane with wanting, maybe. Watching him reveal that gorgeous body of his was causing a serious meltdown. By the time he'd pulled off his boots and started to unbuckle his belt, she had to bite her lip to keep from moaning.

"But if you don't like something, then you say so." He stripped off his jeans and his briefs in one smooth movement.

She gazed at his bold erection and her voice grew husky. "And if I really like something?"

Awareness blazed in his eyes. "Feel free to tell me." He crossed the short distance to the bed.

"I love seeing you, all of you." She reached for him. "I want to—"

He stepped back a little. "Wait. If you touch me, I'm liable to explode, and I don't want to. Not yet." His hungry gaze roamed over her. Then he looked into her eyes. "Will you let me…explore?"

Her blood pumped wildly through her veins, making her dizzy. In the past they'd had to rush and she'd never had the chance to discover this side of him. "Yes," she whispered.

He eased down on the bed, his eyes hot, his skin flushed. "I feel like this is the first time for us."

She nodded, feeling that way, too.

"You…you're different tonight. The little-girl curls, and that black lace, it does what you said, and it…it makes me want to do things…."

She nodded again, too excited to speak.

"You can stop me any time you want."

But when he leaned over and kissed her on the mouth, she certainly didn't want to stop that. As he delved deep, his kiss changed in a subtle way. He used his tongue more suggestively than ever before, giving her an inkling of what he planned to do with her. Oh, my. She hadn't known he had those thoughts, either.

She arched upward, wanting her lace-covered breasts in contact with his bare chest. He held himself back, bracing his arms on either side of her head while he licked and nibbled at her mouth. She wasn't surprised when he unfastened the front catch of her sexy little bra.

After all, he'd kissed and fondled her breasts before. Ah, but never this long and thoroughly. He'd never leaned back to watch the expression in her eyes as he toyed with her nipples.

"Your eyes turn navy blue when I do this," he murmured. "I never knew that."

"Yours are almost black."

"I've never…I've never wanted you this much." His powerful chest rose and fell rapidly.

She wrapped her arms around him and tried to pull him down to her. "Then let's—"

"No." He was unmovable. His gaze drifted to the triangle of black lace that barely deserved the name of panties. "Not yet."

Heat surged through her.

He glanced back into her eyes, and his voice was husky. "I want to know how you taste, Kendra."

She felt a flush spreading over her skin but she met his gaze boldly.

"I've always wanted to," he murmured. "But we were in the back of the truck, and besides, I thought that you might not—"

Her voice trembled. "I do."

His breath caught. When he kissed her again, there was a fierce note of possession as his mouth settled over hers.

She gave herself to that kiss more fully than ever before, and he seemed to sense it. His touch was sure as he pulled away her panties, his movements unhesitating as he ended the kiss and slid down between her thighs.

And then—another kiss, the most intimate kiss of all, showered her with sensation. Gasping, she writhed against the soft blanket. Cupping her bottom in his large hands, he held her fast. Helpless to do anything but absorb the incredible pleasure he was giving her, she surrendered to the most shattering climax of her life.

As her world spun out of control, he eased up beside her and gathered her into his arms. "I love you," he whispered, holding her tight. "I love you so much."

Words were impossible for her. She wrapped her arms and legs around him, wanting to merge her body with his, to become a part of him. He'd given her so much, but she needed even more.

"Hold on," he murmured in her ear. "We'll get to that part." Disentangling himself, he reached over the side of the bed.

She was lost without his warmth, the strength of his arms. The sound of a drawer scraping against its mooring filtered through the wild beat of her heart. A moment more, and he was beside her again, urging her to her back, moving over her.

She gazed up at him, and at last the words came. "I love you, Teague."

"I know." He thrust deep inside her. "I know."

A tear seeped from the corner of her eye and fell with a soft plop to the pillow. "What will we do?"

"Tonight we'll love each other." He looked deep into her eyes. "And then...then we'll see."

TEAGUE WANTED THE NIGHT to go on forever. Kendra had always made him hot, but in the cozy confines of the truck, she became so spontaneous that he couldn't get enough of her. He should have realized a long time ago that she needed more privacy before she could really let go. But in a town like Crystal Creek, that kind of privacy was hard to come by unless you were married.

And married was what they should be. They belonged together, and this night proved it. Still, he was no closer to a solution to that problem than ever, despite knowing how deeply he and Kendra loved each other.

To be fair, he hadn't had much time to think about solving problems. He'd been swamped by erotic needs ever since Kendra had whipped off her clothes and showed him that fantasy set of underwear that barely covered her secrets. He'd never forget how she'd looked standing there smiling at him.

Then again, he'd never forget how she'd looked without the black lace, either. He'd stroked and kissed every inch of her in the past five hours. In one night he'd learned more about her responses than he'd discovered in months of quick sex in the back of his pickup. He'd been missing a hell of a lot.

She'd paid the same kind of attention to him, and each time he'd struggled to hold back his climax for longer than he'd ever thought possible. The reward had been extended periods of amazing pleasure, followed by orgasms that had rocked him down to his toes.

Considering how constant their lovemaking had been all night, it was a small miracle they weren't right in the middle of another round when his cell phone rang. As it happened, they were cuddling and regaining their strength when the unwelcome sound intruded.

He cussed softly under his breath and rolled over to look at the watch he'd laid on a nearby shelf. Three-fifteen in the morning, for God's sake. It better not be his buddies playing a joke on him. "I should have turned it off. Sorry."

"Who could it be?" Kendra sat up.

"I don't know." He considered not answering until he remembered that he'd given his mom this number. It could be some sort of emergency. Swinging his legs to the floor, he found his briefs and put them on. "Stay right there. I'll bring the phone from up front."

She ran a hand up and down his back. "I'm not going anywhere."

He turned and kissed her quickly. "I'm counting on that." If only she meant that she would never leave him, but he didn't kid himself that she'd made that kind of life-changing decision yet. But she might have, and soon he'd ask her.

Ducking through the curtains, he grabbed the cell phone from the holder on the dash. "Sloan," he said, answering it as he slipped back through the curtains and sat on the bed next to Kendra.

"Teague, this is Scott."

"Scott?" He frowned and put out his hand to Kendra. She clutched it and sat up straighter, her expression tense.

"I tried to call Kendra and got no answer." Scott's tone was cheerful. "So I took a chance that you might know where she is."

"I might." Teague turned to Kendra with an encouraging smile. Scott wouldn't be sounding so happy if anything was wrong.

She relaxed a little, but she still looked worried.

"Well, if you happen to talk to her," Scott said, "you can tell her that Suzette had her baby, and it's a girl. Around midnight Val and I acted on a hunch and went down to check. The baby was nursing like a champ, and Suzette looked very proud of herself. They're both doing fine."

"Suzette had her baby and she's fine," Teague repeated for Kendra's benefit, thinking that she wouldn't want to talk to Scott and reveal that she was in the truck with him at three in the morning. "That's gr—"

Kendra grabbed the phone. "She had her baby?" she shouted into the mouthpiece. "When?"

Teague grinned as Kendra jabbered away to Scott about the birth. Apparently her reputation wasn't as important as news of the gerenuk. He was so relieved that all had gone well. Kendra might decide to ride with him to Dallas to baby-sit mother and baby. If he got that lucky, he'd show her the time of her life once they got there. Yep, once he had her in Dallas, she'd soon get over this obsession with Crystal Creek.

Kendra said goodbye to Scott and pressed the button to turn off Teague's cell phone. She was beaming. "Isn't that terrific?"

"It sure is." He cupped her smiling face in both hands. "And while you were talking, I had an idea. How about if you come along on this trip to make sure Suzette's okay? I can show you my apartment and take you to eat at this great little restaurant I found."

Her smile faded. "And how would I get home?"

He noticed that she'd used the word *home* to describe Crystal Creek. She hadn't asked how she'd get *back*. She'd asked how she'd get home. "If my next trip's in this direction, I can bring you. If not, the bus would—"

"Teague, what are you trying to do?" Her eyes searched his.

"Fix it so we can have some more time together." Lots more time. Forever.

She curled her fingers around his wrists and gazed at him with a plea in her blue eyes. "We could have all kinds of time together if you'd take the job at the Flying Horse."

His hopes began to wither. Then he thought about the sexy underwear and the new hairstyle. He thought about the enthusiastic way she'd made love to him tonight. He'd brought a rose, chocolates and a real bed. She'd brought Frederick's of Hollywood and zero inhibitions. Both of them had been after the same thing—to change the other one's mind.

He sighed, his heart like an anvil in his chest. "It's no good, Kendra. We've had a wonderful time tonight, but it's no good. I don't want to wrangle ostriches and you don't want to leave Crystal Creek.''

Her eyes glistened with tears she blinked away. Slowly she nodded. ''I guess that's the way it is, then.''

He felt his heavy heart crack down the middle. ''Guess so.''

CHAPTER SEVEN

KENDRA FELT OBLIGED TO work the next morning to take care of the clients she'd rescheduled the day before. Keeping a smile on her face and a steady hand with the polish required all her concentration, but she was a professional. She'd be pleasant to her clients and give them an excellent manicure even if it killed her. It very nearly did.

But the worst part of her day lay ahead. During her lunch break she would drive to Hole in the Wall and say goodbye to Suzette and her baby. Teague would be there, of course, and she'd have to put on a show of cheerfulness for Valerie and Scott. They knew she'd spent the night with Teague, so her performance would be tricky. She'd try to act like a woman who took her fun where she could find it and didn't worry about tomorrow.

If only she could be that kind of woman, she might not feel as if someone had dragged her through a knothole backward. Once she'd realized that Teague wasn't about to change his mind about the ostrich wrangling, she'd alternated between anger and grief. The anger was directly mostly at herself. She'd gotten her hopes up when she should have known that Teague was too bullheaded to see the wisdom of working for Mary and Bubba.

Anger had helped her through those last moments

with Teague as she'd dressed and prepared to leave the truck. He'd insisted on walking her home, which was the most miserable two blocks she'd ever covered in her life. After he finally left, she gave in to grief. There was no way around it. If she stayed in Crystal Creek, she and Teague were finished.

Because of that, she'd asked him not to attend Shelby and Nick's wedding, after all. Seeing him at an occasion like that would be too much for her. But she had to face him one more time, plus deal with losing Suzette and the baby. The elation of knowing that both animals were fine had disappeared quickly as the truth sank in—now that Suzette had given birth, she and her baby would be leaving. Kendra thought she was mentally prepared, but she wasn't.

Valerie had suggested she come out early in the morning before going to work so that she could see the new arrival. Kendra had wanted to drive out and do just that, but she'd decided not to. The more she saw of the baby, the harder it would be to let the little creature go. Better to see Suzette and the baby once, before they left for Dallas, and then put them out of her mind.

She'd learned from Valerie that Teague and Scott planned to round up the rest of the animals first and have them all loaded by noon. Last of all, they'd put both gerenuks in the special crate Teague had built, and they'd wait until Kendra arrived to do that.

Valerie had also said that Kendra could name the baby if she wanted to. Of course she would love to, but that didn't seem like a wise idea, either. No point in naming a little animal she'd never see again. Jack Bennett might not believe in naming his exotic animals, anyway. Kendra didn't want to think about Suzette and her baby having to adjust to a strange place, so she blocked it out of her mind as she drove to the ranch shortly before noon.

Ever since she'd left Hole in the Wall four months ago, the drive back brought sadness, but never more than now. Chances were she'd never come out here again. As if to mock her, the sky was a perfect blue and the oaks and wild grass looked green and lush, much as they had when she'd first seen them. She loved the undulating road and cherished each hill and granite outcropping.

She forced herself to ignore the dirt road on the right that had been she and Teague's romantic parking spot. Then the billboard advertising Bluebonnet Meadows came into view, and as always her heart ached at the changes bulldozers and backhoes had brought to the rolling rangeland that had once been Hole in the Wall dude ranch.

She drove past the model homes under construction and on past the lodge. She might as well park next to the action. Teague's big black truck was sitting down near the pasture with the trailer backed up to the gate. He and Scott had apparently created a temporary chute with large sheets of plywood and scrap lumber, and Scott stood by the gate waving his hat and yelling to help direct traffic.

Teague was mounted on one of Scott's horses, a large bay gelding. Man and horse were stirring up quite a bit of dust in the pasture as they herded the exotic animals through the chute and into the truck. The clatter of hoofs was punctuated by Teague's sharp whistle and his rhythmic *hup, hup, hup* as he wheeled his horse this way and that, a cowboy in action.

As Kendra climbed out of her car and stood watching him, her vision blurred with tears. Whether his father had brainwashed him or not, this was what Teague loved, and he was poetry in motion on the back of that horse. She'd seen Bubba chase those ostriches around, and it looked nothing like this. Unfortunately she understood Teague's reluctance to throw in with Bubba. Perhaps she'd been selfish asking him to give up so much for her.

The thought of leaving Crystal Creek made her stomach churn, but she wondered now if she could be happy here without Teague. Their night together had shown her how deep and thoroughly they were capable of loving each other. She didn't have a ton of experience in such matters, but she suspected that trust and devotion like that were rare.

She could be a manicurist anywhere. Yet no matter how she tried to talk herself into living in a big city again, the idea horrified her. She knew what urban living was like, and she didn't want that. She was amazed that Teague could tolerate it.

"Hey, Kendra!"

She turned and saw Valerie coming down the steps of the lodge.

"Hi, Val." Kendra pasted on a smile, determined to get through this with some grace.

Valerie came to stand beside her. "If they'd sent a truck driver who knew nothing about herding animals we would have been in trouble," she said. "Scott and I could never have managed to get the trailer loaded by ourselves."

"I'll bet you could have borrowed somebody from the Double C or the Circle T."

"Well, sure, but having Teague do it is very handy." Valerie glanced sideways at Kendra. "Is there, um, any chance Teague's moving back here?"

"Nope." Kendra tried to make her answer sound breezy.

"Oh." Valerie gazed at the scene in the pasture awhile longer. "Are you thinking of moving to Dallas?"

Kendra sighed. She couldn't do breezy, after all. "I've tried to talk myself into the possibility, but…I love it here so much." Emotion tightened her throat, which meant she needed to change the subject. "How did they manage to separate Suzette and her baby from this rodeo?"

"If you can believe it, Teague put a lead rope around Suzette's neck and led her over to the round pen. The baby followed, of course."

Kendra immediately turned and looked over at the round pen near the barn. "They're in there?"

"Uh-huh. Want to go see?"

"I sure do." As she walked with Valerie over to the round pen, she thought about Teague managing to put a lead rope on Suzette. He would have had to use a lot of patience and kindness to accomplish such a thing. She wished she could have seen him do it. Then again, it was just as well she hadn't been around while he was showing off his gentle, sweet behavior. She loved him way too much as it was.

TEAGUE KNEW THE MINUTE Kendra arrived. Despite all the concentration he needed to work these animals and avoid getting himself or Scott's horse gored with a wicked set of horns, he was aware of Kendra climbing out of her car, aware of her watching him.

He hadn't slept after leaving her at her door. He hadn't even gone back to the truck. Instead he'd walked until daylight, and he wasn't much of a walker. All the while he'd turned everything over in his mind. He still couldn't imagine himself as an ostrich boy, but he couldn't imagine himself without Kendra, either. They'd become a part of each other during the night, knit together like the strands of a well-made lariat. He'd never get loose from her, and she'd never get loose from him.

But she belonged here in Crystal Creek. Walking the deserted streets in the early morning hours, he'd finally realized that for good. He'd been wrong to ask her to move. Yet he couldn't make a living here, at least not the kind of living he wanted to make. For the first time, though, he'd begun to wonder if being without Kendra was worse than wrangling ostriches.

No doubt his daddy would have said that no woman was worth giving up your calling for. But his daddy hadn't needed to make that kind of choice. Teague's mother had hated the danger of the rodeo, but she'd known not to challenge her husband's decision. Kendra wasn't like his mother, Teague had thought with a weary smile as he'd returned to his truck in the early light of dawn.

Now he would be leaving in less than an hour, and he still didn't know what to do. Slapping his coiled rope against his thigh and whistling sharply through his teeth, he edged the last of the animals up the ramp and into the trailer. As they'd arranged, Scott released the sliding door, caging the restless creatures inside. Time for Suzette and her baby.

Scott swung the gate wide and Teague rode through it and over toward the round pen, his mouth set in a grim line. He wished he could load Suzette and the baby without Kendra being there. Taking them away from her didn't seem right, but he couldn't do anything about it.

Val leaned against the top rail watching Kendra inside making over the baby. He didn't blame Kendra for want-

ing to get her hands on the little creature. She was pretty
damn cute—all big eyes, ears and impossibly long and
spindly legs. Suzette acted nervous, but she was allowing
Kendra to stroke her baby.

Teague dismounted and tied his horse to the top pole
of the round pen. God, he didn't want to do this. Post-
poning the inevitable, he watched Kendra with the little
gerenuk for a while. But that was no good, because his
throat was tightening up the longer he stood there looking at the picture they made together.

Val sighed and glanced over at Teague. "I guess
you're ready."

"Yeah."

Kendra looked up. "It's time?"

He nodded.

"Okay. I'll help you."

"Thanks." He had to admire her grit. Her voice was
steady and her eyes were clear. She was tougher than
he'd given her credit for.

"I'll bet you could use a carrot or two," Val said.
"I'll go get some from the kitchen." Then she called
over to her husband, who was walking toward them.
"Scott, I think it would be good if you phoned Bennett
to tell him we're nearly loaded up here."

"Sure." Scott changed direction and headed for the
lodge along with his wife.

Teague figured Val was giving him one last chance to
be alone with Kendra, and he appreciated that. He
slipped through the rails of the pen and walked slowly
toward her, taking off his sunglasses as he went. "I'm
sorry about this," he said. That covered a whole bunch
of things, including taking away the two gerenuks.

"I know." She gazed at him, her expression brave.

Her eyes were red from crying, but she wasn't crying now. "Me, too."

"Should I...call you when I get them there safe and sound?"

She seemed to consider that. "Call Scott and Val. They can let me know."

He flinched. She didn't want to talk to him again. Well, that was her decision, but it hurt like hell. "Okay." He took a deep breath. He'd never been a coward and he wasn't about to be one today. Maybe she didn't want to talk with him ever again, but she had no choice about it now. "I love you."

"I know." She swallowed. "I love you, too."

Then they just stood there staring at each other. There was nothing more to say.

From the corner of his eye he saw Valerie coming back with the carrots, and he thought of an addition to his statement. "I always will love you," he said. "No matter what."

"Same here."

He nodded. "Val's here with the carrots."

"Then I guess we'd better get those two in the crate, huh?" With that she walked over to take the carrots from Val.

They managed to coax Suzette in with less trouble than Teague had expected. Her baby followed, and he swung the hinged gate shut. The operation proceeded efficiently after that. He brought the truck around, and with four of them working they managed to open the back door and slide the crate inside before the other animals could react.

Teague shook hands with Scott and touched the brim of his hat as he said goodbye to Val. So far, so good. Then he looked at Kendra and nearly lost it. She stood there like a soldier facing a firing squad, and the calm resignation in her eyes was more than he could handle.

He'd meant to at least say goodbye to her, but he couldn't get the word out. Swallowing hard, he walked to his truck and climbed in. As he drove away, he watched her grow smaller and smaller in his rearview mirror. He was going in the wrong damned direction.

KENDRA GOT THROUGH THE afternoon on autopilot. Physically she was at Curly Sue's, but mentally she was on the road with Teague, Suzette and the baby. As she'd driven back into town after Teague had left, she'd realized that Crystal Creek was the same, but she had changed. She would always love this Texas town that had given her a sense of herself, but her home was with the man who'd gone to Dallas this afternoon.

At the end of the day, she waited until Angie had headed off to a fund-raiser in Austin and Sue's last client had left. Then she sat in Angie's chair and turned to Sue. "I'm giving my two-week notice."

Sue sent her a hard look. "You're going to Dallas?"

"I have to. If that's the only way Teague and I can be together, then I have to do it."

"I hope you're making the right decision."

Kendra massaged her temples. "All I know is, nothing's right if Teague and I aren't together. I thought staying here was my top priority, but it's not anymore." She gazed at Sue. "Teague is."

Sue nodded. "Okay, but promise me you'll sleep on this before you do anything drastic."

Kendra smiled wearily. "I'll sleep on it. But nothing will change. It's kind of a relief, finally knowing what I have to do." Then she stood, gave Sue a hug, and left the shop. By her calculations, Teague should be getting to Bennett's place about now. She should have been with him.

BY THE TIME TEAGUE DROVE through the entrance of Jack Bennett's sprawling compound, he knew one thing for sure. If he had to wrangle ostriches to be with Kendra, then that's exactly what he'd do. He and Kendra belonged together, and every mile he'd put between them had been another mile too many.

Once he made this delivery, he'd return the truck and quit his job. Then he'd head for Crystal Creek and straighten everything out. Kendra still wouldn't have Suzette and her baby, but she'd have him, and he'd work to make sure that was more than enough.

Jack Bennett's house reminded Teague of Southern mansions he'd seen on runs to Louisiana—white with big columns out front. A compact little guy in a big Stetson came down the wide steps as Teague approached, unsure where to put his rig. The guy waved him down, so he braked the truck and climbed down from the cab.

The man came forward and stuck out his hand. "Jack Bennett."

Although Teague had expected Bennett to be bigger, he could tell the guy was rich just by looking at his hat and his snakeskin boots. He shook Bennett's hand and wasn't surprised the grip was firm. "Teague Sloan, Junior," he said.

Bennett's gaze sharpened. "You wouldn't by chance be the son of Teague Sloan, champion bull rider, would you?"

Teague liked it when people remembered his father. "I would."

Bennett grabbed his hand again and pumped enthusiastically. "Well, son, it's a pleasure. Are you on the circuit?"

"No, sir, I'm not. I was set to do that, but when my dad died, I promised my mom I wouldn't put her through that kind of worry again."

"That's understandable. Listen, before we unload those animals, I need to ask you something. I have this rodeo museum I'm setting up, and I'm collecting all sorts of memorabilia. If you or your family have anything relating to Teague Sloan's career and you could bear to part with it, I'd give you a good price."

Teague thought of the box of buckles and decided not to mention them. They weren't for sale. He'd carried those buckles around ever since his dad's death, as a reminder of what a legend his father had been.

"I can promise excellent care and top security." Bennett's voice softened. "I know it might be tough to consider letting go of a family treasure, but I can guarantee it'll be safe with me. I've installed more alarms and sprinkler systems than you can shake a stick at. Besides that, if you let me display whatever you have, people from all over the world will see it."

Teague shook his head. "Sorry."

Bennett sighed. "Well, if you ever change your mind, you know where I am. Now if you'll drive the truck down that little lane over there, I'll lead you around to the gate into the pasture where I'm going to put those animals for now."

"Sure thing." Teague was glad Bennett hadn't kept after him. Teague's boss wouldn't like it if Teague upset the great Jack Bennett.

Bennett pulled a cell phone from a holster attached to his belt. "I'll get on the horn and have some of my men meet us there. I can hardly wait to see that baby gerenuk.

Hardly any wild animal preserves own a gerenuk, you know, let alone a mother and baby. Common as rabbits over in Africa, but they generally don't fare well in captivity." He turned away from Teague, spoke rapidly into the phone and snapped it back into its holster. "Okay, I'll meet you by the gate. When you get to it, just pull on past. Then you can back in."

"Sounds good." Teague returned to the truck and drove slowly down the lane behind the stocky man who wanted to amuse himself by collecting rodeo souvenirs and rare animals. Teague knew why Suzette had survived at Hole in the Wall. Kendra had given her a sense of security. Teague wasn't so sure how Suzette and her baby would do up here with Jack Bennett.

The whole deal was a damned shame. If Kendra had owned pets all her life, that would be different. She'd weather the loss of this one okay. But Suzette was the first animal Kendra had ever loved, and Teague had been the one to take Suzette away. He couldn't even promise Kendra that the two gerenuks would be okay. Without Kendra around, they might not.

He drove past the gate where several cowboys stood waiting. As he backed toward the opening into the pasture where Suzette and her baby would be abandoned to an unknown fate, he remembered the way Kendra had tenderly stroked Suzette and her little one in the round pen. Damn. Damn it to hell. There was only one thing to do. He'd thought he couldn't, but now it seemed almost too easy.

Climbing down from the cab, he walked to the back of the trailer where Bennett stood. "You know that stuff of my father's you wanted?"

Bennett nodded, looking surprised. "You changed your mind?"

"Not exactly. What I have is all his prize buckles, if you're interested."

Bennett whistled. "I'll give you top dollar, son, if you'll part with them. Top dollar."

"I don't want money," Teague said. "But I sure would like to do a little horse trading."

KENDRA ANNOUNCED TO Sue the next morning that she was definitely moving to Dallas. She'd wait until Sue found a replacement, though, because so many of the ladies in Crystal Creek had become accustomed to having their nails done.

By noon both Sue and Angie seemed to be reconciled to Kendra leaving, but they'd made it clear that they didn't like it much.

"I don't want to stand in the path of true love." Sue massaged shampoo into Cynthia McKinney's blond hair. "But I just don't feel like this is the right move."

"Maybe you won't be in Dallas all that long, Kendra," Cynthia said as she leaned back into the shampoo bowl. "I sure wish we had an opening for Teague right now at the Double C, but none of our hands have talked about leaving. That could always change, though."

"You'll be back," said Angie, who was between clients and had asked Kendra to give her a manicure.

"Well, of course I will. Teague and I wouldn't miss Shelby's wedding."

"No, I mean you'll be back permanently one day," Angie said. "You belong here."

"I belong with Teague."

Turning on the handheld spray, Sue washed the suds from Cynthia's hair. "Well, Kendra, there will always be a spot for you at Curly Sue's."

"Thanks. That's good to know." Kendra's throat

tightened, as it had been doing quite a bit recently. She knew her decision was the right one, but she was already starting to miss Crystal Creek and all her friends, and she hadn't even left yet.

Coming back for Shelby's wedding, no matter how much she wanted to be there, would be tough on her. Blinking furiously, she pretended interest in something outside the window to give her a moment to collect herself before she dripped salty tears all over Angie's maroon nails.

And there, through the scrolled pink letters spelling out the name of the shop on the plate glass, she saw Teague's pickup truck. In the back was the crate he'd built to transport Suzette.

She leaped up, not caring that she'd knocked over several bottles, and raced for the door. Something had happened to Suzette, or to the baby. That was the only explanation. With a sob she tore out to the sidewalk and collided with Teague coming into the shop.

"What happened?" she wailed. "Is Suzette—"

"She's fine." Teague steadied her. "I've fed her and watered her. She and Fifi are a little tired of that crate, I'm sure, but otherwise they're in perfect shape."

Kendra heard the words, but she couldn't stem the tears streaming down her cheeks. She gulped air and tried to speak. "Why…are they here?"

He wiped at her cheeks with his callused thumbs. "Don't cry, Kendra. Everything's okay. I traded my dad's buckles for them. Suzette and Fifi belong to you, now. To us."

"Fi-Fifi?" Kendra couldn't make sense of it, and now, besides crying, she'd developed the hiccups.

"She's already two days old. She needed a name, so I picked something I thought sounded French."

"But...*hic*...how are we...*hic*...going to keep them...*hic*...in Dallas?"

He frowned at her. "What do you mean?"

"I'm moving...*hic*...with you to...*hic*...Dallas."

Teague stared at her for a long moment. Then he began to laugh. "No, you're not."

"I...*hic*...am so! I need to...*hic*...be with you!"

"Oh, Kendra." He cupped her face in both hands. "You don't know what that means to me, to hear you say that. But you don't have to live in Dallas. I quit my job. If Mary and Bubba will still have me, I'm ready to ride herd on those ornery ostriches."

Her tears flowed faster. She could really have it all. But she couldn't let him sacrifice everything for her. "No. You hate...*hic*...ostriches."

"I love you more. Kendra, this is where we fell in love, and this is where we belong. We'll live here, raise our kids here, and make sure that Crystal Creek stays as special as it is right now."

"You're...*hic*...sure?"

"More sure of anything than I've ever been in my life. Now stop talking so I can take care of those hiccups." With that he lowered his head and kissed her, right there in front of Curly Sue's Beauty Parlor.

Her hiccups disappeared as her heart overflowed with more joy than she'd ever imagined would be hers. She was home, really home, at last.

EPILOGUE

KENDRA HAD NEVER attended a western wedding, but she had a feeling Shelby and Nick's would be a perfect introduction. Ushers in black tuxedos, black string ties and black snakeskin boots directed her and Teague around to the huge flagstone patio at the back of J. T. McKinney's elegant ranch house. J.T. himself had offered to give the bride away, since Shelby was fatherless and a good friend of Lynn, J.T.'s oldest daughter.

Lanterns and tiny white lights flickered in the gathering twilight, and pots of daisies lined the low adobe wall surrounding the patio. At the far side of the enclosed area, several rows of white folding chairs faced an arched trellis decorated with fragrant jasmine. Nearer the house, linen-draped tables were set for four, and each table held a centerpiece of tiny orchids wreathing a candle protected by a glass hurricane shade.

Kendra didn't realize she'd sighed with longing until Teague squeezed her hand and leaned over to whisper in her ear.

"Ours will be just as pretty, sweetheart," he said.

She glanced up at him, feeling guilty that he'd noticed her envious sigh. "All that matters is that we'll be married," she said. "This is very nice if you can afford it, but—"

"Do you think for one minute that Bubba and Mary will let J.T. outdo them?" Teague asked in a low voice.

He grinned and glanced over his shoulder. "Check it out. They're taking mental notes, even as we speak."

Kendra glanced back at the Gibsons, who were trailing them by several feet. Sure enough, Bubba wore a very calculating expression and Mary was studying everything carefully. Kendra leaned closer to Teague. "I know they said we could have the wedding at their ranch, but I don't think they should come out of pocket for it, and we certainly couldn't pay for this kind of wedding."

"I understand how you feel, but if the wedding's going to be at the Flying Horse in two months, you know darned well that everybody in Crystal Creek will be comparing, and if you don't let Bubba and Mary have their way, you'll force them to feel second-rate."

"Then I'll figure out how to economize." Kendra paused as they reached a small table where J.T.'s youngest daughter sat, looking very grown up for nine years old in her blue lace party dress. "Aren't you beautiful, Jennifer!"

"Thank you." Jennifer smiled, obviously pleased with herself. "You need to sign the guest book."

"Of course." Kendra took the pen Jennifer handed her and wrote her name. In only two months her name would change, and she shivered with delicious anticipation at the thought of becoming Kendra Sloan.

"See my fingernails?" Jennifer displayed both hands for Teague. "Kendra did our nails, all the people in the bridal party, which means me, too, because I'm in charge of the guest book."

"And you're doing a real fine job of it," Teague said as he signed his name underneath Kendra's.

Bubba came up behind Teague. "We're gonna have canopies at our weddin'," he muttered.

Teague turned to him. "Canopies? You mean those little crackers with some kinda spread on top?"

"No, that's *canapes*. Don't you know nothin' about high society, boy?"

"Guess not," Teague said with a smile.

"Well, we could use some canapes, too. But I'm talking about them things they have at the fair, just poles and a roof over it. That way, if it should happen to rain, we're covered. If J.T. had ended up with rain tonight, he'd a been in a real pickle. We're not lettin' that happen at our event."

Somehow Kendra kept from laughing. "That's a good thought," she said. Teague had been right. Bubba wasn't about to be upstaged by the McKinneys. Fortunately she was creative and could probably find ways to cut costs on things like centerpieces and other decorations. She just hoped Bubba didn't decide to have the bridal party ride in on ostriches.

Once they'd all signed the guest book, Tyler McKinney, J.T.'s oldest son, appeared to show them to a seat. Kendra already knew that Shelby had decided not to have a bride's side of the aisle and a groom's side. Nick hadn't been in town long enough to collect any friends who weren't Shelby's friends first. As for family, Nick's mother and two brothers wouldn't be attending. All of them still felt loyal to Brian Fabian, and Nick's defection from the Fabian camp had caused a problem with his mother and brothers.

The bride and her attendants had spent the morning at Curly Sue's, and the sad situation of Nick not having his family here for his wedding had been thoroughly dissected. Shelby said that Jack, Nick's youngest brother, had called to say he would come, but Nick had advised him not to rock the boat. Nick's mother was upset about not coming, too, but she still felt great loyalty to Brian Fabian, the man who had been her employer and helped all her sons through school.

The most disturbing part of the conversation this morning had centered on Nick's brother Mel. A nasty rumor had it that Fabian might send Mel in to finish the job that Nick had abandoned. Everyone prayed that wouldn't happen. Even Fabian couldn't be that nasty, or so they hoped.

Kendra pushed that worry from her mind as she noted with pleasure that Tyler had led them to seats right next to Dusty Turner and Claire Page. Claire had become a client, and the two of them spent every manicure appointment discussing their upcoming weddings. Claire and Dusty were getting married in Claire's hometown of Boston at Christmastime.

As Kendra slid in next to Dusty, he greeted her with a smile and reached over to shake Teague's hand. Now that Teague realized that Dusty was no threat, the two men had become friends.

"Let me switch places with Claire," Dusty said. "Then you two ladies can talk weddings."

"Now that I see how gorgeous a ranch wedding can be," Claire said as she exchanged seats with her fiancé, "I'm a little sorry we decided to get married in Boston."

"But it's the right thing to do," Kendra said. "Your parents would be crushed if you didn't."

"They would," Claire agreed, brushing a strand of blond hair from her cheek. "But it means we won't have it outside, that's for sure!"

"It'll be beautiful," Kendra said. "Poinsettias and pine boughs and your attendants in green velvet."

"I really hope you and Teague can make the trip."

"We're sure planning on it." Kendra tucked her small

evening purse under her chair. "I understand J.T.'s talking about chartering a plane."

Claire nodded. "He told me. He also said Crystal Creek might get its own airport in the future. I know everyone's upset about the growth, but you know, a small airport would be so nice."

"It would. I—" Kendra stopped speaking as the minister walked from the side yard to stand under the jasmine-covered trellis. "I think they're about to start," she whispered.

Nick Belyle followed the minister and stood to his left, followed by his best man Dave Chapman, an old friend from Nick's college days. Hutch Hutchinson was Nick's other attendant.

"Don't they look great in those western-style tuxedos and string ties?" Claire murmured. "I'm thinking of having Dusty and his friends dress like that. After all, they are from Texas."

"Good idea," Kendra said. As she looked at Nick standing so proudly at the altar, she imagined Teague there instead, and a lump formed in her throat. She glanced at him and discovered he was watching her.

He took her hand and laced his fingers through hers as he silently mouthed *I love you*.

She squeezed his hand. Every day she awoke to a sense of wonder at all she had—a home, a man who loved her and a tight circle of friends. At last she belonged somewhere. Inner peace had allowed her to forgive her mother and reach out to her. Ginny Burton had promised to be at Kendra and Teague's wedding.

Kendra could hardly wait to show off Crystal Creek to her mother. Of course the town wasn't perfect, and it had some tough adjustments coming up. But this wedding was an example of the town's flexibility. J.T., one of the biggest proponents for keeping the town as it was, had offered to host a wedding for Nick, a man who had helped change it.

The wedding processional began, breaking into her thoughts. Bridesmaid Nora Slattery, Shelby's boss at the Longhorn, started down the aisle in a Victorian cowgirl dress of pale green lace and fringe. Next came matron of honor Lynn McKinney Russell in a similar dress in dusty rose.

Then, as the music swelled and the guests stood, Shelby glided down the aisle on the arm of J. T. McKinney. The long fringe on her ivory lace dress fluttered gracefully in the slight breeze, and the delicate material of her veil couldn't disguise her radiant smile.

Kendra turned her attention to the bridegroom, whose eyes shone with happiness. Then she glanced around at the assembled guests, folks who had spent the past few months agonizing and bickering over the future of Crystal Creek. All of it seemed forgotten as they basked in the joy of this moment.

Finally she turned to look into Teague's eyes. "Crystal Creek is the best place on Earth," she murmured.

"Yes," he said softly, holding her gaze. "It is now."

HARLEQUIN®

AMERICAN *Romance*®

presents a brand-new series by

Cathy Gillen Thacker

The Deveraux Legacy

Steeped in Southern tradition, the
Deveraux family legacy is generations
old and about to be put to the test.

Don't miss:

HER BACHELOR CHALLENGE
September 2002

HIS MARRIAGE BONUS
October 2002

MY SECRET WIFE
November 2002

THEIR INSTANT BABY
December 2002

And look for a special Harlequin
single title in April 2003.

*Available wherever
Harlequin books are sold.*

HARLEQUIN®
Makes any time special®

The Trueblood, Texas
tradition continues in...

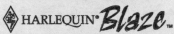

TRULY, MADLY, DEEPLY
by Vicki Lewis Thompson
August 2002

Ten years ago Dustin Ramsey and Erica Mann shared their first sexual experience. It was a disaster. Now Dustin's determined to find—and seduce—Erica again, determined to prove to her, and himself, that he can do better. Much, *much* better. Only, little does he guess that Erica's got the same agenda....

Don't miss Blaze's next two sizzling Trueblood tales,
written by fan favorites Tori Carrington and Debbi Rawlins.
Available at your nearest bookstore
in September and October 2002.

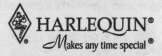

HARLEQUIN®
Makes any time special®

Harlequin invites you to experience the
charm and delight of

COOPER'S CORNER

A brand-new continuity
starting in August 2002

HIS BROTHER'S BRIDE
by *USA Today* bestselling author
Tara Taylor Quinn

Check-in: TV reporter Laurel London and noted travel
writer William Byrd are guests at the new Twin Oaks
Bed and Breakfast in Cooper's Corner.

Checkout: William Byrd suddenly vanishes and while
investigating, Laurel finds herself face-to-face with
policeman Scott Hunter. Scott and Laurel face a painful past.
Can cop and reporter mend their heartbreak and get to the
bottom of William's mysterious disappearance?

HARLEQUIN®
Makes any time special ®

Visit us at www.cooperscorner.com   CC-CNM1R